LIVE WIRE

A Novel

KYLE TOUCHER

Let the world know:
#IGotMyCLPBook!

Crystal Lake Publishing
www.CrystalLakePub.com

Cover art:
Kenneth W. Cain—www.kennethwcain.com

Layout:
Lori Michelle—www.theauthorsalley.com

Edited by:
Mark Coombs

Proofread by:
Sydney Ngxokela

WELCOME
TO ANOTHER

CRYSTAL LAKE PUBLISHING
CREATION

For Loraine Toucher, who was called away early.

ĮNTEᴿVĮEW Į

DEFENSE INTELLIGENCE AGENCY
CASE No. NB-18266-00
October 16, 1993 08:06 HRS

D.I.A. INVESTIGATOR: Agent Julia C. Oberon
LOCAL INVESTIGATOR: Detective Sergeant
Hector L. Castillo

Subject Interviewed at Albuquerque, NM
Police Department Medical Detention
Facility.

SUBJECT: Barlowe, Nicole Lynn.
FEMALE CAUCASIAN, AGE 34.
SYSTEMS ANALYST, MEDUSA ENGINEERING
CORPORATION
ADVANCED PROGRAMS AND DEVELOPMENT
BOSTON, MA.

CLASSIFIED.
PRESS BLACKOUT.

BEGIN TRANSCRIPTION

Oberon: Before we start, Miss Barlowe, I want you to be aware that you are under no legal obligation to speak to us. Do you understand that?

Barlowe: Yes, I do.

Oberon: This is merely informal questioning, and if you do wish to have legal counsel present, we can stop until that is made so. I am not law enforcement; I am with the Defense Intelligence Agency. Do you follow?

Barlowe: Yes, absolutely.

Castillo: There is an entire herd of corporate lawyers downstairs, flown in from Boston and New York, I'm told. You have not been charged with anything, nor at this time do I have any intention to do so. Merely asking questions here, Miss Barlowe. A lot happened on the night of October 14th. Would you like any of these lawyers present?

Barlowe: Lawyers? Already? Makes sense, I guess.

Castillo: Do you consent to questions?

Barlowe: You bet.

Castillo: You are an employee of Medusa Engineering Corporation?

Barlowe: I was . . . well, I doubt I am anymore.

Castillo: For how long, may I ask?

Barlowe: Coming up on eight years. I was part of the '80s hiring blitz. Pentagon money arrived in Hefty bags, it seemed. Most anyone that rolled out of MIT with a GPA above 3.8 and solid credentials was snatched up by Medusa Engineering. I thought I'd arrived, you dig?

Castillo: And what are those credentials?

Barlowe: Computer Science my parents are in debt to the ceiling for that and the company paid for Applied Physics. I also dabbled in Cryptology because I love a puzzle.

Oberon: Let's talk about what happened the other night the fourteenth.

Barlowe: You'd never believe it.

Oberon: There's a stack of law degrees in the lobby that want to know.

Castillo: Whatever you remember, Miss Barlowe.

Barlowe: Dragonfire started out fine, then it all went sideways. How's that?

Castillo: A great start. Your work was conducted at the Very Large Array, the radio telescope observatory outside of Socorro, just south of here. Medusa Engineering has a partnership with them?

Barlowe: They leased us star time, and we, in turn, solved some computer problems for them. We did not use the radio telescopes *as* telescopes in the traditional sense at least that's what I was told. Inter-departmental chatter was *verboten*, you know.

Castillo: Compartmentalization.

Barlowe: It's how anything nefarious is run. Keep everyone on a need-to-know basis until it all goes to hell. Compartmentalization equals Plausible Deniability. What follows is an entire legion of employees acting like that fat Sergeant Schultz from *Hogan's Heroes*. [IMITATES GERMAN ACCENT] I know *noth-ing!*

Oberon: Somebody knows something, and today you're it. The VLA disaster is all over the news. NASA and DOD are making statements, but The Defense Intelligence Agency is making the inquiries. *Several* dishes are offline, and—

Barlowe: Offline? That's a nice way to put it.

Oberon: You're certainly lucky to be alive, Miss Barlowe.

Barlowe: A cop told me that just yesterday. You can't see it because of the bandages, but I'm rolling my eyes.

Castillo: Consider yourself in Federal protective custody. Doesn't get more secure than that. Guaranteed.

Barlowe: The *Titanic* had guarantees.

Castillo: Can you tell us what happened at the VLA?

Barlowe: Dragonfire was so utterly far out, no one sane would buy the conference room pitch. But Medusa Engineering has their reasons and I've come to realize those reasons are very, *very* old.

Oberon: That's the second time you used that term *Dragonfire*.

Barlowe: Just like in the military, each project has an internal code name. I honestly don't know its real designation. That said, even if I were to disclose what I know about it, I was fed so much bullshit I may be lying to you and not know it.

Oberon: Try me.

Barlowe: We'd be here until doomsday, and my face hurts.

Oberon: We have painkillers.

Barlowe: Let's say it had to do with capturing CME particles, isolating certain elements, then, via some technobabble no one would fully explain to me, relay it back to Earth via the DragSat II satellite. Back to Earth for well, for whatever it was they were up to in that black tent. And that goddamn tent operation is responsible for all the blood and fire, I guarantee it.

Castillo: CME?

Barlowe: Coronal Mass Ejection, a sun burp if you want to be cute. An explosion occurs on the surface of the sun, an ungodly spew of plasma escapes through a hole in its magnetic field the corona and it blows out into space at *crazy* speed. This was a particularly fast one, and we had thirty hours to scramble our pocket protectors to New Mexico and get the gear calibrated before the wave got here.

Castillo: That's some *Star Trek* stuff.

Barlowe: Aye, Captain.

Oberon: What were they looking for?

Barlowe: I'm at the kids' table, lady. Even with my highbrow degrees, I just wrangle data and look for patterns. You may have to go all the way up the rope if you want real answers but you'll reach senior players like Blasko Thorpe and chances are you'll hang from that rope. Your best bet is their barking Doberman, Armand Jenks. If Jenks made it out alive it was likely at the expense of everyone else.

Castillo: You work for the Science Mafia? That's a little much.

Barlowe: Let's just say I didn't know then what I know now. *La Coven Nostra* may be a better term.

Oberon: I'm no astronomer, but it seems unlikely something requiring the use of radio telescopes would take place during such a huge weather event.

Barlowe: Well, it didn't start out that way.

Castillo: Yes, the electrical storm. Less than an hour ago, the National Weather

Service sent us some pretty wild satellite photos of the Socorro and outlying area, all snapped on the night of October 14 into 15, between the hours of 6 PM and 6 AM. "Never has the formation of a cyclonic depression over a continuous landmass been reported, captured, or documented," they said. I had to ask what the hell *that* meant, and some egghead there told me cyclones, hurricanes, whatever you want to call them, only form over water.

Barlowe: And he's correct. An artificial event, Detective Castillo. I didn't go to cop school, and even *I* figured that out

Oberon: Moving up the timeline, you still maintain that later that night you were at Thompson's Kwik Gas on Route 60?

Barlowe: I do. All of this began at the Socorro VLA but it sure as shit ended at the Kwik Gas. When the kid and I ended up [GASPS] Wait. [SHOUTS] *The kid . . . is he okay?*

Oberon: Kid? What *kid* are you referring to?

Castillo: You were brought in alone, Miss Barlowe.

Barlowe: Yes, *the kid*. A boy twelve maybe? A real trooper, that kid. Marooned at that gas station with his old man. The cop *must* have picked up both of us. Honestly, after all that chaos, all that fire, the wound in my neck, all of it, there's blank spots small ones but I did *not* walk out of there alone. No way. Where is he? [RAISES VOICE] *My God, where is he?*

Oberon: Miss Barlowe, Deputy Youngblood's statement made clear that your state of mind when he picked you up approximately eight miles from the filling station was one of and I am quoting here " incoherent, near catatonic, suffering from severe burns."

Barlowe: My eyelids were burned off. So if you want to talk about the deputy's assessment of my behavior, I'd start there. Your Deputy *had* to have been the last to see him.

Castillo: Deputy Youngblood's write-up mentions only you, Miss Barlowe. No young boy.

Barlowe: I'm *not* imagining that kid.

Oberon: The burns; you were injured at the filling station?

Barlowe: I was injured all bloody night long, lady. The gas station was just the end of the line.

Oberon: This young boy you mentioned, is there a chance you became separated *before* Deputy Youngblood spotted you? Trauma is a twitchy thing, Miss Barlowe, *Doctor Barlowe*. Events get shuffled, memories scrambled.

Barlowe: It was all pretty insane at the time, I'll admit. My current trauma is *you* creating doubt. I know what happened. I was there. *That Deputy is lying.*

Castillo: You said just a minute ago that you experienced memory loss. *'There's blank spots, small ones'.* Seems, well, contradictory to what you're saying now.

Barlowe: It was me and that boy. *That* I recall.

Castillo: We have Deputy Youngblood's report.

Barlowe: Yeah? Well, do better, TJ Hooker.

Oberon: Anything else we're missing?

Barlowe: Just the giants.

-7-

STORM SIGNAL

"**L**IGHTNING, DAD — DEAD AHEAD,**"** Caleb said.
Caleb's eyes never left the windshield as he wrapped the headset's cable around his Walkman. He rarely saw towering thunderheads in his native southern California, and upon witnessing this searing bolt of plasma, New Mexico had his full attention.

Behind the wheel, Pale Brody kept an eye on the fine line of the eastern horizon. An endless procession of high-tension towers guarded Route 60, while above, distant, bruised, and bloodied, the clouds shed a curtain of rain, which set to work in smearing that perfect boundary between earth and sky. The lightning flashed again, enormous and impressive. He silently congratulated himself for changing the wiper blades on his '68 Fleetwood before leaving Los Angeles.

"That was just *huge*," Caleb said. "I can't wait to pass through it. I guarantee the day will not be able to get any cooler than *that*." He jabbed his index finger toward the sky show.

"You're right, Playboy," Pale said. "From here all the way to the Atlantic, the thunderstorms are really something else. We used to drive right through some certifiable whoppers back in the day. Did I ever tell you that in Nebraska we almost got caught in a twister?"

Caleb turned away so his father would not see him roll his eyes. "I've heard that story a couple times."

"That's why I change it every time I tell it, buddy."

Back in the day for Pale meant when he anchored the lead guitar position in a band called Mac Daddy. Mac Daddy was a mid-level hard rock outfit out of Pasadena, signed to a major label subsidiary. Pale likely would never have joined a band like Mac Daddy—his guitar pastor preached Hendrix over Page—but the club scene in LA had only one lane in those days, and if you wanted to play pro, you drove in it.

Fun days nonetheless, those road trips, as Mac Daddy roamed North America, played loud, played hard, drank absolutely *everything*, and met absolutely *everybody*.

Caleb was just past the toddler stage when it all became airborne, and Valerie remained at home base with one eye on their son and the other scrutinizing the label's A&R guy. On a few occasions, Pale flew Valerie and Caleb out for shows in New York, Denver, and Miami. Those times had been good. Never rock star spectacular, but good.

Four years into the band's slow but steady climb up the ladder, they suffered a self-inflicted, humiliating blow. In 1988, Mac Daddy released a highly mocked, syrupy MTV power ballad called "I Wish You Missed Me," right as tastes began to change. Their upcoming album, *Relentless Boulevard*, absolutely died in the stores because of it, and the label tossed Mac Daddy like incriminating evidence.

The second whack in the balls came a month later, right in the middle of rescue negotiations with Capitol Records. Because of *Relentless Boulevard*'s dismal performance, Mac Daddy was replaced in the direct support slot for a major act's European tour; not bumped down a peg to opening band, just *gone*. Upon *that* news, Capitol stopped returning their manager's phone calls, then canceled future meetings. Within four months, the wounds proved fatal. The band split up.

Five years later, with the Nineties pendulum firmly set toward grunge and his marriage in the rear-view mirror, Pale hit the road for Austin, son in tow, eager to enter the world of record producing. Pale's old pal Billy Gaines and his crazy talented batch of post-punk-chicken-pickers were set to record a follow-up to their debut record, *The Tornado Alley Cats,* which had made some real noise on the alternative charts. It was not only gracious of Billy to ask Pale to produce their sophomore effort, but it couldn't have come at a better time, as Los Angeles was filled with ghosts; the house he was forced to sell, the shuttered clubs on Sunset, the handful of friends who had lost it all to drugs. If The Tornado Alley Cats' second record made waves, it could really kick-start a new career. *Produced By Pale Brody*—a future he could get behind.

"I'm glad we didn't fly—we'd have missed all of this," Caleb said. He squirmed as he did when his dad took him to see *The Empire Strikes Back* re-release on the Fox lot. The Imperial Walkers on the big screen blew his mind. "Just *look* at that."

Here on Route 60, part of Pale's slow road to Texas—when they could have just powered through on Interstate 10 and hooked a left at San Antonio—the scenic route revealed its treasures as God took X-Rays of the world. A purple river delta of lightning flooded the sky.

"Behold!" Pale said. He turned to his son and wiggled his eyebrows. "There's going to be a hammer—"

The hammer whacked the Cadillac square across the nose. Caleb had heard thunder a few times at home, rumbling far away in the San Gabriel mountains, but he'd never experienced such deliberate, solid brutality—and his dad was friends with the guys in Slayer.

"That's just crazy loud!" Caleb said, eyes wide as pancakes.

"Really is," Pale said. "Pretty deafening for a storm so far away. Maybe it's closer than we think."

Caleb leaned toward the windshield. The sun was nearly finished for the day, and soon it would light the underside of the storm, a promise of magnificent color.

"Sound at sea level travels at seven hundred sixty miles per hour," Caleb said. "We're about . . . what in New Mexico? Sixty-five hundred feet, maybe? So, it's a tad slower, seven-fifty, I'd guess, but that's still pretty fast. So maybe you're right about it being closer than we think. I love it, though."

"How the hell do you know all that?"

"I actually pay attention in school, Dad. That and, well, The Learning Channel is more awesome than you think it is. There's physics, biology, astronomy, all kinds of great stuff."

Pale shook his head and thought, *did he grow up when I wasn't looking?* "How come I never knew you were so smart?"

"Lots going on, I guess."

Pale sighed. Caleb had endured a lot of bad news since his mother's abrupt departure and had witnessed both parents at their worst. Still, the kid brought home A's and B's, had more than a passing interest in Yolanda Rivas two blocks over and had never kept a library book past its due date. His stomach wormed at the thought of uprooting his son, but the compass pointed to opportunity, and it had to be followed. Best of all, Caleb seemed to understand.

"By the way, I took one of your Marshall amps apart last year." Caleb tried to keep one eye on his father and the other on Route 60's descent into heavy weather. He wasn't sure how the old man would take the news his son had been screwing around inside a vintage1972 Super Lead, but currently emboldened by the compliment, if he was going to brag a little, now was the time.

Pale frowned, but his eyes smiled. "No, you didn't. How the hell could you do that? You were *eleven*. I never even saw a screwdriver until I was twenty-seven."

Caleb nodded. "I did. I mean, not all the way like unsoldering everything, but I took out all the power tubes, cleaned the contacts, all that. I removed the whole thing from the chassis and fixed a speaker output connection that was close to failing. I figured out how the effects loop you had installed works by reading one of the amp-nerd books you bought—but never opened—and also became fascinated with re-biasing. I didn't have the gear for that or the desire to electrocute myself, so I scrapped *that* idea."

"Dismantling that amp would have bought you a one-way ticket to military school, but amazing work nonetheless. Your mother always said you were born with special skills. When I was your age, I was into T. Rex and Little League."

"Most kids my age are into weed, Soundgarden, and *Penthouse*." Caleb watched another jab of God-fire plunge into the desert.

Voice drained of boyishness, Caleb said, "And, well, Mom never really . . . got it."

"She had a hard time of it, you know," Pale said.

Caleb scoffed. "Sure."

"What's *that* supposed to mean?"

Please, not now. The ride's been great, the storm is awesome. Not now, Caleb, please.

"Nothing."

Pale felt compelled to plead his case, a man in a traffic stop.

"Your mom, and hell, me too, I suppose, expected the good times to keep rolling. I think she was holding out for the beach house and the Benz. We never made it past Tarzana and Hondas."

Pale thought: *But it was far more than homes and cars or the rock star wife-life. It sidewinded beyond depression or anxiety.*

After a while, she turned her back on her maternal instinct and had the audacity to blame her son.

Caleb shrugged. "She was weird. When she came home with those fortune-teller cards and mint cigarettes, I knew something was way wrong."

Tarot cards and Kools, Pale remembered. Valerie sulked in the guest bedroom for hours, greasy-haired and cross-legged on the bed like some strung-out Yogi, sheets twisted into a battlefield. Many times he'd walked in to find her with her face buried in her hands, muttering cosmic hippie nonsense. She obsessed over cards such as The Hanged Man, The Magician, The Tower, and The Fool. *The soul is in the blood, Pale*, she'd said while laying the cards out in a carnival huckster's version of solitaire, fingers yellowed, eyes exhausted and rheumy, the room hazy with smoke. *And that's why Caleb marked mine.*

A crack of thunder snapped Pale out of his unpleasant daydream. "Caleb, seriously. She loves you."

Caleb bent his face into a smirk.

"She had a strange way of showing it," he finally said. "I was there when you weren't, and Mom was . . . preoccupied."

"Playboy, let's not wade into the 'you weren't here' swamp."

Caleb remained unmoved when his mother finally packed her bags and split. On several occasions, prior to her withdrawal into the guest bedroom, he'd witnessed parents sloppy drunk, a pair of arguing idiots on public display while the valet at El Cholo or Musso and Frank brought the car around, followed by the silent, tension-filled ride home. By the time Mom stopped coming home on weekends, followed by lame excuses about "losing track of time with the girls," Caleb knew the writing was on the wall. He never suspected that she had another man, although he couldn't say the same for any suspicions his father may have had. Caleb's instinct was pure and unfiltered: she simply didn't want anything to do with *him,* and Dad was part of the package. Not long after, Tarot and menthol. She never ate. She stopped doing laundry—and you could forget about cooking.

The old man smartened up, cut off half his hair, put the brakes on the booze, and resumed running sprints at the park. With Mac Daddy cold in its tomb—with only a failed power ballad to keep it company—Dad began to receive road job offers from bands that had steady work. *Jimmy's in rehab, can't tour. Mark's wife is nine months pregnant; he won't travel.* Caleb finally figured out his father truly believed he'd be able to salvage the marriage if he stayed put and figured that later he'd be able to put his own band together if things turned around at home—so he passed on the gigs.

Caleb knew his father made a point to sound as hopeful as possible around the house. He never complained about the situation or the loss of income and dutifully manned the bilge pumps in an attempt to keep the SS Brody afloat. But when he was alone in his little home studio, Caleb could see the truth on his face as he sat behind the console, staring into nowhere with the guitar in his lap, amp buzzing, expended reel spinning, the tape leader slapping.

Despite Dad's efforts, it wasn't enough to stem the tide of Mom's detachment and isolation. She'd punched her time card a while ago, ate pills like tic-tacs, and once the Ooga-Booga Express arrived at the guest bedroom station, she covered the mirror in bizarre cutouts she'd harvested from various magazines, installed blackout curtains, hung weird little talismans, burned sage, the works. She smoked Kools as if they'd fallen under threat of a moratorium and flipped Tarot Cards like a dealer at the Bellagio. She only looked at Caleb if she absolutely *had* to speak to him.

Caleb had never told his father, but when he watched Mom back her car out of the driveway for the last time, he was relieved to see her go. Even before the meltdown, she'd always been on the icy side, kept him at arm's length. What loss was it to have her gone?

He'd always known he didn't belong to her.

Within a year of her departure, Dad had done several sessions around town (from prog-rock to pop, it all paid nicely), word got around, the phone rang more often, and things looked like they'd smooth out. When the discussions for Austin began, Caleb hoped it would pan out for the old man because neither one of them genuinely minded leaving LA. Caleb knew he would miss the ocean, but the world was covered with water. He'd find another sea.

"Yeah," Caleb said. "Let's talk about something else."

Pale nodded and smiled. "Next time, try the Fender Champ for your science projects. I can afford to lose that to experimentation."

"Give me a little time, and I'll turn that runt into a growler."

Caleb turned his eye to the electrical towers, which in his

imagination resembled colossal prisoners, *a Louisiana chain gang of captured robots*, he mumbled to his father. New Mexico lay bleak and unhurried beneath those giants, resigned to whatever punishment the sky saw fit to dole out.

Caleb said, "I can't wait, this is going to be intense." He whipped his hand around and snapped his fingers, a trick he'd learned from his father's guitar tech. "Showtime," he added.

Just as the words left the boy's lips, the leading edge of the storm flashed alive with forks of feral energy.

"This is the coolest thing I've ever seen, Dad. Seriously."

"Cooler than rummaging through your old man's Super Lead?"

Caleb shrugged. "Once you've looked inside the magic Marshall box, the mystery is gone. So don't make me choose."

"Listen up, Playboy," Pale said. He fished around for his nicotine gum. One left. Once Valerie had begun smoking like the 1950s Pittsburgh skyline, he'd become less enamored with his fealty to Camel filters. But a monkey on your back always dug in its claws, and after several setbacks, he had finally left that gibbering little imp at the side of the road. He glanced at the fuel gauge. "The old gal's tank is getting low, and unlike hers, mine is full. I'm also out of this shitty Nicorette gum, so keep your eyes peeled for an exit."

"Roger that."

"The weather guy said it would be high eighties and clear today, but what do you think, Mr. Speed of Sound?"

"I think we hit the weather jackpot, so who cares?"

When Caleb saw one of the electrical towers take a direct hit, the flare so dazzled his eyes it was like paparazzi inside the Cadillac.

"Wow!" Caleb said. "Did you see that? *Did you see that tower get hit?*"

Pale had seen it, and for a moment, his balls tightened. A half-mile away or so, one of the hundred-foot giants had been jabbed by a spear from heaven. Sparks blew from the impact, but the tower stood fast. Wires swayed; dust blew. Soon the rain would find them.

"No, I missed it," Pale said. He knew Caleb wanted to file a report. "Tell me about it."

"The lightning just came down like . . . like *a missile*. It hit the tower like Ba-*Boom!*" He flipped his fingers out and raised his hands to simulate an explosion. "Millions of sparks—and that glow!"

Caleb tossed the Walkman into the back seat like a toy outgrown. He pressed his hand to the passenger window, a starfish in an aquarium. In a minute or so, the stricken tower would be at their side, and there was no way he was missing that.

"These desert thunderstorms can get pretty wild, but in my experience, they pass quickly," Pale said. "Enjoy it while it lasts. But we need fuel, and my whiz reactor is about to go super-critical."

"Maybe we could just find a bridge, like in that awesome tornado footage you see on the news. People park under bridges, and the sound gets all crazy. You can pee in the bushes."

"Keep your eyes out for an exit, buddy. Bridge will be the last resort."

Caleb shrugged. "Might be more fun under the bridge."

Pale grinned. *More fun? This kid is fearless.*

"This is it!" Caleb said.

As Pale slowed the Caddy, Caleb rolled down his window. The injured tower stood in dim silhouette, a mighty steel lattice. At the crown, where the impact had occurred, the tower sustained an enormous black scar. The raw power coursing through that lightning strike had been tremendous, but the tower endured.

The wires hummed. At their connection point, a faint glow was still visible.

"What's that ray-gun-looking thing between the wire and the tower?" Caleb said, marveling at the giant.

Now that Pale thought about it, the dual rows of glass discs *did* kind of resemble a ray gun from an old science fiction movie.

"Insulator," Pale said, "Supposed to keep the power from running into the tower instead of flowing through the line. That would break the circuit, I guess. We have similar ones on the telephone pole behind our house, well, the *old* house, but these insulators are just gigantic."

"They're still glowing. Man, they must have taken a real beating."

The air felt alive, crisp, prickling with tension—everything to Caleb seemed to be on the precipice, like the apex of a roller coaster. He turned to his father.

"Smells like . . . like electricity? Is that possible?"

"Ozone," Pale said. "The smell of a thunderstorm."

"What happens if lightning hits the car, Dad? We're metal too."
Pale snorted. He threw up the index and pinky devil horns.

They both laughed, partly because it was mildly funny but mainly because the storm showed it could become a close, dangerous reality. Caleb put his window up, and Pale put the pedal down.

A quarter mile later, Caleb spotted a rusted sign that read:

THOMPSON'S KWIK-GAS
3 MILES
NEXT RIGHT

Caleb pointed. "*There's* our exit plan."

"Right on time," Pale said, but his voice was drowned out by rapid bashes of thunder, artillery fire from a sky-borne adversary.

-2-

OTIS AND THE CANARY

BY THE TIME the big red Cadillac pulled into Thompson's Kwik Gas, the wind had throttled up. Debris and loose paper skated across the gravel yard of the filling station, chased by tiny dust-devils. Caleb watched as a toppled trash can coughed up a salad of soda cans, hot dog wrappers, and blue paper towels.

"Man, this place is old school," Caleb said.

Beneath the slanted, fifties-era awning stood four gas pumps past their prime, complete with rotary indicators and manual levers. Fluorescent tubes glowed above, struggling in the omnipresent static electricity. The color fluctuation produced a weird funhouse effect, and Caleb wasn't sure if he dug that or not. A few yards away, an old swing sign advertising Chesterfields—*Put A SMILE in your Smoking!*—swayed like a man at the gallows.

As Pale pushed the door open the wind defied him, nearly slapping him back into the driver's seat. He crabbed out of the Caddy and dug for his wallet while Caleb, already at the pump, nabbed the hose.

"Hey!" Caleb said, "The wind's warm like the Santa Ana."

"That's a little freaky," Pale agreed.

Santa Ana winds were hot, dry, miserable, and threatened fire, never accompanied by clouds, let alone thunderheads.

At the horizon, lightning raged.

"We would have missed *all* of this on an airplane," Caleb reiterated.

"Or we could have flown through it, which might have been worse. Listen up, Caleb—keep your eyes open. If I don't pee right now, I'm going to burst, but I'll be right back."

Caleb scoffed. "I'm not six," he said. He flipped up the pump's manual lever and pulled down the license plate, exposing the fuel cap. "I'll be fourteen next July. And look, we're the only car here." "Stay in the car until the tank's full. I know the storm is cool, but with the wind and everything . . . or your . . . just sit tight." Pale handed Caleb the Visa. "In case I take longer. Back in a flash."

I almost said, "or your mother will kill me," but she likely wouldn't have noticed if you'd gone missing.

A memory dashed through his mind, Valerie dumping the contents of her nightstand into a paper bag, flustered and hurried, hair askew, suitcases already in the hall, clothes poking from the seams as if their escape had been thwarted. She wore her rabbit fur vest. A cigarette bobbed from her lips.

We both know he's not right, Pale, she said as she rolled the grocery bag shut.

What's wrong with you? Pale fired back. *You're his mother, for God's sake.*

Caleb rolled his eyes as his father jogged toward the illustration of a pointing glove that read PIT STOP.

"Fill 'er up?" The old man's voice came out of nowhere. "Welcome to the wide-open between Pie Town and Datil, the only gas on Route 60 until Magdalena."

Startled, Caleb whirled around.

Thunder crackled. As the wind toyed with an aluminum sign, it tapped a madman's rhythm. *I Believe In Crystal Light Because I Believe In Me!*

"Fill 'er up?" the old thing repeated.

White kinky hair beat a retreat from the man's forehead, and crags like the dry riverbeds of Mars flowed from the corners of his eyes. He clearly hadn't shaved in a few days, but the unkempt appearance stirred no anxiety in the boy. The man's teeth, the few stubborn enough to remain in his head, were soured with the same tint of yellow that had conquered the whites of his eyes. He was as black as a witch's cat.

"Sorry if I scared you there, son," he said. "I know it's hard to hear over the wind and such."

"It's fine," Caleb said. He handed the old timer the hose, flipped his eyes over to the restrooms, and back. His father was already inside. "I had it all ready to go, though, Mister. You take Visa?"

"These old pumps, you know, they can be fussy. Some machines, I find, all they'll *ever do* is disobey. Your pop has a fine old road schooner. I'll bet he treats her real nice. And yes, I take plastic, paper, and gold." His face stretched into a wide, friendly grin.

Caleb nodded. "The Caddy used to belong to my grandpa, but he died when I was little, so my dad has always had it. My mom called it Red Zeppelin."

Across the road, a blade of wind howled through the scaffolds of the electrical towers. A dust devil the size of a bus whirled past. In the far away, the sun suffocated behind the wall of the storm. It coughed one last ray of orange into the sky before it choked.

"Name's Otis Thompson, and this is my place," he held his hand out to indicate the filling station and his double-wide, which poked out from behind the mini-mart. Next to the trailer stood an enormous satellite dish that looked more like a spider web than an antenna.

Caleb watched the old man, who began to squeegee the windshield. Probably habit, but full-service gas was something he'd very rarely seen, so he let it go and watched the show.

"Caleb Brody. My Dad's in the restroom. He'll be back right away."

"I was securing the air hoses when I saw you and your pop pull in here. The first thing I thought: I wonder if they'll have the sense to stay off the road for a bit because the sky is bound to open up, nice and wide."

"I think the storm's pretty neat, Mister," Caleb said.

"Love is always fascinating at first."

Caleb's expression was unreadable. "The hot wind is weird, though."

"Let me be true to tell you, I saw a Winnebago get hit by lightning once right here in front of my Kwik Gas. It flashed white for a second, then *Pow!* Exploded just like a grenade. *That* was some heat!"

"Wow." Caleb grimaced and took an unconscious step backward. "That's gnarly."

"Everyone got electrocuted, too," Otis said through a sigh. He moved to the passenger side of the windshield and got to work. "You've never heard such screaming. A Really tragic scene."

He finished with the windshield and began to start on the rear window. "Desert weather moves fast, don't you know, and I don't mind if people hole up when the sky becomes crabby. Happens all the time. Better safe than sorry, as they say, and I could use the company. I never close up shop, though. No-sir-eee."

Caleb couldn't shake his uneasy feeling about the wind. He'd been in Hawaii once with his folks, and yes, it rained even when it was eighty degrees, but this was different. This was a *fire* wind, and fire wind blew the sky clear—never clouds, and never lightning.

"It hasn't rained a drop on us yet," he said.

"It will," Otis said. He set the hose back, plunged his hands into his pockets, and rocked on his heels. "It'll howl through here like the Devil in a speedboat, then be on to bother someone else."

Pale, fresh from the restroom, picked up the pace when he noticed the old man in the gray jumpsuit chatting up his son. Under the fritzing fluorescents, the big red Fleetwood looked the color of blood. He crushed his empty Nicorette pack and dropped it into the trash can next to the fuel pumps.

"Two points and right at the buzzer," Otis said. With Pale's Visa, he tapped a peppy rhythm on his calloused fingers. "Twenty-two dollars and fifty-five cents."

"Thanks for taking care of everything," Pale said.

"I was just telling your boy here that it's alright by me if you folks wait out the storm. They don't last too long, and the market is stocked to the rafters. You also look like a man that could use a nicotine refill. Don't smoke anymore myself, my Ruthie saw to *that*, but I understand the habit, sure enough. Takes courage to quit, but that gum tastes awful. I'll have to run inside to run the Visa, Mr. —" He read the name on the card. "Mr. Brody. Follow me, and you can grab your gum and such."

Pale said to Caleb, "You want anything from inside? Pop, chips, nuclear reactor schematic?"

"I'm fine—"

A blazing sword of skyfire stabbed the desert, cutting Caleb off in mid-sentence. A second later, a cannon blast of thunder rolled across the New Mexico plain. The clouds opened, and down fell Otis' rain, pushed by Caleb's fire wind.

Caleb hopped back into the Caddy and watched his father and Otis dart across the yard to the mini-mart. A moment later, the exterior lights popped on.

Night and the storm arrived in tandem.

"My offer is still good, you know," Otis said. "It's wet 'n wild."

Pale entered his PIN on the Verifone reader. He pocketed his gum, thanked Otis for his offer, and stepped outside. When the wind grabbed the door and the needles of driving rain stung his face, he immediately regretted his decision.

Headlights approached. Pale could hear a big rig's diesel engine knock and grumble as the driver downshifted. He double-timed it back to the Caddy, relieved to be beneath the awning.

Pale stood at the passenger door as the eighteen-wheeler hissed to stop. The Peterbilt and the trailer it towed, both painted a blaring yellow, boasted they were the property of the Canary Trucking Company, Omaha, Nebraska. On the trailer, a winking cartoon bird wearing a trucker hat presented an eager Thumbs-Up.

The Caddy's passenger window fell in a grumbling, electric whir.

"Dad, it's getting pretty bad. I can barely see a hundred yards down the road." He nodded toward the big rig. "Even the trucker pulled off the highway."

A tall figure clad in a hooded rain slicker scaled down the big rig's cab. Head lowered against the rain; he approached the Cadillac. In one hand, he carried an enormous black flashlight.

Pale had experienced many a Maglite-toting State Trooper back in the road dog days, blasting their vehicle with light, searching for drugs, guns, and drugs. There had been several pullovers and a few close calls, but all the Officer Friendlies had ever found was a tiny bag of weed in Minnesota and a twenty-year-old groupie so desperate to leave Syracuse she chose Mac Daddy as the avenue of escape.

Pale turned and nodded, barely able to conceal his misery from the wind and rain. "Hi there. Something we can do for you?"

"I don't mean to interfere," the trucker began, his Native American accent unmistakable. Water ran down the slope of his nose in a shiny line. His eyes were so brown they were nearly black. Big black braids dangled from his hood like sleeping kingsnakes. "But you look like you're getting ready to head out. Not a good idea to be on the highway. Road is uneven, the low spots will fill if they haven't already, and that means hydroplaning, especially in a boat like yours. Best to stay put for a while."

A mammoth thunderbolt brained one of the transmission towers. Hot light spewed from the target as a crowbar of thunder yanked everyone's ears open. Insulators glowed orange, then blue, and finally buzzed themselves back to normal.

"*Jeeezus!*" the trucker gasped. "See what I mean, Paleface? A few miles back, I saw that happen multiple times. *Purple lightning.*" Looking directly into Pale's eyes, the trucker raised a breadstick of a finger, which sported a turquoise ring nearly the size of an egg. "For your boy's sake, at least."

The trucker shoved his flashlight into his slicker and hightailed it to the mini-mart.

Paleface? No way this guy recognized me. He was just being facetious.

"Dad, everyone's telling us to stay put. We should listen."

Otis had put a touch of fear into Caleb (even though he thought that story about the Winnebago was kind of spooky-cool, actually), but the Indian trucker, his expression as he looked right into his dad's eyes, for some reason, sealed the deal. Besides, it might be fun just to sit and watch the storm from the big picture window in the mini-mart, toss back a couple of dogs and a bag of chips, and maybe sneak a peek at a naughty mag if the situation presented itself. One thing was clear to Caleb: you could not get entertainment like this on an airplane. *Ever.*

"Let's stay awhile. Huh?"

Pale felt like an idiot. *The old guy and the trucker must be just shaking their heads and having a good laugh at the clueless California twinkie.*

The rain and hot wind just didn't jibe. Pale wanted to be out of here, but that massive submarine of a car, its ancient drum brakes, and how it handled like a B-17 with its tail blown off would be nothing but stress on a slick road and gusting winds. *Hydroplaning*, the trucker had said, and he had the sense to steer his big yellow canary off the road and wait it out. Was he willing to put Caleb into that peril, especially if he fled now with his ego bruised? A pussy would run into the storm out of embarrassment; a man would see his son's safety.

"Grab your stuff," Pale said. "We'll rustle up some mini-mart vittles and watch the show."

Pale thought about his guitars in the trunk—he never liked to leave instruments in the car, especially in heat or humidity. But the delay would likely be minimal—how long could a desert thunderstorm really last—and he'd just hump his fiddles into the motel later.

"We'll probably be done with all this in an hour," Pale said. "Then it's up the road to the motel in Magdalena for the night. French toast in the morning. Let's make it happen."

"Win," Caleb said.

The track of Route 60 yawned wide as night took dominion, the road slick now with long sleeping oils. Across the road from Thompson's Kwik Gas, the wind moaned the name of every ghost through the chain gang of electrical towers, daring the storm to spill its worst—be it from God, Magician, or Madman.

-3-

DEVIL WIND AND THE MOTHER OF FRANKENSTEIN

OTIS TRIED TO find a weather report, a news update, *something* on the radio, but the storm cast a curtain of interference over the area, so a clear signal was not in the cards. For a few seconds the little radio picked up some Ranchero music and a Country station, but both fritzed into static and a jagged snaggle of tones, as if the Emergency Broadcast System had run amok.

Wincing and rubbing his temple, Otis gave up and shut the radio off.

"That was ugly," Pale said. For a moment, the sound conjured a memory of his mother crying in her bedroom. The images scattered like sand in the wind when the radio was silenced.

"Sounded like Tyler Beans tuning up," Caleb said from across the store.

Tyler "Beans" Grady was Pale's long-time guitar tech. The man was a fantastic luthier, he could diagnose and remedy guitar disasters at the drop of a hat and kept Pale's entire rig running like a thoroughbred. Beans, however, could not tune a guitar by ear for his life. Pale once told him, *Beans, you've discovered the key of H. Nice work.*

And to Pale, that's what this noise was like; a keyless, dissonant blasphemy.

"Sorry about the radio, everyone," Otis said. "No news is good news, I guess. And speaking of beans, I'll get some fresh coffee going. Chief Big Wheel over here likes it dark and muddy, isn't that right, buddy?"

"Swampier the better, Gas Money," the trucker said. "You still have any of that Ecuadoran Hi-Test I was hauling a few months ago? One cup of that stuff makes you stand up straight and shit bigger than Texas."

Otis chuckled. "A few pounds of it managed to fall off your truck."

"The same." He winked at Pale and leaned into his ear. "If you can't sample the goods, why haul them?"

Pale nodded. He was reminded of the guitar strings he'd swiped as a kid working at Dorian's Music in Hermosa Beach. He'd sold only one guitar that summer and his commission had been shit, but he bagged a mile of strings and a ton of free lessons.

"You call him Gas Money?" Pale said.

The big Indian shrugged. "Well, just *look* at him."

"I dress for success, Big Wheel," Otis said. He unzipped his jumpsuit and offered the trucker a friendly middle finger salute.

Thunder rolled; the rain flowed in curtains. Several jabs of lighting dazzled their eyes with blue spots. Otis was surprised the power was still on and wondered how long their luck would hold in that regard. Backup consisted of an eight-kilowatt gennie in the shed out back and the battery-powered emergency lights required by law. He worried about his brand-new satellite dish out there in all that wind. If that baby hit the deck, he'd have to either call the service guys in Las Cruces or spend a hell of a time fixing that mess. Either way, he'd miss his shows.

Pale, who had taken roost next to the trucker in folding chairs they'd set up between the Frito Lay rack and Slush Puppie dispenser, assumed the man was named Ken—his belt buckle spelled the name out in big iron-block letters detailed in turquoise. Hard to miss.

"Your name's Ken, I'm guessing?" Pale said, pointing to the belt. He held his hand out. "Pale Brody."

The trucker's eyes went wide for a second.

"Your name is really *Pale*?" he said, shaking Pale's hand. "Shit, buddy, sorry about the paleface comment. That's *never* happened before."

Pale grinned. "It's a nickname, actually."

"Well, I was just working a little Apache humor on you, bud. Old habits from the Rez, you know."

Pale shook his head. "It's fine. Name's Pete. Peter. A thousand years ago, in the schoolyard, I used to be called Peter Pan. I was sick as a pig for a couple weeks, and when I came back to school, I looked like death. I was re-christened *Peter Pale*. Pale just stuck."

The trucker looked at his belt buckle then raised his eyes. He folded his arms over his chest and wiggled his eyebrows.

"*Ken*-osabe," he said, then gave a short, curt nod.

"You're shitting me," Pale said.

The Indian laughed. "Of course I'm shitting you!" He turned and looked at Otis, who was busy with the coffee. "Gas Money, my man, where do you find these people? Ha! The name's Ken Lightfeather. Who's the papoose?" Ken poked his thumb at Pale's son, who was watching the light show from the plate glass window. "I saw the California plates on the Caddy, so I'm thinking the sky show is new for him."

"That's Caleb. Yeah, it's all a big spectacle. Caleb, come and say hello to Ken Lightfeather."

A little of the conversation was getting through, but to Caleb, the thunder and window-rattling muted most everything. Crunching Pringles didn't help, either. He turned at the sound of his name.

"Say hello to Ken Lightfeather," Pale repeated, holding his hand out like a magician introducing his lovely assistant.

"Hi, Mr. Lightfeather," Caleb said. "Thanks for helping us make our decision to stay."

Ken nodded. "First big thunderstorm?" he asked.

"I've seen lightning before, but nothing like this. I mean, the color, the—"

A wallop from the sky squashed all conversation. Ingots of light strobed in blazing succession, immediately followed by colossal anvils of thunder. Caleb backed away as the window flexed, immediately sorry for his recklessness. A lone thunderbolt followed and scored a direct hit on one of the electrical towers opposite Route 60. The effect was blinding but enthralling, and for a moment, he saw the wires sway—as if the tower had flinched.

The lights flickered. The hum of the refrigerators stuttered.

"Oh Ruthie, we're in the thick of it now," Otis said as he poured Ken's stolen coffee. "Back in the seventies we lived near Tampa, and after hurricane Darlene, we had a power failure that lasted eight days. We'd never played so much cribbage by candlelight."

Pale stood. "Keep your distance from that window, Playboy."

Caleb blinked and shook it off. He turned to his father and offered a wide smile. "Just surprised, but that was *awesome*."

Pale looked at his watch, a Movado Valerie had given him on their final anniversary in 1990. "We've been here nearly an hour."

Ken shrugged. "Been on the road since age sixteen and seen some mighty skies." And that was true. The highway offered far more opportunity than the Arizona Rez, so when a young, aimless, and eager to get away Ken Lightfeather had accumulated a hundred dollars in tens, fives, and singles, he hitchhiked as far as Boise. Even though Ken fit in there less than he did at home with his old man, he worked like a dog on ranches, tractor repair shops, and finally bars until he'd saved enough dough to enroll in a trucking school in Twin Falls. By the time he was twenty, he had his Class A CDL. A year later, he could drive an eighteen-wheeler outside of Idaho, and the road opened wide.

"Tornadoes in Oklahoma. Ice storms in New Hampshire. Hurricanes in Florida. Fires in Yellowstone. Desert thunderstorms are a weird breed, don't you know? Some fuck ya fast like a jackrabbit; others stick around and make trouble. This one was coughed out of the east—it's a troublemaker."

Pale said, "Like it came out of nowhere."

"That it did," Ken agreed.

"Especially this time of year," Otis added. "Eastern storms are rare. Also, that purple lightning is new to me. And if it keeps beating on the power lines, it's apt to get awfully dark in here."

"That the wind is hot, like the Santa Anas we get in Cali," Pale said. "I don't care if you're from San Dimas or Mars—that's a dry, hot wind and completely impossible for it to be in tandem with rain. You can't shake the weird off *that* stick."

"Bizarre, late monsoon," Ken said. "A strong one, sure, but a late one."

"Yeah, but aren't those humid and thick, you know, like the tropics? This is the damnedest thing, arid wind with driving rain—it doesn't make sense. I may be a guitar player that barely crawled out of high school, but even I know that's impossible."

"Every storm is different. Here in the desert, there are lots of old, old memories. Rain summons them from the dirt, then they do what they will. Spend enough time on the Rez—and believe me, the road always leads me back there—you'll know what I mean."

"Ghosts?" Pale said. *I have enough of those, thanks.*

Ken shrugged. "One way to look at it. We're all connected to the spirit world, Paleface. Even you. Even your boy. Hell, even my man, Horatio T. Gas Money."

Spirit world, Pale thought. *Valerie played with those freaky tarot cards, The Hanged Man, The Devil, The Tower, smoking incessantly and muttering like a homeless person.*

"Hard for most white folk to grasp how ancient this place truly is," Ken went on. "A lot of people think history begins with sailing ships and triangle hats. By the time you Puritan boys lost your mind with the Salem witch trials, the Red Man coalition had long figured out the cycle of the weather, the herds, the moon."

Otis sipped his coffee. Fascinated though the young man was with the storm, Otis also preferred the boy away from the window. He knew that California types became lawyer-happy if they got so much as a splinter in a woodpile, but he honestly did not want to see anyone get hurt by any misadventure. He'd experienced enough of that already.

His own son Franklin, a Marine Lance Corporal, had died in the 1983 bombing of the Marine barracks in Beirut, and that malignant tumor of loss would never be removed. He loved his son and missed being a father.

On the heels of that horror was the loss of his wife, Ruthie. Otis didn't know it at the time, but she'd chosen slow suicide the day of Franklin's burial in Arlington National Cemetery. *Why do we have to leave him there, Otis? Alone and anonymous . . . just one in a sea of all those white gravestones. We left our son with murdered strangers, our son who could have been a professional ball player. Now look, now look at him.* She'd said it over and over again through a face melting with tears and running makeup.

It began on the drive back to Florida. They'd stopped at a Piggly Wiggly for fuel, and Ruthie returned to the car with her first haul: an entire box of Ring Dings, a couple rolls of Sweet Tarts, and several bricks of Bit O' Honeys, all chased with Mountain Dew. Already heavy (though she was a panther of a woman until the age of forty), diabetes swept through Ruthie Thompson unabated, and within five years, she had eaten herself to death.

Living alone had its haunts. Otis often dreamed of everyday life back in Tampa; Ruthie's scrapbooking in the living room with piles of photos and glue sticks, Franklin's friends over after baseball practice, their cat Lucius lounging atop the console television. His sweetest reverie, though, was their lazy floats upon

Green Willow Creek. During a cicada year, about eighteen months before they married, Otis and Ruthie had discovered a clearing nestled between two gorgeous willows, and it quickly became their private cove. Ruthie always packed a basket of goodies, and Otis paddled the raft he'd fashioned from pallets before laying a short trot line and hauling supper out of clear, singing water.

The blare of the alarm clock inevitably dragged him back to his double-wide on Route 60, where photos of Franklin in his baseball uniform and Marine Dress Blues now hung, and the blankets Ruthie had crocheted lay draped over the sofa. No cat snoozing on the TV, and the scrapbooks slept in boxes shoved into a closet. As for the cicadas, they couldn't be heard this far from Florida.

Otis rubbed his temple and sighed. The irony did not escape him that when he sold everything in Tampa, moved to the exact opposite environment, and opened a one-man operation, it would be in a business similar to the ones in which Ruthie had begun her decline. It helped that the road always brought something new to keep him distracted. The occasional repeat customer, plus road friends like Ken Lightfeather, were welcome disruptions when intermittent survivor's guilt gripped him, ghosts be damned.

"Since it's a good night for a ghost story," Ken said, "did you know that your Santa Ana wind is actually called *Santana*? Heard that on a game show." He turned to Otis and laughed. He downed the rest of his coffee.

"As in Carlos?" Pale said.

Ken's face went leaden. "As in derived from *Viento Satanás.*"

Pale and Caleb both knew a little Spanish. It was almost unheard of not to know at least *some* Spanish if you'd lived in southern California for any length of time. If, at the very least, you couldn't order properly in a Mexican restaurant, you might as well pack your shit and move to somewhere like Delaware or Connecticut.

"*Devil Wind*," Caleb said from across the store.

"Exactly," Ken said, jabbing his mammoth index finger and turquoise ring in Caleb's direction.

Otis added, "Ruthie used to say that Old Scratch uses the wind to call out the names of the damned—and if you hear yours, you're in a fight to the end."

An enormous purple flash blazed through the mini-mart. Before anyone could react, the thunder was on them, the sound of a derailing locomotive. Everyone flinched, and Caleb actually cried out.

The wind took a turn for the ferocious. The Chesterfield sign ripped from its gallows and flew away like a Kleenex. Ken's rig swayed on its suspension. Pale wondered if any flying debris had injured his Caddy.

"Jesus!" Pale barked. "Caleb, get away from that glass!"

Buried within the steer call of the wind, Caleb heard a metallic, creaking ache. He imagined a giant rusty hinge and cocked his head, the Pringles can forgotten.

"Did you hear that?" Caleb said, but his voice was swallowed by a follow-up thud from the sky.

"That one was a monster," Ken said. "But this will blow over soon, Mr. Los Angeles. It always does. Sometimes, though, it takes a minute for—"

"Did anyone hear that?" Caleb said again, now wheeled around. "Sounded like a . . . I don't know . . . a groaning?"

"Whatcha mean, Playboy?"

Caleb raised his shoulders in a frozen shrug. "I don't know, Dad, but it was *not* the wind. Something else. *Metal.* Maybe something collapsed . . . I don't know."

Another powerful barrage rocked the Kwik Gas. Everyone stood up. The lightning struck again, then a third time, splitting off into three jagged talons of energy. It tapped three of the towers—*Bam! Bam! Bam!*—a magician's finale.

Caleb saw worms of violet light move through the towers' connecting wires, a pulsing, visible Morse code igniting each insulator in the chain. The insulators swelled with light, a purple/orange glow that reminded him of sunset over the Pacific. Above, the storm roiled black as crows. The vapor swirled within a gargantuan, skyborne cauldron.

Otis barked, "The Mother of Frankenstein—right on top of us!"

Caleb was at his father's side before the last crack of thunder subsided. Pale pulled him close.

Ken whistled.

"But we'll be in the dark soon," Otis said. "Bet on it." He flicked his head toward Ken, who followed Otis' gaze to a shelf packed with flashlights and batteries.

The trucker turned to Caleb, whose expression had changed from fascination to worry. "Don't fret, *Kemosabe*. We have everything we need right here, isn't that right, Otis?"

"You bet," Otis said. "Make some flashlights happen, Ken. Let's be ready."

"Roger that, Gas Money."

A shockwave of wind followed. As the walls quivered, the Hamm's sign listed to one side. One of the beverage coolers popped open. A few bottles of Yoohoo fell to the floor.

Outside, a piece of the awning's sheet metal peeled up and flapped like a fish on a hook. The long antennae on Ken's big rig bent in the arc of an angler's greatest tale. One of the side mirrors beat a broken kite's death throes on the cab.

The wind brayed through both awning and tower.

"This is deep shit," Caleb said. Pale didn't argue.

The storm erupted into a rapid-fire frenzy. Ten thousand photographers and a hundred broken church bells went to work at once, overloading retina and eardrum.

Lightning penetrated the awning. The edges of the hole sizzled away to glowing, molten slag. The thunderbolt connected with the concrete below, then wormed across its surface before it found one of the metal pillars, climbed it, and winked out.

Pale recalled one of the Japanese movie monsters he loved as a kid—the three-headed space-dragon.

King Ghidorah's fire moved like that, he thought.

The air tingled with ozone, the hair on everyone's arms standing up like thorns. Pale's old metal fillings injected aluminum foil misery into his skull. Otis' artificial hip became a ball of agony. Ken suddenly thought Oklahoma twisters weren't all that bad after all. Caleb wondered if there was a basement.

Another swarm of lightning crawled over every metal surface, a tesla coil gone completely mad. A wicked scar of light scrawled across Ken's Peterbilt like Zeus signing a document, the cartoon canary's face sizzling away into bubbling paint and smoke.

On its side and huffing a confetti of garbage, a metal dumpster suffered a direct strike and was flung out of view. Smoke or vaporized debris—Caleb couldn't tell—was snatched by the wind and whisked away.

The light show snuffed out with a deep, audible *whump!* Directly on its heels, an ungodly thunder punch hit the roof like the fist of a monster.

As if an earthquake had struck, the magazine rack dumped its load, shelves spat their wares to the floor, while above, two fluorescent tubes popped from their housings and exploded on the floor. And perhaps in a sense, there had—but Pale's first thought was *No, not Earthquake—Soundquake.* Hadn't some friends of his called their first record that? Probably. His hearing became muddy and thick, like being in the deep end of a swimming pool, down by the drain ten feet down, where you can still hear the garbled voices of your friends above.

The ringing in Otis' skull sent his short supply of teeth vibrating against one another, and the momentary scoop in air pressure had him gulping for air.

Ken's hands went to his ears, reminded of the time he'd found himself in deep trouble and fired his .44 Magnum at a brown bear he surprised at a dumpster behind a truck stop.

Caleb felt like he'd been punched in the sternum, and he pushed that agony from his mind when he returned his gaze to the window. Peering now from a gap between Pale's shoulder and a fallen Foster Grant display case, words clogged Caleb's throat. He'd choked on peanut butter once, and that's precisely what this was like; dry, chalky, heart fluttering with adrenaline. It was surely real, but the words wouldn't come. All he could manage was cram his arm through that gap and point at the impossible.

One of the high-tension towers was moving. Not swaying in the wind, but *moving*, twisting like a man with a foot in quicksand. It leaned to one side with a great, slow effort and pulled a concrete anchor from the ground. At maximum tilt, the transmission lines, still crackling and alive with the pulsing, violet Morse code show, went taught, and for a moment, Caleb was convinced the immense cage would topple. He searched for a rational explanation, wondered if the violent wind and rain had somehow loosened its anchor—it only *looked* like the tower was moving under its own power.

Once the leg was free, the tower shifted its mass. The concrete pylon was driven into the ground with the steel cage's multi-ton weight upon it, and it crumbled like a dirt clod. In that sunset purple/orange, the insulators glowed, bloated with energy as light pulses rocketed through the wires. When Caleb steadied his eye and focused through the slanted rain, he saw several towers following the lead.

"Tell me you all see that," Caleb said. He turned to look at his father, whose face had transformed into a terrain of amazement and disbelief. *"Tell me all of you see that."*

The chain gang had an escape plan.

INTERVIEW II

DEFENSE INTELLIGENCE AGENCY
CASE No. NB-18266-00
October 16, 1993 14:33 HRS
ATTACH TO PREVIOUS INTERVIEW

INVESTIGATORS AND SUBJECT UNCHANGED

CLASSIFIED.
PRESS BLACKOUT.

BEGIN TRANSCRIPTION

Barlowe: Thanks for the break. That meeting with the burn specialists was something else, they informed me that my Oil of Olay commercial deal is kaput. Remember my phone call request? I do.

Oberon: I'm sorry you have to go through this. It's all a terrible tragedy. Are they hopeful? The doctors?

Barlowe: Isn't everyone that bills you?

Castillo: Yeah man, doctors, mechanics, and lawyers. [LAUGHS]

Barlowe: See you at the kegger, dude.

Castillo: What?

Barlowe: Never mind. Happy Hour at Hooters is at four, so we'll get this handled so you can be on your way.

Oberon: Miss Barlowe . . . please . . .

Barlowe: Did I mention I'm on several drugs? Man, my mind is *on fire*. So, Inspector General Agent Madame in Charge Oberon, where were we?

Oberon: VLA. The project called . . . sorry, I have it in the transcript . . .

Barlowe: Dragonfire.

Oberon: Yes, thank you. Dragonfire.

Barlowe: How in detail do you want it?

Oberon: I'll take all you're willing to give.

Barlowe: Are those people that claim to be lawyers still out front? I'll bet one of their opening moves will be to send in a gentle female. She'll try to engage me in some girl-talk. Get real chummy. *Love your bandages, they were a huge hit in Milan this year.* Ha!

Oberon: They're not in the building anymore. You can actually thank Detective Castillo for ushering them out.

Barlowe: Maybe they'll be at Hooters later and you can all do some Jello Shots.

Oberon: Miss Barlowe, please stay cordial.

Barlowe: So, the VLA. After Bobby Greene and his gang over at Sunspot the solar observatory here in New Mexico gave us the alert, we put on our big boy pants and got rolling. Mr. Jenks left a standing order that as soon as a candidate solar eruption was detected, we were on call and expected at Logan within 45 minutes. They had the chartered jet on standby, and the hold had been packed for a couple of weeks. Bobby Greene had made sure we knew well in advance that the current amount of sunspot activity was prime breeding ground for a Coronal Mass Ejection . . . so when I say that plane was ready to go, it was all they had to do was shuffle us dorks into the cabin and hit the gas. The Fun Jet hit the sky, and we were eager to fly.

Oberon: Armand Jenks. You mentioned that name earlier.

Barlowe: Yeah. Jenks has been with Medusa Engineering for a long time. You don't want to run afoul of that mantis.

Oberon: What does that mean, exactly?

Barlowe: You'd know if you met him. If you could stand to be in the same building with him, that is.

Oberon: But he was the man in charge, this Jenks?

Barlowe: Randy Childs, he was the brain-engine behind *our side* of Dragonfire. Smart man, Childs. We all loved Randy. Rolled joints one-handed and could make a margarita out of a Dixie cup and turpentine.

Oberon: So, back to Boston, this is on the fifteenth, the phone rings, and off you go . . .

Barlowe: Correct. By the way, speaking of the phone, I need to call home. My neighbor is watching my cat. He's good, I'm sure, but I told my neighbor I didn't know how many days I'd be gone.

Oberon: We'll arrange that when we wrap up today.

Castillo: You may be gone awhile.

Barlowe: You're still here? Sorry, Detective. I'm glad you're following along, though. So yes, we get on the plane at Logan, and honestly, the mood on the jet was pretty snappy. A bunch of nerds off for a plane ride and a change of scenery. And, of course, *good old-fashioned Space Shit*. We *love* that stuff. Booze helped.

Oberon: So you arrive at ABQ, all ready to roll.

Barlowe: Landed at Albuquerque, and the crew had the Hertz trucks packed to the rafters in about twenty minutes. Yeah, we'd brought in an epic amount of gear. I mean, we had huge road cases full of stuff. You know, like the cases you see at rock shows and such stacks of them. Crammed with computers and huge IBM tape drive arrays, mostly, but there was some other gear I had *never* seen before that had *no* business there. A team I'd never met swooped in, grabbed that shit, and hauled it off. They must have been on a different flight because I did not see them on the Fun Jet.

Oberon: And where were you when this occurred?

Barlowe: I was downstairs in the basement level of the control area. I looked out the window, and there's that other team, running in and out the black tent. All very need-to-know. *Compartmentalized*, to quote Detective Castillo. Dig me? One of those big generator trucks was parked outside as well, and believe it or not, it had a Paramount Pictures logo on it. Medusa Engineering has *a lot* of contacts, you know.

Oberon: How long before your spotting of, let's call them the B-Team, and the arrival of the electrical storm?

Barlowe: As scientists, we tell ourselves we're looking for a specific thing, but usually, it's a dice roll. *Let's see what happens if I do this, will the lab catch fire if I do that.* That's the thrill. But it felt like at the VLA it was *don't look here, you're not cleared to know.* That got my tail up. Remember, I'm a cryptologist too. I *want* to know.

Oberon: So, figuring out your way around the compartmentalization was kind of a way to scratch that itch, you're saying?

Barlowe: Not bad, Inspector. You should sign up for our summer classes.

Oberon: In other words, there was always an undercurrent of secrecy you didn't really fully realize until the VLA?

Barlowe: Well, it's more of an after-the-fact thing, but you're in the neighborhood. Spend enough time at Medusa Engineering, and you'll see a lot of barely-there, knowing nods between the suits. Seriously, these cats were one step away from a secret handshake. Not that I was ever at the MEC Tower in downtown Boston, but even at our joint, R&D Seven in Cambridge, over by the Charles River, whenever Management would grace us with their presence, you had that weird feeling that you had somehow become a pallbearer for the world.

Oberon: Sounds a little dark, Doctor Barlowe.

Barlowe: Honestly, I laughed it off for years. I figured they were just Ivy League racquetball jackoffs with BMW's and daughters named Winston. Yale Skull and Bones rejects. But after a fuck-parade like that shitshow a couple of nights ago, your perspective shifts. Curiosity may not have killed *this* cat, but my eyes are wide open. For good it seems, now that I no longer have eyelids.

Castillo: Cute.

Barlowe: Arthur C. Clarke said something to the effect that magic is just technology we don't understand, you know, *indistinguishable* from magic. Maybe so, but ask your local Hooba-Jooba witch doctor and he'll tell you straight: rituals require blood. *Sacrifice.*

Castillo: Who cares? What of it?

Barlowe: So where do corporation and cult intersect?

Oberon: Alright, I'm not listening to this nonsense. Stop the tape.

Barlowe: Hey! Julie, really

[RECORDING SUSPENDED]

-4-

DARKNESS AND PARALYSIS

THE GIANT WORKED on the fourth pylon.

Pale recalled the tower on Route 60 right before they saw the Kwik Gas sign, how its insulators glowed and buzzed, and the black scar left at its apex by that massive lightning wallop. He wondered if that was where all of this had begun.

"Alright, we're out of here," Pale said as he grabbed Caleb by the shoulder. "We'll double back toward the Arizona line. This . . . this entire thing is impossible."

Shaking his head, Caleb said, "I can't believe it either, but impossible or not, Dad, the towers are on the move, and on the road, we are exposed." He turned to Ken. "Do you think they can see us?"

Ken nodded and looked Caleb in the eye. "That's the exact question to ask, *Kemosabe.*"

How many years had Otis looked out these very windows, or stood on the island beneath the awning and watched the sun set, painting the towers in silhouette? In this brutish Devil Wind storm, had mother lightning had borne a terrible son? His bones vibrated like a tuning fork, the marrow moving through those pipes thick as tree sap. A dollop of intuition rolled in his gut.

"The storm did this," Otis said. "Had to be. We knew something wasn't right with that purple lighting, that dry wind."

"Or worse," Ken said. He resumed opening battery packages, dropping D-cells into the flashlights, and just shook his head when Caleb offered to help. "Old forces out here, for sure. Every now and then, the spirits get restless. It might seem like Apache hocus-pocus-wigwam bullshit to you, but spend enough years on the road, and you'll see what I mean. It gets awfully dark out there, no matter what time of night."

Ken set a pack of batteries on a shelf next to the travel-size Bounce fabric softener sheets. *Outdoor Fresh!* He regarded Caleb for a moment, head cocked toward the metallic ache of the tower reconciling its new life. "In a span of three years, I saw the same dead woman at three different truck stops in three different states. The first time was right before Christmas during one hell of a blizzard, someplace I've never found on a map, Beltane Road, the exit was called. I'll never forget it. The last time I saw her was in this little dump in Colorado, and it was then that she finally *looked* at me."

Caleb took a step back. "Whoa."

"I don't know, man—you've never seen such emptiness. To be true, that brittled my bones and marbled my balls, so now I'm able to tell you from experience—it gets awfully dark out there."

"I've seen a lot of weird shit in my time," Pale said. "Caleb can even tell you. My grandmother's house was haunted to the rafters, but this—"

Fwunk! The refrigerators shut down, and when the mini-mart went dark, everyone was seized by temporary paralysis.

"Stay put," Otis said. "Emergency lights in a few seconds, and there's also a gennie out back. It will keep the fridges on for a while."

"We didn't try the phone, did we, Mr. Thompson?" Caleb said.

Pale wished he had a solution, but getting behind the wheel in a storm of this magnitude, especially a road barge like Red Zeppelin, was madness, let alone with something as unprecedented as the towers factored into the scenario—Caleb was right about that, they were an undeniable reality now—plus absolutely no one knew they were here. And if this phenomenon was happening elsewhere, any fire or police department would likely have their hands full.

"Not as yet," Otis said. "But the telephone still works even when the power is out. If the phone lines are down—*then* there's a problem." He zipped up his coveralls and shifted his gaze to Pale. "I should get about firing that generator up, but Mr. Brody, if you and your son don't mind trying the phone, it's on the wall behind the register."

Just as the emergency floodlights bloomed, Otis' radio snapped on by itself. That non-music blared, the Emergency Broadcast System frequency howling dissonant, ugly nonsense. Warbling static spilled into the mini-mart in a wave of sawtoothed coughs, a sinister Theremin performance broadcast from an asylum. Pale winced, and Ken spat on the floor.

Otis navigated the minefield of toppled soup cans and hostess donuts. He grabbed the squawking radio and held it to show everyone as the device blared. The switch was still in the OFF position.

"God, that's hideous," Pale hissed. He tugged Caleb along, and they made their way to the phone, one of those early sixties wall-mounted jobs; avocado green, handset hanging on a U-shaped hook, dial, the works.

Otis opened the radio's battery compartment and yanked out the D-cells. The noise decayed into an intermittent stutter but did not immediately stop; it took its time, five seconds, say, and growled all the way down. While the sound ebbed away, Otis had a flash of memory: He was in the funeral parlor, picking out a coffin for Ruthie. His eyes settled on the only one leaning upright, as if on display in a western movie's undertaker shop. He chose the one with the white satin lining embossed with roses.

Otis shoved the radio to the side. It smashed to the floor, and a couple of the knobs broke off and spun away. He looked at Ken, who had just finished with the flashlights.

"After that radio performance," Ken said, holding up one of the torches. "I wonder if we should turn these things on."

Pale lifted the handset and dialed 911.

Caleb watched the chain gang. The tower had pulled itself free and took its first pivoting step forward. Insulators aglow, the cage flexed as the giant moved. He wondered if the tower was indeed alive, was it conscious, did it *know*, could it *see*? Was it taking stock of its surroundings as the giant's crown turned from right to left, seeing the world through new eyes as it set bearings? Did the tower possess a mind or thought process, or did the storm, this weird dry rainstorm, and by extension the lightning that, as absurd as the thought seemed, appeared to have animated all that steel, do all the heavy lifting?

That's impossible, it's mindless steel. But they're—

"But they're walking," Caleb said. He almost laughed at the words. "Dad, that tower is actually walking. *By itself.* The others aren't far behind."

Pale, eyes on the old phone, acknowledged Caleb with a thumb's up, then heard the line connect.

First ring.

Thank God, He thought. *At the very least, someone may be able to tell us what the hell is going on or if it's spreading.*

Pale glanced outside. The tower leaned into another step, and another one worked on freeing itself. Beyond that, a *third* giant was also well on its way to liberty. The screech of galvanized steel reached his ears, somehow penetrating the lowing wind and throaty hiss of rain. Birth is always painful, and its story will be heard.

Second ring.

Insulators swelled with light, spilling across the breadth of the cross arms, but stabs of lightning brought it all into view—an army of giants, now miraculously mobilized, slowly marched, destination unknown.

Third ring.

Success! There was a muffled click, then the earpiece trumpeted the same grating noise that had come from the radio. In such close proximity to Pale's ear, it seemed personal, offensive insults directed at him.

GHZRT—!BOK

This snarl of machine language immediately assumed authority, a declaration of indictment. As much as Pale detested that sound, he found it difficult to pull the handset away. It was almost like trying *not* to look at Valerie's tarot cards. They gave him the creeps, but he always *looked.*

Stop being stupid. Drop the phone; lines are obviously hosed. Get busy—your son needs you.

That jumble of noise surfaced an old remembrance. Pale was ten years old, bumbling out of bed in his flannel PJs, stirred awake by his parents arguing in their bedroom. He knew his folks ached to raise their voices but struggled to keep them contained—that alone made it frightening—but he was even more petrified over the idea that their argument was somehow about him.

Like his inability years later to look away from Valerie's cards, he *had* to know. He leaned his ear against the door, shocked as his father said *fuck,* called his mother a *bitch,* then laughed at her muffled sobbing as she muttered the words *stop calling me names just because I know what you're doing.* Pale felt the vibration through the wall as the bathroom door slammed, then heard the angry clatter of keys as his father grabbed them, intent on storming out of the house.

This noise, this vulgarity from somewhere else, was like that night, a glue made of dread that kept him where it wanted while filling his ear with things that poisoned a child's head. This was indeed an electronic Signal, Pale knew, but far uglier—it bristled with intent. His chest and arms crawled with gooseflesh.

From the earpiece, pushed tightly to his head like he was concentrating on a phone call in a busy airport:

$3N-\breve{X}V!\bar{W}$

Dark, *angular*, the language of knives. For the brief but heavy sliver of time, Pale Brody listened. Pale Brody understood.

—*Why don't you just stab everyone?*—

A wave of seasick nausea swept through him as the vile suggestion poured into his mind. His palms and armpits broke out in a yellow, ripe sweat. In the rank terror of the moment, he gagged, and a squirt of tangy bile leaped into his throat.

"Dad, what is it?" Pale heard from far away. He squeezed his eyes shut and tried to pull the handset from his head, but something mined his memories, shuffling through them like a woman rummaging her drawer in search of the perfect accessory.

Dad, what is it? Pale said as the front door banged shut, the opaque glass trembling in its frame. Mom burst into tears and slammed the closet doors repeatedly while screeching "son of a bitch!" with every furious crash. Dad's car roared to life in the driveway, and the big V8 made the tires screech as he sped away. When Pale's little sister, Gwen, a girl still drawing horsies and playing Barbies with her little friends, called out from her bedroom, her voice was thin and afraid. At the sound of her mewling, the quality of light in the house somehow changed because Pale knew that things would be different from this moment forward; both his mother and the house would be unstable. Tension and sadness would now hold dominion.

$!!-Q\check{Z}R\ R_{1}K$

—*Find that screwdriver under the counter. Start with the Negro and work your way up to the Indian. If the boy runs, then do what you have to do, Mac Daddy*—

A tremendous artillery flash from the storm yanked Pale back to the Kwik Gas. Four seconds had seemed like four minutes. He jabbed the receiver back onto its hook, then spit the stomach juice to the floor. A silver line of spit dangled from his bottom lip. His vision exploded into a hippie light show of blue dots and crazy yellow blotches.

He noticed the long flathead screwdriver, a Stanley, on a shelf beneath the counter.

"Dad, you alright?"

Caleb's voice. Caleb is here. *Ashtray stuffed with Kools.* We are in a gas station in New Mexico. Storm outside. *The Hanged Man. A crazy monster of a storm. The Ten of Swords. The Tower*—and there were giants. *Giants*—

"The towers," Pale said as he managed to set his gaze on his son. "There's something else to them, Caleb. *That phone.*"

Caleb was taken aback at his father's eyes—his left eye was dilated; the right was not. He held his father's shoulders and realized he had an additional problem: *I may not be able to rely on him.*

Not knowing exactly what to say, Caleb repeated, "Dad, you alright?"

For a moment, Pale set his forehead to Caleb's shoulder and exhaled. When had Caleb become this tall? The kid had to be nearly five-ten by now.

Yes, think of that. Caleb is almost a teenager. Tall and smart, the boy can fearlessly explore beneath the hood of a Marshall Super Lead. Soon, he'll be ready to make his mark in the world. Quick on his feet, he will make his own decisions—but you will have to guide him. No voice on the phone can make you do anything you don't want—

Even though that terrible signal had been silenced, its malevolent cadence, a hideous gnawing intrusion, squirmed fresh in his mind.

—why don't you just stab everyone—

"Let's get away from that thing," Caleb said. He led his father away from the phone. "That awful sound from the radio, I heard it blasting through the receiver. That had to hurt like crazy. Sit for just a minute while we put a plan together. But now I think you're right, we *should* think about getting out of here."

Pale's mind ran a flickering sideshow. *Valerie unconscious on the bathroom floor.* What To Do? *Scrawled in lipstick on the mirror. Those damned tarot cards strewn about; a witch's poker*

game upended. Caleb gawking at her the way a kid looks at an
ant suffering beneath a magnifying glass. You don't look so—
"You don't look so good," Otis said. He was standing next to
Ken, all zipped up and ready to head out to the generator shed.

Pale looked up to both men and did the see-saw thing with his
hand.

*"The Hanged Man," Valerie said. "Pause, surrender, letting
go." Her voice was muffled, underwater. But Pale could see her
spindly fingers turning the cards on the rumpled bedspread in the
guest room. "Ten of Swords—Painful endings, deep wounds. The
Tower—Upheaval, chaos, revelation."*

Ken handed Caleb two flashlights and said, "What's the story
with the phone, Paleface?"

He put his hand to his hip where his slicker had been tucked
behind a massive Smith and Wesson 629. Most rig drivers carried
at all times, and Ken preferred to have nothing short of a cannon
on hand. That big hawg had come in handy years ago when he'd
surprised a bear rummaging through the dumpsters at a Flying J
truck stop.

Pale shook his head. "It was that shit from the radio, but vile.
Straight into my head like a drill. Hard to put into words."

The telephone receiver uttered one last snarl of squeaks and
bleeps. It sounded far away, like someone shouting obscenities
from the other side of the river.

A telephone call from the dead, or worse, Pale thought. Then,
a revelation. *Eager to get inside my head, in search of a wound to
salt, then demand a ransom in violence to make it stop.*

Otis and Ken turned their heads toward the sound.

Pale heard nothing but the growling electronic jumble. For the
moment, that awful homicide demand submerged, but he knew it
lurked just under the surface, an alligator watching from the
waterline. He assumed Ken would deliver a real nail-pounding or
turn that hand cannon on him if he made a move, yet part of him
wondered how fast he could dart back to the counter and retrieve
the screwdriver.

*You'll have to cut that Indian before moving on to the others.
I'm talking to you, Mac Daddy. Flannel PJs or not, you'll have his
gun, and then you'll rule the roost. We can go back to that night,
and you can settle business with Daddy on the driveway like a
real man.*

-48-

Give the desert its due.

"Sit tight and clear your head," Otis said. He whacked Ken's slicker with the back of his hand and cast his eyes to the magnum. "Cover that peashooter of yours, makes normal folks nervous. You're on generator duty with me, Lightfeather."

The storm punished the world. The horizon flashed with color: the blues of the arctic, the yellows of the sun, the blood hues of fire. Both landscape and tower were little more than silhouettes, massive shapes leaping from the darkness to remind all that the night was vast, the night was boundless, and it crawled with long-dead music and hidden things.

The rain released the voices of everything that had died of thirst in that limitless barren, the Devil Wind carrying their murmurs to parts unknown. Dormant volcanoes, their faces wind-driven and battered, held old secrets deep in the Undervoid, where the molten blood of the world stirred.

The towers marched, pivoting in their colossal strides, the impossible made possible, all under a tremendous, churning vortex. Counterclockwise that growling cyclone spun, the interior furious. Brilliant, luminous spider legs skittered over the clouds, stretching for miles until their life was spent.

Thunder announced that sentence had been passed, the dungeons had been pulled open, and the shadowless nomads that starved there for generations—bound by laws of dimension and the lawlessness of superstition—were set to prepare the way. The Gate. Science and Sacrifice fused in an unpredictable union, and this night was theirs for the taking.

INTERVIEW III

DEFENSE INTELLIGENCE AGENCY
CASE No. NB-18266-00
October 16, 1993 17:09 HRS
ATTACH TO PREVIOUS INTERVIEW

INVESTIGATORS AND SUBJECT UNCHANGED

CLASSIFIED.
PRESS BLACKOUT.

BEGIN TRANSCRIPTION

Oberon: I feel compelled to explain why I called a halt to the interview earlier today, Doctor Barlowe. Getting into a little hoodoo-woo-woo territory, it seemed.

Barlowe: Cute, a joke. You're loosening up a little, Julie.

Oberon: Agent Oberon will suffice.
Barlowe: Castillo here might think he has a shot at you later tonight at the Red Roof Inn if you keep that up. Probably imagining your JC Penny pantsuit draped over the chair while he takes you to Castillo Boulevard if you know what I mean.

Castillo: We can go all night long, lady.

Barlowe: Your sleep deprivation tactic is ham-fisted. Did Castillo think of it? [DROPS VOICE TO IMITATE CASTILLO] *Back in Desert Storm we bagged some of Saddam's guys, and we never let 'em sleep. We eventually got everything out of those Hajis.* Something like that, Julie?

Oberon: So you think Castillo is using wartime tactics on you. Do you think he had cause to do so? Is that what is ham-fisted about it?

Barlowe: Great. Now you're repeating my words with slight changes. Neurolinguistic games, another academic pukefest. Why *do* the intel agencies keep hiring Ivy League mouth-breathers?

Oberon: Actually, I went to Florida State.

Barlowe: Well, go Gators.

Oberon: Seminoles, Florida State Seminoles.

Barlowe: Who gives a shit. You're probably a low-rent psyche major. But dig this: my face doesn't hurt at the moment, but my mind is *fucking sparkling*. Hey, for all I know it's an interrogation drug of some kind. What are the odds of that, Julie?

Oberon: There's still a lot to discuss about the fourteenth.

Barlowe: Keep me delirious by having multiple interview sessions in one day, I get it. What is it? Five, six o'clock? I don't like to miss the news that Peter Jennings is a dreamboat. You strike me as more of a Connie Chung type, Julie. Do you think she's cute? Does Castillo here know you hit for the other team?

Castillo: You're way out of line, Barlowe. Stay on the subject and watch your mouth.

Barlowe: You're interrogating a drugged woman in a medical facility. Well, you say it's a medical facility. Apparently, one without phones. I wonder how that would look splashed all over the pages of the *New York Times* or the *Desert Tweaker Tattler*. Ha! I kill me sometimes.

Oberon: You mentioned a second work area at the VLA, a black tent, separate from the team. Can you amplify that, expand on it?

Barlowe: Never did get my phone call to check on my kitty. Also, I'm sure by now my parents think I eloped with a microbiologist. Phone call, or no dice.

Oberon: We're in the middle of a national security tragedy, Doctor Barlowe. The stakes are real. When we wrap this session, we'll see about your phone call.

Barlowe: You said that last time. I want you to pinky-swear.

Oberon: It will be done. When you even suggested rituals taking place at the VLA, I knew it was time to pull the plug. But you've experienced injury, trauma, exhaustion. Hey, I get it.

Barlowe: Actually, that was the moment to prick up your ears, not kill the session. Come children, hear the story of Project Dragonfire.

Oberon: The US Government takes this very seriously.

Castillo: As uncooperative as you've been, adding the Halloween angle on top of everything isn't going to help this go any smoother.

Barlowe: Oh look, it's bad cop, dumb cop. Stop looking for the Scooby-Doo solution. Do you want to hear the story or not?

Oberon: Absolutely.

Barlowe: I'm going to say some outrageous shit.

Castillo: That'll be different.

Barlowe: It's the nexus of the whole thing.

The seventeen technicians on the Fun Jet were the *real-world* side of Dragonfire, so to speak. The other guys the B-Team, you called them they were on the *other-world* side.

Oberon: Hmmm.

Barlowe: I'm sensing a roll of the eyes.

Oberon: Was there a specific moment during the VLA run that made you realize that the delineation between teams was as you just described it?

Barlowe: The B-Team presence, in general, put my tits in a tangle, but when things were going full-bore, it got *homicidal* in there.

Oberon: Homicidal?

Barlowe: Bet you weren't expecting that, but yeah, real bad news. It's not like murder broke out at the VLA after we all dropped peyote; it was whatever was going on inside that tent. When that garbled, hard noise . . . some were affected, others, like me, were not.

Oberon: Honestly, I don't follow.

Barlowe: That noise *wanted things.*

Castillo: We need you to be straight with us on this, Doctor Barlowe. No more jerking around.

Barlowe: [SIGHS] Well, sorry, Barney Miller, if I'm a little all over the place.

But I have three words for you, Agent Oberon of the Defense Intelligence Agency The black tent.

Oberon: Alright, you have my attention.

Barlowe: I haven't even started with the crazy. We were lucky to make it out of there.

Oberon: You and Dr. Childs . . . what? Escaped?

Barlowe: Fuckin'-A. Oh, shit. Wait. Wait . . . You distracted me . . . you distracted me and made me forget about the boy. You find that cop, that lying deputy? Where's the kid?

Oberon: No mention in Deputy Youngblood's report. We told you that.

Castillo: It's doubtful there was anyone in that patrol car but you.

Barlowe: After all that chaos, you won't lift a hand to find anyone else that may have survived this mess. *What's wrong with you people?*

Oberon: Our mission is to obtain your clearest recollection. When you wander off the rails, it's our job, *our duty*, to point that out.

Barlowe: That makes zero sense. You ask for my recollection, then refute half of it.

Oberon: Stay on track here.

Barlowe: [SIGHS AND FLUTTERS LIPS] I'm beginning to wonder just who it is you're working for.

-5-
LASERS AND BLOOD WORK

"ALRIGHT, DELEON, JAYNE,** and Barlowe get your data dogs ready to hunt," Randy Childs said, "and come presently upon your hour. We'll be underway very soon."

Childs looked at his frazzled but eager team. They were all good kids—well, kids to him—certainly exhausted and definitely pumped. In his experience, that was the perfect recipe for success. The techs had the gear jacked into the VLA's mainframe reasonably quick, and even though the place resembled a hybrid of a submarine (conduits above, keeping critical data lines out of harm's way) and a recording studio (huge anvil cases opened, filled with rack-mounted computers, power conditioners, DAT recorders and the like), the place appeared to be humming along just fine.

Nikki Barlowe stood before a line of giant IBM tape drives. The basement work area looked like the set from an unintentionally campy Irwin Allen show like *Time Tunnel* or *Lost in Space*, and all she needed was a white lab coat and horn-rimmed glasses.

There was ample digital storage available, Dr. Childs took the time to point out before the gear was loaded onto the jet, but Mr. Jenks was very clear that he wanted the analog tape medium to be the primary capture source. Randy Childs protested—as gently as he could without receiving that icy Jack the Ripper stare Armand Jenks was known for—but the boss was adamant. It shall be so. As far as Childs was concerned, Jenks didn't need to know about the DAT backup.

"We're good here, Doctor C.," Nikki said to Childs. She gave him the thumbs up and took her glasses off to examine a smudge. Her hair, a lush orchard of waves that was leaning to gray now instead of auburn, framed a freckled face and sharp hazel eyes. She wore a T-shirt that read *Smile, Cthulhu Loves You!* featuring a cartoon denizen of Yuggoth snuggling a petrified doggie. "Bobby Greene at Sunspot Solar says we're still nineteen minutes out."

Childs nodded. He wore one of those big com headsets Nikki had seen on the heads of pro football coaches. The condenser mic hung below his chin, and the ear cups were almost comically huge at the sides of his long greyhound's face. Cables snaked down his back and hooked to his belt. It all looked uncomfortable as hell.

"When that plasma smacks the magnetosphere, it's going to be quite the light show up north," Childs said. "I've always wanted to see the aurora, yet here we are, in the arid south."

A voice said from across the room: "Yeah, but imagine us later tonight at Don Francisco's, eating until *mas gordo* and drinking until stupid. You want Northern Lights, Doctor C., be advised it's all knit caps and vodka. What a terrible existence. Can't get a decent meal in Scandinavia, Boss."

Gary DeLeon. Smart as they come, but he'd never set a foot anywhere near Norway. A can of sardines was about as close as he had come, and the smell alone left lifelong scars. He sported a big bushy mustache twenty years out of fashion, mainly grown to conceal his unfortunate harelip. He looked like a guy who desperately wanted to resemble the actor Sam Elliot but leaned more toward Truman Capote. "Bunch of mackerel chewers up there," he added.

"I'm willing to make sacrifices, Gary," Childs said. "There's an old saying: 'never pass up the opportunity to drink with Vikings.'"

Nikki nodded toward the window, where a second team had set up a large, black tent. A couple of thick power cables wormed from the tent to the Paramount Pictures generator truck she'd spied earlier, parked next to the Hertz/Penske gear haulers. "What's up with the Special Bus?" she said. "Those cats came in here and whisked the stuff out of the orange cases faster than shit through a goose. Because I'm nosy, I opened one and saw a *stupidly* expensive gaggle of prisms and mirrors. That smells like laser work to me."

Nikki Barlowe knew lasers. A few years ago, she had been friends with some of the nerds at the MIT Plasma Science and Research Center. On weekends, when security was light, she visited the lab, usually with a bucket of the Colonel's Extra Crispy and always with a bottle of booze. The PSRC guys were next-level brain-trust, and not long after the chicken feast and a doobie, the conversation went straight to far-out land: non-visible light possessed temporal properties, gamma radiation as a possible gateway to immortality, future particle beam weapons were closer than most realized, and further esoteric musings Nikki didn't even pretend to grasp. But mostly, they gathered to do stupid shit with an argon laser, like heat up Jiffy Pop and melt embarrassing albums they were eager to purge from their collections. They even managed to spell out *Red Sox Suck* over the quadrangle via a helium laser, an elaborate array of prisms and mirrors—plus two bottles of Patron Silver. It was all goofy, high-tech hi-jinks until someone burned a hole in the wall and set the storeroom on fire—twice.

"I caught a glimpse of something that looked like medical gear," DeLeon added. "Stainless steel this and that. Also, some ugly box with spinny deeley-bobs on it, rubber tubes, gauges, and shit like that."

"Like a blood centrifuge?" Nikki said. "I'm a closet phlebotomist."

DeLeon cocked his head and nodded as if the image had just dropped into its proper ID slot. "Yeah, maybe so. Like a transfusion pump, maybe? One of those Gary Coleman liver machines?"

"Kidney dialysis, you mean. The poor bastard's got kidney disease. Don't you read *People* in the shitter?"

"Well, whatever, it looked like some sort of blood pump."

"That's creepy. What gives, Doctor C.?"

Childs' face tightened. His eyes darted over to the tent and back to Nikki. Always curious as a cop and quick as a fox, Nikki Barlowe had a tendency to ask questions other people would not. She had sniffed out that Fiona Galbretti and Frankie Zenga were doing the nasty in the office supply closet, sometimes twice in one day. Nikki then started asking Fiona in front of everyone if she liked big, hot beef franks or just sweet Italian sausage. Within a month, Fiona and Frankie were snagged doing blow and humping like rabbits in the employee lounge. Frankie was replaceable, Fiona was not, but Childs fired them on the spot. Nikki had been right all along. Zany times at Medusa Engineering.

"Another side of the operation," Childs said. "A different angle on the tech."

"So says Ned Nebulous," Nikki said. She set her hands to her hips. "I could get a better answer from a Magic Eight Ball."

Gary DeLeon elbowed Artie Jayne. Artie's head popped up from behind gear racks, flashlight still in his mouth. He looked like a New England lighthouse.

"I think they see a different window of opportunity," Childs said.

"How am I supposed to interpret that?" Nikki said. "Where's their data feed? I don't know; maybe someone from over there should run a cable into our hut or show up with a stack of post-it notes. Maybe a napkin with a few drawings on it. I have no idea what they're doing in there. *Do you?*"

"They have their own independent system, I'm told, and Mr. Jenks is keeping all of that on a need-to-know footing."

Childs hated to regurgitate office speak to a room full of scientists, and he had no idea how he was expected to break that news once it was right in front of them. But Armand Jenks had definitely considered it.

I do not care what you tell them, Jenks had told Childs after summoning him to his cramped basement office right after the call from Sunspot Solar. It felt odd to Childs that someone as high in the hierarchy as Jenks didn't have a palatial spread on the upper floor of the MEC building downtown, but Jenks seemed to prefer the belly of R&D Seven outside of Cambridge, surrounded by old brick, river rock, and small pools of incandescent light. *As long as the message is this: you do not need to know. They have a job to do, and that is all I require of them. Just make sure the Dragonfire satellite's telemetry is nice and clean when read by the VLA. Failure will be expensive to Medusa Engineering and reflect poorly on you. Any questions, Doctor Childs?*

Of course, there were plenty of questions, but Randy Childs knew that last statement meant *shut up and get on the airplane.*

So now here was an agitated Nikki Barlowe, a curious Gary DeLeon, and the last-in-line savant Artie Jayne, staring at Childs like a kid wondering what dangerous mysteries lurked in their parents' gun safe.

"We deal with the data that comes to us, and they'll do their own thing. My guess is a DOD angle."

Something's definitely cooking, Nikki thought. *Childs my know a little, or a lot.*

"Lasers and blood work," Nikki snorted. "Happens every day at the VLA."

"That rhymed," Artie said. With the flashlight wedged in his kisser it sounded like *hat-hymed.*

A klaxon blared one long, honking tone. It startled Artie, and the flashlight tumbled from his mouth. Nikki flinched. It felt like a reprimand from a robot.

"Alright, it's showtime," Childs said. He twirled his index finger like a member of a helicopter flight crew, a gesture he'd picked up in Vietnam over twenty years ago. "Let's spin it up, then we'll spit it out. After we're pure and secure, the first round of brain erasers at Don Francisco's is on me. Let's make it happen, pussycats."

Childs ascended the stairs, glad to be free of the hot seat. He was eager to settle into his ground-level station in full view of the magnificent VLA. He loved to gaze at the army of radio telescopes; it filled his head with wonder and fond boyhood memories of hopeful science fiction novels.

Back in 1970, he'd read *The Andromeda Strain* on the nervous deployment flight from Fort Lewis in Washington to Yokota Air Base, Japan, and at the time wondered if, as detailed in the novel, science and its blunders harbored the potential for so much danger, how could the jungle be any worse? He was young and generally wrong about everything then—especially volunteering for military service when he could have just stayed at CalTech and avoided the draft.

That pissed off Harry Childs, his father, to no end. Likewise, it infuriated his hippie sister Irene, who'd done her weeks at Haight-Ashbury, followed flower-power bands around like a groupie, then spent the subsequent years referring to her brother as Randy the Warmonger. He supposed that was better than Baby Killer.

Though miraculously unscathed in combat, it propelled him from a naive twenty-year-old to an experienced veteran in less than eleven months.

Faith grabbed him not long after he witnessed the jungle burst into flames from a dreadful napalm drop. The screams of VC soldiers echoing off the valley walls, and the pungent, acrid stink of burning human meat haunted him nightly. The large-scale homicide of which he was a part, even tangentially, had him on his knees that night after the attack, repeating over and over the only prayer he knew. If it came down to it, he'd kill to stay alive, but prayer or no prayer, he wanted to be nowhere near that kind of darkness ever again. He swore at the first opportunity he'd procure a Bible and read it from *In the beginning* to *Amen.*

When Randy Childs' tour ended, and he managed to get shipped stateside—and through God's mercy, assigned to a domestic intelligence unit and stayed stateside—he counted the days until he received his discharge papers and could get back into CalTech with full VA benefits. By then, his mother was dead, his sister lived with a dingbat commune in northern California, and his father was terminal, Godless as ever, and hot with death-anger.

Now in 1993, the klaxon calling all to order and Project Dragonfire ready to roll, Armand Jenks had made it clear that the black tent was just like that napalm drop; not only a no-go zone but something, if stared at or contemplated long enough, would require the faith he'd summoned in the jungle to separate its claws from his hide. Childs wasn't sure what would occur there, but one look at Jenks as he arrived at the VLA in Medusa Engineering's jet-black Bell 206, and he knew the man had more on his mind than keeping his troops in line. He stepped from the chopper with the arrogant confidence of a Mafia Don, dressed in a black suit and perfect fedora. Today he was accompanied by a stern-looking military type, a buzz-cut, square-jawed jarhead in aviator shades with a 1911 on his hip.

To Randy Childs' eye, Jenks stood a waif-thin six-four, maybe six-five. His suits were impeccable; no less than bespoke Savile Row, crafted from only the finest British wool. His narrow neck poked out from his starched collars like a cobra charmed from its basket, supporting an angular chin and an unmistakable Basil Rathbone beak of a nose. His pale blue eyes, despite their cool, arctic hue, could burn a hole into concrete. If the man had ever sprouted facial hair, there was no evidence. It was difficult to pin down his age, and Nikki had once joked over a spliff and a cooler full of Rolling Rock: *Maybe if we cut him in half and count the rings, we'll be able to determine what epoch spawned such a creature.*

Jenks answered only to the corporation's never seen, known-by-name-only executives, who harbored zero compunction about isolating themselves in their lofty thirty-third-floor suites. He made sure things stayed on the rails, and when they did not, Armand Jenks' intolerance for men's foibles was made abundantly clear.

When the initial white paper for Project Dragonfire was

presented to Childs in 1985, he'd been in his own cluttered mad scientist's office at R&D Seven, trying to figure out his new FAX machine. The courier dropped it on his desk.

"This just came from the thirty-third floor," said the courier, a fresh-faced kid who was likely an unpaid intern. "I was told it goes straight to Dr. Childs and R&D Seven, so here I am." He backed out of the room like a member of the Royal Guard.

Twenty minutes later, Randy Childs had stuffed the document back into its envelope, dismissed as nutty, speculative pseudo-science. He had a mind to send it back up the chain stamped *Fucking Ridiculous*. However, an enclosed hand-written note from Blasko Thorpe, Medusa Engineering CEO, read:

Dr. Childs:

You have been selected as Project Dragonfire's technical director. You will answer directly to Mr. Jenks, who will provide you with any required resources, space, and personnel. Although the satellite described in the white paper is nearly completed and will be deployed soon, there is still a generous amount of time to work out the earthbound details. I remind you that your security clearances are still in effect, and Project Dragonfire—in perpetuity—is to be considered above Top Secret.

The enclosed cashier's check for a hundred grand served as an enticing sweetener, and two days later, when Randy Childs exited the thirty-third-floor conference room, he had a preliminary team of eight, a starter budget of eleven million, and a lease on star time at the Very Large Array outside of Socorro, New Mexico—all under a four-year deadline. Plus, of course, a nice tax-free six-figure bonus.

"There are old memories everywhere," Jenks told Childs not long after he'd read the white paper—which, despite numerous inquiries, never had its author revealed. "Old forces, Dr. Childs. *Old commands.* Imagine the handiwork of creation and its shortcuts in the very fuel of the stars. There is an Architect there, to be sure. And his name is Zero."

"From what's in the paper, I'm almost inclined to say Space DNA," Childs said, half-joking.

Jenks offered a harlequin's grin.

"Such things," Jenks said, "keep the mystery alive. The

Dragonfire satellite is scheduled for the next Challenger launch, slated for November. The public will be told the payload is a Spartan Satellite sent up to study Haley's Comet. With Haley's streaming star-child soon visible, the cover story is fortuitous, would you not agree? We have managed to delay that launch until January to tune last-minute details."

Randy Childs just nodded.

Just over a year later, after the *Challenger* blew up seventy-three seconds into the STS-51L launch, Jenks was furious. *Fucking NASA amateurs!* he had thundered from his basement office. Compounded by NASA's two-year plus launch freeze, administrator shuffles, and *that useless pain in the ass Gulf War* as Jenks referred to it, it took far longer than usual for Medusa Engineering to strong-arm NASA into another launch slot. On a few occasions, it was suggested that the European Space Agency handle the lift, but the weight of the new, re-vamped DragSat II device was sure to exceed their launch capabilities.

Shit happens, Childs had said.

The excrement will roll on you if it does not, Jenks responded.

Eight years later, nearly to the day, he stood at the VLA, an absolute monster of technology and logistics, attempting to snare solar ejecta and harvest exactly God knew what—or what God *knew.*

The klaxon blew again. Childs brought the mic to his lips and said, "Good afternoon, Project Dragonfire. This is your Captain speaking. Today's forecast is sunny, with highs in the mid-eighties with a chance of CME. VLA is live. Telemetry from the DragSat Two is nominal. Looks like we're in the pipe."

A tense silence fell over the control room. Through the window, Childs could see Armand Jenks' hand pop out of the black tent, beckoning his stern-looking military-type assistant. The other man did not wear a uniform, but the buzz-cut, creased pants, black shoes, and sidearm were clear enough signal that he was one serious cat. Colonel Nobody also wore earmuffs, the type one would wear at the rifle range or the airport tarmac. The tent flap closed behind him. Ahead, twenty-seven 230-ton radio dishes pointed at the flawless New Mexico sky.

"Let 'er rip," Childs said.

And from the sky, secrets—and sorcery.

-6-
DRAGONFIRE

THIRTY MINUTES INTO Dragonfire and Nikki Barlowe realized she had never seen such a rapid flood of data; it flowed at such a rate she feared she and her assistants would be unable to analyze all of it. The wall of IBM 3480 and 3490 magnetic tape drives whirred like a laundromat.

"The 3480's are running at ninety-five percent," Artie said from across the room. "3490's are spooling up. It's like a tilt-a-whirl in there, Niks."

"You're doing fine," Nikki said over the machine roar.

Three big CRT monitors displayed the information flood—green text and code only a computer scientist could love. On the farthest left screen, a jolt of static caught her eye. She gave the monitor a tap, and it cleared up.

"Cheap Korean shit. Buy American or suffer the consequenc—"

The interference returned with fervor. Scrolling upstream in steady blocks, the data appeared to distort—*displace*—Nikki thought, actually bend as it made its way into the monitor's northern territory as if refracted by liquid.

A moment later the distortion dissipated, but upon clearing, the green text had been augmented, accompanied by something else, as if a passenger had been picked up along the way. Intertwined with the slashes, brackets, underscores, and numbers were arcane symbols that she could not immediately decipher:

```
void assign (float, x float,y)

{
```

55
32 / [illegible]

“permissions” true = 1 false = 0

   Zero = [illegible]
   Shadowless = [illegible]

}

hydrogen—978.332/5
helium—999.660/2

radio—988 ӤלOקμ¥
gamma—$10^{20.04}$
X-ray—$10^{17.5}$ ̈փՓ [ÿ0xycn
M-ray—$15^{32.3}$ ħV̈ eokbbb yu\k

void <<([illegible] Ɖ [illegible] ℕʆ [?% ?])>> [[ELSEWHERE]]

{

// [function definition]

   [illegible]
   [illegible] {[complex]} [illegible]

322
      33
            911
0000 **000** 000.0000
[ELSEWHERE = [illegible] { Ĉ Λ ⊾ Σ ß }
   [illegible]
}

The data stream moved with such ferocity Nikki could barely read it, but, like a conversation heard through a closed door, just enough made it through to cause confusion. *Jesus, what a mess, but part of me feels I should know this . . . but if this is code, it's Farsi for Robots. This looks . . . primitive? That's dumb. But I should see unfiltered DragSat II data instead of this gibberish, and* that *bugs me. Someone upstream fucked up, and Jenks will hit the rafters when he finds out.*

She looked over to DeLeon, who also had his hands full. "You okay over there, Sheriff? I have some monkey business here I can't really identify."

DeLeon didn't look up, but he managed a thumbs up as he popped a Tiparillo in his mouth. He had no intention of lighting it; he'd just chew it until it was soggy—Sam Elliot cool. "Isn't unidentifiable kind of what we're looking for?" he said.

"I mean an embed in the code. I don't know . . . junk data."

"If it's streaming alright we can sift through later, try to make sense of it. I can always write an excise filter and dump it into a trash file. Use it to make a hat for Jenks."

"It's really hauling ass, too."

DeLeon smushed his Tiparillo around until it hung from the opposite side of his mouth. He looked at Nikki through a forest of desk lamps, hanging cables, and monitors. "We're still lean and green in the data stream, you know what I mean? No problems seen, Jelly Bean."

Nikki rolled her eyes. The symbols jerked their way up the screen with the rest of the satellite's data flow. *Hard, angular. Ancient. A dead language? Now who's talking gibberish?*

"When we're back at R&D Seven," Nikki said, "when I have printouts and time, I'll going to find out wh—"

"Weather coming in, weather coming in," Artie called above the din. He sounded like a submariner relaying an order. "Right over us too. Put an eyeball to it, Niks. It's a little weird."

When Nikki looked out the window, she saw a strong breeze buffet the black canvas tent. Two armed guards stood outside, wearing helmets and goggles, holstered sidearms, rifles at their chests. Their uniforms flapped.

That's *a little much,* she thought. *Maybe not Runes in your satellite data odd, but strange—like that black tent. But I'm finally here with my eyes to the stars. Good Old Fashioned Space Shit.*

Beyond, billions in hardware aimed at the sky. The afternoon was late, but cloud cover, not so much as a word about it in the National Weather Service report, began to coalesce above the array. Like Childs, the sight of those monolithic radio dishes brought her back to the piles of science fiction she gobbled up from junior high to graduate school. Defensive weapons, a younger Nikki Barlowe would have imagined those dishes to be, pointed skyward to protect Earth from invasion. *Keep looking—keep watching the sky!* warned the last line from *The Thing From Another World,* and here she was, doing just that.

Fun as it was to stay up late with her brother Rex and watch *The Blob* or *Earth Vs. The Flying Saucers* on channel eight, it was reading Asimov's *Fantastic Voyage* (although she didn't know at the time he had novelized the movie script, not the other way around), plus countless others, that irreversibly implanted her with the tech-bug. The possibilities explored in deep space and time travel stories really put the hook in her. She thought Mr. Spock was the coolest person ever, so much so that she saved allowance money and bought Leonard Nimoy's record, *Mr. Spock's Music from Outer Space,* which she, like nearly everyone else, quickly regretted—although it never ended up in the laser melt-pile at the Plasma Science and Research Center.

Nikki asked for a chemistry set for her eighth birthday when she should have been playing with an Easy-bake Oven or an Etch-A-Sketch, and she was almost insulted at the simplicity of the puzzles in *Highlights,* a children's magazine found at every dentist's office. By the time she was thirteen, Nikki helped her dad build a Heathkit stereo receiver, concocted a fertilizer that increased the yield in her mother's garden by twenty percent, and fashioned a speaker out of a metal trash can lid. That speaker sounded like shit, but by jingos, it worked.

As a sophomore, she was the over-achiever anomaly that hung out with the Deep Purple stoners as well as the dorks who'd joined Math Teens. She began submitting gag articles for her high school newspaper, with titles such as *The Banana Compass: Can We Trust Tropical Fruit When Steering Our Vessels?, Why You Should Live Next to an Active Volcano, Grow Your Own Weasels Before the Russians Find Out,* and the one that earned her a trip to the Dean of Girls office: *The Egyptians Hated Fat Girls—But Put Up With Them Anyway.*

Suburban middle-class life in America was good; Nikki won the lottery, having been born at the time she was. Even though she knew she was different, it never occurred to her to assume superiority—she took people at their word and kept hers, and if they proved to be clowns, she walked away. Boys acted like monkeys, and they had their charm, and she occasionally relented, but technology and its precisions always obeyed . . . until they didn't.

Every now and then the fractal nature of everything intervened, and the roads got crooked—and wicked fast at that.

She watched as a few dark clouds gathered above the array. Cloud cover was something that happened gradually, you turned away, did your thing, looked again, things had changed. To Nikki this resembled a time-lapse, like those she used to watch on *Nova* on their old Zenith, when the UHF antenna worked properly.

"Artie, you're right, that *is* weird," she said. "I'm not crazy about the speed at which these clouds are gathering, but I would think they wouldn't affect anything, so tough titty."

"Roger that. Titty is tough," DeLeon said.

Artie, still in his office chair, wheeled himself down the aisle of IBM drives, legs out, arms up, a kid at Disneyland—until he arrived at his workstation.

"Tape spooling hard," Artie said. "But as far as that weather goes, relative air mass will be an issue, Niks—I know at least that much. If the VLA crew can adjust for the opacity, wind, signal refraction, whatever, we should be able to stay in the green like we are now."

On the left screen, more of the indecipherable ramblings, popping on and off in luminous green characters while digits cycled, and lines of computer language scooted up the screen real estate in dense, rapid blocks.

The first jab of lightning surprised Nikki, but the mighty punch of thunder caused the entire team to flinch at their consoles. A moment later, Nikki, DeLeon and Artie popped out of their seats like little prairie dogs. Eyes glued to the window, they watched as cloud cover stirred in slow motion, a warped iris of tendrils.

Lightning wormed from the cloud bank. It met the ground with a tremendous, purple flash, overloading their retinas, searing their cones and rods with sheets of impossible light. Moments later, a second rip of thunder announced its arrival with a deep, concussive blast.

"Jayzus!" a wincing DeLeon said. "How the goddamned hell did that just come out of nowhere?"

Batting her eyelids, Nikki shook her head.

Nowhere? Sorry pal, how about Elsewhere?

"If we take a direct hit, that could zap all the gear," Artie said. He tilted his head to the noisy wall of IBM boxes. "Also, if the VLA crew can't make adjustments for the weather, this entire job is probably screwed. Either way, Jenks will lose his shit. Maybe eat us."

Another barrage ignited the clouds, a feral network of horizontal veins. Thunder slugged the VLA again, far angrier than the opening salvo.

"Artie has a point," Nikki said. "A strike could fry this hardware. EMP for thee and me."

DeLeon shook his head. "You'd figure they get a bundle of electrical activity out here, Niks. Let's not sweat it and get distracted." He hoped he sounded believable, but the Tiparillo bobbed in his lips like the needle of a VU meter. Sam Elliot would not approve.

"I'd like you to be right about that," Artie said. "But where did that storm come from? Weather sat images were clear as a bell. And come on, *nothing* forms that fast."

Wicked fast? Nikki thought. *The road just turned crooked, didn't it?*

Nikki planted herself in front of the line of big CRT monitors. The data stream moved in frenetic, vertical fits, so rapidly now that her eyes could barely catch the unknown language—that's what she decided to label it—as it breached the DragSat II telemetry. The rate it banged the tape drives was about as heavy as the system allowed; the cooling fans had switched on, but the machines pumped serious BTUs.

"I've still got some weird shit on my monitor, fellas," Nikki said.

"Need a Kleenex?" Artie said. He reached into his pocket and pulled out a cellophane, travel-sized package of tissues, but he had one eye on the gathering storm. "Don't leave home without 'em."

"Dork. No, I mean this *unreadable* weird shit."

"Any change from a minute ago?" DeLeon said. He was at the window now, hands on the glass. He was surprised at the warmth.

"Just piles of it, *more* of it. Started at maybe ten percent, now

I think we're over fifty." She looked at DeLeon, whose expression had turned grave. The Tiparillo no longer wiggled beneath the canopy of his mustache. "I'm serious, dude. It's taking over the job."

Nikki looked at a sky rife with bruises. God rays shone through jagged holes in the stormfront, gargantuan circus spotlights illuminating the dishes, and miles away, the massive gridwork of an electrical substation sheathed in moving shadows. The entire color palette of the desert had changed.

A purple flash dazzled her eyes. At first, she thought it to be another gouge of lightning.

"Woah," Artie said. "Did I just see that? *Did that come from the black tent?*"

"What in fuzzy fuck?" DeLeon said.

"Laser," Nikki said. "Had to be."

"You weren't joking about all those mirrors and prisms," Artie said.

Nikki held a high, tight shrug. *I'm just sayin'.* "What the hell else could it be?"

DeLeon said, "I don't kn—"

A slow, drowsy baritone, the howl of a waking giant, resounded through the basement data room. It wormed through their minds, this audible tumor, spawning a snarl of unpronounceable syllables.

No one moved or said anything for a few seconds.

"I didn't imagine that," Artie said.

"Neither did I," DeLeon said.

"None of us did," Nikki said. "Boys, there's no way that can't be related to the garbage on my monitor, the lang—"

Less than a thousand yards away, the radio dish designated EA16 suffered a direct lightning strike. The impact flare birthed a fountain of sparks which spewed trails of glowing slag, purple/orange plasma hot as a welder's torch.

"Fuck me in tube socks," DeLeon said. He stepped back from the glass. "I should be nowhere near this window."

"Sit tight, I'm going upstairs to talk to Doctor C.," Nikki said. She was up the stairs and gone.

Randy Childs was not pleased. The longer he looked at the black tent, the more he realized he'd been played. Project Dragonfire—

whatever its true ambition—unfolded there. He and his team had likely been farmed out to NASA for some shitty subcontract work, which served as a perfect cover for the VLA time. The whole thing carried the stink of Pentagon black budget, or worse. NSA? CIA? Hell, who knew? It wasn't that Childs had any objection to doing military work; he'd served not only in the Infantry but in the Vietnam hot zone. What chapped his ass was that he'd been chumped. No wonder the 1985 white paper seemed so much bullshit—it was bullshit—but the hundred grand in shut-up lube made it a lot easier to beer-bong the swill and assume the role of hapless dupe. That prick, Jenks.

After the first lightning impact, cloud cover rapidly closed the sunshine gap. A number of the distant dishes bathed in the God rays now crawled with storm shadow.

Without an ocean to fuel the cyclonic action, the weather defied explanation. Childs had little room to speculate on its genesis, other than Dragonfire directly, no matter how far out that idea was to him. The wind brayed against the control room glass, peppering it with dust and debris.

Even though I took a hundred grand to go with the flow, what if the flow becomes dangerous?

Just as another bright whack of light blasted from the tent, Nikki popped up from downstairs. She looked as nervous as the doggie on her Cthulhu T-shirt.

"Niks," Childs said. "It's a little crazy up here. What's cooking below?"

"Weird shit all over my monitors, freaky noises, nervous nerds, and screeching tape drives. You know, the usual. Listen, on top of all *that,* we're a bit worried about this psycho weather out of nowhere. You saw the dish take that smack to the face?"

"Oh yes I did."

"And that monkey business in the tent stinks like shit, too. You saw that purple flash? I *told* you those mirrors and prisms meant laser work, I'm sure of it." She pointed to the window. "Right after that little light show, the storm begins to close the gap right over us—that *can't* be a coincidence."

Childs nodded, then adjusted his gigantic headset. "Agreed," he said.

They watched as Nikki's words blossomed true. Irising over the VLA, the burgeoning storm's interior flashed alive with purple and green. Jagged rivers crawled over the cyclone, splitting off and impaling the ground. A few more wiggled away to juicier targets, the substation a few miles into the gloom, a high-tension tower or two in the darkening haze of Route 60.

Soon, like an eclipse, the cloud cover achieved totality. To the west, the sun seemed little more than a suggestion.

"You *do* have the authority to pull the plug, right?" Nikki asked. "I'm just saying, we may be headed there, so it's good to be ready for it. Jenks will shit a gopher, but he'll get over it."

A second later, the rain spigot opened. The wind grabbed hold and drove it sideways.

"Holy smokes," Childs said. He turned his head to the weather monitor display. "Niks, look at the weather feed."

The weather station monitor read:

Wind: SxSE 57 mph
Temperature: 95.6F
Relative Humidity: 9.3%
Barometric Pressure: 27.33

"That's a hot wind with a storm ceiling," Nikki said, pointing at the monitor. "Pressure and humidity in the basement. Even *I* know that's not right—a nine percent humidity while *raining*. That's absolutely impossible. Either the weather station is on the fritz or . . . dammit, what's going on in that tent? What the hell are they doing in there?"

Childs stood up. "*Jenks* is what they're doing in there. But you're right; I'm real close to putting the brakes on this. I don't like it."

"I know Jenks will have your ass in a sling, but I really think you need to consider it."

Or worse, Childs thought. *Blasko Thorpe and Armand Jenks residing on my south side will make every effort to assure that I'm ruined; they'll take their hundred grand's worth of retribution. Attention: career suicide clean-up on aisle four.*

"Why on earth would anyone need anything like mirrors, prisms, and medical gear when studying a CME?" Nikki said. "Doesn't that set your hairs on end? And if not, what do you know that the rest of us don't?"

Childs felt beads of sweat erupt on his forehead. *I took a fat check to look the other way, that's what I know.*

"Again Niks, I was left in the dark on this second crew Jenks put together."

This much was partially true. Randy Childs was paid to not ask questions, so he didn't. On more than one occasion, Childs had heard Jenks through his shitty basement office door, either murmuring to himself or on a call. The details were foggy, but a few terms popped up repeatedly: *The Gate, The Discoveries of Crosius*, a glacier near a place called *Exeter,* and some mountain he'd never heard of called *Walpurgis Peak*—but all mentioned in direct relation to Project Dragonfire. Childs did his best to pretend he wasn't listening, but at night—after a bourbon or two—he was unable to put it out of his mind, because the truth was staring him in the face.

They're looking for something, and they paid me not to notice.

Noise and light blared from the tent. Beams found every possible exit. The two armed guards, though pummeled by the weather and abused by the crushing light, made sure to keep their distance from the thick eels of power cables.

"*Woah,*" Childs said. "The power running through those cables must be tremendous."

Nikki said, "Of course it is. It's juicing the goddamn laser, or whatever the hell else is in there. Why else would they need power *and* security like that?"

Fucking Jenks, Childs thought as he lifted the condenser mic to his mouth. His voice buzzed through every speakerphone in the building. "Attention everyone, this is Dr. Childs. I'm implementing a yellow alert, repeat, we are now at a yellow alert status. Be on standby for an emergency shutdow—"

A low, awful bellow wound its way through the control center, followed by a brutal electronic noise that roared through everything that would resonate: headsets, computer speakers, desk tops, wooden shelves, the water in the sparkletts cooler, even the glass that separated them from the wild weather.

Nikki covered her ears. Several screaming team members ripped off their headsets. One of the Medusa Engineering techs, Kristen Irfrate, Nikki thought her name was, pushed herself away from her station and threw up. Kenji Hurosawa picked up a pair of scissors and eyed it in a way that made her very, *very* nervous.

To the west, the sun began its descent. It burned hot and lethal behind the storm, the clouds glowing, swollen with brilliant veins of lightning. Soon the sun's hue would change from blazing orange to the sanguine red of sacrifice, accompanied by this ugly score from everywhere yet nowhere. Again she imagined this grating, dissonant noise, which seemed to be driving quite a few of her colleagues batshit with misery, the aural interpretation of the symbology she'd seen on her monitor. If *that* was true, then whatever levers Jenks had pulled in the black tent were of a very sinister, and possibly *off-world* origin. The very thought made her heart thud beneath her sternum.

One of the VLA employees, someone Nikki did not know, leaped to his feet and slapped his palms to his lips, agonizing how there were "Nails in my mouth! My God, my mouth is filled with nails!" As he dropped to his knees, nearly in tears, mouth agape, tongue dangling, Kenji Hurosawa eyed him like prey.

The monitors vibrated, binders flipped to the floor, soda cans tipped then bubbled over. At the sight of pens and coins scooting across desktops, Nikki was crazily reminded of her brother's ancient electric football game.

GZrt-Ru- !!Bŏk

The enemy voice croaked a dark seduction into Randy Childs' mind—*Strangle her. The disbelief alone will make her eyes bulge. You can bathe in her last scream—*

Childs ripped his headset off and tossed it aside. It dangled from the cable and the ugly noise raged from the micro-speakers, a tiny demon gnawing at his ankles.

He fumbled with the cord until he managed to disconnect it. He spit bile onto the floor and looked up at Nikki, who also looked like she wanted to puke.

"Did you hear that?" Childs said.

To Nikki, the man looked like he'd just watched his dog die.

"Did you hear *what it said to me?*"

The military guy at the tent, he wore ear protection, Childs thought as his hands scrambled over the desktop until he found a pair of cocktail napkins. He wadded them up, dunked them in cold coffee, and crammed as much wet paper as he could into each ear.

Nikki shook her head. "I heard garbage, ugly electronic garbage. But look at everyone else."

One of the dish techs, gripped by the voice in his head—the one that whispered old memories—stood up and said, *"I miss you, Delilah!"* then plowed his face directly into the glass of a CRT monitor. After its surface split into a spiderweb crack, the man fell back into his chair, his face brutalized and eyes bulging like ping pong balls. Pausing no more than a second, he grabbed the leading edge of his desk and pulled hard, wheeling himself into the monitor again. There was a loud *pop!* accompanied by a jet of sparks and blue smoke from the rear vents. The poor bastard ground his face into the smashed glass, then took hold of the enormous screen and yanked it like a man struggling to put on a turtleneck sweater.

Blood poured out of the monitor, soaked his shoulders, pooled on the desk, then dripped to the floor like syrup. From inside the plastic shell of the screen, Nikki heard one last whine: *"I miss you, Delilah!"*

The suicidal tech's body stiffened then he slumped to his knees, face permanently crammed into the monitor. He twitched. If he wasn't dead, he would be soon.

Billy Urus, a friendly Jewish kid from Brooklyn and new to Medusa Engineering, sprang up from his station and looked at Nikki, his face warped with shame, his tongue white. A trickle of blood ran from his left ear.

"She *dared* me, you know!" he screamed. He examined his hands like they were foreign objects, then wiped them on his shirt. As buried trauma twisted his face, Billy's mouth yawned open, his lips deformed into a weird, snarled ellipse. His eyes watered. Snot dripped.

"I didn't know the bum was just asleep . . . It was a dare . . . I wouldn't have stabbed him if I'd known. I thought he was already dead." Billy pulled at his lips, stretching his mouth into an unspeakable width. The carpet of his tongue rolled out.

"Billy, slow down," Childs said.

"But I enjoyed it," Billy said through his stretched mouth. It sounded like *buh hi henoii et.* "I never could tell her how I *enjoyed* it. She dared me, and I wanted to make her happy, prove I was no sissyboy."

"Good God, Billy, *please stop*," Nikki said.

"I didn't know . . . *vagrant* blood would feel so good . . . so *different*."

The raging, brutal noise tore through the room.

Billy drove his thumb into his eye, then twisted away at it like a man scooping the dregs from a can of beans. Howling and laughing simultaneously, he pulled the thumb out and jabbed the bloody pulp over his shoulder like some sort of crazed baseball umpire. *You're outta here!*

"His soul leaked all over me."

Billy stumbled backward until he thumped ass-first into his work area. After he used his index finger to draw a horrible red smile on his face, he looked like a Gacy painting.

"Time to leave," Nikki said as she pulled Childs away from the consoles.

Chaos had taken roost. A chair went flying past, followed by a stapler, a telephone, someone's shoes, and a huge five-gallon Sparkletts water bottle.

Kenji Hurosawa jumped on the man with nails in his mouth and plunged the scissors into his back. A woman leaned against the wall and worked on her tongue with a pair of wire cutters. Someone kept screaming *He knows I did it, he knows I did it!* Kristen Irfrate, covered in puke, jabbed a pencil into the back of her hand.

Hideous and accusatory, the Signal assaulted every living thing in the VLA. The secret chambers of hearts opened and out poured scarlet shame. Something that needed its blood resuscitated by machine, something that bellowed in a language ancient enough to have been snuffed out by the Great Flood, had been conjured in the black tent.

Outside, the storm grew incensed. Childs and Nikki looked over to the tent, which took whipping but remained standing. The guards stood fast, faces low, rifles slung. The ground cables continued to spasm, tentacles of a struggling squid.

A sheet, a physical, visible *sheet* of purple light screamed out from the gap where the tent met the dirt. The guards immediately dropped as if someone had thrown a switch. The sound, so hot on its heels it may very well have been in tandem with the flash, was an even more dreadful variant of the ugly barrage of tones that had moments earlier seeded darkness and driven men to suicide.

Nikki and Childs fled; behind them, nothing but screams.

When they reached the basement stairs, Nikki turned her head to look. Billy Urus was busy with his other eye yet seemed to be looking directly at her. Behind him, Kenji Hurosawa's bloody scissors rose, then fell. Rose then fell.

"They want my shadow." Billy gurgled, his mouth filling with scarlet, his new clown face rearranged. Blinded and yet still never losing track of Nikki, Billy pointed directly at her with a slick hand that had been dipped in dark red paint. *"Because they can't have yours."*

Nikki felt like sand had been poured into her throat. She didn't know whether to speak or scream at the sight of the blind prophet, but when a knife whizzed by her face and embedded in the wall, she yelped and dug her nails into Childs, who pulled Nikki along, the two of them bumbling down the stairs.

In the basement corridor, they could already tell things had made a turn for the worst. A streak of blood smeared the Pepsi machine, and the snack dispenser was overturned. The janitor's closet door hung open, and several mop handles were split into jagged stakes. The fire extinguisher station's glass had been shattered, and the item was missing. A boom box sat on the janitor's cart, blasting the vicious signal, cranked so loud the speakers were breaking up. Bloody footprints led back into the bullpen and had squashed several packs of Ritz crackers and Hostess ding-dongs along the way.

They gazed down the corridor. A few yards away stood the exit, but outside was sixty-mile an hour winds, hot rain, and worst of all, that wicked black tent.

"We go?" Childs said. "I mean into the bullpen, not outside."

Nikki nodded. She crazily wondered if her cat was okay all the way home in Boston. "They're our friends. We have to at least try," she said. "God almighty, what is happening?"

They pushed the door open to a horrendous scene. Gary DeLeon held the missing fire extinguisher over his head, bushy mustache drenched in scarlet and snot, shirt torn like a swashbuckler's. Arched in his chair sat Artie Jayne, head cracked watermelon. Artie's lips and bridgework dangled like horrible wind chimes, and his trusty flashlight shone from his lap. Most of Artie's natural teeth were on the floor, along with his glasses and a weaponized section of broom handle. One of his Reeboks was untied.

"Jesus, Gary, no!" Childs screamed.

DeLeon hissed. He reared back with the fire extinguisher, one of those big steel jobs designed for heavy-duty work, and dropped it onto Artie's cheek. The man was still alive, and his scream blended terror and resignation, childhood fear and the adult awareness of death. His entire body heaved as the chair set sail on its wheels, rolling backward like it was in some Carol Burnett skit.

-78-

Childs, channeling the formidable linebacker he was before he volunteered for the Đồng Nai Province, rushed DeLeon. He slammed into the man, driving their weight into Nikki's work console. The monitor displaying the bizarre symbols tumbled away.

Slipping in Artie's blood, the men crashed to the floor. They grappled, flailing and grunting, smeared in scarlet muck. The other monitors fell and fritzed out.

Still, from everywhere, that dissonant noise blared in intermittent, buzzing pulses, a robot with a speech impediment and murder in its eye. Each time one struck, DeLeon howled and snapped at Childs with his teeth, but for now, Randy Childs' improvised earplugs were holding, and the horrible signal was little more than a muted gibberish.

Childs grabbed the broken broom handle and pressed it to DeLeon's Adam's apple. DeLeon gagged, his face round as a blowfish. He let go of the fire extinguisher hose, and it rolled away.

In Gary DeLeon's mind's eye, he was back in the boy's locker room at Cresthaven Junior High; that prick Carlos "Mad Dog" Mendoza singling him out for his harelip, calling him Rat Face, then in the showers, towel-snapping his ass and tip of his dick. Carlos laughed and pointed, said a bunch of insulting shit in Spanish he didn't think the twelve-year-old Gary DeLeon could understand. But Gary DeLeon *did* understand; he knew the insults cut to the quick as Carlos referred to him as *afemenado, maricon, joto*, said that he wore panties, jerked off to pictures of Leif Garret, got his harelip from sucking off bums in the street. How badly he wanted to beat Carlos's face in, use a twenty-pound dumbbell from the school gym and pummel that punk's ugly mouth until his crooked teeth clattered onto the gym floor like marbles. Carlos would be free to choke on *his* blood, then call for *his* mommy and wet *his* pants.

The voice from everywhere and nowhere knew. It tunneled inside DeLeon's head and stirred the shame, resurrected it from ashes, made it whole and real, then brought it to life through the lens of a child's eye and the wounded pride of an unsatisfied adult. He'd beat Carlos's ass but good today; used that fire extinguisher to extinguish that motherfucker, and pronto. *Adios, El Fucko.*

Childs squatted on DeLeon's chest. He balled his right hand and delivered a flurry of punches, further soaking DeLeon's mustache into a tacky red mop. His nose now pointed to the left.

"You killed Artie! What's wrong with you?"
"I killed *Carlos*," DeLeon gurgled. "Adios, El Fucko."

Nikki was suitably horrified by everything, which turned the trip to New Mexico and the chance to engage in some Good Old-Fashioned Space Shit into an unspeakable nightmare. She looked out the window and saw, through a series of powerful lightning strikes, Sharon Voorhees, one of the software engineers Jenks had assigned to Dragonfire from the very beginning. Sharon was a few yards from the black tent, beating a man senseless with a shovel. Scrambling on all fours, the dazed victim seemed bent on escape, but the wind, confusion, and terror proved overwhelming. Sharon Voorhees kicked the poor slob square in the ass and then cleaved his neck with the spade. He dropped like a bad habit.

For the second time in under five minutes, Nikki grabbed Childs in an effort to pull him away. He resisted at first, his primal urge to exact retribution for Artie a powerful lure, an enticement to stay and finish the job.

"*Up!*" Nikki screeched. "Leave him, Randy. Gary's lost his mind."

Childs complied. Outside he saw Sharon, soaked to the bones, and perched on the unknown man's back in a gargoyle's squat. She stabbed the spade into the ground, eyes bulging, tongue flicking.

Gary DeLeon rolled over to his side and began to blubber, "Carlos you fucker. Mad Dog, you motherfucker. Adios, El Fucko . . ."

The wall of IBM tape drives whirred—screaming almost—the heat barreling out of them unable to be mitigated by the struggling fans. Soon, Nikki knew, there would be smoke, and, if things were not dealt with, fire.

"Forget the big tape spools; Jenks is on his own," Childs said. He wiped DeLeon's blood from his hands then pointed at the anvil cases full of rack gear. "Grab the DATs. There are external drives, and I'll take care of those. Fuck Dragonfire and Jenks. If we make it out of here, we'll stick these drives in a vault somewhere, then blow the lid off this shitshow. Toss everything in Artie's tool bag, and we're gone."

Nikki reached into the bank of DAT machines and pulled all the cassettes. Childs yanked the drives out of the bays and stacked them like library books. After Nikki dumped all of Artie's tools, they dropped the entire mess into the canvas bag and zipped it up.

On its side, in red Marks-A-Lot, Artie had drawn a caricature of Armand Jenks, clenching a cigar in his teeth and wearing a sombrero.

Near the bank of IBM racks, Artie was still slouched in the chair, just as bloody, just as dead, a discarded ventriloquist's puppet.

"Sorry, Artie," Nikki said as she handed the bag to Childs. "I'm sorry for what happened to you, old buddy."

Childs nodded. He looked over at DeLeon, who was still bleeding from his nose and mewling like a toddler. "We're out, Niks."

By the time they hustled to the end of the basement corridor, Nikki was panting, and Childs was in the middle of a post-adrenaline rush. The bizarre audible assault had subsided for now, but the thunder still played a heavy game, splitting the sky. The firehose of rain against the steel door blended with the awful wounded steer call of the wind into the roar of whitewater rapids.

"It's goddamn hell outside," Nikki said. "We have no jackets, no boots. Nothing."

"Well, it's *bloody* hell in here," Childs said. He glanced back at the corridor. He hadn't noticed the dead body slumped underneath the bank of payphones. The other missing broom handle stuck out of the woman's ear. "Just get out of the building. Soon as we're clear, we find any open vehicle."

All it took was a nudge, and the wind did the rest—the door was snapped away and banged against the cinder block. Hot needles of rain stung their skin.

At the western horizon, the sun's exit promised night, the entire expanse of the VLA heavy with twilight, flashing clouds, and the silhouettes of gargantuan dish antennae.

Childs led the way with the tool bag slung over his shoulder, head lowered, Nikki in tow. The Hertz trucks weren't too far away and likely unlocked, as techs and movers had been running in and out of them until showtime. If fate could take a second to smile upon them, keys may still be inside.

Lightning spidered overhead, radiating from a bright central core. It snaked for miles in search of targets as far away as the horizon. In the distance, somewhere near the electrical substation, Nikki thought, she saw a monstrous blue flash, followed by several more in rapid succession. She was reminded of the Desert Storm air war footage she and the rest of the world had watched live a couple of years back. It scared her then, and this scared her now.

"It's war," Nikki said.

"Or something like it. Closest truck, get to it, and keep an eye out for Voorhees."

They stumbled over one of the fallen guards, and Childs nearly went down. It was hard to tell if the man was dead, but it did not go unnoticed to Childs that the guard had a holstered Beretta, spare mags, and a rifle slung over his shoulder. It also meant, of course, that they were closer to the black tent than they realized.

Childs wrangled the rifle away and pulled the pistol from the holster. He press-checked the chamber; there was a round in the pipe, ready to fly. He handed the handgun to Nikki. "Take this. You know how to use a gun?"

Nikki nodded. "My dad taught me."

"Drop the safety with your thumb and you're ready to go, but keep your finger *off* the trigger until you *have* to shoot. Grab the mags."

Nikki took the magazines and slid them into her jeans pocket. She knew enough from her old man to keep her index finger on the frame, use both hands and stay at least ten feet away from the target. It certainly felt a lot better to have a way to fight back if Sharon Voorhees, for example, made a surprise appearance. She hoped it wouldn't come to that.

"You two. Stop!"

Jenks.

-7-
A WORLD OF HERTZ

THE SHED BEHIND the Kwik Gas had seen better days, and it didn't take well to the wind. The corrugated metal roof had lost a few of its rivets over the years and made a hellish rapping noise that mingled with the sounds of flapping tarps, wooden crates filled with rattling pop bottles, and a relentlessly banging gate. The latch broke last summer, and Otis never bothered tending to it.

"Funnel's under the bench," Otis said, raising his voice to be heard over the din. With a grunt, he hoisted up a five-gallon gas can.

"The best thing about being holed up at a filling station is the lack of fuel problems," Ken said. He stuck the funnel in the gennie's fuel receptacle, and Otis set to pouring the gas. "And you have beer."

"This baby will power only a few things, but if it comes down to it, we can always manually pump fuel out of the underground tanks. Truck came last week, so I'm right next to full."

Ken poked his head out of the shed and watched the pivoting tower wander on the far side of Route 60, its progress slow. It was an impossible sight, this behemoth moving under its own power (a pun that did not escape him), tethered to the herd via glowing insulators and buzzing wires—but seeing was believing. After years spent on the road, most of it at night, it had become difficult for ghost, miracle, or abomination to salt his eye. True, Ken Lightfeather had never witnessed a living giant in any form, let alone a goddamn high-tension tower out for an early evening stroll, but jaded was jaded—just never enough to ever let his guard down. The first order of business had always been survival.

The Old Conflict, he thought. *The Oldest Conflict.*

When he turned back to the generator, Otis met his eyes. In the glare of the flashlight, the old man looked like he'd been carved from dark wax.

"I can't even begin to explain it," Otis said.

"Not sure anyone can," Ken agreed. "The easiest guess is the storm. Yeah, the storm caused it." Ken lowered his voice and dropped his eyes to the generator. "Maybe," he added.

"That wicked monsoon blew through last year, remember that?" Otis said.

"I do. We ate burritos and listened to Al Green."

"Bill Withers," Otis corrected.

"Right. At the time we both thought that was the big daddy of them all. Now look at us."

"Running would be stupid. The weather's too insane, and who knows how many giants there are. Electrical towers, walking on their own. If Ruthie could see that!" Otis uttered a small volley of nervous laughter. "I'm here to say if I wasn't so freaked out by it, I would think it's ridiculous."

"I wonder how far this goes," Ken said. "Aren't they all connected by wire? I mean at some point, maybe it just, you know, ends."

Otis shrugged. "I know there's a big substation forty or so miles up the road. Near Socorro, the astronomy field. The big radio dishes."

"I haul past them all the time, but I never really *looked*, you know? Aside from that, what do you think the story is with Mr. Los Angeles and Junior? He looks rattled. Kid seems alright."

Otis set the can down. "Whatever came through the radio slammed him extra hard on that phone. If he loses his cool, it'll be bad with a kid in tow. Gotta keep it together when there are kids involved."

Ken unconsciously set his hand on his sidearm. He leaned over the generator and said, "I thought of bad shit when I heard that noise. Didn't you?"

Otis looked at Ken's right hand set on his Smith, then back to his eyes.

"How so?"

"Old times."

A single candle in the bedroom, the bent, scorched spoon covered in wax, his wife Little Star incoherent as their daughter

Bibi cried in a filthy diaper. The litter-strewn living room filled with nodding junkies.

"You know it didn't end well when I came back to the Rez."

"Old times," Otis repeated, but his voice was brittle. Old times meant he preferred to reminisce about the raft he'd built out of two-by-fours and palettes, how he and Ruthie had floated down Green Willow Creek to their secret sunset picnic spot, how they used that raft for weeks until it became water-logged and sank —

In the car after burying Franklin, Ruthie bawling, empty and hollowed out. Her face a hood of grief, suffering the years to come in a single afternoon. Why do we have to leave him there, Otis? Alone and anonymous . . . just one in a sea of all those white gravestones.

Otis shook his head. Ken was right; that ugly Signal, an Emergency Broadcast System tone gone haywire, introduced his nerves to a cheese grater, stirred loss and renewed weight on his heart. There were decades of life worth remembering instead of all that heartache between Franklin's death in June 1983 and Ruthie's funeral just before Christmas in 1988. A sound, a frequency, capable of conjuring all that old hurt; how could that possibly be so?

Ken reached for the generator's pull cord. "This desert is long on disaster. It has a history you people would call *witchy.*"

Otis snorted. "You people?"

Ken laughed. "You know what I mean. A lot of blood spilled here, ancient days, before and after the Indian Wars. I don't care if it's New York City or the Reservation—we're all living on a battlefield. The Old Conflict. You dig me, Gas Money?"

"Ruthie would have been right out there on Route 60, Holy Bible and a gris-gris in one hand and a fist in the other, demanding that the giants return to whatever pit they came from."

"I'll take all the Juju we can get. From God Almighty to Black Cat Bone."

Otis stuck his head into the gap between the shed and the rear of the mini-mart. On the far side of Route 60, moving a little faster than the last time he'd seen it, a tower, easily a hundred feet tall, dual cross arms lit by fiery insulators, groaned as life bent its frame and tested its limits. Lightning streaked above in mighty electric rivers, allowing temporary sight of the mother cyclone's enormous breadth. The rain showed no sign of letting up as an impossible dry wind whistled through the cages. He managed a glimpse eastward. More towers on the move.

Ken said, "Let's fire this old girl up and get back inside."

Caleb slapped his dad on the back when the hum of the refrigerators resumed. "Back in business," he said. "You want something to drink?"

Caleb handed Pale a Seven-Up, and they watched the towers go on their way, mesmerized by the sheer scale and the absurdity of it all, pivoting from one crushed anchor to the next. Neither purpose nor destination was apparent, but the overall sense of discipline was—there was order, there was strength in their union, and Caleb's mention a couple hours ago that the towers were some sort of chain gang wasn't too far from the mark.

How soon—or if—the battalion of towers came to an end was impossible to know. They had seen hundreds, if not thousands, of these structures as their lazy road trip wound through the Mojave and other moonscapes until they hit the 191 South. They met Route 60 in Springerville, Arizona, near the New Mexico border, and Thompson's Kwik Gas not long after.

Now they were in a world of giants that had somehow found a way to broadcast old terrors, whisper poisoned thoughts, and urge atrocities. The number of these behemoths could be endless in the desert; if this had spread to the cities, only chaos would come from that.

"Eventually, the rain will let up," Pale said. "It's been going full throttle for a while now. When it does, we'll jet out of here."

"And go where?" Caleb said. Lightning flashed, illuminating marching cages and slanted, bitter rain. "The towers are coming from the direction we're headed. Do we turn around? Try to outrun them?"

"We'd have to turn around. They move slowly, so we can be ahead of them in two minutes."

"Unless there's more coming from the other direction," Otis said from behind. "Anything we haven't seen yet could be worse than what's already out there."

Ken stuck his finger between Pale and Caleb, pointing at the towers, marching more or less parallel to the highway. They couldn't tell how many of them had passed by now, maybe five or six, maybe eleven or seventeen.

"For the moment, it's a case of the devil you know," Ken said.

"We can't just sit here," Pale said. He wasn't sure if he wanted to be on the road or just far from that hideous phone. The old-style handset eyed him from its hook, silent, cord dangling, waiting like a snake in a hole.

There's a screwdriver under that counter with your name on it, Mac Daddy.

Ken said, "I don't like it either, Paleface, but the road is a no-go zone."

"If they notice us," Caleb said, "just imagine what could happen."

"Let's not borrow trouble, son," Otis said.

A hard *whunk!* punched through the din of the storm. Everyone's heads turned to the window like the crowd at Wimbledon. While their attention had been focused on the distant towers, there had been no awareness of the vehicle until they heard the impact.

The truck approached from the east, fishtailing and sliding, the yellow eyes of its headlights throwing long beams in the rain. A flash of lightning revealed a big box truck, and Pale could make out the Hertz/Penske logo on the side. They'd used similar mules to haul the band's gear all over North America.

"That's *the* worst thing to drive in the rain," Pale said.

"Horse trailer is worse," Ken said.

"But what the hell are they doing?"

"The same thing you were contemplating," Otis said to Pale. "They're running."

"If we have the juice, try flashing the exterior lights," Ken said. "Maybe get their attention so they can get off the road in one piece."

Otis flipped the exterior light switch, but the storm had far greater resources.

A salvo of lightning revealed a tower in *pursuit* of the truck. The giant, approaching from the east, closed in, sweeping one of its massive legs into Route 60, blocking the truck's route. The driver attempted to swerve out of the way, but the turn was short, the road slick, and the truck's rear end clipped the tower.

Already top-heavy and susceptible to wind, the boxy Hertz's situation was dire. After impact, it slid, and for a moment the driver's figure could be seen as his hands repeatedly crossed one another, attempting to correct the wheel.

"They saw him," Caleb said. "Why else would the tower be in the road? I knew it. *They can see!*"

By some miracle or skill, the driver straightened it out, and the headlight beams now aligned parallel with the road. The pursuing tower leaned into another step, bringing its leg down directly behind the Hertz truck. A second tower, approaching from the west side of the Kwik Gas, near the entrance Pale and Ken had used, changed trajectory with shocking speed. It swung into the road in front of the fleeing vehicle, digging up chunks of asphalt like a backhoe.

"It did that on purpose," Otis said.

"Intent," Ken added. "No doubt about it."

The Hertz was caught between two steel predators, one emerging from the dark gulfs of route 60, *Tower East*, Ken and had labeled it in his mind, and *Tower West*, now in front of the awning.

On the road below, rear tires locked up as the brakes engaged. The dwarfed truck appeared doomed, collision unavoidable.

The driver yanked the wheel to the left, and the truck's passenger side whacked Tower West in a vicious diagonal. Despite the flooded road, the tires screeched, spraying a silver rooster-tail of water. The impact made an ugly, brutal noise, the bellow of a wounded machine. The front quarter panel crumpled like a concertina, killing its headlight. Even with the panel partially collapsed around the tower's cage, it looked, for a second at least, like the driver might wrangle out of the mess.

Tower East, the one behind the vehicle, pivoted its bulk and swatted the side of the big yellow Hertz truck. It rode for perhaps two seconds on its left wheels until physics declared victory, tipping the vehicle onto its side. The driver-side mirrors folded beneath, and the corresponding headlight popped out like a glass eye, tumbling away. Window glass shattered into a spreading carpet of diamonds. The windshield on the passenger side suddenly exploded into a radial crack, and Caleb could see some poor soul tossed about inside the cab.

The truck slid to a halt. That was all she wrote.

Ken looked at Pale. "They're in deep trouble," he said.

"Or worse," Otis said.

The sprained front axle twisted skyward, tires spinning but slowing. The rear wheels whirred as the engine growled, and

Caleb's thought was that the driver's foot had somehow been pinned on the accelerator. He could see a second person struggling inside the cab, obviously the passenger who had cracked the windshield.

Though the driver was now motionless, the towers were not. They closed on the truck with slow, massive strides—one from the east and one from the west—steel shrieking, insulators hot, the wind casting a terrible spell through the latticework.

Caleb bolted for the door, but Pale moved fast and snared his son by the arm.

"You stay put!" Pale barked. He jerked Caleb from the door with a strength only reserved for parenting.

"Come on," Ken said. "We all go, but the boy stays here."

Otis pulled the door, and the wind did the rest. The storm pushed into the mini-mart in a hot wave, tumbling the churro display and sending the scattered newspapers and magazines flying around like a flock of deranged birds.

Otis hit the pavement in a sprint, flashlight in hand, his unzipped jumpsuit filled with the wind. The old man could hustle and was all the way to the pump island before Ken.

Pale pushed Caleb back and indicated with his eyes the boy's spot was by the big window, but Dear God, nowhere near *that phone.*

"Once I'm out, pull the door shut, then get away from it, Playboy. Sit tight—I love you, Caleb." Pale spun and fled in pursuit of Ken, no jacket, boots—just adrenaline.

Caleb watched his father dash into the chaos. Providence was kind, and a brief lull in the wind allowed him to pull the door shut. He did as he was told and watched as the three men ran into the storm like rescue workers after an earthquake, while on both sides of the truck, lumbering giants, steel beasts a hundred feet tall and weighing one hundred and fifty tons, moved in.

Once Pale reached the island, he saw Red Zeppelin seemed to be alright, but should the storm send debris or one of the towers maim his car, there was very little he could do about it. For the briefest moment, he lamented the probable loss of his guitars, then felt a sag in his heart that Austin and a new avenue in life for Caleb—whom he did not want to attend high school in dope and gang-laden Los Angeles County—may not be possible. The Tornado Alley

Cats and all that gig promised could be snuffed out if this all went bad.

He looked up through the hole in the awning. The world had gone insane; an electrical tower was now a titan on the move. The cross arms swept as the giant pivoted toward the crash site, and the wires brimmed with violet throbs of God-fire. The insulators, the spear of discs that looked like some sort of Art-Deco attachment, shone in their fierce purple/orange plasma glow.

Lightning strobed, illuminating the monster in all its glory, and it was then, as the tower scraped the awning, a spear of noise skewered Pale's mind. Tower West—not just the wire connections, but *the cage*—hummed. Beneath that wormed the *Signal*, that ungodly garble of Machine Speak, Knife Talk, and Murder Song.

His mind opened. Pale *remembered*.

There's something wrong with him, Pete. Valerie's voice from years ago. *He will not show it to you, only me.*

That phone had broadcast madness to him, conjured old hurts, and suggested blood as an escape valve, and now the tower wedged a crowbar in that valve and yanked it wide open.

Mom passed out on her bed, mouth open and snoring, a bottle of Valium and a burning cigarette on the nightstand. Her wedding album lay open, pictures removed and tossed like pick-up-stix.

X̱ƀv 'lK̓!

Why don't you run back to the store and grab that screwdriver, get in that truck and stab everyone?

Otis made it to the truck first, but it was Ken who hopped onto the right fender and shone his light into the cab. After dodging debris and leaping over an orphaned truck tire, Pale, mind half-occupied with old terrors, grabbed the passenger side mirror and hoisted himself up to peer inside.

A woman lay crumpled against the driver, an older man still snared in his safety belt. Blood leaked from the left side of his face, either from the broken glass, road rash, or both. Though the driver appeared unconscious, the woman moved her leg and shoulder, then raised her hand to shield her eyes from Ken and Otis' flashlights.

"Open the door then, push it to me," Ken said, raising his voice over the wind. The rain was an abusive blanket of hot needles.

Pale swung his leg up, perched himself on the passenger door, then moved to the space where the cab met the bed. He slipped a couple of times—his Nikes were clearly not designed for this type of work or weather. The wind bullied him.

"Faster, goddammit!" Ken screamed. "The towers!"

Pale didn't bother to look back. He'd already had his memories looted, and if he looked directly at either of the approaching giants, he might freeze, scream, shit his pants, or all three. He worked the door handle and managed to pull the door up like the trapdoor to a dungeon. As he pushed it up, the wind fought to press it back down, but Ken managed to take hold.

"In you go, Paleface," Ken barked. "Gas Money is too old for this."

Fresh from its scrape with the awning, Tower West hammered a leg into the road. Purple/orange plasma spewed from the insulators, streaming down the transmission lines tethering it to Tower East. The overwhelming presence of electricity caused everyone's dental fillings to shiver.

Pale scrambled into the cab. The woman howled as his weight fell clumsily upon her. The cab was a wet slippery mess, smeared with grime and intermittent blood. An orange tool bag hung from the long manual gear shifter. She had a handgun—Beretta from the look—tucked into the waist of her jeans.

The truck rattled as Tower East dropped its weight into the road. The sheet metal protested, and the remaining glass trembled. The trap would close in under a minute.

"Can you move?" Pale said. "Is anything broken? Can you *move,* lady?"

"I think so," she said. Her eyes were boiled eggs, and her lips were pulled back from her teeth in a grimace. However long her ride here had been, it had to have been terrifying. She looked at the comatose driver and back to Pale. "Help him, he's hurt!"

Pale pulled her up by the waist. Otis gave her outstretched arm a good hard tug, and she clambered up, stepping on Pale as she did so. She slipped once, but when Pale looked back, her feet had cleared the threshold. He set to freeing the driver, but his weight pulled against the taut seat belt. Luckily, the release was on the right, so Pale pulled the lever.

The driver fell free and slumped into a heap. The man was breathing, which was good, but he appeared to be out cold. Thunder tore the sky a new asshole, the towers were close to snaring the wreck in a bear trap, and Pale knew his time was next to zero.

"Just pull as hard as you can!" Otis screamed from up top. "Crouch down there if need be and tug like there's medicine in it!"

Pale slapped the driver. "Wake up, man!"

"No time, hustle!" Otis screamed, then turned his head.

The legs of the giants moved with deliberate furor, threatening to crush the truck or send it spinning. They buzzed and hummed, mammoth, raging wasps, just thirty yards from their target.

Pale thought, *if a tower so much as touches this truck . . . that Signal . . .*

He slapped the driver again. There was a flutter of eyelids, and his lips moved.

Pale positioned himself as best he could with one foot on the transmission hump, the other on the back of the bench seat, and pulled. The man's eyes popped open—they were screwy, but he was conscious for now—and finally, Randy Childs was able to participate in his own rescue.

Fifteen yards. Tower East was very close now. Steel bellowed, and the Devil Wind howled in agreement.

Otis grabbed both of Childs' wrists, Ken grabbed Otis, and Nikki Barlowe popped her head in from the side. Her hair looked like an oil slick.

"Push, Randy, you tough bastard!" Nikki screamed. "And buddy," she said to Pale, "grab that tool bag. It's important."

They dragged Childs out of the truck, screaming as his gut and thighs labored over the metal threshold. Pale heard them all collapse on the pavement. He fetched the bag and tossed it out the do—

Wham!

The entire world went sideways. The truck upended, and Pale felt like a bug in a rolling soup can. His shoulder slammed into something; the steering wheel, the emergency brake, he didn't know. When the vehicle came to rest, he lay across the transmission hump, dazed, soaked, and disoriented. He looked up to see nothing but the crisscross of steel and the pulsing glow of the insulators. The electric buzzing resonated everywhere; the truck's sheet metal, the steering wheel, the windshield. The cheap speakers, mounted in the doors, crackled with noise and ugly garbage.

He knew the towers—those goddamned towers—were about to broadcast the death note into the crippled Hertz truck and straight into his skull.

VQ!ᴙŹǦ! 'Bok

Valerie's voice in his head, a hybrid of whisper and the thrum of insect wings: *Look at me, Pale. I'm a dead woman walking the longer I stay.* She wrapped a rubber band around her tarot cards. *Just like what you told me about your father. I'll whither if I don't escape.*

Pale's mind tried to rationalize and categorize it, give it a name as the Signal grew in ferocity.

It's a doom frequency, a death radar. It knows how to scoop Valerie's voice out of the past.

FҚŽD—!VQℲ)!

Time became elastic, fluid, oozing at variable speeds through the maze of his life as the Signal violated every soft corner.

You don't know what he does when you're away from home, Valerie said one night after a half bottle of Captain Morgan loosened her tongue. *You don't know about the drawings in the bathroom mirror, in the steam, the same symbols I felt him outline on the wall of my womb as I carried him. You've never seen him watch the sky in the middle of the night. He points at the stars and knows them by name. Did you know I saw him freeze a* National Geographic *special on TV just so he could gawk at a Montana glacier? I don't mean on a VHS, Pale. He did it with his mind, he froze the image on TV with his brain. Who can do such a thing? What five-year-old does that?* Valerie passed out moments later and claimed to recall none of it the following day. That was all the permission Pale needed to dismiss it.

!Fjh—Ш v

The tone squeezed Pale's skull. He recalled Caleb's birth on a sweltering night in July and how Valerie gave Pale that accusatory look as she lay slick with sweat and exhausted, her feet still in the stirrups: *I did this for you—he's yours, not mine—and now you owe me.*

ₔҚŭ̱ҟ !—

Valerie had written a death letter in lipstick on the bathroom mirror. *What To Do?* it read. Tarot cards lay everywhere, the alchemy and incantations of the Middle Ages laughing at him from a green bathroom rug. *The Magician. Ten of Swords. The Devil.* Propped against the bathroom scale: *The Tower.*

Żď džy!

Pale huddled with his sister Gwen next to the Christmas tree, frustrated by their inability to wake their mother. She'd been glued to the cushions since the night before—Christmas Eve, no less—where she drank until unconscious. They'd tried to give her a small gift they'd bought for her at the Thrifty drug store, a bottle of Jean Nate, something they thought she'd enjoy, something that might make her smile even a little bit. She was having none of it. Now, on Christmas morning, she opened one eye, saw their faces light up with hope, then rolled over onto her side.

GὼN—! U

The banished Shadowless Ones fell, snarling through that sightless nowhere, until their descent was broken by the tender infant spine of Primal Earth.

The soul is in the blood.

The truck endured further assault as the towers had their way with it, a rodent shaken into delirium within the jaws of a dog. But when the entire vehicle left the ground, it was then that his mind plunged into darkness, and true, end-of-the-world terror seized him.

Though caught between worlds, for the first time ever, Peter "Pale" Brody truly feared for his life.

ĮNTERVĮEW ĮV

DEFENSE INTELLIGENCE AGENCY
CASE No. NB-18266-00
October 16, 1993 20:24 HRS
ATTACH TO PREVIOUS INTERVIEW

INVESTIGATORS AND SUBJECT UNCHANGED

CLASSIFIED.
PRESS BLACKOUT.

BEGIN TRANSCRIPTION

Barlowe: Gee, I sure wish today could go on forever.

Oberon: Sorry to pull you out of your room.

Barlowe: I doubt it.

Oberon: I know today has been arduous, but we really need to get the facts in the can. You understand that a good portion of western New Mexico is in blackout conditions.

Barlowe: That'll last for weeks. You must have been a sympathy hire. Did your dad work there and get you a summer gig, then they just kept you on? Seriously, Julie, I harbored high hopes you'd be a sharper cookie. In fact, your performance is so bad, I don't believe you are who you say you are. Turn in your SAG card.

Oberon: Here's my badge.

Barlowe: My eyes are bandaged, Mrs. Columbo.

Oberon: Detective Castillo can vouch for me.

Barlowe: I suspect him absent. I don't smell Aramis or sense his need to dash out to Outback Steakhouse with *the bros* for a bloomin' onion.

Oberon: [SIGHS] Earlier, you were brazen in your candor concerning Medusa Engineering. Is there a way we can get back there, Doctor Barlowe? The black tent?

Barlowe: Where we *definitely* talked to Jenks.

Oberon: He was in the tent?

Barlowe: You listen the way old people fuck. Rarely and slowly.

Oberon: Just making sure we're copasetic.

Barlowe: I think people misuse that word, *copasetic*, with the same fervor as *mortified*.

Oberon: Smart ass.

Barlowe: Our cozy chat with Mr. Creepshow takes us all the way to the fireworks. Things moved very quickly after that. *Ha! Things moved!* Get it? I kill me.

Oberon: The Air Force 377th Special Operations Group has been calling next of kin for two days. *Who. Called. Them. In?*

Barlowe: You get testy when it's late, and you're really a brick if you can't figure it out by now.

Oberon: I'll order your pain meds stopped. A couple of days screaming under that face wrap of yours should straighten you out. Want to try me? I've had enough of your mouth.

Barlowe: Yet you constantly encourage me to speak.

Oberon: I just need you to say the words, not imply them. For the record.

Barlowe: Randy Childs had seen real combat, but I had not. Our exit from the VLA changed that. You want all the details, then pull up a bean bag chair and light a spliff, because baby, it's going to get colorful.

-8-
THE AWAKENER OF STARS

AT THE SOUND of his master's voice, Childs froze.

He's well trained, Nikki thought.

Nikki and Childs stood in the fresh gloom of sundown, yet caught in the glare of Armand Jenks. He wore a black raincoat cinched at the waist, and a black fedora shielded his arctic blue eyes. Nikki thought that was a pretty good trick, keeping his lid attached in forty-mile-per-hour winds.

Above, the storm bellowed. Below, the black tent's sound and light display were temporarily suspended. Work lights shone through the tent flaps, and the chatter of raised voices let Nikki know that things were likely not over yet.

"Mr. Jenks," Childs said. He sounded like a kid caught peeping into the girl's locker room.

"Why are you not on station?" Jenks said. His voice, colored by an accent no one had ever been able to precisely pin down—a hybrid of London money, Boston power, and Southern guile—defied the wind.

"You're kidding," Nikki said. She realized she had the Beretta in her hand and tucked it into the waistband of her jeans. "It's a slaughterhouse in there. *My friends are dead.*"

Jenks ignored her, then raised one eyebrow at Childs.

"You are the Dragonfire technical director," Jenks said. He barely flicked his head toward Nikki. "Your mouthpiece here is in charge of data security. I expect the tape spools to be on the plane to Boston tonight. Leave the gear here; it is obsolete anyway. I do not care what you have to do to get it done."

Childs shook his head, then adjusted the rifle's sling.

"It's all bad in there, Mr. Jenks," Childs said, raising his voice to be heard above the wind, something Armand Jenks, for whatever reason, did not have to do. "Whatever we processed from Drag Sat caused one hell of a . . . I don't know . . . *frequency resonance.*"

Jenks' mouth collapsed into a thin dark line. He dipped his head, and water streamed from the brim of his hat. When he looked up his eyebrows crunched into the M shape children use when illustrating seagulls in flight.

"You have not been released from your responsibilities."

"I say different," Nikki said.

Jenks flicked his hand in dismissal. *Away, pest.*

"We're not going back in there," Childs said. "People are *dead. How could you not know?* We're leav—"

Jenks interrupted. "These are old forces we are dealing with, Doctor Childs. And it is our intention to understand the mind of God, He that set these forces in motion, and any that use, serve, pervert, or exploit them. Old commands. There are Rules."

"What the fuck does *that* mean?" Nikki said.

A blast of lightning ignited the sky, and each mammoth dish leaped from the murk, radiating purple/orange from its central receiving antennae. When twilight returned a second later, only those points of Dragonfire glow remained visible, glaring at Nikki and Childs, the eyes of distant, nocturnal predators.

"None of this is normal," Childs said. "Whatever took place in this tent drove half of the people in the control center insane. It *sounds* batshit to even say it, to accuse it. What *is* Dragonfire, really?"

"I've told you several times," Jenks said. "Old forces. Old commands." Jenks looked up to the storm. The razor rain didn't appear to bother him in the slightest. "The world positively swims in them."

Child shook his head. "That white paper was nonsense. I took the money."

"Wait," Nikki said. "What *money?*"

"Do you not stand in awe, in reverence to the majesty of The Gate?" Jenks said, then snapped one of his mantis arms outward, pointing toward the distant radio dishes. Lightning flashed to clarify his point, illuminating the snarling cyclone above the array.

In the spill from the tent's work lights, Childs saw the stress of the day on Jenks' face; sunken cheeks and eyes painted his already extreme features into a hollow, scarecrow mask. After years of working with the man, Randy Childs suddenly noticed Armand Jenks did not have eyelashes.

Jenks continued, "What voice summons such things? Lights in the sky herald more than saviors, Doctor Childs. The comets brought doom, and the eclipses brought terror and sacrifice. Dragonfire *is* the Great Summoner, the Awakener of Stars, the—"

Jenks stopped speaking like a wire had been cut. The wind brayed.

"Just get the job done," he finished.

Why was so much of it unreadable? Nikki thought as her mind raced to recall the blurred, enigmatic code as the Dragonfire data poured into the system. *Because it's in another language. A dead language, a secret language.*

She took a step toward Jenks. *No wonder the data appeared so arcane as it streamed across the monitors.* A gloating Jenks had just said it himself, *Dragonfire is the Great Summoner, the Awakener of Stars. Sure it's cryptic—especially if you don't know shit about the occult.*

She scoffed. "On the monitor, that was . . . what? Some secret language? It's a *ritual*, isn't it?"

Nikki realized she had her accusatory index finger just a few inches away from Jenks' face.

Jenks extended his king crab of a hand. With his fingertips, he poked Nikki in the shoulder as if disciplining a dog. It hurt like a cop's billy club, and she stumbled backward. She looked up to see breath fog from his lips.

"Shadowless," Jenks said.

"You killed our crew," Nikki said. Her hand went to the pistol.

Jenks actually smiled. To Nikki, it was like finding out you were the special on an alligator's dinner menu. "Language, Doctor Barlowe," he said. "And if you use that pistol, prison."

Nikki had to say it. "The rest of us think we're here for science, but you're using technology to stir the cauldron. Hedging your bets? Seeing which avenue leads you to where you want to go? There's blood in the control room—all of it is murder. You creepy bastard, *do you know what you've done?*"

I think I just got fired, Nikki thought, and laughed.

Jenks let Nikki run her mouth.

"All that nonsense I couldn't read on the monitors came from *somewhere else*, didn't it? Some *when* else, maybe? That explains the Hollywood generator truck. You need all that extra juice to—shit, who knows—drive those lasers, open your Gate? *Just what are you bleeding in that tent?*"

Nikki tried to blow past Jenks toward the tent, but his raised palm stopped her like a child warned. Childs tucked the rifle into his shoulder, pointed it at his boss, and leaned in.

"You have your assignments," Just as the words left his mouth, the noise from the generator truck swelled to a roar. The cables flopped near their feet like spasming snakes, and an ugly lowing, the cry of a wounded bull, emanated from the tent. Then, a purple flash.

Childs flinched. Within a thicket of agonies, a decades-old memory surfaced.

He was twenty-two, crumpled in the chair next to his father, who lay in St. Augustine's ICU ward. Wires, tubes, and pins had turned his father into a sinister art project. The morphine drip was useless, Harry Childs' mind was gone, and the machine that monitored his vital signs—huge and noisy in those days—squawked and beeped erratically as the final seconds counted down.

Pop opened his eyes. Randy Childs, who was already a combat veteran and still six years from his doctorate and the need to shave daily, saw only bewilderment and a child's fear of the unknown stare back at him. There was nothing beyond this life for Pop, no white light. He'd stomped through his time rudderless and faithless, and now that candles were being blown out, he realized just how dark it was soon going to be.

Randy feared God had turned his back on this unrepentant man. There would be no smiling Christ in his white robe, no welcoming of family and lost loved ones, only the void of nowhere. Pop was to be snuffed out like a matchstick in the middle of space, a solitary photon far away from its mother star. His eyes said it all, and the yellow reek of fear broke from the invalid's pores, an unconscious warning to anyone willing to listen.

Pop gripped the sheets, his lips parted as best they could with the ventilator tube occupying his mouth. If he was about to say something, there would be no way to get it out, so his frightened stare into the abyss was all that Randy Childs would be able to take with him. His pale, anemic lips were cracked Mojave clay, his skin a discarded parchment left in some cave to dry out and lay

LIVE WIRE

forgotten—a Dead Sea Scroll of a man's life. Maybe someone would dig it up one day, but all that remained would be fragments, a puzzle to be pieced together, revealing the unfinished portrait of a man they could barely tell had ever been there at all.

Now, at the last second of his father's life, his mother already in her grave, his sister unavailable and blissfully unaware, off in some deteriorating hippie commune in Humboldt County, it became the responsibility of the son to usher his father out of the world and attempt to keep him from the trap he'd set for himself.

As this wounding memory skewered his heart, Randy Childs' soul soured around a nail carved from a witch's bone.

"He *knew* he was damned," Childs said, but he sounded like he was talking to himself. "But part of him was all right with it, all right with being snuffed out for good and not moving on."

"The final stage," Jenks taunted. "When he realized that only *Elsewhere* waited on the other side."

Childs looked up at Jenks. A ghastly version of Punch from the ancient Punch and Judy shows looked down on him with the devil in one eye and Charles Manson in the other.

"The soul is in the blood." Childs said. "Is that why you needed a blood centrifuge? Is that what it all means?

"The world is stained with it by the millions. Now you know."

We're just here to do the job, the goddamn Dragonfire job. But it's not about the satellite, it's not about the Coronal Mass Ejection, it's about opening a wound in the world, reaching in and seeing what filthy bugs are eating the—

Both the rifle and Childs' head dropped.

You had until the very last second, Pop, and you remained obstinate.

He leaned on the rifle, mourning Harry Childs not only as his father but a man who willingly succumbed to emptiness.

Jenks turned to Nikki. His hypnotist stare softened to a smirk, then the first hint of a grin.

To Nikki that was the lip-licking smile of a killer on the road, a hitchhiker with a knife in his sleeve, leaving fresh wet clues at the rest stops.

Nikki thought of Billy Urus, clawing at his bloody guilt mask while spooning out his eyes. He'd kept his mouth shut for who knew how long about a murder, a *goddamn homicide* of all things, just to impress a girl. What a horror to live with, and what reckoning when Jenks' Dragonfire ritual popped the lid of that one. Once again she tugged Childs' arm, but this time to pull him away from Jenks.

"We're out of here, Doctor C.," Nikki said. "*Gone.* Away from this crazy warlock. We stick to the exit plan."

Jenks scoffed at the term *warlock*. He raised an index finger in warning.

"Before the lights go out for good, I'll have your shadows."

Nikki turned to Jenks. She pulled the pistol but didn't raise it, she just wanted him to see it. "Next time, asshole," she sneered and crammed the gun back into her waistband.

"No evidence, no crime." Jenks tipped his hat like Bogart at his best. "*Never* pull a weapon on me again." He turned and walked back into the tent just as another massive tornado of light erupted inside. Something in that black tent screamed, and as Nikki and Childs moved toward the Hertz trucks, she heard Jenks raise his voice.

"*Get it under control, Taymour!*" he shouted. "*Call it in.*"

-9-
THE 377ᵗʰ

ALTHOUGH NIKKI PROTESTED, Childs insisted on driving the Hertz truck. The second one they came to was unlocked and still had the keys in the ignition. It was a blessing to be out of that horrendous weather.

"You alright?" Nikki asked. She had one hand on Childs' shoulder and the other on the big, thin steering wheel. "Bad moment back there. Looks like Jenks got into your head."

"All of that without the aid of the Signal," Childs said. He pulled the wet cocktail napkins out of his ears.

Childs let out a long exhale. Water ran through the lines in his skin, and at that moment, he surely looked older than his fifty-three years. He gazed into the vast New Mexico night, where the lightning brought the giant dishes into view then snatched them away.

"You're not going to beat my face in with that rifle butt, are you?" Nikki said. She attempted a smile, but it was like trying to walk through fall leaves without making any noise.

The final stage, Jenks had croaked in that unidentifiable accent. *When he realized that only Elsewhere waited on the other side.*

"Honestly, I don't know," Childs said, Jenks' voice worming through his skull.

He started the engine and hit the wipers. They didn't do a lot, but it was better than nothing, and at least the road leading from the VLA to Route 60 was paved and well maintained.

"Just checking. A girl can't be too careful. Did I ever tell you about the time I broke a date's nose when he tried to get to second base just after we pulled into the movie theatre?"

Childs fumbled with the gear shifter. He hadn't driven stick in a while. "You're choosing *now* to tell that story?"

Nikki blew right past that. "What a *chooch* that guy was, and I left him blubbering bleeding. My dad picked me up, and at sixteen years old, he bought me a congratulatory beer."

Childs managed a wan smile. "That's my girl."

"True story, so remember, I'm armed, buddy."

"If we make it out of here, we're going straight to Don Francisco's in Magdalena and getting absolutely shitfaced."

"I'll drink to that. Wish we'd shot Jenks in the balls, though. That would have been classic."

"Let's get."

"Agreed. Move it." Nikki settled into her seat. She buckled up. "Do your seat belt and blow this taco stand."

As soon as Childs switched on the headlights, there stood Sharon Voorhees. Soaked, thin as a rail, she wielded her shovel like a broadsword. She'd pulled her shirt to shreds, revealing flesh pale as death, no breasts to speak of, sternum and ribs visible as if someone had skinned a xylophone. Her left eye was a glazed, dark marble; the right was swollen shut. Nikki had seen the horror film *The Evil Dead* years ago on VHS, and to her, there was no way Sharon would have been passed up during the open casting call.

"Jesus, Mary, and Joseph," Nikki said.

Sharon brought the spade down on the hood with a sharp *clang!* She dropped the shovel, and as she was bent over looking for it, Nikki said, "Punch the gas, Randy. Knock her skinny ass out of the way."

"It'll kill her," Childs said. He still had his father's death in his mind, staring blankly into the big empty, the doom as clear on his face as the crazy was on Sharon's.

Sharon popped up like a spring-loaded marionette bent on homicide. She smacked the quarter panel on Nikki's side and brought the shovel up again. The strained tendons on her neck throbbed.

"Do it!" Nikki yelled.

Childs dropped his foot on the accelerator. There was a deep revving noise as the V8 wound up for the pitch. They remained stationary, the engine screaming. Sharon flipped the shovel around, clearly intending to use the handle as a club to break the windshield.

"It's in goddamned neutral!" Nikki screamed. She yanked the gearshift. The machine made a terrible grinding noise. "*Clutch, dummy!*"

Childs hit the clutch, and Nikki pushed the shifter up into first. Sharon Voorhees, who had beanie babies on her desk and a crush on Bruce Willis, fumed with long-buried rage. She tossed one scrawny leg on the bumper and hoisted herself up onto the truck's hood. Her ripped shirt flapped in the Devil Wind. Nikki saw the woman was wearing argyle socks.

The truck lurched forward when Childs released the clutch, and for a second, they thought Sharon would manage to hang on. Not to be, however, as the inertia of the truck, the slick surface, and the high winds made quick work of the poor wretch, and down she went beneath the headlights. Childs yanked the wheel to the left, and the truck pulled away, engine roaring. He dropped it into second gear, and they fishtailed out of there.

"I didn't feel a bump," Nikki said. She looked over her shoulder but couldn't see anything. "There was no bump, right? If we'd run her over, we'd have felt a bump, yeah?"

Childs nodded. "She slipped off, Niks. She's somewhere on the ground—"

The first blaze of cannon fire startled them both.

Diagonal streaks of yellow slammed into the ground. No less than a quarter mile away, plumes of earth billowed as a fireworks show of sparks assaulted the base of a dish.

Childs flinched and yanked the steering wheel. The clumsy truck swayed.

"What the hell was *that*?" Nikki said.

"Tracers," Childs said. His voice was toneless.

Another flurry of fire screamed from the sky. It was followed a second later by a horrific belching sound.

BRRRAAAP!! BRRRAAAP!!

"Gunship," Childs said. He ducked a bit so he could peer through the windshield, past the sun visor, just in time to see another intense barrage from the Vulcan cannon. "Holy smokes."

An explosion of sparks and debris spewed from the already wounded radio telescope. It had endured a terrible volley of fire, the death of a thousand cuts. Its central antenna blew into pieces, steaming flames and residual Dragonfire glow.

With night pressing down on the VLA, the flash of the impacts coaxed other dishes from the gloom. Sitting ducks, all of them.

"What. The. *Fuck?*" Nikki said.

Childs looked at her. His eyes were big as ashtrays. "Good question," he said.

"Will they shoot us?"

"An even *better* question."

Another cloudburst of tracers streamed down—but from the other side of the array. In the distance, a massive light show bloomed as a second dish sustained catastrophic damage. Ten tons of glowing steel spun away, dragging with it a ferocious plasma trail.

Lightning flashed, and there it was. A chubby but enormous prop-driven aircraft banked onto its left wing, angry cannon barrels extending from its port side. Four Rolls-Royce turboprop engines growled in the coming night. The gunship fired again, this time unleashing the 105mm Howitzer.

A second later, that same dish was obliterated in a massive, concussive explosion.

"God almighty, there's *two* of them," Childs said, but he sounded relieved. "Behold, Niks, the AC-130 Spectre. It turns left, it blows shit up, that's all it does. Someone is putting a stop to this and getting shit handled."

"Jim Dandy to the rescue," Nikki said. "If we're lucky, they'll grease Jenks—"

The shockwave, a bulldozer of sound, smashed into the Hertz. The windshield rattled, the mirrors shook. The truck's hood trembled like they were on a hard mile of wrong road. Again, Childs had difficulty keeping the vehicle straight.

"*Jeee—Zus!*" Nikki had never heard an honest-to-God explosion before. One hand went to her sternum, the other to the panic handle above the glove compartment. "That was awesome!"

The distant fireball dissipated, but in its fading glow they could see the decapitated remains of the radio dish. A massive broken-bowl section leaned on snarled steel. Debris burned all around it.

Childs remembered the flat-top guy who had stepped into the black tent just before showtime, the guy with the rifle range earmuffs. Briefcase. Black shoes, straight posture—military all the way. Childs had figured out the earmuffs were so Colonel Nobody would not be affected by the Signal and become corrupted—or possibly assault Jenks—which led Randy to stuff his own ears.

But the presence of a military accomplice in the black tent meant that Medusa Engineering had operatives in very high places when it came to Project Dragonfire, people who could give real orders—*People Who Could Get Shit Handled.*

"Oh Goddammit, why didn't I see that?" Childs said. "It was *Jenks* who ordered the strike. He's scuttling the ship. Or at the very least, he ordered someone else to call it in."

"*No evidence, no crime,* was the last thing that lizard said to me," Nikki said. "But even I can't believe he has that type of pull, Doctor C."

"He's got a military ally in the tent with him. You saw buzz-cut guy?"

Nikki couldn't specifically remember buzz-cut guy, but a worse thought occurred to her. "*Shit*—Jenks is nutty as a truckload of filberts; he'd have zero compunction about trying to take us out once they're finished with the VLA."

"You think so?

"Oh, shit yes. I think he's a pentagram-dancing nutbag."

Childs pushed the pedal down, and the truck revved. The windshield wipers indeed had their work cut out for them. With visibility in the toilet and the asphalt exorcising months of road oil, Randy Childs had a far harder night ahead of him than getting his buzz on at Don Francisco's.

Lightning revealed one of the gunships, banked on its port wing, coming around for another pass. Even over the wind and road noise, they heard the engines.

"When I was a kid in Vietnam, and this was in 1970, I saw these AC-130 gunships operate. They were extremely lethal then, and even more so now."

"Thanks for the pep talk, Sarge," Nikki said.

"A couple of years back at the end of the Gulf War, these birds and the A-10s *smoked* the Republican Guard on the Kuwaiti highway of death, if you remember that slaughterhouse. But if you're right about Jenks turning those things on us, if so, then we are certainly finished. When the Spectre shoots at you, you die."

"Well, screw Darth Jenks. He's not going to smoke Nicole Barlowe and Randy Childs. No highway of death for us, buddy." Nikki smoothed her soaked hair and brandished the Beretta. "The shit I see during a typical workday."

They hit a pothole, a deep one from the feel of it. They bounced around in the cab like those crash test mannequins Nikki saw in the old driver's education scare films like *Red Asphalt* and *Mechanized Death*. Childs banged his head against the driver's window.

"This truck is a useless piece of shit, Niks. I never thought I'd miss my Volvo."

They passed the tourist gift shop, and the exit was coming up fast. Once they hooked a right and headed toward Route 60, they'd be wide open. Even in the awful conditions of the storm, Childs pointed out, they'd still be vulnerable to the AC-130's FLIR and targeting systems. If they were on the hit list, it would only be a matter of time. Childs knew that death would be severe, sudden, and certain.

The sky rumbled with engine noise and crackled with thunder.

The gunships, one headed south, the other northbound, fired simultaneously. From opposing forty-five-degree angles, blazing tracers wreaked havoc below, peppering the ground with intense yellow flashes that lit the interior of billowing dust plumes. More dishes suffered the onslaught. A mammoth fireworks show played out beneath the cyclonic eye of the storm.

The northbound gunship fired its Howitzer *and* the Vulcan cannon. Two-hundred-thirty tons of radio telescope blew apart, and the machine died on the spot. Its support structure toppled in glorious slow-motion like a miniature in a Godzilla movie, monstrous pieces spinning, trailing fire, glowing with the rabid purple/orange signature of the Dragonfire effect.

This time, Nikki had her fingers in her ears before the deep blast rattled her skull. Childs was likewise prepared and held the wheel true as the second shockwave swatted the truck.

Absolutely impossible, this wild hour at sunset, but it was so, and though Nikki and Childs thought they'd seen it all, it was the counterstrike from the VLA that truly astounded them.

From perhaps a mile away, two magnificent purple beams shot into the sky—not straight like lasers, but jagged and toothy, *like fury*, Nikki thought at the time—and clipped the upturned starboard wing of the southbound gunship. A gash appeared, spewing sparks and puking smoke. The gunship rocked, then leveled out. Its engines throttled up with a feral snarl, and it banked in the opposite direction, fleeing the scene.

"*Fuck me!* Did you see that, Nikki? Did you *see* that?"

"I did," Nikki said, her voice eerily flat.

The second gunship opened fire. Its Vulcan cannon screamed, followed by rapid punches from the Howitzer.

Brilliant fountains of sparks and fire painted the twilight. Over the array, the cyclone raged, the lightning brutal, as if the storm was soon to be a player in the Battle of Socorro.

And maybe it will be, Childs thought. *The Awakener of Stars, Jenks had called it. The Gate. Jenks and his blood machine ritual opened a pathway to something awful, and its influence—*

Before the lights go out for good, I'll have your shadows, Jenks had told them. The very thought of the man's voice and eyes made Randy Child's balls crawl up into his body. He swallowed a deep breath and tried to concentrate on the road, but his eyes insisted the sky show was not to be missed.

A tremendous crab of lightning spread across the belly of the storm. Instead of radiating outward to parts unknown, the forks rushed toward a central point, directly over the VLA. They merged in a brilliant flare that lasted less than a second.

A piston of plasma fire slammed into the earth. Upon impact, snarling tendrils crawled across the desert floor, plasma rivers scouring new channels in which to run. Immeasurable power surged through that strike and lit the underside of the cyclone in its entirety, as if a gargantuan lantern had been set down in the middle of the VLA.

The rain shimmered silver, and every dish became visible.

Nikki and Childs, stunned, could only watch. The presence of electricity was nearly intolerable. The hair on Nikki's arms stood up like cactus thorns, stimulating her skin with tiny waves of static. Randy Childs felt his scalp tingle. His vision, for whatever reason, was the clearest and most crisp it had been in decades.

Each plasma river found its target—every surviving radio telescope. The raw energy spiraled upward through tons of steel until it fully encompassed the reflector dishes. The receivers, held above the dish by steel arms, began to glow hot as thermite, dripping molten plasma, which gouged holes through the dish's concave surface.

Nikki watched the dishes move in unison, tracking the gunship. It was impossible, she knew; these behemoths weighed over two hundred tons and could not possibly move that fast nor operate with any hive mind intelligence. But thanks to the infusion

from the storm, they *did* move that fast, they *did* operate with
intelligence, and as the newly energized dishes drew a bead on
their attacker, she had a ridiculous thought.

Mr. Sulu, lock phasers on target.

A snake pit of ragged beams squirmed from the VLA and into
the sky. The light threw huge shadows all over the desert and
turned the slanted rain into silver ingots.

"We really are on Mars now, Doctor C."

"I can't stop looking at it," Childs said.

The beams coalesced, unifying into a massive wad of light. The
flare swelled into a pulsating mini sun, the thorax of an impossible
plasma spider with each leg tethered to a radio telescope. The core
dripped plasma in huge, glowing ropes, and despite the rain,
ground fires ignited where the molten slag fell to earth.

A searing Deathbeam, surely more powerful than the twin
ribbons that had sent the first gunship fleeing, rocketed outward
from that blazing mass and slammed into the northbound AC-130.

The incredible force shoved the seventy-seven-ton aircraft off
its trajectory, yawing starboard, pitching upward—but not before
the gunship managed one last blast from the Howitzer.

This final cannon shot landed a direct hit beneath a radio
telescope tethered to the Deathbeam. A thunderous explosion
obliterated the rotational mechanism, and the dish slid from its
supports like a giant soup bowl. Dragonfire napalm spilled from it
like sand.

The turboprops roared bloody hell as the aircraft fought to stay
airborne. The pilot attempted to level out, but the force against the
airframe was tremendous, and soon the angle of pitch and roll
pushed the aircraft past the point of recovery.

Deathbeam terminated with a deep *Zoorrf!*

Although the destruction of this enormous wok blazing with
Dragonfire plasma appeared to have broken the Deathbeam chain,
it was not enough to save the AC-130 Spectre.

A brilliant ribbon of fire ignited in the early evening murk.
Fuselage compromised, the wings separated like angry lovers. The
tail slinked away in shame. Atomized jet fuel burned, and fire
followed the doomed pieces in bright, violent ropes. Tumors of
black smoke spread everywhere.

"They're utterly fucked, Niks," Childs said. He forced himself
to look away and tried to focus on driving.

The ordinance went up all the way down.

As if the light display in the sky was not enough to sate the world's appetite for theatrics, thousands of twenty-millimeter rounds and every remaining Howitzer shell detonated in a booming mid-air popcorn frenzy. It was like the Fourth of July had a tryst with Armageddon, and for the brief time they parented, their offspring was glorious.

A few stray bullets peppered the wet road with lethal hail, and the asphalt danced with impacts. Nikki ducked, holding onto the panic handle.

Face between her knees, Nikki said, "This would be one hell of a way to die after all the shit we've seen."

Childs heard shrapnel penetrate the cargo hold in the rear, but a more fearsome danger was the out-of-control Howitzer shells. Luckily, they seemed to spiral off in a direction opposite the road, off to carpet-bomb the wilderness.

He saw one of the crew members falling in flames, then deployed his parachute. Soon the chute was consumed by fire, and he dropped like a stone.

Nikki watched the aircraft die.

The nose and fuselage corkscrewed toward the ground, pieces snapping off and tumbling away, fire bleeding from its wounds. It slammed into the base of a dish with an awful noise, the ugly sound of war and the undeniable cathedral clang that reminded her that death still had plenty of business to attend to this night. She thought of the flight crew, still strapped to the chairs, screaming as the ground came fast and terror overwhelmed them. A cold sickness spread in her gut, bowels, and veins as she imagined them torn to pieces by debris and vaporized by fifteen-hundred-degree flames.

"Oh God, Randy, how many people just died in that plane?"

Childs shook his head. "Can't recall, Niks. Ten? Thirteen, maybe?"

"That fucking cunt, Jenks. I wish we could go back. I'd shoot him in his shitty face."

The wreckage was legendary. Several of the radio telescopes were decapitated, one of them sheared in half. Nikki, eager to push the horror of the mass death she'd witnessed from the forefront of her mind, was reminded of a broken Franklin Mint commemorative plate, still proudly on display in her grandmother's hutch; the lady just loved Clark Gable and couldn't let the item go. This dish was like that, and Nikki reminded herself that if she made it out of this—*goddamn* if she made it out of this shit show—she'd find Grandma a new one.

Fire, rain or no rain, burned everywhere, strewn throughout a multi-mile radius. All surviving dishes still glowed hot with the Dragonfire effect, and above, the mother cyclone showed no sign of relenting.

"I hear engines," Childs said.

Not a half-mile from the truck, a massive explosion. The sound was cacophonous, rife with sudden fury and a deafening air-rip.

Nikki looked over her shoulder to see the first Spectre gunship had circled back. Fire, streaming from its starboard wing, engulfed one of the engines. To her, it looked like a warrior angel bent on recompense. Below the aircraft, a dish crumbled in flames.

The returning Spectre flew nearly level and at a far lower altitude than its last pass. Nikki thought the plane doomed in the face of such overwhelming power, and she knew that *they* knew. If this AC-130 crew were going down, it would be with all guns blazing.

"*Yes!*" Nikki shouted. She made a fist and jabbed it toward the windshield. "Go get 'em, fellas!"

The storm retaliated. Lightning crawled across its roiling surface, strobe lights of purple and white, a paparazzi of chaos, illuminating the suicide run of the 377th Air Wing's last remaining AC-130 Spectre Gunship. Lightning struck the plane, repeatedly jabbed it with enough volts and amperes to kill a hundred elephants—but the aircraft remained on course. One thunderbolt connected with the windshield, spawning a terrible flare and a weird blue spitball of flame. Yet, the remaining engines throttled up in their savage Comanche howl.

The guns opened, and tracer fire spat in ferocious, angry bolts. The Howitzer bellowed as many times as the gunners could manage, each round connecting with the base of a dish, leveling a couple, but inflicting severe damage everywhere they landed. Fiery debris clouds belched from the impacts. The Devil-Wind snatched them and whisked the entire mess northward.

"I don't know if it's wonderful or terrifying," Nikki said.

The dishes locked on. They moved like a predator's eyes, tracking the Spectre for the kill. Nikki could see their central receivers, now misshapen slag, launch their crooked, luminous arteries into the air. They slammed into one another with a tremendous wallop of light and electric noise, then leaped full bore into the aircraft's center of mass, directly under the port wing.

Ammo expunged and engines at full throttle, the plane disintegrated. It tore to pieces in a bloody line of red and orange fire, blooming in the night like the swan song it intended to be. The port wing snapped upward like a final salute, then twisted out of the fire trail.

Flaming wreckage slammed into the ground and tumbled for hundreds of yards. The tail skidded out of the fiery mess, flinging dish debris, pushing desert mud, and dragging burning jet fuel.

The enormous heat turned the inside of the Hertz truck into an oven. Nikki screamed. Childs barked something incoherent. Everything was alight in fire and lightning, the entire world ablaze in the fury of war.

Childs floored the truck and swerved, but better to take their chances in a road accident than smothered in airplane fuel. Behind them, the Very Large Array was half in ruin, and two combat aircraft and crew had burned to death. On the horizon, the very last gasp of daylight.

The Very Large Array—and by extension Armand Jenks and whatever he'd conjured through Project Dragonfire—seemed to have won the battle.

The turn to Route 60 lay less than a mile ahead. The wipers fought with tenacity, and the headlights barely cut through. Childs held fast, stayed on point, and navigated the slippery road.

"East or west?" Childs wanted to know as the intersection loomed. "Which way, Niks? *Which way?*"

"West! Away, gone. Chase the falling fucking sun, I don't know. *Anywhere* but here."

Childs pulled the wheel left, and they swerved onto Route 60. Sweat dripped into his eyes, his heart felt destined for seizure, and his bladder bloated to the size of a cantaloupe. But when he looked into the passenger side mirror, he knew the show was not over yet, and any relief he sought from the night's terrors would have to wait.

"Dammit, one more trick," he said, then pulled to the side of the road.

"What in sheared, hairless *fuck* are you doing, Randy?" Nikki said. She punched the naked aluminum ceiling of the cab. "God*dammit*."

"It's in your mirror, look."

Nikki leaned and looked into the big door-mounted rearview. She could see the remaining dishes in motion again, glowing and throbbing, building toward another discharge. The ruined ones looked like broken, neglected teeth.

"They're going to take us out!"

Childs shook his head. "No, no. They're pointing *past* us. *North*. This is something else."

"My God, what now?"

A series of luminous, gossamer tendrils erupted from the array. They sailed upward, swaying with the underwater grace of a mermaid's hair, seeking one another until twisted into a grand, vertical double helix. As they weaved together, the edges burst pinpricks of light. A massive tentacle of plasma, its borders blossomed with millions of shimmering micro-stars.

"Elegant," Nikki said. "I hate to say it, but it's actually beautiful."

"Notice the helix, Niks. DNA structure. I knew it. *I goddamn knew it.*"

The helix tentacle reached toward the storm, the leading edge fanning out into spider-thin angel hairs. Billions of tiny fireflies danced around a gargantuan, braided hydra. Colors within and beyond the visible spectrum swam through the helix in gradients an artist could only hope to imagine.

"Jesus, Niks," Childs said. "Look at it. Colors that have never existed before."

There it stood, a pillar of glowing magic, tethered to the remaining radio telescopes of the Very Large Array by soft, lustrous ribbons, wavering in the fierce winds like a sea anemone in the gentle currents of the reef.

The thing's interior began to pulse, emitting a nearly sub-sonic signal that caused the truck to resonate. Every loose screw rattled, every piece of plastic clicked and clacked. Nikki felt pressure in her ears and pain in her teeth.

"Oh God, no," Nikki said, recalling the sight of Artie Jayne slumped in his chair with his lips dangling by fleshy threads. Dread pressed its palm against her breastbone.

The core of the wavering tentacle swelled with brilliance, and what was an ineffable purple became a searing white. The hum leaped from a rumble to a shriek.

"Not again, Randy, dear God, not again." Nikki relived the young tech plunging his face into the monitor and corkscrewing his face into the glass. *I miss you, Delilah!*

She looked over to Childs, sure she'd see him behind the wheel with wild eyes, the rifle barrel in his mouth, or worse, pointed at her.

But Childs leaned forward, looking past Nikki into her mirror, watching the helix float above the smoldering battlefield.

The helix curled like a swan's neck, leveled out, then soared just above the damaged dishes and flaming aircraft wreckage. The connecting tendrils had all but faded, and within a few seconds, the horizontal weave sailed independently of the VLA. It wormed its way over the desert at an altitude just above that of the ruined dishes, illuminating everything as it passed.

The solid core flared, so intense Nikki could hardly look at it. The outer ghost of the tentacle remained alive with shifting gradients and swimming, swirling particles. As it moved in that shallow sine wave, the dishes hummed with the fury of a thousand generators.

It bolted to the north, blurring past with a bright screeching wail. An ugly gulp of air, a muffled sonic boom, sounded as the atmosphere rushed to fill the vacuum left behind.

Nikki shrieked and spat out one of her dental fillings. Childs saw his father's eyes close for the last time and heard his EKG monitor emit the flatline tone.

"It's escaping," Childs finally said. "Dragonfire, or whatever it is . . . it's *escaping*. My God, it's on the run."

The electrical substation, also to the north, a massive gridwork of steel, transformers, and power distribution circuits—and a good four miles as the crow flies from Randy Childs and Nikki Barlowe—took the impact.

And at that moment, absolutely everything stopped.

The rain. The wind. Even the mad insect buzzing of the VLA itself immediately ceased. The entire desert seemed to hold its breath—only the idling V8 and the breath of the truck's occupants could be heard.

The headlights gawked at total desert darkness.

Nikki rolled down the window then leaned outside. Childs did the same. Without the hot Dragonfire wind, the evening was cool and moist, almost like October back home in Boston.

They waited.

The sound of fire behind them. Caterpillars of dark smoke wafted by. Jet fuel and cordite.

Ozone—

"You think maybe there's som—"

There was no explosion. There was, instead, an *absorption*, followed by an energy discharge visible for miles. The brilliant display dwarfed the union of Deathbeams, and it made the gunship's mid-air execution look like a display of obnoxious casino lights.

The entire visible spectrum blossomed upward into a translucent jellyfish dome. It shielded not only the electrical substation but a generous handful of acres around it. To Nikki, it looked like a drop of Universe Oil had splashed into a great pool of light, stirred, then filmed in slow motion, an old hippie light show on a massive scale, a psychedelic peyote weekend crammed into a few seconds.

She saw the master helix and all its secrets, incredible plumes of interstellar gasses—the galaxy womb—then wondered how anything so stunning could be so detestable and horrible, how it could drive men to murder or self-mutilation.

Childs knew. The entire substation was alight and alive, saturated with everything DragSat II had captured from the Coronal Mass Ejection and made readable to the VLA. This was what Jenks was talking about all along, back in R&D Seven when Childs received the original Dragonfire white paper. He had laughingly told Jenks *Space DNA*, and Jenks had looked at him with his usual wry smirk of well-kept secrets. The helix-snake and this staggering light show confirmed it all.

Such things keep the mystery alive. There is an Architect. And his name is Zero.

Is this Zero? Childs wondered. *The absence of anything? The Nothing of Elsewhere?*

The jellyfish dome contracted as suddenly as it had expanded. The condensation climaxed in a sun-bright flare that blinded them for a few seconds—just enough time for the sound to roar across the plains. It was a crack in the spine of the world, the rage of Odin

LIVE WIRE

stabbing Zeus in the gut—yet a mere sliver of the Wrath of God himself.

Nikki dropped back into her seat and said, "When we were drinking and having a good time on the Fun Jet, no one could have imagined *any* of this." She looked down at her filthy clothes, muddy shoes, and the 92FS in her waistband. "Now look at us. Witnesses to murder, suicide, warfare, valor, and *whatever in fuck that was*, all before sundown."

"If we're lucky," Childs said, "that's the slamming shut of a fissure between worlds. The closing of Jenks' gate."

"Shit, I'd like to believe that."

"So would I."

The lightning resumed, and when it flashed, they both saw the eye of the cyclone had relocated directly over the substation. The storm followed its master, and it stared down like an accusing eye.

"That was quick. Not shut after all, Niks," Childs said.

"Well, it's *in* the substation now," Nikki said. "If anyone is there, they're going to start killing one another. If they survived that blast."

Childs nodded. "Wouldn't surprise me. Whatever Jenks released seems to have plans, doesn't it?"

"I hope the money you said you received was worth all this shit, the releasing of some blind, idiot force," Nikki said. "I don't doubt you were in the dark like the rest of us, but you were told to shut us up if we began to notice things, right?"

Childs signed. "That was never specifically put into words. I was told to not ask questions and keep things on schedule."

"Close enough."

Old forces, Dr. Childs. Old commands.

"It's more than the blind idiot force you mentioned; it reached into me and stirred up a lot of old dust. Just look at what it did to Gary DeLeon."

Nikki had seen and heard enough. "For some reason, all it did was shake my fillings loose. Jenks seemed unaffected too, but he's an alien. '*Before the lights go out for good, I will have your shadows,*' Jenks said. Who talks like that?"

Nikki remembered there had been plenty of shadow-talk when the blood and projectiles began to fly in the VLA Control Center's no-holds-barred psychedelic freak-out. But what remained foremost in her mind was the nice kid from Brooklyn, Billy Urus, wracked by terrible, long-standing guilt, who gored his eyes like Georgie Porgie, or was it Jack Motherfucking Horner?

They want my shadow, because they can't have yours.

Was Billy able to pick up that I appear to be immune? Does he know—or did that signal allow him to know—something I don't?

"I'll likely never understand it," Nikki sighed. *But you grok part of it: You were used for something diabolical and never knew it.* "Let's just go. Screw this place."

Childs dropped the truck into first, and they squirmed westbound onto Route 60.

"Again, we should have whacked his skinny ass while we had the chance," Nikki said. "With all that slaughter, no one would have known it was us. Next time I see him, it's a Beretta to the frontal lobe."

"Too good for him. I'm pissed too, Niks."

"That goddamned tent, all that creepy noise, that crazy shit on my monitor. It was in front of us the whole time, wasn't it? Do you think he's some Devil worshiper, an Aleister Crowley fanboy? Because I sure as shit do."

"Worse," Childs said. "He's one of them but with unlimited resources."

"We all got played." Bad as it was, it was cathartic to say it out loud. "Bunch of nerd chumps, us."

"I agree."

"Medusa Engineering, I now realize, is bad news all the way around. What's your take on whether there was something, I don't know, something *else* in that tent? I'm sure it was something that needed blood or had to be drained of blood, maybe. What the hell screamed in there as we were leaving?"

A blur of light caught Nikki's eye. The transmission cables leading from the substation were aglow, the all too familiar Dragonfire signature began to spread its cancer through the electrical grid.

"Oh great," Nikki said. "Look out my window."

Childs tracked the pulse as it streamed through the transmission lines, straight into a massive herd of one hundred-foot-tall cat-head towers. As the signal impacted each of them, a flurry of purple/orange sparks spewed from the contact points and insulators. A second later, they glowed plasma-hot. Even at this distance, they could hear the crackling and deep, warbling hum as thousands of kilovolts surged into the grid.

"Infection," Childs said.

After the battle of Socorro, Nikki thought she'd seen it all. She laughed when she saw the steel tower writhe and twist like a man with his foot caught in a bear trap. It was terrible and frightening, but at this point, and after so much, it was best to roll with it so she didn't lose her focus, hope, and mind.

"You really don't see that every day," Nikki said.

Childs shook his head. "I wish I had something profound to say. Or glib, and I'd even settle for stupid."

"We landed in Albuquerque but woke up in Fucksville, my friend."

"That'll have to do."

By the time the big Hertz truck reached the next mile marker, another tower had begun the slow process of pulling itself free. The cyclone resumed its ferocious assault on the New Mexico desert, and Project Dragonfire was back in business.

Night had arrived in full.

"Go West, young man," Nikki said. "For here there be giants."

At that exact moment, and forty miles west at a small, run-down establishment known as Thompson's Kwik Gas, Pale Brody stood next to his Cadillac's passenger window. He watched as a stranger in a yellow slicker and carrying a big Maglite approached from his Peterbilt. From the passenger seat, Caleb Brody looked up at the stranger with wide eyes and hoped the man would convince his father that the road was a dangerous place to be.

-10-
RESCUE AND REMEMBRANCE

CALEB WAS NOT one to remain idle. Otis Thompson was one tough old man, Caleb thought, perched atop the toppled truck, risking his life for strangers. His father dropped into the tipped vehicle, the big Indian Ken perched up top with Otis leaning to peer inside, ass in the air.

The towers closed on the crippled vehicle.

I was right all along, Caleb thought. *The towers can see them. Maybe not with eyes, but they see.*

Caleb scanned the mini-mart for anything of use. Chili dogs, no. The Slush Puppie dispenser, not a chance. Beer nuts and Funyuns were also a no-go. On the wall next to the motor oil, funnels, and Prestone coolant hung heavy nylon ropes. He pushed the toppled magazine rack out of the way and snatched one. On the shelf next to the rope, a pair of bright red steel tow hooks. He attached them to his belt loops.

"Forty feet," he said, reading the rope's cardboard label. "A little more than twice the length of the Caddy."

Turning from the shelf, Caleb noticed Otis' feet sticking out of the truck's open door, Ken's boot planted on his rear end. The old man reared up, and out popped a woman who looked like she'd escaped a dungeon. Even at this distance, there was no missing her giant, terrified eyes, face wrapped to her skull like a wet chamois, and her soaked, grimy clothes.

Although Ken's flashlight shone into the interior, rain and the damaged windshield made it difficult for Caleb to see inside the cab. Vague shapes moved about, so he knew his dad was still on mission. Before too long, another set of hands emerged, and Otis and Ken struggled to drag that man, a dazed older guy whose face looked like it had met the business end of a cheese grater, free. They lost balance, and the three men tumbled onto the concrete like the Keystone Kops. Caleb was slightly horrified that his first instinct was to laugh at the slapstick display, but before he was aware, he had the rope unpacked and coiled over his shoulder. Lowbrow comedy could wait for less urgent times, and Caleb leaned into the door.

He flinched at the first slap of wind, stunned at the ferocity, the heat, the needle-like rain. A small, cowardly part of his mind demanded that he return to the market, but ahead lay the battered Hertz with two buzzing monsters on a collision course with his father.

The crazy lady clambered back onto the truck. She cupped her hands around her mouth and yelled something inside. A second later, a bag sprung out of the cab like a buoy. She caught it, then looked up to see the approaching tower. She slung the bag and leaped to the concrete, leaving his dad inside to fend for himself.

Tower West—the one that had scraped the awning, screeched as its apex and upper cross arms turned, tracking the fleeing woman. She darted between the Cadillac and Ken's big rig, never once looking over her shoulder, and a second later, she was completely hidden.

"You ungrateful bitch!" Caleb screamed. *"My dad just saved you! Go back for him!"*

Above, two towers; one with its attention diverted, the other fully emerged from the dark of Route 60 and into the Kwik Gas exterior lights, eager to pulverize the maimed Hertz truck. Insulators blazed bright as a theatre marquee. The sound pierced through the braying wind and hissing rain, the crackling buzz of all the crazy gear in Dr. Frankenstein's laboratory magnified into a cacophonous insect bellow. Had Caleb seen a giant wasp crawl up that tower, wings humming, stinger dripping venom, it would have made more sense to him than this ambulatory steel giant.

Tower West, perhaps done with its human distraction, simply lost between vehicles, twisted back with speed Caleb thought not possible, returning its attention to the truck. It swung the nearest leg, pillar, strut—Caleb wasn't exactly sure what to call it—in a sweeping arc. It smacked the truck's exposed underside, an angry drunk abusing a dog. The vehicle slid but was stopped cold by the mass of Tower East. The sound was ugly and brutal but not as terrifying as Caleb's glimpse of Pale tossed about inside, limbs flailing.

Otis and Ken were on their feet by the time the truck slammed into Tower East, but the semi-conscious man was not, and they dragged him toward Ken's big rig.

Caleb bolted, sprinting against the wind-driven rain. The rope slapped at his side, and the heavy steel hooks felt like cinder blocks on his belt loops.

"Dad!" Caleb screamed. "Dad, get out of there!"

It was Otis who noticed him first.

"Get gone, boy!" Otis yelled. "We'll grab your pop. Get inside!"

Caleb would have none of that. He reached to his belt loop, grabbed one of the hooks, and then did his best to thread the rope through the eyehole. The wind was a demon's hand pressing against him, the rain a series of infuriating slaps, but nothing compared to what awaited his father if the hundred-foot buzzing giant saw fit to punish him further.

"Kid, get inside!" Nikki Barlowe screamed. She darted from between the Cadillac and the Peterbilt, pawing at Caleb's shoulder. He pulled away.

"He fucking *rescued* you!" Caleb spat, not rewarding her with so much as a glance. "The least you could do is help me rescue *him*."

She watched him secure the rope in the hook. "What're you doing?"

"Whatever I can."

Caleb resumed his dash toward the Hertz, but before he could take three strides, two things happened: Ken's hand was on him like a grizzly claw, and Tower West, straddling Route 60 and the gravel yard of the Kwik Gas, impaled the hollow box of the Hertz's cargo bed.

Caleb froze. His knees wobbled as his jaw fell open. A scream swelled in his diaphragm, then roared, jagged and primal, from his throat.

"DAD!"

The cargo box collapsed. Metal squealed, and plywood splintered into the road, spilling everywhere.

The moment the tower's galvanized steel made contact with the Hertz's frame, that monster insect hum escalated into a full-throttle roar. The giant leaned, pivoting sideways. The wires tightened.

"It's winding up to change direction! It'll drag my dad wherever it goes!"

Ken's bear paw remained on the boy's narrow shoulders, and just as he pulled Caleb back, Tower West's leg swung around like a sailboat's boom. The captured Hertz truck obliged the change, scraping and sparking against the concrete, missing Ken and Caleb by just a few feet. The windshield's frame bent, the glass flexed, and the spiderweb crack spread wide. The wheels bounced like goofy party favors.

The awning's two support beams, slanted, stylish, late fifties-era steel girders that should have been painted ten years ago, swayed as the twisting giant once more struck the upper frame. All but one piece of sheet metal up top was gone, the lights still miraculously burning but dangling like stranded circus performers.

Instinct prevailed, and everyone turned tail. Otis and Nikki leaned Childs against Ken's big rig, and the new figure skating team of Ken Lightfeather and Caleb Brody glided backward in matching strides.

Steel met steel with another awful noise; first, the hum and buzz were amplified upon contact, and second, that goddamn Signal. It wormed its way into the awning, the panels of Ken's truck, Pale's Caddy, everyone's bones, and of course, the steel frame of the Hertz.

—ʃDžp—\!!Bok

Wracked with sobs, a dazed Randy Childs cried out.

Directly behind Caleb, Ken Lightfeather screamed.

Above the Devil Wind, Otis uttered a deep, agonized moan.

From the Hertz, another awful series of cries from his father.

That ugly dissonant machine noise now roared back full throttle, and Caleb, unaffected by all of it, had no idea how to make it end.

ᛞ𝚔KG—Kx Ŗbo!

Ken winced. He threw back his slicker, and his hand went to the big Smith on his hip. His mind dipped into the dark.

He was back inside he and Little Star's desperate shithole trailer on the rez—*the pills and liquor dependency grinding his will and self-esteem into the basement; Little Star's heroin addiction and the prostituting to keep it going; walking in the door after weeks on the road, strung out on bennies and tequila, to find the place reeking with junkie squatters and some pincushion insect in bed with his woman, her face and legs a constellation of bruises; a burnt spoon covered in wax on the nightstand, and the candle burning so low as to threaten fire; Little Star dangling unconscious from the bed, the sheets stained with puke and piss, her eyes so far away he wondered if he'd ever see their true light again.*

There was no time for Caleb to spare, as Tower West had changed course, towing its nuisance payload. It bent a portion of the awning's frame as it twisted away, unleashing another flurry of agonies. The final piece of sheet metal was freed, and the wind sent it sailing.

Tower West moved toward the highway, eager, it seemed, to fall back in line with the others. The connecting transmission lines tightened, pulling on the cross arms as if restraining an unruly dog. The giants swayed and brayed during their slow trod back to the road, back to the circuit, back to the chain gang, where there was order.

Even as a giant dragged his father across the road, Caleb's mind whispered, *The circuit . . . where there's order, where they stand as one . . .*

D3Kh −BŬŐk!

Ken released Caleb. He buried his face in his hands as his skull accused: *You took any job after that just to be away from home— you left your little girl, your precious baby girl Bibi with her—*

Erect a barrier, a sliver of Ken's rational mind hollered from some aspect of his mind the Signal had not reached. *Build a wall, think of something else, think of something good that happened before—*

—before you left Little Star alone, that knife-voice shrieked, *before you abandoned both your girls, and Little Star slipped all the way down—*

Ken imagined a wall of old bricks, the alley behind Fat Bear Liquors on the Rez, where he used to hang after cutting class. Jolene Swimming Horse had her father's Kodak Instamatic and took his picture next to the empty kegs. He was smiling because a *girl* wanted to take his photo—

—so far down, she drowned in her own puke.

Ken dragged other images from that secret corner of his mind. He imagined cellophane tape, and with that, he stuck a handful of old Polaroids to the brick, the phases of his life, fragments, some captured on film, others imagined as to how they would *look* on film.

⟨ᏖᏢ ᏇᎠᎬᎥ⟩–?

Otis, now near Nikki and Childs, slammed his eyes shut. His teeth chattered, and guilt churned in his gut.

Ruthie the behemoth snoring in her recliner, pizza boxes stacked like encyclopedias, snack wrappers on the end table, a half bottle of Hawaiian Punch on its side, pooling around a photo of Franklin in his baseball uniform.

Franklin, no more than seventeen in the photograph, shifted his eyes to meet his father's. He opened his mouth to speak, but black smoke spilled from his lips like motor oil, ran down his uniform, and pooled around his Adidas cleats.

You always thought I looked great in my Marine Dress Blues, Franklin said through the billowing, black oil smoke. *I was in my bunk at the time, so sorry to disappoint, Pops, it was just skivvies and dog tags that day.* He raised his Louisville slugger and pointed it at his father. *The flying rebar cut me diagonally, you know, like a Samurai. Just before it all turned to fire, I swear I saw my own guts. They're never purple in the horror movies, but mine were. You've never heard such screaming, hard men screaming for their mothers. Fire ignited their hair, eyes boiled out of their faces.*

Otis stumbled backward, nearly fell, and righted only when Nikki grabbed him by the shoulders. His jaw trembled.

The Hertz truck—and Pale—were in serious trouble. Caleb could only guess how badly his father would be flung around inside, let alone pulverized if he wasn't rescued. He turned to Ken and showed him the nylon rope with the red hook—a big scarlet question mark with a forty-foot tail.

"Can you hook the truck?" Caleb said.

Ken kept his face in his hands. The banshee noise from the awning, and the terrible movies it played, had his mind in a vise as it pounded on Ken's brick wall. The Polaroids flapped like leaves— but held.

It's almost working, Ken thought.

Caleb slapped the hook against Ken's chest and said, "Can you find some way to get the hook on that goddamn truck so the tower can't pull my dad away?"

Ken pulled his face from his palms, eyes fluttering.

How many days was your daughter in that sopping diaper?

*How many days had she gone unfed, screaming her throat raw?
And where were you?*

He reached for the faded photo of his mother, Gloria
Lightfeather, in her waitress uniform, clowning for the camera with
a shotgun in one hand and a coffee pot in the other . . .

Caleb smacked him again. "No time, we have to do something!"

For a moment, the Signal retreated, muffled behind the brick
wall like insane, noisy neighbors. Ken finally saw the boy holding
the tow hook lashed to the rope, hair plastered to his face, eyes
desperate.

Good, God, his old man is still in that truck.

Ken grabbed the rope, then noticed the second hook dangling
from Caleb's belt loop. He yanked it free, then jabbed it into Caleb's
hand.

"Get this hook on the other end of the rope," Ken said.

Caleb immediately began to thread the rope through the
second hook.

"Now look at my rig, there's big-ass towing loops on the front,
they're welded to the frame. Slip the rope through that a couple of
times, then hook this to the steel loop. Understand, *Kemosabe*?"

Caleb snapped his head back to the big rig. The big sturdy loops
were below the headlights. A wave of hope buzzed through him.

Ken took off, rope in hand,

*—You left her alone. You left her alone when she needed you
and she died—*

and was at the truck before the tower lurched into its next step.
He jumped, hook held high, Michael Jordan going in for a lay-up,
and hooked the front axle. He pulled on the rope with all his
weight, and the suspension resisted. When Ken looked back, he
saw Caleb already in front of the rig, threading the rope through
the loop.

Lightning exploded overhead. The thunder was right in line, a
succession of colossal cannon blasts.

Tower West tugged, the truck's body panels rattled, and the
windshield bulged—cracked to shit—but it held. If Paleface was
conscious, Ken believed the man would have kicked it out of the
frame by now.

The tower bellowed. The Signal bored into Ken's mind.

FʌG—R2 !Ĉɔ

Maybe you should go in the truck and deal with him. He

probably paid good money to lay with Little Star when you were on the road. Brought her drugs, tied her off, then shot her up in your bed. Laughed at Bibi in a shitty diaper. You should puncture his lung. Then take his eyes. Take his eyes and poach them like eggs.

Eyes, yes, eyes. Ken saw on the wall a snapshot of Little Star in the cab of an old Freighter he used to lease, applying her mascara in the rearview mirror. *Think about her lovely brown eyes . . .*

"Let go!" Ken screamed back, unsure if it was directed at young Kemosabe or the demon harvesting his terrors—but nevertheless, the thunder swallowed his voice. The Oldest Conflict had found him, and the desert wanted its due. The parched earth was never satisfied, as every battlefield required sacrifice, required blood.

Take his FU¢ḳĮŇĞ eyes.

There was no slack to spare. Tower West moved, and as the truck jerked, the hook slid on the axle and slammed into the wheel. The rope went taut.

Ken saw the boy spring straight up like a jack in the box, mouth wide open, staring at his hands. The immediate tension not only startled him, but harvested a little skin as a trophy.

Caleb watched as the tower attempted to pull away. The insulators raged, and the giant struggled, leaning back to shift its weight on a rear leg. Miraculously, the rope and hooks held. The axle bent, the wheel twisted and dipped. The tower committed one last effort to free itself, and tore the remainder of the cargo bed to pieces.

At seventy-three years old, Otis presumed he was beyond swashbuckling rescues and life-risking adventures, but conditions had changed. The world had gone nuts in as little as two hours, so his only recourse was to adapt as new conditions were imposed upon him. There was now a new adversary to consider, one that reached into his mind and rummaged through his secrets, summoning the ghosts of Guilt and Shame.

Monsters were real—not only these leviathans, lumbering in their Seven Dwarfs off-to-work-we-go unison, but the seditious parasites that waited patiently in the silt, under rocks, nestled beneath the deadfall of a man's soul. The monsters that didn't come out until he was vulnerable in dreams were now free to roam when that ungodly electronic roar rattled his skull. Alive and well, this unseen cadre of ghouls preyed on weakness and regret, eager to gorge themselves on dishonor and grief with the same greed a vampire bat laps up blood.

SHRṇ−ʔɔÁk!!

The Signal opened his mind's eye.

The suicide bombing of the joint American and French military barracks in 1983 killed over three hundred service personnel sent as peacekeepers during the Lebanese Civil War. Two trucks, driven by either Hezbollah, Iranian, or Islamic Jihad fighters, Otis never really found out, penetrated security and detonated two massive explosions. The Marine barracks had been hit so hard the building actually left its foundation, then collapsed upon itself while ravaged by fire. Franklin had been in the barracks at the time and lost his life along with 219 other fellow Marines. Ten years later, and the wound had not scabbed over.

Mr. Thompson, this is Colonel Robert Dennings, United States Marine Corps, First Battalion, Eighth Marine Regiment. I'm afraid we have some tragic news. Approximately sixteen hours ago, your son, Lance Corporal Franklin Morris Thompson, was killed in a senseless terrorist act against our brave forces in Beirut—

Though the bombing had been on the news, Otis and Ruthie prayed Franklin had not been affected. Otis knew Ruthie could hear Colonel Dennings' voice, even though he had the phone snug to his ear. She stabbed her hands into the air like a gospel singer caught in the fervor of services, her head shaking back and forth as her mouth opened into an ellipse of pure suffering. Otis listened as his heart merged with his Adam's apple, and Ruthie dropped to her knees on the kitchen floor, rattling the table and knocking her tea and saucer to the floor. Her palms slapped the linoleum, and when Otis had the phone back in the cradle and his life scarred forever, Ruthie crawled on all fours toward the living room, sobbing Franklin's name, praying for Jesus to show mercy upon him.

You encouraged him, she accused from the living room. She tucked her ankles under her thighs and sat there like a Buddhist monk. *You're the one that told him he'd have a better future in the Marines as an Officer. He was nineteen, he looked up to you. You said he'd be a man that demands respect. Now look, Otis. Now look! He died in that God-awful explosion. He died in flames.*

The words *he died in flames* dissolved into a pitiful, hollow squeal. Otis squatted and tried to take Ruthie's hands but snatched them away, pawing the end table for a framed picture of Franklin instead. Not his recent Marine portrait, in his dress blues in front of the flag, but a high school baseball photo, taken the season he'd hit six home runs and Natasokie High won the State Championship. Otis and Ruthie had hosted a big barbecue for all his teammates after that victory; a band played, and the cops came to tell them to keep the noise down.

She clutched the frame to her breast and uttered a sound only a mother could make.

Otis, they'll want to bury him in Virginia, far away from home. They'll want him in the ground with strangers. He could have gone to Florida State, he could have played ball. He'd be in the major leagues by now, he'd be a star first baseman on the Cardinals, maybe the Atlanta Braves. He'd have a pretty wife and a nice house. You told him the military was safe . . . safe, you said . . . because Vietnam was over, and they wouldn't ship him off to get killed in some jungle.

Otis looked up. Tower West pulled the wounded truck, screeching Ruthie's accusations while dragging that poor man into the road. Every metal surface indicted him of forcing his son into the career that killed him, and narrowed his vision to the inescapable radius of Ruthie's judgmental eye. It drilled into his psyche.

'!Hu!ḳ —ĴИƘ

What chances did Franklin have other than his average grades and God-given athletic talent? Now he's dead. Now he's dead because of you, because of the President, because of Eye-Rain-E-Uns.

Behind Ruthie, Franklin's baseball trophies sparkled in the morning sun. Two feet in front of Otis, A crumpled version of Ruthie, boneless and forever heartbroken.

You did this to him! He joined the Marines to please YOU! YOU, OTIS!

Otis surrendered to tears—but raised his hand. His open palm became a fist, tightened into a ball of heartache, then solidified into a boulder of rage.

You did this to him! Now Franklin's dead!
DEAD!

In the horrific onset of this new reality, where Otis Thompson's son no longer existed and the blame was his, Ruthie's mewling helplessness sent waves of anger through him. It angered him that the accusation was at his feet. It angered him that she may have been right. It angered him that he was about to take his self-loathing and disgrace out on a defenseless woman whose heart had been broken, who he'd sworn to love and protect—

Debris flowered into the air as the tower ripped its leg free. Otis watched Ken Lightfeather tumble out of the way as the tower tore the entire box section of the Hertz to pieces. The string of memories immediately came to an end, as if the most dreadful reruns imaginable were interrupted for an urgent bulletin—

Newsflash: Your son will always be dead, and you'll die too if you don't get that man out of the truck and everyone inside.

Plywood shrapnel spun away as the Tower West extracted its leg from the mess. The Hertz logo flew into the wind like a weird, sawtooth Frisbee. The rope held, and the eviscerated truck did not move past the edge of the highway.

Now with its partner free of entanglement, Tower East pivoted toward the road, and scraped one leg out of the gravel yard and onto Route 60. With an air of hard, idiot arrogance, the twin giants stalked away to join the rest of the chain gang. Above, the storm flashed and growled, dumping rain and coughing wind in great, searing gusts.

The truck's back was broken, its frame bent into a vague V-shape. Although part of Ken felt relief that this portion of the night's horrors was over, another dreaded what he'd find inside. Paleface had been in that truck for over two minutes—and bombarded with the Signal.

Ken felt as if a vise on his head had finally been released. The ghosts would always be there—he could manage those—but the dark commands and bloodlust came from Elsewhere, and although its demands were powerful, grounding himself in the positive anchors of his life and the task at hand—concentrating on the bricks behind Fat Bear Liquor and rescuing the boy's father—allowed him to push them away. This time. He didn't know what would happen if it got a hold of him again, but he was pretty damned sure that wall would need reinforcements.

Ken climbed the snarl of wreckage and pulled his flashlight.

The first thing his flashlight beam found was a pair of formerly white Nike runners, now covered in grime. Broken glass littered the space as if a smash-and-grab had taken place, and spots of blood painted the radio, the panic handle, the driver's side door. Paleface lay crumpled over the transmission hump and crammed head-first into the footwell, one shoulder on the brake pedal, the other against the seat. His head rested directly on the door speaker, mouth open like he'd been frozen in mid-scream. Minute glass gems were embedded in his hands, arms, and neck.

He was directly on that speaker, Ken thought. *That Old Voice must have gored his mind but good.*

Ken looked back to his rig and waved at Caleb, who released the hook. The rope went slack. Caleb gathered it as fast as he was able and lit out for the wreck.

Otis surfaced from his misery, watched the boy run past, dragging the slack. Ken was up on the bent frame now, shining his beam into the cab.

Ken managed to pull the door open (much more manageable now without the glass catching the wind), and in he dropped like an intrepid cave explorer.

Otis chased Caleb to the truck and stopped just behind him.

"Up you go," Otis said. He grabbed Caleb by the waist and boosted him onto the fender. The sheet metal was as battered as Otis felt, but it would hold until they could get the boy's father out of the truck. The young man stood, ignoring the wind, and gathered enough rope to send it down to Ken. Otis climbed up and peered over the edge.

"What an awful ride, Paleface," Ken said.

As Ken pulled, Pale's eyes sprang open, but his mouth did not move; it remained in that mute, terrified yawn, a hooked trout in his last seconds on the riverbank. Ken looked up just as the rope came in, hook and all.

Caleb watched the big Indian loop the nylon cord around his father and fasten it with the hook. Ken gave it a good tug and motioned for them to pull. As his father began to lurch upward, limp, bloody, eyes wide and mouth paralyzed in that dreadful silent scream, Caleb realized that not only were their Austin plans dust, but there was a good chance he'd lose his dad and wind up alone.

INTERVIEW V

DEFENSE INTELLIGENCE AGENCY
CASE No. NB-18266-00
October 17, 1993 06:44 HRS

D.I.A. INVESTIGATOR: Agent Julia C. Oberon
LOCAL INVESTIGATOR: Detective Sergeant
Hector L. Castillo

Subject Interviewed at Albuquerque, NM
Police Department Medical Detention
Facility.

SUBJECT: Barlowe, Nicole Lynn.
FEMALE CAUCASIAN, AGE 34.
SYSTEMS ANALYST, MEDUSA ENGINEERING
CORPORATION
ADVANCED PROGRAMS AND DEVELOPMENT
BOSTON, MA.

CLASSIFIED.
PRESS BLACKOUT.

BEGIN TRANSCRIPTION

Castillo: I know yesterday was a long one, Doctor Barlowe. Hopefully we can wrap all of this up soon.

Barlowe: That would be nice. I'm expected at my book club. We're reading *Incompetent Bureaucracy Fucksticks*. Up and at 'em, you little scamps.

Oberon: You never stop with the mouth, do you?

Barlowe: Well, this is an interview, isn't it?

Castillo: Agent Oberon and I are of the opinion the severity of the incident on the fourteenth has left you in a state of Post-Traumatic Stress

Barlowe: Better watch out, the FBI is bound to snatch up a couple of bright bulbs such as yourselves.

Oberon: That was quite the escape story.

Barlowe: Let's review: I witnessed homicide, suicide, and two, count 'em, *two* airplane crashes. I didn't have time to stop in the VLA gift shop.

Castillo: Terminator 2 type shit.

Barlowe: Again, kegger, dude.

Oberon: Let's talk about the gas station. You state you made it to Thompson's Kwik Gas, a good forty miles away from the VLA. I'd assume that drive was difficult in that weather.

Barlowe: Difficult? The drive sucked. The towers sprang to life the entire time we bolted down the highway like a spreading disease. Just when we thought we might be clear, one of those goddamn things would be standing in the road. I can tell you this, Randy was not in the best frame of mind by the time those two towers cornered us. There's a Signal buried in all that moving steel; it harvests any old ache. Scary shit. *Personal* shit.

Castillo: So whatever happened at the VLA could get inside your head. That's absurd.

Barlowe: Whatever *escaped* the VLA can get inside your head. That alone should make anyone suspect of what it is Medusa Engineering gets up to. Like the both of you, *they are not who they say they are.*

Oberon: You're saying it's a living thing, this Dragonfire?

Barlowe: Hell, who knows? What matters is at this point of the tale is the broad stroke: Armand Jenks and his black tent gang conjured something.

Oberon: Look at it from our POV, Doctor Barlowe. We deal in concrete facts here at the DIA and the people to whom we report count on that.

Barlowe: Concrete facts? The people to whom you report *are the problem.* You should have heard that satisfied twat, Jenks. Who says cryptic shit like that unless they're proud of what they've done?

Castillo: That would make Medusa Engineering complicit in mass murder.

Barlowe: I suppose no more than Raytheon or IG Farben, yeah?

Oberon: You sound like some kid at Berkeley.

Barlowe: When Medusa Engineering first hired me, then paid for those additional degrees, I thought I'd hit the lottery. I used to think the name was cool…like metal band cool. Defense, Biotech, Nanotech. Shit, you dig deeper, I'm sure they're up to their nuts in Goldman Sachs and every other Wall Street gang.

Oberon: Yeah, they're a major player. What's your point?

Barlowe: Add it all up. Here in the dark I can finally see Medusa Engineering for what they truly are. I'm fairly sure it's a rub-it-in-your-face cover for a cult. Since they're based in Boston, perhaps they're Irish, an *O'Cult*. Oh man, I still got the funnies. Great drugs, Julie.

Castillo: Conspiracy?

Barlowe: Worse. *Implementer*. Tell me, what did they find at the VLA? I'm sure that tent was hustled out of there. There was no way to miss all that carnage, however.

Oberon: We were shown a select series of photographs.

Barlowe: [IMITATES MALE VOICE] We have *Top Men* working on it right now, Dr. Jones. [LAUGHS] Jesus, you two. Did they find you at some recovering actors studio in Duluth?

Oberon: You're a real wise ass.

Barlowe: Also, I've noticed there's no TV blaring in my room. The orderlies zip their lips when I ask them to flip on the news. Sounds like quarantine to me.

Castillo: No TV, sorry. You're in the detention wing of the hospital.

Barlowe: Detainment, then, not quarantine. And you won't allow me to call and check on my cat or phone my parents and let them know I'm alive. I haven't forgotten about that *or* the kid. You're obviously trying to get me to say some magic phrase to fit your narrative not solve your puzzle. That's what I think. If you do not give me what I want, I will stop cooperating. In full.

Oberon: We just want the truth, told to the best of your recollection.

Barlowe: And you have it. Plus, my brilliant insight.

Oberon: All right, all right. Let's regroup.

Barlowe: Kiss my ass.

Oberon: You're not going anywhere, Doctor Barlowe and neither are we, so why don't we pick up on the situation on Route 60? Yesterday you said, "it began at the VLA, but sure as shit ended at the Kwik Gas." I'd be interested to hear that story while it's still at least partially fresh.

SILENCE
DURATION: ONE MINUTE, TWELVE SECONDS.

Oberon: Doctor Barlowe?

Barlowe: [SIGHS]So you want the home stretch, all the way to the finish line?

Oberon: After you and Doctor Childs were rescued from the stolen truck

Barlowe: [SCOFFS] *Stolen.* Good God, you want to add grand theft auto to the tally?

Oberon: After you and Doctor Childs were rescued from the *crashed* truck

Barlowe: Those men, and that boy, the one you keep telling me does not exist, showed a lot of moxie. And what did they get for their efforts, braving that mess with the towers overhead? They got a fat dose of the Signal, plenty of wounds, and something you wouldn't goddamn *believe* standing on the hill come dawn.

Castillo: Why don't you just tell us.

Barlowe: The summer I turned fifteen, when I made the decision that I wanted to go to MIT and learn all this crazy shit—which in Oberon-speak is 1972—my parents happened to bust me with a half-ounce of juicy Thai stick. To teach me a lesson, they thought I should learn about *responsibility and* *earning a living*, so my mom got me a job at the shitty Burger King across town not the nice brand new one a few blocks from home. Bus rides and transfers, working weekends, dumb people like Castillo, absolutely miserable. However, come August, I'd made enough dough to buy a *half-pound* of Colombian gold, and I turned a huge profit my junior year in high school. The point I'm making is that I made the best of a shitty set of circumstances and years later, in a run-down gas station with a bunch of guys who had also taken an ass beating like me, I did the same thing.

-77-

JAILBREAK, THE SHED, AND A TASTE OF DEATHBEAM

EVERYONE WAS FRAZZLED.

Otis and Caleb propped Pale up against the beer cooler, his mouth still open in that awful mute terror, eyes almost comically wide, like an audience plant in a county fair hypnosis show. Soaked to the bone, Otis took off his hat and wrung it out. Caleb grabbed a package of shop towels and a tin of Band-Aids from the shelf. He set to tending to his father's wounds.

"Well, that was some shit," the woman said. She was on her feet next to the older, semi-conscious man she'd sat next to the Slush Puppie machine. "Evening, everyone. Name's Nikki Barlowe. My friend here is Randy Childs. And I'd say we all have a hell of a problem."

"You two just rob a bank?" Otis said, nodding toward Nikki's waistband pistol, the bag around her shoulder, and Childs' M-16 now leaning against the cooler.

"No, but I see how you can say that. Listen, I can't thank you all enough for pulling our asses out of that truck." She nodded toward Pale. "Especially our friend here, who seems to have taken the worst of it. Those things mean business. They goddamn tried to kill us for the last twenty or so miles."

Caleb looked at Nikki. Like all of them, her hair was plastered to her skull, clothes soaked and slick with grime. If she'd had makeup on today, it was long gone now. He did not want to stay angry with anyone, as he had far more critical things to deal with. He used his nails to remove a few of the glass beads from his father's skin and to tug hard on a few of the bigger pieces. Pale didn't react at all.

"That's your dad, yeah?" Nikki said to Caleb.

"Yes, ma'am," Caleb said, but his voice was not as polite as his words.

"Your father is very brave, my friend. We're alive because of him. Looking at him right now I'd say he appears susceptible to . . . well, you know. Sensitive to . . . *the Signal.*"

Caleb turned to Nikki and nodded. "For sure. The phone freaked him out, I saw that."

To Nikki, the kid's dad looked like he may not come back from wherever the Signal had moved him. It reminded her of a distant cousin Alvin she'd heard about through the rabbit warren of family gossip. Apparently, this poor soul was permanently locked away in a mental institution near Walpurgis County, rumored to be catatonic and mute after a horrific experience involving an airliner crashing into his neighborhood.

United Flight 1564, Spokane to Atlanta and caught in terrible turbulence (which the DC-10 could have endured), mysteriously suffered catastrophic engine failure over Walpurgis County—then dropped from the sky as a corkscrewing, smoking torpedo. It slammed into the Twilight of the Ozark Apartment Homes, the fuselage splitting in half as it leveled two buildings full of sleeping tenants, flinging corpses like confetti. Cousin Alvin launched himself into the rescue efforts—but the following afternoon, he was found in the slanted ruin of a parking garage, performing CPR on a body that was burned beyond recognition.

His hospital experience likely wasn't any less traumatic, and the scuttlebutt around the table at Thanksgiving was that Alvin was gone for good; cross him off your Christmas lists, write him out of your wills.

"I am sure as hell freaked out, lady," Ken said. He slid to the floor and dropped his wrists to his knees. "It gets in your head, stirs up bad blood. The desert wants its due." He looked over at Otis. "How're you feeling, Gas Money?"

Otis' face tightened. A few minutes ago, he'd relived the worst day of his life while an impossibility literally towered before him. He turned to Ken, who wore the old-as-the-hills expression of the man at the bar, preparing to drink his thoughts into the basement.

"Like shit, Big Wheel," Otis said.

The lights flickered, dimmed, then resumed.

"You're on a gennie?" Nikki said, glad to change the topic.

She'd seen enough bad blood stirred up for one day. "We never would have veered toward your place if we hadn't seen the lights. By then, the towers followed every move we made. I'm sorry if we led them to you."

Otis poked a thumb over his shoulder. "Yeah, there's a generator out back. Time for a refill, looks like. Fuel goes fast. And don't worry, you didn't bring the towers to us. They were already here."

Well, Nikki thought. *About that . . .*

She reached into the cooler and grabbed a tall boy. "I'll pay you later. You're Thompson, I'd guess." She cracked the Hamm's and sucked it down. "Name's on what's left of the sign, and you're the only one in coveralls. Plus, the big guy calls you Gas Money."

"I am, Miss Barlowe."

She looked at Childs, who seemed to be coming around. The Signal was one thing, but taking the whack to the truck's A-pillar when it pitched over had done him no favors. He was bound to carry one hell of a shiner around his left eye. Nikki reached into the freezer, squatted, then pressed a frozen burrito against it.

"How long have all of you been here? It all started for you just after sundown, right?"

"Just about," Otis said. "Storm gathered and blew not long after the rain hit us. The lighting hit the towers like a hammer. Caleb here saw the first of them move not long after sunset. Watched a tower pull itself right out of the ground. Damnedest, and I mean *the damnedest* thing I ever saw."

"Oh, believe me, I've actually seen worse," Nikki said.

"The Old Conflict," Ken said.

Old forces, Dr. Childs. Old commands.

"The soul is in the blood," Childs said. He grabbed the frozen burrito and looked straight at Pale, then shifted his gaze to Caleb. If the situation hadn't been so odd, it might have been funny. "That's the message. Spilled blood, spilled souls."

He's close, Nikki thought, *but not dead-on. Somewhere in my inner junk drawer, I know precisely what that blood hokum means. All that arcane shit on my monitor, just before everything went crazy, whatever was in the tent—screaming.*

Cradling his face, she examined one nasty case of road rash, but his eyes didn't look too far away. After a little rest, he'd probably be ready to roll. But, of course, roll where, exactly?

"How're you feeling, Doctor C.? Do you think you can stand?" She flipped the bird. "How many fingers?"

Childs' eyes snapped straight ahead. "The only one that matters," he said, then offered a weak smile.

"Correct. Let's try to figure out what's next." She grabbed another beer, then turned to Otis. "Think we can refuel that generator of yours? Certainly no shortage of go-go juice around here."

"He's a doctor?" Otis said, meaning Childs. "Maybe when he's feeling better he could look at the boy's dad. He really had his bell rung in that Hertz truck."

"Well, technically, I'm a doctor too, Mr. Thompson, but we're not medical doctors. We were at the VLA up the road. You know, the observatory in Socorro."

"Spacedoctors," Ken said.

"We planned to stop and have a look at that tomorrow," Caleb said. He managed to pull out another small piece of glass, wipe the wound, then cover it with a Band-Aid. "I saw pictures of it in a *National Geographic*. It's pretty cool, all those radio telescopes that look like giant radar dishes. You can see to Forever."

Well, kid, tonight it's a magician's wand, Nikki thought. *Armand Jenks, also known as Fuckface the Magnificent, had his matinee performance go a little haywire at the end.*

"Well, you're right, young man, that's the place, and it's definitely cool," Childs said.

"Shame it's not there anymore," Nikki added.

"*What?*" Caleb's back straightened.

"That's impossible," Ken said. "The towers? The towers did it?"

"Let's just say it was taken out by other means," Nikki said. "We grabbed this here bag, a couple of guns, and we were out of there like it was on fire. Well, I guess technically, it *was* on fire. Jesus. What a scene." She raised the can to her lips and took another long, deep swallow.

"Taken *out?*" Otis said. "What the hell does *that* mean?"

"It means they know more than they're telling," Ken added. "Has to be." He waved a hand toward the window, through which the glow of the insulators could be seen, moving along in single file. The remnants of the Hertz truck lay like roadkill.

The adrenaline coursing through Nikki Barlowe suddenly subsided, and she slid to the floor next to Childs, her back also against the Slush Puppie dispenser.

"Shit," she grumbled. Nikki guzzled her beer, belched with zero embarrassment, and dropped her head. "I'm dead tired."

"Tell us about that noise," Otis said. "Wherever it's from, it's doing damage here. Came in through my little radio, then the boy's father got a full dose of it on the phone. Sounded like the Emergency Broadcast System tone—sort of—then it all went monkeyshit, miss. Total monkeyshit."

"Punched it full throttle when the tower made contact with the pump island," Ken added. "When it scraped its steel frame, the noise was unbearable. You recall some real dark times, think about doing some seriously bad shit. I get the feeling you two know something we don't."

"I didn't *feel* anything," Caleb said, still working on Pale.

"You're lucky, *Kemosabe*," Ken said. He grabbed one of the shop towels and dried his face. "I managed to push it back a little. Had to dig deep, I'm here to say."

"But I *know* that something is trying to break through. It was like when I could smell the electricity earlier today when we saw that tower hit by lightning. I can tell without *seeing* it. I know how weirdo that sounds." Satisfied that he'd removed as much glass as possible, he sat next to his father and tossed the filthy towels away.

Caleb added, "There's something else. Here, with us."

Nikki thought, *You should have seen it escape the VLA in a pretzel-twist of gorgeous purple light. Appealing in its beauty, rotten in its mission.*

"Actually, you're in the X-ring," Nikki said to Caleb. "I'm like you in that way. I don't hear it like they do, either. But I know it's foul, and whatever the hell it is has nothing but bad intent. I call it the Signal."

Caleb continued, "The storm is more than a storm. Its eye is a hole, a tunnel."

Childs and Nikki exchanged a glance. They both remembered Jenks with his hand out, like a salesman offering a fabulous deal on timeshare condos. *Do you not stand in awe, in reverence, to the majesty of The Gate?*

Ken pointed at Pale. "I think it moved through your dad like a freight train while he was in that truck."

Pale looked every inch his nickname. His skin was like hotel sheets, teeth almost yellow against his bloodless pallor. His jaw had loosened somewhat, and by now, Caleb could at least attempt to close it without encountering the tight resistance of locked tendons. His mouth fell back open, but at least it was no longer in that spooky state of living rigor mortis.

"We should get out of the store," Otis said. "This close to the road is far too close to *them*. Maybe get everybody over to my trailer out back."

Nikki looked up. She raised an eyebrow. "They'll kick a trailer over as easy as they boxed in our truck, buddy. Although mindless, they're dead serious, contradictory as that sounds."

Otis wrung out his soaked cap. "It's not really a trailer, more of a double-wide, a mobile home, bolted to a foundation and everything. All I have to do is throw a switch on the main breaker box, and the gennie will run the house instead of the store. Had an electrician set it all up a couple years back."

"I'll help you fill her up again," Ken said. He looked to Childs and Nikki. "Gas Money's right, as long as we're stuck here, we should get as far away from the road as possible."

"There are towels and blankets and such. Maybe get everyone dried out a little. Grab whatever food and water you want—we may be there a while." He turned to Caleb. "There's a couple of couches, too, young man. One big enough for your Pop here, and your friend too, Miss Barlowe. *Doctor* Barlowe."

"Nikki is fine," she said. "And thank you very much for all your help. All of you."

Caleb shot Nikki a look. Without getting up, she slid over next to Pale.

"I need to tell you again, your father was very brave," Nikki said to Caleb. "We wouldn't have made it out of there without him."

"Maybe you could have gone back for him," Caleb said.

"Honestly, young man, I'd just been chased twenty miles by those things. I'm not trying to excuse anything, but I was a little out of my mind. I'm sorry if, well, if I appeared self—"

"We should just drop it," Caleb said. He managed a smile. It was anemic, but it was there. Staying angry would not help anything.

"Okay then," Otis said. He looked at Nikki, then to Childs. "But once we're settled, we need to know what you know. See what you've seen. The world just went nuts all around us, and now after watching what happened with your truck, we definitely know we can't just drive outta here."

Otis swept his palms upward, a teacher gesturing for his class to stand for the pledge of allegiance. "So that's it. Giddyup!"

Childs stood at the rear exit, very similar to the steel door he and Nikki had escaped through at the VLA. As they prepared to leave, he'd gobbled a handful of Tylenol with a Hamm's chaser, then tore into a bag of Fritos like he'd been stranded on an island. His big ears were still covered in grime, and despite the frozen burrito's best efforts, his left eye was Tyson-punch swollen. He had his rifle over his shoulder once again and shifted its weight as he set his hand on the door's big sliding bolt.

"Let me know when you're all ready," Childs said.

"You okay to take point?" Ken said from behind. "You took a hell of a whack in that truck."

In front of Ken, Caleb and Nikki stood with arms around Pale. Caleb had a touristy tote bag from the store over his shoulder that read *I Love Me Some Desert THUNDER!* in big crazy electric letters. It was stuffed with chips and Cheetos, bottled water, and all the beer and Hostess sweets Nikki could cram into it. She still had Artie Jayne's canvas tool bag slung over her shoulder, from which a cartoon Armand Jenks grinned in his sombrero. She tilted back the last of her beer and tossed the can aside, then switched on the torch Otis had given her. Otis stood adjacent to Childs, his keys in one hand, flashlight in the other.

"You bet, Ken," Childs said. His voice was a little shaky. "Otis says it's just a few yards, and then we're up a couple of steps and done."

"There's an exterior light out back," Otis said. The lights dimmed and stayed that way. He gave his flashlight to Childs. "But not for long. We have seconds now before the fuel's gone. You'll see the double-wide ahead and to the right a tad. I'm sure the puddle there is enormous now and watch out for the furniture and fire pit, it'll be easy to trip over them. And, if it's still standing, keep an eye out for my satellite dish."

"Roger that," Childs said.

"You have a dish—that's just marvelous," Nikki grumbled. "Who knows what the hell that thing may be thinking."

Otis nodded. "Yes, ma'am. Big ten-footer. I get all the shows. Ruthie used to watch all the true crime stuff back in the day."

"There's a doozy broadcasting from The Devil Dimension you wouldn't believe."

Otis turned to her. "You think my dish is part of it? Or could be?"

Nikki instantly regretted saying anything. "I don't know, pops, just running my mouth. Let's bust outta here."

Pale's voice floated above them, singing a Thin Lizzy song he loved as a kid. *"Tonight there's going to be a jailbreak . . . ."*

Caleb smiled. "Nice to have you back, Dad."

Otis put a hand on Childs' shoulder. "Let's go."

" . . . some of us won't survive . . . "

Caleb's smile faded.

The lights went out.

They tumbled into the Devil Wind.

The rain had, for whatever reason, subsided for now, but the few yards between the Kwik Gas and Otis Thompson's double-wide was a soupy mess of gravel, mud, and debris. Childs led the way with the flashlight; the first thing it shone upon was a pair of hubcaps scooting over the ground like a pair of maimed UFOs. A rake followed, then an old metal watering can.

Otis and Ken broke left for the shed, its steel roof jabbering its non-stop clatter. They disappeared into the rickety box, and the loose gate banged behind them.

Childs turned back and raised his voice. "Lots of stuff flying about. Stay close." He found Otis' trailer with the flashlight beam and bolted toward it. Mindful not to pull so hard as to trip up Nikki, he leaned in and pushed against the mud. If luck or God was with them, the run to the trailer would take only seconds.

"Dad, move!" Caleb said, nudging Pale with his shoulder. Pale's legs were still rubbery, and he and Nikki had to bear most of his father's weight as they dashed through the mud. The heavy bag slapped Caleb's back, and he nearly went down, legs splitting like a cheerleader's when the puddle proved much deeper than he thought.

They saw the behemoth in a flash of lightning, and Nikki recognized it immediately. A gargantuan cat head-style tower stood behind the double-wide, the same kind tethered to the substation— the place the helix escaped to from the VLA.

Although its distance was difficult to determine in the intermittent light, the tower was too close for comfort. It stood a hundred and fifty feet tall, its breadth easily the length of Ken's big rig, buzzing like a colossal yellowjacket with meat on its mind. A bolt of wind screamed through the cage, and its message was clear: things had changed, there was a new sheriff in town, and everyone had better get in line or suffer terrible consequences.

"God almighty," Nikki said.

"It fucking followed us," Childs added, but his voice was snatched away by the wind.

Pale looked up to see the blazing purple/orange beacon of the insulators, and he pulled against Caleb and Nikki. He dug his sneakers into the mud, then tried to push backward, appearing to pedal in place. He looked over his shoulder, but all was dark shapes and flashlights bouncing around inside the shed and the snarl of the storm above. Muddy grime covered him to the knees.

"No!" Pale shrieked. He managed to grab Nikki's shoulder. He brought his face so close she could smell his breath. "The Threshold! *The Gate!*"

When the words of Armand Jenks spilled from Pale's mouth, something in Nikki clicked. *I was right, by God—if this isn't black magic it'll do until the black magic gets here.*

"Close," Childs barked. "Almost there." He moved through the mud as he'd been taught in basic training, the way he'd dealt with marshes and quicksand at the Quang Tri River. A couple of the guys had gone down; one drowned in mud. But they'd made it to the other side, despite heavy enemy fire. A half-hour later, the napalm drop that changed his life turned the jungle behind him and his squad into a screaming funeral pyre.

Despite the agitated protest from Pale, "Don't go near it, don't even look at them!" Nikki held fast. The boy held up his end, a little more cautious after he nearly went down in the puddle. Together they kept Pale in time with Childs, trying to maintain focus on the three steps leading to the double wide.

The tower leaned into a plodding, bovine step. The steel bent and groaned, the wires swayed from the inertia and Devil Wind. From the insulators, a bolt of luminous Dragonfire—just as Nikki and Childs witnessed at the end of their VLA escape—sailed down the length of the transmission wires in urgent, humming pulses.

!ŊĐ—!ķœ Ó⊂!

The Signal. Pale screamed. His mind, a clutter of agony and ecstasy as hands rummaged through his memories, went white.

Mom blotto and nearly boneless at the dinner table, [Pale as a teenager finally figuring out the simple solo from Black Sabbath's "Tomorrow's Dream", eager to phone Sean Barber and tell him he'd finally nailed it] *chewing with her mouth open, mashed potatoes, and broccoli tumbling to her plate.* [The first time a gorgeous girl clocked him non-stop on stage, and how nervous he was when she spoke to him] *She's already spilled her wine,* [Stealing a six-pack of Schlitz Malt Liquor Bull from a Seven-Eleven on a dare] *and the stem glass sits in a dark stain on the tablecloth like a one-legged bedwetter.* [Fraulein, Valerie's beautiful calico cat, giving birth in the cubby-hole underneath the stairs while they both cried in amazement and joy] *Already petite, she's down at least fifteen pounds since Dad left, cheeks sunken, clavicle visible.* [Tumbling and rolling on a Slip-N-Slide in Johnny Markway's front yard while their parents drink beer from a cooler, smoked Viceroys and Kents, and summer seemed to last forever] *Not long after the announcement that he's leaving California for good, her hair thinned into fine, brittle fibers.* [But Dad, I have to wear my hair long if I'm going to be a guitar player]

A half-cooked pork chop lays on Pale's plate, inedible, covered in far too much pepper. His sister Gwen sits stiffly in her chair, hoping her big brother will be able to find a way to get them both away from the table before the blubbering and profanity resume. [There's trick-or-treaters at the door, and his mother, lovely in her Tinkerbell costume, is all smiles as she compliments their get-ups and passes out fun-sized Snickers] *Gwen hasn't touched her dinner, either. Outside, Hollie, their spaniel, barks.*

Eyes bleary and sad, Janice Brody points a fork at her son. [Pale and Gwen count their change as the ice cream truck rounds the corner, they have enough for two Sidewalk Sundaes and a candy necklace they'll split]

"It's all ruined now," she says. Her voice is warm, slippery yogurt. "We're on our own, Little Man. Money, a nice house, pussy—whatever drives you—it's all made out of bullshit." [He looks to the backyard, where he sees Dad, like a film running from a forgotten epoch, whistling as he grills burgers and dogs, fragrant smoke plumes like dragon's breath] *When I kill myself, you're*

going to live with your aunt in Provo, your sister somewhere else. Then you'll know what alone means."

Pale looks at his sister, who has somehow morphed into Caleb at six years old. He still has his little boy's haircut and nearly featureless face. He's wearing an extra-small Mac Daddy T-shirt, and what should be a fork in his right hand appears to be a crude rendering of an electrical tower made from his mother's silverware. It snarls like a jackal.

When Valerie, who he will not meet for another twenty years, speaks through his mother's mouth, Pale sees the words spill from her lips in a wispy white fog.

"When your own wife turns her back on your son, you'll know what I feel. You think he's with you, but he's with Us now, she tried to tell you, but you didn't want to hear it. We'll all be Shadowless in our last raving days, Mac Daddy."

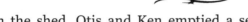

In the shed, Otis and Ken emptied a second gas can into the generator. The tank was nearly half full when the lightning struck, and the shape of the massive cat head tower leaped from the murk.

"Holy shit," Otis said. He threw the switch in the breaker box. When the generator fired up, there would be rear external lights, and power would be restored to the trailer. "That tower's different. It's one of those big bastards from way down the road. Which means things have spread pretty wide."

"We shouldn't get anywhere near that thing," Ken said. He looked like a man that wanted to be anywhere else—and fast. "I think if something that big broadcasts like the other one did at the awning, it'll blow a huge hole in us. But I might have found a way to push it back a little; I don't know how long that will work."

Ken conjured his brick wall. There were quite a few more Polaroids taped there now. It gave him a mild sense of relief.

The area became alight as the purple plasma buzzed the transmission lines.

They heard Pale scream.

The deep, ugly hum rattled Ken's skull—bricks in a clothes dryer and a punch between the eyes.

—*T! bÕŁK!*

A snarl of memory so dark swelled inside Ken he jolted backward and yanked the generator's starter cord. The machine roared awake, spitting exhaust. The cord wheel's safety screen was long gone, and as the cable retracted, the handle became snared in the motor, and the metal snagged and screamed. Sparks flew out.

As Otis opened his mouth to say *I'm still pouring gas, you idiot!* The shower of sparks met the gasoline vapor near the full port's opening, and a rose of fire bloomed toward him with a hot, urgent *woof.*

Even as Little Star choked to death in the torture garden of his memory, Ken pushed Otis away from the generator and managed to slap the cap on the fuel tank—but that curl of flame moved fast.

Otis' batted at his face like a man who had just stepped into a curtain of spider webs. His eyebrows singed, but his clothes may have ignited if his jumpsuit hadn't been soaked through.

"*Goddammit*, you oaf," Otis spat. He gave Ken a full dose of Florida Stink Eye. "What the hell were you thinking?"

Ever stab a man in the neck? The Signal rasped. *Ruthie will show you how to make him bleed fast. She is here, with Us, and she knows all the details.*

Otis pulled his shoulders back and raised his upper lip in a sneer.

Ken stiffened. He had about five inches and eighty pounds on Otis, not to mention an age advantage of nearly thirty years. He tried to conjure his wall. Nothing came. Instead, he said, "Cool your jets, old man," voice stern with warning.

Why don't you just crush that old sack of shit to death? That disembodied thing hummed into the crawlspace of Ken's ear. *Crack this man's skull and watch his mind spill out. Put that in your peace pipe—then know his dreams.*

Whatever its identity, luring Ken to violence, simultaneously it taunted Otis—but now in *Ruthie's* voice. Otis could sense his wife's presence somewhere in the shed, just out of view, buried in the shadows and woven into the voodoo rhythm the storm played upon the roof.

thumpthump—

Franklin's not truly in a grave—all we buried was an empty uniform and a few charred bones we were told were his.

Although Otis appeared to be glaring at Ken, what he truly focused on stood behind the trucker. Ruthie's unearthed coffin, somehow here in New Mexico instead of God's Grace Baptist Internment Garden outside of Tampa, was propped up the way it was in the funeral home showroom, like an item in an old Dodge

City undertaker's window. It leaned against the crooked shelves in a pool of ugly storm light.

Now the intermittent clang of the roof matched the blows coming from inside the casket. Old Florida dirt sloughed away with every strike. Through the lid of the casket, Otis heard every muffled word of Ruthie's jagged resentment.

—thumpthump thump—

Listen up, I got me some new friends!

thumpthump thump (thump)

Franklin and I will keep a sour eye on you. Those Others, The Shadowless Ones, have a plan for the future—and you're not in it. Eternity has been canceled

—thump thumpthump thump—Ruthie's fist and the corrugated steel in tandem, the rhythm of cardiac arrest—

None of Nana's Juju can keep the Devil away, no gris-gris will ward off the Soulhunters and the Eaters of Prayers.

—thumpthump thump thump—

It's time you learned how to really draw blood.

Otis turned his eyes away from the coffin with its thudding lid, crumbling dirt, and the furious ghost inside. His flashlight beam fell on an old Garden Weasel, something he'd seen advertised on TV, bought on impulse, and left next to a long-dead bottle of miracle grow, back when he thought he'd be able to raise a few fresh greens out here in the inhospitable desert. He picked it up and tested its weight.

"Ruthie would never speak like that," Otis muttered as he examined the garden tool. "My Ruthie was a good, God-fearing woman. She loved me on Green Willow Creek."

He twisted the Garden Weasel, examined all those tiny blades, then looked at Ken. "Do you think death drove her insane?"

Ruthie growled from her deadbox, *Gore this Apache savage, and I'll pretend to forgive you. Swing it the way Franklin handled that Louisville Slugger. The soul is in the blood, and you'll see that Indian's all over your shed.*

Ken watched as Otis' eyes turned glassy and the corners of his mouth edged south with impending sobs. But what really held Ken's attention was the Garden Weasel. A dozen pointed blades, tiny spinning shark's teeth, caught the light.

Otis tapped the tool into his other hand, the snaggle of the tiller's bite-sized fangs whirring. Ken's spine filled with ice water.

"It had to be," Otis said as he took a step forward. "Death is always the culprit when it comes to very bad things."

That gun of yours is a pussy's weapon, the Signal chided Ken. *A real man would grab a brick or the jaw of an ass—go totally old school, Chief Lightfeather, connect with your heritage and spill the blood. Little Star will see you finally manned up.*

"Otis, drop the weapon," Ken said. He tried to push through that awful gibberish, find the alley behind the liquor store where a girl once took his picture. "Think about what you're doing, pal."

. . . let's talk about your lifestyle . . .

As dangerous as Otis appeared to be with the dirt tiller, it didn't escape Ken that Otis seemed to be focused on a spot over his shoulder. Ken risked a quick glance to the rear. Nothing of interest, just cluttered shelves and a cracked garden hose.

Otis could not keep his eyes off that coffin.

They banged in unison, the demands of both storm and ghost urgent and primal.

—thumpthump thump—

"Hey, old buddy," Ken said. *"Gas Money.* Set the tool down. Let's not let this get out of hand. It was just an accident, that shit noise got in my head and—"

—fucked up on Xanax and tequila at eight in the morning, staggering all over the Rez wearing nothing but sneakers. You beat the tar out of that tourist real good. His pregnant wife screamed. When you backhanded her into the dirt, she broke her wrist. Did you really have to go the extra mile and piss all over them in the dirt?

Ken pushed again. He squeezed, and there, emerging from the dark, among the discarded boxes and drained kegs, the brick back of Fat Bear Liquor. The Polaroid he wanted was here somewhere, it *had* to be.

A typist in the dark, Ken's calloused fingers tapped the photos until he found it—next to the picture of his little Matchbox truck, the one he'd found by the bus stop—the photo was of that pawn shop in Stillwater, the place he'd purchased Little Star's engagement ring. The ring was still in the glass display case, the price tag attached. $385.00, a fortune, and he'd kept it hidden in his rig for over a week until he got home. For a moment, his early morning, nude anger romp in front of the Rez's general store vanished.

Ruthie pushed the coffin open.

Otis screamed.

She'd shredded the casket's silk lining. Curtains from a haunted house flapped in the Devil Wind and brushed the ridges of her ghoul face. The ribbons danced against the peaks of her cheekbones, fluttered over the flat plain of her forehead. Even from where Otis was standing, with her eye sockets vacant and jaw unhinged, her tongue resembled neglected leather. Ruthie's bridgework, which replaced the teeth Otis had knocked out, fell to the floor of the coffin years ago, but now that the casket was leaning upright, it tumbled from her shoulder. Her remaining teeth looked like a tiny Halloween diorama, a child's depiction of a cemetery. The table-cloth-sized burial dress, filled now only with her mummified husk and an artificial hip, was a mildewed old rag.

The sob, so heavy inside, broke the dam, and Otis's face, scorched and waxen, fell.

Ken snapped his head around again, positive he'd missed something. Pop bottles rattled in a wooden crate. The pages of a magazine fanned like a team of speed readers was having their way with it. The cracked hose writhed like a snake in its death throes.

Otis, you miserable puke, if you blubber now, this goddamn Indian will get the drop on you.

"The weapon, Otis," Ken said. *Drop it before I can't hold this demon back any longer and do something terri—*

—life on the Rez is no life at all for you and your junkie trash woman. Only a mongrel coward lives feckless in some desert rat hole given to him by his conquerors—

Otis dropped the Garden Weasel to his side but did not let go.

"Good man," Ken said. He concentrated on the day that ring caught his eye in the display case, white gold with little diamond chips set into a raised setting. Little Star had never seen a diamond before.

—a good man looks better with his head smashed in. Little Star is here, with Us. We keep her in the most depraved street corners of the cosmos, those crooked alleys, carved from nightmares harvested from a thousand stars—

Ruthie leaned out of the casket.

In one hand, Ruthie held a high-tension tower fashioned from twigs and twine, something a child would make in crafts class. In the mangrove of her other hand, a long sewing pin of carved bone.

Dirt tumbled out of her ruined mouth, crumbs of a brownie she'd never be able to finish. Her dislocated jaw clicked and clacked. That desiccated leather strap in her mouth wagged as she spoke.

I gorged myself, it hurt like a motherfucker, but I wanted you to see the steady poison at work. You needed to suffer longer than Franklin. Now, look. Am I the sleek panther you remember?

Otis' right hand—which years ago removed two of his wife's teeth and fattened her lip but good—raised the Garden Weasel. He stood there like Van Helsing with a hammer.

The Shadowless Ones snuffed out the stars just to get here, so honor them, give the desert its due.

Mouth open, yellow eyes bulging, Otis rushed Ken Lightfeather.

Ken backed away, stumbling over a rattle-can and a roll of duct tape. He reached out to steady himself and grabbed a stack of rickety shelves. Junk, tools, and other shit clattered to the floor.

Instead of dirty shelves, Otis saw Ken's hand plow into Ruthie's emaciated shoulder. Her bones snapped like twigs. Dust and dried bone chips crumbled away. Ruthie whipped her head toward Ken and snapped her little graveyard teeth at him. Her tongue lashed.

"Don't you touch her!" Otis screamed, and before Ken could take another breath, Otis, the Lady's champion, swung the Garden Weasel and caught Ken's cheek at the jawline.

Ken howled. His catcher's mitt of a hand stabbed outward and seized Otis' wrist. A couple of the tiller's fangs were still lodged in all that soft meat between mandible and cheekbone, burrowing around as he struggled to push Otis away. He squeezed, blood now hot with adrenaline, until he was at the threshold of shattering Gas Money's bone.

Otis, screaming his war cry, launched his left fist, attempting to jab Ken in the nose. Ken dodged the blow, and the inertia of that move allowed him to twist free. His skin tore, and blood ran warm. He slapped a hand to the wound and stepped backward.

"Otis, *what* the *fuck!*"

Ken's hand came away red, the blood ran down his neck and onto his slicker.

Now, Chief! The Signal screamed at him. Wherever that pawnshop in Stillwater had run off to, he didn't know; there was nothing in this shed but blood and Gas Money. *Now's the time, show Little Star you're a stud and crush that spearchucker's skull . . .*

Ruthie continued to snarl, biting the air between her coffin and Ken. *That blood is going to taste mighty good, go git some!*

Ken flipped his slicker back and flicked the holster's retention strap open.

Otis lunged again—no real plan, just blind rage—the Garden Weasel high over his head, twirling blades spitting Ken Lightfeather's atomized blood.

Ken's arm extended like a striking cobra, and Otis walked right into it. He found his neck wrapped in enormous fingers, turquoise ring and all, and a half second after that, the black mouth of a .44 magnum was pressed to his eye socket. Ken didn't let up on the pressure, either. It hurt.

Signal or no Signal, Otis stopped.

. . . Oh this is your moment of triumph, Red Man; old-school, desert-prairie payback. We'll cop an eight-ball, then tap a vein and reminisce . . .

"They . . . *it*...wants me to *end* you," Ken hissed. His breath sprayed all over Otis' face, hot and rank with terror. His tongue was white with plaque. "I *should* take a piece of you."

Kill him! Ruthie screamed. *But first take his goddamn balls with that dirt knife. Do it!*

Ken pulled the hammer back.

Otis, who was near-sighted, watched in crystal focus as the cylinder turned. Each monster hollow point bullet looked like a torpedo in a launch tube. In the fuzzy background, Ruthie spat obscenities and held her little tower made of sticks out for him to see. In the other hand, the bone needle.

Don't you quit on us, Ruthie growled. *We'll tear Franklin's skin off all over again.*

Ken pressed a little harder. It hurt Otis a little more.

Sack up and shoot!

"Don't make me listen," Ken whispered. His teeth clenched. His eyebrows pulled together into a collection of fine dunes. The tendons in his neck looked like the erosion marks of Devil's Tower. The roof banged in that prison riot frenzy.

Although Otis stood still, his entire body trembled. Ripe dread surfaced from his pores.

"Big Benny's Pawn and Loan in Stillwater, Oklahoma," Ken breathed.

Piss on that fucking redneck dump. Shoot . . .

The pad of Ken's trigger finger squeezed ever so slightly. There was certainly no competition-tuned trigger on his big S&W 629, but it wouldn't take *that* much effort for it to break.

. . . you can fuck the bullet hole when you're done . . .

"You have to push back, Otis. Listen to me . . . push back with something in your life that isn't so goddamn horrible. Find something, dig hard, find something."

Ken closed his eyes. Although he had no intention of dropping the revolver as long as Otis held the Garden Weasel, he *pushed;* bored through that electronic witchspeak and returned to the brick alley. Next to the Polaroid of the ring in its case, a creased, worn photo of their kitchen lit by a single flame, the night of the engagement ring, Little Star's mouth wide open in surprise. Desert honeysuckle breeze passed through the rustling curtains, the votive candle flickered on the table, and Little Star kissed him in between each time she said *"Yes,"* over and over.

Do NOT defy us . . .

Otis fought. He reached into a box, that little tin where his nightly dreams slept during the daylight hours, possibly the only place he had left to himself where the Signal had not managed to level with a shame-scythe. Ruthie's voice became a trumpet.

Just slice his crotch open, do a little preemptive birth control . . .

[WHEN FRANKLIN WAS SIX, I TAUGHT HIM TO RIDE A BIKE; THEN WE WENT TO WOOLWORTH'S FOR A MILKSHAKE.]

I thought about poisoning your toothbrush after we got home from Arlington . . .

[AT SEVENTEEN, DOROTHY WASHINGTON WAS THE MOST BEAUTIFUL THING I'D EVER SEEN, SHE KISSED ME, THEN SHOWED ME HER PANTIES BEHIND THE OLD MILL SAWHOUSE DANCE HALL]

The explosion tore Franklin in half and he lived through it, then the fire boiled away all his body fat into a running, stinking soup—

"Oh God, Ruthie, stop!" Otis screamed, and brought the tiller down.

White pain crunched his eyes into slits, and he had to tug once to pull the Garden Weasel free—from his own thigh. The Signal was cut off like a spigot.

Sort of.

ΨℏÅ3Ŝ [[!

Otis pushed Ken's gun barrel out of the way and watched as Ruthie spasmed in her deadbox. She turned to look directly at him, and that was when he saw the eye, her familiar, wet, brown solitary eye, surface from the gloom of her vacant socket and retake its rightful place. Blood vessels swelled dense and red until her sclera was a raw, bloodshot egg. The pupil, a huge black disc of a dreamless void, narrowed into a pinprick of malignant hate. The other socket remained capped with cobwebs.

It's the Old Conflict, just like the Indian says. Her voice had changed, the Ruthie imitation losing cohesion while the *true* voice, the Signal, pushed forward. *Every world we consumed was the path that brought us here.*

In lock-step with Ruthie as she plunged the bone-needle into her little voodoo doll electrical tower, Otis whacked the Garden Weasel into his sternum. His tongue popped out; Ruthie's tongue wagged like a dragon's tail. The jaundiced balloons of his eyes bulged; Ruthie's sole eye swelled from that skull-hole to the size of a summer plum. He made a thick, choking sound; Ruthie laughed like a hyena.

[WILLIE AND I FISHED ALL DAY OFF THE COPPERHEAD PIER, WILLIE CAUGHT A CATFISH, BUT AN ALLIGATOR CAME UP OUT OF THE WATER AND SCARED US BOTH]

The coffin lid slammed shut.

Ken Lightfeather did not see Ruthie's coffin close, but he *heard* it; the whoosh of the heavy mahogany door, the creak of the hinges, and the firm thud as it slammed home. Ken realized the membrane separating dimensions, realities—whatever, he didn't know what the hell to call them—had thinned here in the generator shed. They'd nearly killed one another at the behest of the Signal, and now was definitely the time to leave.

No one gets out of here alive, Otis! Ruthie, or the thing that pretended to be Ruthie, said in that buzzing, sawtoothed growl, now muffled by the casket. *You can't push us out for long.*

[I DRANK WHISKEY WITH CURLY BOSS RIGHT BEFORE HIS CAREER TOOK OFF, HE TAUGHT ME AN E CHORD . . . I MADE A RAFT OUT OF STOLEN PALETTES, WE FLOATED ALL THE WAY PAST DILLON'S HOLLER TO OUR SECRET COVE ON GREEN WILLOW CREEK]

Outside, an enormous crash resounded. The generator shed suffered an intense jolt; shelves dumped their contents, the shitty gate banged. Face bloodied, Ken seized the opportunity and grabbed Otis, and it took more than one pull to drag the stiff-legged man from the shed.

Now in the Devil Wind, Ken saw that Otis' outdoor furniture and cinder block fire pit were shredded, and a metal trash can had been flattened. He watched the cat head tower sweep its leg directly past the fleeing Paleface, Kemosabe, and the Spacedoctors. It drove its weight into the muddy yard, dragging with it something that may have been a motorcycle or a cement mixer in an earlier life. Hard to tell.

Ken's mind rang: *They should have made it to the trailer by now . . . were we in the shed only a few seconds, a minute—tops. Time moved differently in there.*

Paleface and the Spacedoctors dropped onto Otis' small wooden porch, the boy twisting just in time to shield his collapsing father. In the hard, single fluorescent light bolted to the rear of the mini-mart, they looked like a roadhouse fight caught in a cop's spotlight.

The tower's rear legs had yet to clear the double-wide. The twin points of its crown slowly turned toward Otis and Ken, then groaned as it strained to pull one massive leg from the mud. Now that anything was possible, Ken felt the tower *glare* at him.

Ken whirled Otis around. The Garden Weasel, which had done its bloody damage, fell to the ground. "You have to snap out of this," he said. "Goddamn tower's right on top of us again."

Brilliant plasma screamed down the transmission lines, blaring its ungodly Signal into the desert. The air grew surly with dread.

It felt to Ken as if his skull sprouted barbed stingers, piercing the tender curd. His eyes tightened from internal pressure as that throat from Elsewhere opened and screamed until raw. Gun still in hand, he pressed his palms to the sides of his head and squatted to his haunches.

SoÞ Ḵ!ṇ—Bρи!

A curled, glossy photo. He hit a home run in grade school, they used the dirt lot by the taxidermy shop as their baseball diamond—He patted the wall for it, fingertips like clumsy gloves over all the old prints.

You sure won the chickenshit home run derby that night. Little Star's lungs filled with puke and bile while you fled with a screaming baby in a station wagon full of toys and baby clothes. She was in withdrawal; she was trying to quit—and you quit her.

"That's not fucking true!" Ken screamed.

It was days before anyone went to collect Little Star's body. Tribal Police never knew—but Bibi knows. We talk to her through her menses because the soul is in the blood.

Childs reached down to help Caleb with Pale. The men clambered to their feet while the wind flung the scraps of Otis' outdoor furniture in all directions.

Nikki watched as the big Indian threw his head back and screamed *that's not fucking true!* face bloody, hands pressed to his head. He held a huge cannon, a Dirty Harry gun, something that shoots through engine blocks. In the glare of the fluorescents she could also see the old man—Otis, she recalled—blubbering like a schoolgirl next to Ken, his face twisted, chest and thigh both stained bloody.

Ken straightened, holding the revolver with both hands.

He pointed it at the tower.

Oh shit, don't do that, Nikki thought.

"Holster that weapon!" Nikki screamed, but the wind took most of it.

Ken pulled the trigger.

A Smith and Wesson 629 chambered in .44 magnum is a beast of a handgun, so when the crushing report came, nearly as brutal as the detonations from the storm, both cylinder and barrel spat fire. More air-pressure disruption than sound, that cannon roar, and despite the impossible conditions of that night, gunfire is gunfire, and everybody flinched.

The first round went ass-wild. Ken's second shot, however, scored a direct hit on one of the insulators, which jettisoned sparks as it cracked in half. It dangled like broken neon. The attached wire sagged, humming and snarling, but did not let go.

"I said holster that goddamned weapon!"

Nikki heard a grating noise, separate from the Signal, like the whine of an immense servo. She immediately thought of the monstrous targeting motors at the VLA, and how they hummed as the radio telescopes tracked the gunships.

She turned to see the receiving antenna of Otis' satellite dish display the first signs of Dragonfire glow. Heat radiated from it, noticeable despite the Devil Wind. It began to spread down the aluminum support rods toward the main dish.

"I bloody *knew* it," Nikki said.

Childs, still holding Pale Brody up like a cop rousting a drunk, looked at her, then the dish.

The reflector dish, a ten-foot spiderweb of a thing, lit up as Dragonfire infected it from the main receiver, which now was so bright he could barely look at it.

Childs screamed to Ken and Otis, *"Get out of there now! Split up!"* He reached for Nikki's waistband and fell back, and tugged her down with him. For the second time, the four of them lay in a dog-pile on Otis Thompson's porch.

Bright as day, a *purple* day, the Deathbeam illuminated the area between the Kwik Gas and the double-wide.

The jagged energy snake struck the ground directly in front of Otis and Ken. Smoke boiled up from the wound. The sizzling edges of the impact scar glowed like the insulators above.

With that purple flash, the ramshackle gate splintered into flaming streamers. The sound was a bizarre hybrid of a high-voltage hum and the crack of falling trees.

Ken and Otis rag-dolled backward into the shed. Limbs flailing, they collided with a hard clatter into the already leaning shelves and stacks of junk. Otis rolled into the shadows by the generator. Ken lost his grip on the magnum and ended up on all fours.

The Deathbeam had screamed past Nikki in its wailing, banshee shriek, and her hair felt like tiny boiling wires. Although it discharged for perhaps a quarter of a second, to Nikki, it felt like the slow motion of nightmares, that ineffable sensation of time-compression when everything ebbs to a crawl, but the presence of inescapable danger is insurmountable.

Childs was on his feet immediately and shouldered the trailer door open. He turned and reached down to grab Nikki.

"Holy *shit!*" Caleb yelled. Adrenaline swelled through him, and in one swift motion, he pushed his staggering father into the trailer and followed. "Jesus Harold Christ, what *was* that?"

"Goddamn," Nikki said. "Goddamn, Randy, this is bad news."

Childs pulled her up and flicked his head toward the open trailer door. "These two are inside," he said. He pointed to the shed and the glowing patch of mud at its threshold. "But we can't leave *those* two out here with the tower. They saved us, we owe them. Let's go."

The satellite dish sagged, the Deathbeam's heat a serious tax.

The glowing main receiver hissed as it cooled, the smell of ozone everywhere.

"C'mon," Nikki said. She took off, and Childs followed.

The belligerent giant swung its leg out of their path. It smeared past Nikki and Childs with a deep *whooosh,* scraping up mud and spraying filthy water. Nikki looked straight up to see the twin spire of the cat head silhouette, and dangling there, the broken insulator. It sent a glimmer of hope through her.

They can be injured, she thought. *If we had enough firepower, who knows what we could do? I'd kill for one of those gunships about now.*

The tower scraped the far corner of the mini-mart. A ribbon of sheet metal sheared away, exposing the building's wooden frame. It also took out the lone exterior light, and they were plunged once more into darkness.

"Enemies on all sides," Nikki said.

When Nikki and Childs arrived at the shed, careful to leap over the molten slag, they found Ken squatting, flashlight in hand, looking for his gun. He looked up at Childs, neck slick with blood, his big brown eyes sparkling. Otis sat upright on a set of tires. In the spill from Childs' flashlight, Otis looked traumatized, like someone who had just spent weeks in solitary. His eyebrows were practically gone, and his face was beaten with agony. Blood soaked through his coveralls on his thigh and chest, where he had stabbed himself with the Garden Weasel.

The generator murmured and coughed exhaust. The Devil Wind continued to work over the steel roof.

"Jesus, you okay, buddy?" Nikki said.

Otis shook his head. "No."

"Let's get you back to the trailer. That Deathbeam nearly smoked you both."

"Her coffin was right here," Otis said, pointing to where the crooked shelves formerly stood. They now resided on the floor, along with their contents. "And that's not the worst of it."

Otis stared across the yard, where it was good to see the lights were on in the trailer and the boy moving about inside, but dreadful that his satellite dish now was an enemy agent.

"She wanted me to kill Ken," he said. "Slash his neck with that garden tiller. Ken, I'm sorry, buddy. I'd never do anything like that. You know me."

Nikki and Childs exchanged glances. If there was such a thing as telepathy, it happened then as both of them conjured the image of Gary DeLeon standing over Artie Jayne with a bloody fire extinguisher. *Adios, El Fucko!*

"But we know how to push it back now, don't we?" Ken said.

Otis moaned. Ruthie in her coffin had really torn the rags from him. What hideous thing in this storm would make her speak like that?

It wasn't her. It was Them.

Nikki helped Otis to his feet.

"What does he mean by that?" Nikki said. "Push it back?"

"Tell her inside," Otis said. He felt his pelvis creak and his shoulders pop. "Let's just get inside. I've had enough of this damned place."

"Nice shootin' out there, Tex," Nikki said to Ken as she led Otis past him. "I should have told you earlier that they fight back. You're lucky it just grazed you. The Deathbeam can be a real bastard, believe me."

"Shine the light, would you?" Ken said, he didn't care to whom. "I'm not leaving here without my gun."

Childs illuminated the concrete floor. The place was wrecked, paint cans and debris tossed all over the place. No sign of Ken's gun just yet, but when he looked right outside the threshold, where the beam had struck the ground, the mud had cooled and was now like a sheet of obsidian. The stubborn gate was all over the yard in smoking splinters.

"Close one," Childs said to Ken. "You're lucky all you lost was your Smith."

You left her alone and she died . . .

Ken grumbled, "Oh, I've lost a lot more than that, Spacedoctor."

-12-
WHISKEY AND TWIZZLERS

CHILDS LOOKED AT his watch; almost eleven o'clock. He fingered the yellowed curtain aside and watched wide cat head towers stalk Route 60. The rain had not resumed, but the wind blew like hell. Behind that mayhem, the hand of Armand Jenks.

Wherever that asshole is, Childs thought, *I hope the Signal has him, and he's reliving his mother being gored by a bull.*

"We still have quite a few hours before sunup," Childs said. "Since Mr. Thompson has been kind enough to let us shelter here, we should get some rest. Everyone's exhausted."

"How are we going to get out of here, mister?" Caleb said.

"The road is the only way out. What's our vehicle situation?"

"My rig, for better or worse, is still out front," Ken said from the kitchen. He stood at the sink, cleaning his Garden Weasel wounds with paper towels and a bottle of hydrogen peroxide. "Also, Paleface's big Caddy might be a little on the battered side by now, but I'll bet it's still good to go. Full of gas, too, I'd reckon."

"I have an observation," Nikki said. She sat in a wooden chair next to Otis' La-Z-Boy, a bowl of bloody water in her lap. A pile of used paper towels formed a tiny Pike's Peak next to her feet. She dabbed one of Otis' thigh wounds. Soon as they were clean enough, she was set to plaster him with gauze, Band-Aids, whatever was available.

"That tower we just encountered," she went on, "is from way down the road. And by that, I mean about as far as Socorro. And there are plenty more of them where that one came from. By dawn, I can't imagine how many of those things will have stomped through here."

"I noticed that too," Otis said, a little self-conscious in his boxers in front of Nikki. It felt good to be tended to, however, good to have someone take care of him. He hadn't realized how much he missed it.

On the end table stood a photo of himself and a lovely 1980 version of Ruthie, all smiles on their little anniversary getaway to Savannah. Franklin's high school baseball portrait lived next door, and adjacent to that, an unopened bottle of Old Grand Dad. A larger photo of Franklin, in his Marine Dress Blues, hung on the far wall, next to a shelf that bristled with the boy's athletic trophies. Otis sucked air when rubbing alcohol met open flesh, and he grabbed the whiskey bottle's neck like a gear shifter.

"Hey!" Otis hissed.

"Suck it up, you old greaser," Nikki said. She looked at him and winked.

"You only see the really large ones next to the substations," Ken said. He shut the water off and leaned against the counter. With several pieces of butterfly tape now on his face, he looked like a man who had shaved in the dark. "I swear, it's like the entire grid just decided one night to get up and go for a walk."

Otis twisted around and looked at Ken. He'd really done a job on the trucker's face. Guilt, as if he needed any more, gnawed at him.

"I'm really sorry about that Garden Weasel, Ken," Otis said. "That thing, that noise, whatever it is . . . made me *see* Ruthie . . . "

Ken spat into the sink. His bristles were still up, but on a night such as this, who was really to blame? "Dead wives club, pal."

"Well, sorry just the same."

Ken walked over to the La-Z-Boy. He stood on the other side of the chair and put his hand on Otis' shoulder. The old man's bones were a little too close to the surface these days. "Don't take that gun in your eye personal-like."

"Jesus," Nikki said. "Remind me to never step into a shed with either one of you." She looked at Ken and handed Otis the isopropyl. "You're not too far off the mark about the grid deciding to get up and stroll the desert."

Nikki stepped away from Otis, past Childs, and pulled the curtain all the way open, revealing the mangled rear of the mini-mart and beyond, the giants on Route 60.

"Behold, friends—a by-product of reckless fuckery," she said.

An impossible scene: high tension towers on the march, their wires swaying as the sky swirled in a flashing cyclone. The listing frame of the awning poked above the mini-mart's roofline. The rear corner of the store hung open like a stab wound.

Childs looked at her and said nothing, but his expression said: *Shut up, Niks. They don't need to know.*

"I think everyone needs to know," Nikki said. "I think you'd all like to hear how the billions of dollars in radio telescopes were used to test—well, honestly, I'm not sure exactly *what* now—some dangerous technology that may have, if you'll stay with me here, had *outside help.* I also think now would be a good time to speculate on how a bunch of goddamn steel towers, whose only job is to hold wires out of the way, are walking around like soldiers. Anyone? How about you, Caleb? You seem bright and open to new things. Hit me with your best shot."

"I honestly don't know," Caleb said.

"X-ring, buddy. Hard to fathom? You bet. Unless you've seen the helix and heard the *Signal*, that is, and then you know there's some dark players on the scene. Otis, Ken, care to chime in on that? Rough minute in that shed, yeah?"

Otis shifted in his seat. He looked at Ken.

"I found a way to block it, somewhat," Ken said. "You have to move your mind in the opposite direction. It's hard, and I mean real hard, but it helps."

"Ken's right," Otis said. "When it comes in and digs up the bad, try to remember the good."

Childs took a deep breath and adjusted the rifle sling. "Shine a light," he said. He remembered kneeling in his unit's forward base the night the napalm run incinerated forty VC fighters, repeating the Lord's prayer over and over in an attempt to blot out the sound of screaming men, burning jungle, and horror stench of napalm and human meat.

Otis said, "Yeah, that's it. But it's harder than it sounds."

Ken nodded, and it hurt like hell. Butterfly tape would hold only so long. He needed stitches.

Pale watched Nikki with darkening eyes and waited. Hadn't he done something similar out there in the mud as the Signal tortured him at his mother's dinner table?

"I'm sorry if that struck an ugly chord," Nikki said, "but what we're dealing with is both real and unreal. At the VLA we saw the worst of it. Maybe it's easier to fight this far from the black tent, I don't know. But we are still in dangerous water."

Thunder exploded in the deep desert, and Otis' cheap windows shuddered in their frames. Nikki stood with her hands on her hips, now looking at her ruined shoes. Her life near Boston, hanging in the pubs with other tech-heads after a long day at Medusa Engineering, smoking a joint on her rooftop deck, jogging on the shaded streets of Cambridge, all suddenly seemed to her like stupid, naive things now that she knew what stalked the world.

"Two things, everyone," Otis said. He reached past Franklin's baseball photo and grabbed the bottle of Old Grand-Dad. "If we're going to find a way out of here together, we're going to need a plan. And we have to get on the same page if we're going to draw that plan up."

"What's the second thing?" Caleb said.

"I'll be needing pants."

Otis popped the cork and tossed it over his shoulder. It hit the kitchen linoleum and rolled away. The message was clear: *we're finishing this bottle.*

"Do we need glasses or not?"

Ken stuck his hand out. "Not."

Otis put the bottle to his lips and tilted back. He made a satisfied *ahhhh* sound, motor-boated his lips, then passed it to Ken.

Ken dropped his voice as low as it would go. "Thankum heap-plenty."

"Watch that firewater, Big Wheel."

"Might blow my whole paycheck in one night," Ken said, then took a healthy pull, then showed pain in all his face holes. He hadn't had a drink in years, since the night he scooped up Bibi and fled that trailer on the Rez, but if tonight was not cause for exception, nothing could be. "Whatever will I tell the wife?"

Ken passed the bottle to Childs. "Bottoms up, Spacedoctor."

Childs took a slug like a pro. He held the bottle out until either Nikki, the kid, or his father grabbed it.

"Doctor Barlowe to the booze ward, STAT," Nikki said as she grabbed the whiskey. "I like to call this a reverse boilermaker, fellas." She opened a Hamm's, took a swallow, then chased it with bourbon.

"There's cigars, too," Otis said.

"Oh, shit yes," Childs said.

"Caleb has snacks for days in his desert thunder bag," Nikki said. "Isn't that right?"

Caleb reached in and pulled out chips and Cheetos, Nikki's Hostess goodies, and a big-ass pack of Twizzlers.

"Dibs on those Twizzlers," Ken said.

"Sorry, Pal," Nikki said. "We share heap-plenty."

Ken laughed. Childs smiled. Otis grinned and grabbed his little humidor from the shelf below the end table. He held an array of maduros out like a Vegas dealer fanning a deck of cards.

Caleb opened the Cheetos and passed it to the right, opened the chips, and passed them to his father. Pale stared into it like a man who'd lost something in a well.

"Lay's Chips, Dad," Caleb said. "Salty and unhealthy, just like you like 'em."

Pale chewed with his mouth open. After a horrified look from his son, he seemed to remember his etiquette and before long, grinned like a six-year-old with a forbidden treat. He didn't hit the whiskey (although under the circumstances, Caleb kind of wished he had), but he gobbled down a Twinkie and a Ding-Dong.

Childs accepted the cigar-cutter from Otis and snipped the end of his stogie. "Holy shit, this is a *real* Partagas. Cuban."

Otis shrugged. "I still know a lot of folks in Tampa, and Tampa has more Cubans than stars in the sky. I wouldn't be surprised if you couldn't buy Cuban cigars from vending machines there."

Childs struck a kitchen match, then turned and burned. By the time he blew out a plume of cigar smoke and had his cherry nice and bright, the bottle had come back to him. He had booze in one hand, a Partagas No. 4 in the other, and the horrors of the day were, for the moment, elsewhere.

"Give your pop a Twizzler, Caleb," Nikki said. "They're junk food magic. They'll fix his wagon."

"Anyone ever drink whiskey through a Twizzler straw?" Ken said.

Nikki frowned. Cheetos had turned her lips and fingertips orange.

"Do I need to try that?" she said. The cutter and lighter had come to her, and for a moment, hands full, she found herself in a bit of a quandary.

Ken shrugged. "Couldn't hurt."

Soon the room was chattering, drinking, and smoking cigars. Ken performed a bar trick he hadn't done in years: he balanced a Cheeto on his fist, flicked it upward with his thumb, and caught it in his mouth. Everyone laughed, including Pale. Nikki dared him to blow a smoke ring, then flick the Cheeto through the ring. He immediately shook his head and declined, citing "it is forbidden by tribal law."

Childs twisted a figure-eight out of a Twizzler and referred to it as Infinity Licorice. Otis gathered everyone's cigar rings and made a paper chain. Nikki attempted to sing AC/DC's "Back in Black" in German, with Pale humming the guitar parts and Caleb keeping time on the coffee table. She was booed.

The wind and lightning did their damnedest to disrupt the impromptu party, but for an hour so, terror was not at the forefront on their minds. It began to quiet down once the cigars were done, and the bottle lay empty on the carpet.

Ken found himself a spot next to the air conditioner. He lay with his eyes open, apparently lost in thought. Childs propped the M-16 against the end table, grabbed some couch real estate, then shut his eyes.

Nikki, who found herself in a beanbag chair, looked to the sofa where Pale and Caleb sat. The kid's father slowly turned his head toward the brooding Indian.

All those guys, Nikki thought, *Randy, the trucker, and this dazed fucker look like they received a stern talking-to this evening. I still don't know why I seem to be immune to the Signal. Is there something wrong with me? If so, thank God for that.*

The boy looked straight at her. His fatigue was an easy read, and likewise the concern for his father. But there was something else to that expression, and damned if she could lay a finger on it, especially now with a head full of booze and exhaustion.

The kid's immune too. I haven't heard a spooky-peep outta him. I may have been weird when I was young with my face in books and electronics diagrams, but had I witnessed even half *of this, I'd be shitting in my hat. This kid is remarkably unfazed.*

"Those Others like the stagnant water of your past," Pale said, his voice rusty nails. He shifted his gaze from Ken to Caleb. "Every horrible moment of my life. My father stormed out of the house with my mother's broken heart still on his heel, I relived it as real as when I was eleven. That look in Valerie's eye the night you were born. Do you know what that look said, son?"

Caleb stammered. He felt not only immediately put on the spot but creeped out by his father's croaking demeanor.

"She chose *that* moment to say it all to me in a look, one small change of expression, and all it conveyed was contempt."

Pale raised a hand into the old spidery Bela Lugosi pose and swept his accusing finger toward Nikki and Childs. "*They* let it loose. You hear me for real, Caleb—everything's about to change, and it'll never come back. There will be no happy ending and string ensemble at the end."

Caleb's face sagged in disbelief. "Why would you say that?"

"She resented you, *she was afraid of you,* and I was too stupid to see it for what it was. I told everyone she wanted to be a famous rock and roll wife, but when the band seized up and I couldn't provide that lifestyle, she punched out. Even I believed it. I *told* myself to believe it. And I'll tell you: *Those Others* know it in the deepest detail. But you knew before I did, Caleb."

Caleb's throat felt like a circle of dry sticks. "Dad. Dad, please stop it."

"The lid has been torn off the Devil's toy box, son. Now they're free to roam through whatever medium they see fit; the speaker, that old phone, every scrap of metal in that God-forsaken asshole of a truck. Two minutes passed here, but an eternity in that truck while they forced the damnedest things, the damnedest conclusions into my mind. But not yours. *Why is that?*"

So, I'm not the only one who noticed, Nikki thought. Had not three beers and four whiskeys worked their magic, she might have shivered at Pale's soliloquy.

Pale's features hardened. His California good looks soured into those of a barfly, caved in from years of rounds on the house. Shadows sought the ski slopes of his cheeks and the fluvial lines on his forehead. The constellation of Band-Aids Caleb had applied didn't help.

For a second there, Caleb thought he saw his father's breath fog.

Ken's skin erupted in gooseflesh. Whatever seized Paleface in the Hertz had left a worm in Pale's mind to serve as spokesman. Mr. Los Angeles, with his scruffy hair and rock'n'roll jeans, had morphed from singer to sage.

"We all confess when the night falls," Pale continued. "You know what they showed me, Those Others? Do you know what lurks in the belly of every major mountain of the world? Do you know that out there, just past the shield of heaven, is *Elsewhere*, a place that's vile, ugly, and wrong?"

"I do," Ken interjected. "If the desert is anything, it's a battlefield. The Godless places in the infinite are sure to be the same. The Old Conflict."

"Here in our little, tiny bubble," Pale said as he tapped his temple, "if we keep the lights on and our minds shut, where we can keep it at bay. But now they're in the wild, looking for a host. I think they—*The Shadowless Ones*—are harvesting ugliness, seeking a sour—but emotionally blank—place to nest. They rummage through us and move on. We're inhospitable and therefore tormented. When they've found it, they'll blot out the light of the world. Their machines will breed underground."

"Jesus, fella," Otis said, roused from approaching sleep. "Way to bring down a party."

Otis would never forget Ruthie's coffin propped up in the shed like the final scene in a vampire's lair. *The Shadowless Ones snuffed out the stars just to get here, so honor them, give the desert its due.*

Pale set his hand on Caleb's shoulder. "When that Gate fully opens, it's all over. These are *Old Forces*, Caleb m'boy. *Old Commands.*"

At those words, Childs' eyes popped open. To hear someone else use that exact term made his teeth grind and Nikki's stomach roll. Right now, as far as they were concerned, Pale channeled Armand Jenks, and that was cause for alarm. Childs shot her a look, then tilted his head toward the rifle.

Should I shoot this guy? that said. *He may be dangerous.*

Nikki's face went wide. She mouthed the word *NO!* as widely as possible.

"Dad, you're talking crazy," Caleb said. His voice cracked a little, but his expression never changed. "It was terrible in the truck, I know."

Pale said, "Two minutes in a truck to you, but a *century* to me. The sound, that Signal—think of it as a call looking for a response, and the response is ambiguity. If you're sterile, you can be inhabited. If you receive, you're to be tortured. The towers are just a vehicle; the real enemy is always the one you can't see. They'll find who they're looking for."

Caleb stood, then moved toward Nikki. "Dad, please stop. You're freaking me out."

Nikki reached out and set her palm against his back. Caleb settled into her touch. She could feel his elevated pulse.

"That's because it's real. It's a gleeful sadist."

To save power, a single lamp burned, and in that low campfire light, they listened to the wind scream between the mini-mart and the trailer. Beyond, the steady, heavy strides of the towers.

Pale leaned back into a bar of shadow and sighed. Nikki and Childs watched as the hollows of his cheeks slowly returned to normal, and the lines on his forehead and around his mouth began to flatten. He exhaled one last wisp of icy breath.

At the sight of Pale's breath exiting his mouth and the direct use of another man's words, Childs thought, *Jenks knows we're here.*

"We were given this planet as a gift," Pale said in a voice that sounded to Caleb to be near normal but heavy with the onset of sleep. "They want to take it from us, but God alone decides that. Until then, we fight, even if it all ends in fire."

Pale's head dropped, and a few seconds later, he began to snore.

Ken rolled over and was out like a light. Otis, who had laughed all the way through a drunken Nikki taping his wounds with band-aids, lay in his recliner, mouth open, breathing steadily. Nikki sat slumped on her beanbag like a bored kid at church. Although her eyes became quite heavy, she and Childs watched Caleb.

Caleb fished into the bag of Cheetos and laid several of them out on the coffee table. He doodled a bit, making various shapes, and soon he found he'd arranged them into the rough shape of an electrical tower. Next to it lay Childs' Twizzler sculpture and Otis' paper chain. He laid the paper chain at the end of one of the cross-arms, dumped more Cheetos on the table, and fashioned a second tower, connected to the first with the cigar rings. He held the figure eight on its side, the Infinity Licorice.

"It's a circuit," Caleb said softly." An infinite loop." *The circuit . . . where there's order,* he remembered thinking as the two towers abandoned their assault of the truck and moved back in line like good little soldiers. *They're a chain gang.* He turned and looked at Childs and then to Nikki. "It's a circuit. A loop. That's it. *That's* the answer."

Childs raised one eyebrow. If he didn't sleep soon, he'd be out of his mind by dawn.

"I should have thought of that," Nikki said. Her voice was far away, on the edge of consciousness. "But I have *got* to close my eyes. Good thinking, Caleb. I should have thought of that."

Though well past midnight yet eternity until dawn, the towers roamed. The night had one last card to play, and by the time the sun broke the horizon, Dragonfire would come calling.

-13-

THE SPIDER AND THE ESCAPE PLAN

OTIS WOKE TO the sound of distant cannon fire.

Childs popped up and grabbed his rifle. He was at the window and had the curtains parted before Otis, whose leg had stiffened overnight, could crab out of his chair.

"What is it?" Otis said as a dream crumbled; the old house in Tampa, Ruthie clipped coupons at the kitchen table. She wore her cat's eye glasses.

Childs shook his head. "Sounds like artillery, but different. It's still a couple of miles away, at least. Can't see much with the store in the way."

Ken pulled himself from the floor. He slalomed between the legs of the others still flaked out on the sofa and Nikki snoozing in the beanbag chair. The room was filled with stale cigar smoke and deep breathing. However, their power conservation efforts paid off as the lamp still burned.

"What gives?" Ken said. He grabbed his braids and flipped them over his shoulders. "Doesn't sound good."

In the faraway, a series of deep, cavernous booms. No rhythm, just random thuds. They could still hear the generator running in the shed.

"All I can see is the glow from one tower about a hundred yards across the highway," Childs said. "But it's burning like a son of bitch, I mean crazy bright." He turned and checked his watch. His teeth were fuzzy, and he really wanted to drag a toothbrush over them. "It's just after five. Sun'll be up soon. I don't know what's making that noise, but it doesn't sound like the towers."

"We shouldn't wait to find out," Otis said. "Ken, you with me?"

Ken stretched and pulled his 629. He opened the cylinder and checked it. Two rounds gone.

"You coming, Spacedoctor?" Ken said to Childs, who nodded.

"What's going on?" Nikki said, voice full of molasses. The sound came again, a muffled series of deep booms. "What's that noise?"

"Stay put, Niks," Childs said. "We're going to check it out. You'll need to pull the door shut behind us. Stay with these two. We'll be a couple minutes."

Childs reached into Nikki's bag, rummaged through the pile of Dragonfire DAT tapes, and grabbed a spare magazine. He put it in his back pocket, charged the weapon, and verified the safety was on.

Otis opened the door.

The wind blew hot and steady, and the rain had yet to resume. Childs stepped out with the rifle at the low ready, his infantry training never more than a few inches below the surface.

Ken followed, revolver drawn. His slicker flapped and snapped.

Otis stepped onto the stairs and turned to see Nikki behind him, watching the tower across the road. He followed her gaze. The insulators were far brighter than he'd seen the night before, nearly lighting the entirety of the giant with their radiance. To the right— *East*, Otis corrected—the random artillery thunder.

The tower twisted into its next step.

"What the hell do you have in mind?" Nikki said.

Otis offered a half shrug. "Follow your friend here, run out to the other side of the store, see what we can see."

"Remember the Deathbeam," Nikki said. "If you boys have to shoot, don't do it anywhere *near* that thing." She flicked her head to the warped shape of Otis' satellite dish. Whether it held any Deathbeam juice in reserve, she didn't know.

Otis hurried and caught up with the others. Even in these last moments of darkness, Otis could see the huge gouge the passing giant had carved into the corner of his business, and for the first time, he actually thought about an insurance claim and what the hell he'd say to the State Farm guy. It all seemed so distant and absurd that he laughed in spite of it.

Just as they reached the gnarled corner of the mini-mart, Childs raised his hand and everyone stopped.

"Stay low," Childs said over his shoulder. "If we see anything crazier than walking electrical towers, we beat it back to the trailer. You tracking?"

Ken and Otis nodded.

"Also, if you see another person, Ken, you cover my six with the magnum and I'll get their attention. We square?"

Ken and Otis nodded again.

Another series of booms resounded, solid as stone but definitely eastward.

As they came around, the first thing they saw was the rear of Ken's rig. It still looked to be in pretty good shape despite its lightning encounter and a night of assault from flying debris. One mirror dangled from the driver's door.

The awning had been stripped to its frame. The old fuel pumps leaned like loose teeth, dials smashed, hoses on the ground. Pale's Cadillac was where he left it, now with a nasty crack in the windshield and filthy as a hobo. An enormous scrape had been carved into the passenger side.

Beyond, at the edge of Route 60 and the westbound turn-in to the Kwik Gas, the dark paper cut-out of the destroyed Hertz truck. Its spine had been snapped, the cab a topography of dents. The plywood bed enclosure was spewed all over the gravel and the road. Childs stopped for a second when he saw that.

"Good God," Childs said. "That's what's left of the truck?"

"You bet," Ken said. "That tower tore the bejesus out of it after Mr. Los Angeles fished you out. He was stuck in there for the ride. Lucky to come out of that alive— thanks to Ken and the boy—even if the Signal got the worst of him."

The Thompson's Kwik Gas sign endured, pock-marked and beaten. It creaked in the wind, swinging from heavy chains. Childs found himself reminded of the old poster for *High Plains Drifter*.

To the east, where the first whisper of daylight would soon hiss into the sky, a V-shape of transmission lines extended into the gloom. Over a rise in the desert they ran, toward the battery of sound. Dozens of towers were linked to these power lines; one group marched past the Kwik Gas, the other to the northwest, two mule teams with different destinations.

"Look at the insulators," Childs said. "You can nearly see the entire tower by them."

The glow was bright as a searchlight, the hum a chorus of drones in the hive. Childs knew if another purple bolt of Dragonfire rage were emitted with the insulators at such ferocity, anyone sensitive to the Signal would likely become unhinged, including himself. The last thing he needed was his dying father reaching for him with his pale fingers, mouth crammed with tubes.

And still, the arrhythmic tribal drums, the resilient pounding from miles away, tugged on the edge of his mind.

I should know, Childs thought. *Increased luminosity, raging power, dozens of towers, a lot of them cat-heads. I should know . . . I should know what this means.*

"I don't know plasma from a ham sandwich," Otis said. "But my bones tell me these towers are more dangerous than the others."

"Look at the power lines," Ken said. He pointed over Childs' shoulder to where the trajectory of the wires suggested they meet over the land rise. "Eventually, those two bands of lines meet. Didn't the lady—*Nikki*—say these were definitely the towers from miles and miles away? So where do the lines end?"

BoomThud ThudBoom

A minute sliver of dawn overtook the horizon-bound darkness. Faint silhouettes of mesas and hillsides were now visible. Over a mile away, a tower crested the ridge, insulators bright as day. To its side and behind, the horns of a second tower's apex. The wind howled low and long, a bull with its neck trapped in the slaughter chute. The sign banged against its gallows. The Cadillac's suspension creaked.

Ken glimpsed it first: a horizontal gridwork of steel, clearly not a tower, but listing slowly side to side as it revealed itself over the rise. Buried in the haze, the slow seesaw motion reminded him of the oil pumps he'd seen through Oklahoma, Wyoming, and Texas. Sometimes farmers would paint their elliptical heads like grasshoppers. Sometimes kids would ride them.

"Jiminy Jesus," Ken said. "What the hell is this now?"

Soon, several spires crested the hill, spaced apart by tens of yards. The boxes from which they protruded were stacked into tall pillars, like weird art-deco totem poles. Transmission lines swayed with every clumsy, thunderous step, splitting off to the wandering towers. More gridwork followed—some vertical, most horizontal, but a gigantic cage nonetheless—but certainly not in the busy criss-cross fashion of the towers. This was a frame, a substructure built to support other things.

When the fiery grid of its insulators first became visible, Childs lowered his weapon and stared. Ken and Otis watched as a delayed expression of realization came over the Spacedoctor.

"Goddammit," Childs said. "Of course, of-fucking-course. Has to be." He used the M-16 to point at the enormous shape. The snaggle of steel rose over the hill, bristling with hard edges. "That's the source. *That's Dragonfire.*"

"I see what it is now," Ken said. The crowd of insulators bled light like a formation of low-flying UFOs. As the vast horizontal grid climbed to the apex of the land rise, they heard the first hint of its baritone electric hum. Lightning flashed, and the dead center of the cyclonic eye hovered overhead, the storm's distant edge lit by the emerging sun.

To Ken it was so surreal it looked fake.

"Looks like scaffolds and transformers and stuff like that," Otis said. "Am I seeing that right?"

"Exactly," Ken said. He looked over to Childs. "Say true, Spacedoctor."

"It's the substation, fellas," Childs said, shaking his head. "It's the goddamn *substation*, and it followed us here all the way from just outside the VLA. *This* is the source of the towers. *This* is the nexus."

"Wait, this is the one to the north of Route 60? By the telescopes?" Ken said.

"You said 'say true', and I'm here to tell you so."

"We need to go, gents," Otis said as his tongue turned to chalk. *Ruthie is in there somewhere, and there's room in her coffin for me.*

"In a second," Childs said as he eyed Ken's rig. "Nice jalopy."

"Modded with twin turbos. Just looks like hell right now, that's all."

"Rock and roll guy's in the Caddy?"

"Yeah. Paleface and his boy."

"I have a Silverado King Cab behind the trailer," Otis said. "Unless one of the towers had its way with it—I haven't looked—but we should already be saddled up and the hell out of this place."

Just as they turned back for the trailer, a tower approaching from the east stopped dead in its tracks. They looked up to see its cage begin to turn, that aching steel shrieking like a hyena. The apex shifted direction toward the Kwik Gas.

"They made us," Ken said. "I'll bet the spider on the hill knows now, too."

Eastward and atop the hill, more of the sprawling substation's vertical protrusions clawed out of the dawn. Light strobed from the site, illuminating the belly of the storm. Wires swayed in the wind.

The tower held its position, the cross arms slowly moving from side to side, wires humming like Dr. Frankenstein's lab. Even at this distance, they could feel the heat from the insulators.

"Go!"

Otis led the way, legs pumping, chest heaving. Even with his punctured thigh howling, he leaned into the turn around the mini-mart and toward the double-wide, leaped over the fallen light fixture and dodged the shrapnel of his garden furniture. Ken and Childs came in hot on his heels.

Leading with his shoulder, Otis banged into the door just as Nikki pulled it open. He tumbled inside and almost ended up on top of Caleb, who was still half-asleep.

"Whoa," Nikki said. "Doctor C., where are we?"

Childs waited for Ken to shut the door. "It's the goddamn *substation*, Niks."

It took a second, but when she realized what she'd been told, her eyes opened nice and wide.

"Good Lord, no," Nikki said. "*Jenks*. He followed us."

"Not sure if it's Jenks or just Dragonfire itself. But the towers we're seeing now are *all* connected to the substation. That's the source, Niks, just as we saw it last night. We all need to be gone."

"Let's get ready," Nikki said. She threw the tool bag over her shoulder and slid the pistol back into her waistband. Without thinking, she pulled Caleb off the sofa. "Rise and shine, champ."

"Hey!" Caleb protested. Nikki had him like an angler on one of those cable TV fishing shows. "I have to pee."

Nikki said, "Drain your vein and grab your dad. Come to think of it, everybody have your morning whizz—we are *splitsville*."

"Wait, back up," Otis said. "*Just as you saw it last night?* What did you see?"

"We saw it hit the grid," Nikki said. "As we fled Socorro, we saw the substation hit with . . . well, at Medusa Engineering, we call it Dragonfire. The Helix. I honestly don't know exactly *what* it is, but we dragged it into the world through the VLA, and that homicidal bastard *escaped* into the power grid. And now . . . "

"Holy shit," Ken said. The way Nikki looked at him and her immediate urge to flee told him everything he needed to know. She wasn't bullshitting. At all.

"Now it's here," Childs said. "There's not a lot of time, shit, probably none. We ended up drunk last night and never made an escape plan."

"The plan is *Get The Hell Out*—at least now that the sun's up, we'll be able to see," Ken said. He holstered his gun and patted his pockets for his keys. A couple of his butterfly tape bandages had popped off, and his Garden Weasel wounds leaked. "I'd rather not take another dose of the Signal. My man Otis can't either."

Otis nodded. "Hurts to walk, but I'll run like my ass is on fire."

"I think your big rig will hold us all," Childs said. "If we had to, I suppose we could smash through one of them."

"Contact means Signal," Otis said. "When that tower touched the awning and your crashed truck, it got very dark; you were lucky to be unconscious. Just look what it did to Mr. Los Angeles."

Caleb returned from the toilet, zipping his pants. He'd even washed his face and borrowed a mouthful of Otis' Listerine. "It's a circuit, remember," he said. He looked down to his diagram made from Cheetos, cigar rings, and a Twizzler. "The towers are linked." No one heard him, or if they did, they ignored it.

Nikki looked at Childs. "Old Timer's right," she said.

"You have ear protection?" Childs asked Otis. "Shooting range earmuffs, that type of thing? If the substation broadcasts, especially this close, who the hell knows what kind of trouble will surface."

"Sorry, not at all," Otis said.

"Seemed worth asking, as it appeared to work for someone on Jenks' detail."

Early sunlight crept through the curtains, and the lamp had gone out—which signaled the generator was out of fuel. Night was over, and it was time to go.

"Colonel Nobody," Nikki said. "Look at the time, we figured the lot of you didn't need all the gory details. But whatever we let onto this planet, into our reality, is inhabiting that substation. Fucking ridiculous as it sounds, that's what's happening. Armand Jenks and his little coven of weirdos is responsible for every death. We should have shot him in the face when we had the opportunity."

"Hardcore, lady," Ken said as he exited the bathroom but

remembered that just a few hours ago, he'd had the barrel of his 629 pressed against Otis' eyeball.

"You'd agree if you'd been there. From now on, I will *never* hesitate."

The cross-talk became a jumble of noise and near-panic; Otis nervously ranting about the absurdity of it, Ken attempting to see it through the lens of logic, Nikki's venting anger at Jenks, Childs' full-bladder urgency to build a coherent plan.

"It's a *circuit*," Caleb said again. "A circuit can be *broken*."

"Caleb is right," Pale barked. No one had noticed he'd risen to his feet; the homeless rock and roll street preacher with a face full of Band-Aids, dirty hair, and even filthier clothes. He set his hand on Caleb, then looked at Nikki and Childs. "I said *Caleb is right.* Listen to him."

The conversation ceased. Caleb swallowed big, licked his lips, then pointed to the coffee table.

"They're tethered," Caleb said. "It's a loop. I know it looks stupid, made out of Cheetos and all, but when you look at any closed system—cameras in a bank, my dad's guitar rig, and in our case, grid electricity—if you break the connection, *the system fails.*" He flicked away the chain of cigar bands, and brushed the second Cheeto tower away with the side of his hand. "Now that tower is all alone. Cut off from the others."

Caleb held up Childs' figure eight, the Infinity Licorice. "It's a loop, an infinite loop. So, if everything is connected to the substation, then we cut the towers off from the source. The Hertz truck you guys were in was not big enough, and they ran you off the road. But . . . "

"But that big ass Peterbilt could get the job done," Nikki said. She looked at Childs. "Good lord, it's that simple?"

"So we're obeying a Cheeto diagram," Childs grumbled.

Caleb shrugged. "If someone smashes into a power pole in our neighborhood, the lights go out. What's different here? They're just big, powerful, and super scary—*that's* the difference. We all saw the purple signal run through the wires and light up each tower. My dad and I saw a tower hit by lightning before *any* of this started. Where else would the power have to go if the wires were out of the picture?"

Pale laughed. "If you want your guitar to stop buzzing, you ground it. That's where the *Signal* goes—to ground."

"If you trip up a tower, the lines snap and it ends?" Ken said. "Really?"

"It *can't* be that easy," Otis said.

"That looks great on paper, Kid," Childs said. He stood at the door and set his hand on the knob.

"Yeah, well, we were told that about Project Dragonfire too," Nikki said.

"It won't be easy, but the *idea* is simple. You said it yourself, Dad—*unless they're stopped, they'll find who they're looking for*—and if it's really that bad, well . . . "

"Fuckin-A, *Kemosabe*," Ken said. "Big brain on your boy, Mr. Los Angeles. But Nikki is right, the Caddy should be the escape vehicle. The *rig* should be the weapon."

All eyes went to Ken Lightfeather.

"You sure about that, Big Wheel?" Otis said.

"It's the only way to *be* sure."

An avalanche of noise rattled the windows; the eye of the storm was nearly upon them. Lighting spread from the infectious cyclone in a series of searing crab legs. If they didn't move in the next couple of minutes, the spires of the substation would be too close to the Kwik Gas, and the noose might tighten for good.

"Let's hit it!" Childs barked.

"One last thing," Nikki said.

"Goddammit, Niks, shut the hell up and move!"

"Thirty seconds, this affects you too, Randy. We go west, toward anywhere but back toward the VLA."

"Oh hell yes," Otis added.

She put a hand on Pale's shoulder. "You don't look ready to handle that big Caddy just now."

"I don't know if I'm right for the job," Pale said. "I'm sorry, Caleb. I'm sorry for all of it. We should have just stayed on the easy road to Austin. That could have been a song title."

"Please, Dad, stop talking like th—"

Childs interrupted, "You two can hash it out down the road tonight."

Ken took his slicker off and tossed it aside. He wore a black shirt with a glorious eagle embroidered in beads. His black braids hung like ropes. On either side of his eponymous belt buckle, rattlesnakes were tooled into the leather.

"I'm ready for the fight," Ken said. "If we don't stand up, we're fucked. This is the Old Conflict, and if the desert wants its due, then I'll have the desert's ass."

Caleb thought Ken was the bravest person he'd ever met; the way he stood his ground in the face of the tower, how he'd hopped into the truck after his father had been trapped inside, and now he was willing to solo it on the road. He'd seen *The Road Warrior* on HBO, and here he was for real.

"I head east, you head west. I'll fishtail the trailer and hopefully trip up one of the towers, then unhitch the cab and scram. I put that spider in the rearview and meet you all down the road. We find a bar, get shitfaced."

"Deathbeam will be a problem," Nikki added.

"It's *all* a problem," Pale said.

"All right, everyone, it's showtime," Childs said. It didn't occur to him that he'd just repeated the exact phrase he'd uttered as the Dragonfire test went operational, but it wasn't lost on Nikki Barlowe.

He whirled his index finger again like a member of a chopper crew. "Wheels up."

-14-
LIVE WIRE

WHEN NIKKI SAW the substation, walking on its own in a disjointed series of epic, clumsy strides, she actually stopped and admired it. The thing was positively giant, easily over a hundred yards wide, fashioned from a grid of scaffolds and beams, which in turn supported vertical hives of transformers, circuit breakers, and a herd of insulators.

The structure ascended the hill like a wounded crab, edging one corner forward in a series of disjointed stabs, then waited as the tremendous weight settled. Wires and spires swayed, and the substation did not attempt further steps until all motion subsided. The insulators emitted a fierce, nearly blinding version of the Dragonfire glow seen on the towers. Here, at the source, their power was ten to twenty-fold.

Soon it would be on the downslope, right smack dab in the middle of the road, perhaps a half-mile to the east of the Kwik Gas. Whether the force inhabiting the substation was Jenks' Awakener of Stars or Those Others Pale mentioned, they could have been one and the same; Nikki had no way of knowing, and she harbored zero interest in finding out.

Nikki stood with the others between Ken's rig and Pale's Cadillac, all momentarily transfixed as the inanimate yet alive structure crawled over Route 60. Directly above, the malignant storm, stirring counterclockwise, the walls of the eye alive with purple flashes. Thunder rolled so frequently that they hardly noticed it anymore.

"You cannot help but be impressed," Nikki said. "It's evil and weird and horrible, but that is truly amazing."

"No time to pat yourself on the back," Otis said. Pale dropped the keys into his hand, and he limped around to the driver's door of the Cadillac.

Otis looked at the damage wrought upon the concrete island. "Oh, shit. No, no. That's not good."

Childs peered over the Caddy's rear end. Two of Otis' old-time gas pumps had been twisted from their mounts, leaving the channel which connected them to the underground reservoir exposed. Even in the Devil Wind, the pungent smell of gasoline was everywhere.

"Do we cap that before we split?" Childs asked. "Can it be done quickly, or is it even necessary?"

"I don't know if it would matter," Otis said. "I'd rather deal with the insurance man than take my chances with *that* thing." He looked at the incredible grid-spider squatting atop the hill. Raging light flashed from it in spastic intervals.

Ken climbed into his Peterbilt. He cranked up the huge turbodiesel, then rolled down the window and leaned out, waving his hand until he had Caleb's attention.

Caleb hustled over to the truck. It was pretty beat up, the headlights cracked, one of the turn signals missing, the top of the trailer section scorched from lightning. Ken twisted the dangling mirror from its mount and handed it to him.

"Might need this to reflect that Deathbeam if things go sideways," Ken said. "You never know."

Caleb smiled, but they both knew the Deathbeam would not be stopped by a mirror. "Be careful, Ken," he said.

Ken grabbed his aviator shades from the visor. He fogged the lenses with his breath, wiped them with a rag he kept in the console, then began to undo his braids. When he was done, a flood of jet black, straight as an arrow hair spilled over his shoulders and onto his chest. Caleb had been around a lot of longhairs in his time, but Ken's slate-black mane was unlike anything he'd ever seen.

"When going into battle, it's important to look cool doing it. No warpaint available today."

Most of the butterfly tape holding his wounds together had either been peeled away by the wind or dislodged by his own movements. Blood began to seep.

"Not too sure about that," Caleb said. He held the mirror up so Ken could see.

"Damned if Kemosabe doesn't have a point," Ken said. He

dabbed two fingers in the blood and smeared a twin line from his forehead to his lips. "The old ways will never fail you, buddy. Remember that."

Caleb climbed onto the step and held his hand out. The wind grabbed Ken's hair and obscured his face. To him, Ken looked like the ultimate badass.

"Unhitch that trailer fast as you can," Caleb said. "I'll make sure we don't leave without you."

Ken took Caleb's hand into his huge mitt, shook it, then wiggled his eyebrows.

Down the road, a sole flat-top tower, a massive rectangular beast that had no other towers between itself and the substation, dared him like an opponent in a boxing ring. The Devil Wind screamed through its skeleton, but beneath that, the first low rumbling of the Signal.

"I'll do my best, *Kemosabe*. Watch out for your old man. Make sure to tell him and Otis to think something good when the bad comes. I don't think the Spacedoctors knew what they were getting into, hard to say. But tell them, too."

"I sure will, Ken."

"All right. Let's get this handled."

Caleb tapped the door with the severed mirror. "See you soon."

Ken blew the air horn, and that grabbed everyone's attention. He gave the thumbs up, then put on his aviators.

Nikki watched Ken and Otis exchange a look. Otis pumped his fist in the air.

"*Chief Big Wheel!*" Otis shouted.

"*Gas Money!*" Ken shouted back.

Ken gave Otis a salute worthy of an officer, then revved the diesel. Otis hopped into Red Zeppelin's driver's seat.

"Time," Pale said. He opened the Caddy's rear door. Childs slid in behind Otis, followed by Nikki. Caleb opened the door for his father, and Pale climbed inside. Caleb was last.

The substation spider, busy positioning itself into a battle stance, coughed a dangerous, dark buzzing noise, a clear warning of intent. A few of its spires, through which several transmission lines fed into the towers, swayed like a sea anemone. Flat-Top, the closest tower guarding the substation, began to move just as Ken's Big Rig pulled in front of the Cadillac.

The Peterbilt nudged the wrecked Hertz truck, pushing its

corpse to the side. The big rig rolled into the road, black exhaust belching from the polished chrome smokestacks. Ken honked again.

"I can't believe you pulled me out of that thing," Pale said, finally getting a good look at the husk of the box truck. It looked like a robot had suffered a dreadful skydiving accident.

"Dad, it was good you went in there to rescue everyone, isn't that right, Spacedoctors?" Caleb said, enjoying the use of Ken's words.

"We would have died in there," Childs said. He gave Pale two good firm pats on the shoulder.

"Hear, hear, Mr. Los Angeles," Nikki said. She reached over and ruffled his hair. Pale and Caleb smiled. "Now let us do something for you. Let's get the fuck out of here, Otis."

Otis fired up the big V8. The fuel gauge tilted all the way to *F*.

"Seat belts, everyone," Otis said.

Pale said to Caleb, "Right as Those Others showed me their intent to use all of us as soul meat, *you* came and rescued your old Mac Daddy."

"Otis and Mr. Lightfeather too, Dad," Caleb said. He thought of Ken Lightfeather in his rig, bloody warpaint, shades on and hair down. Brave as a bullet and looking cool as can be. "The Kwik Gas Family rolls hard."

"Fuckin'-A," Nikki agreed.

Caleb fastened his belt. He reached over and secured his father as well.

Pale shook his head. The experience inside the Hertz truck had stirred the edge of his memory. *Valerie knew about you. She told me, but I dismissed it. It's the crux of everything.*

"U-turn time," Otis said as he dropped the big machine into drive. "*Westward!*"

Childs rolled down his window and leaned the rifle barrel on the sill.

Nikki grabbed him by the wrist and said, "*Punch it, Thompson!*"

Otis stomped the gas, pulled into the road, and cranked the wheel to the left. Everyone leaned like the old camera-tilt gag when the Enterprise crew endured a Klingon disruptor punch to the hull. As Otis began to straighten out, Caleb was shoved against the door by his father's weight.

Did Dad undo his seat belt?

"God will see this evil pushed back into its hole," Pale said.

"Well, that hole is right above us," Nikki said, leaning against Childs.

She looked up to the storm, lit the color of blood by the rising sun. A wild spawn of lightning cracked from the edge of the eye and spread across an ocean of turbulence.

Ken kept his hands on the wheel at nine and three o'clock. If it was good enough for Indy 500 drivers, it would do the job when it came to confronting monsters. He put his foot down and ground the rig into eighth gear. Ahead he saw Flat-Top begin to pivot. Wires tightened as it dragged one leg across the road.

The stereo snapped awake. The display glowed a brilliant purple, and the Signal poured into the cab. He'd tapped into a morning drive-time show from Hell, hosted by Baal and his sidekick, Suicide.

"Back for more?" Ken said.

A trumpeting of machine language and ugly shapes blasted from the speakers, but now far more intense—and what occurred in the shed had been no picnic. As traversed the distance from Ken's ear to his mind, it was translated into English, hissed and spat with every foul intention imaginable.

Ǧɴ—DŽÒᴜ—Bok!?

You could have stayed. Been a goddamn man instead of a blubbering Fucksissy. She trusted you. That's what you laughed about in the mirror. When your smile cracked and you looked like a wolf.

—!RɣR(t) !ᴎ!

Take that gun and enforce the law—ZƎÐF^—Shoot yourself in the asshole! Turn this truck round and kill all those white men—C1ꞰꞰ<— listen to their bones snap beneath your wheels. Wear their blood

—(souls)—

like real Apache war paint.

Ken slammed the machine into eleventh gear. Power growled in that familiar diesel engine rattle. The turbos wound up.

Fuck that woman senseless, then eat the kid and scalp the nigger. Yeah, baby . . . that's how we get into some old-school frontier ooga-booga!

He pushed back, his mind conjuring the brick wall covered with Polaroids: a picture of himself as a pudgy nine-year-old, attending an Apache Days street fair in Harrison, a half day's ride from the Rez. His mother had a booth, she sold jewelry to tourists. He wore a bath towel as a superman cape. He bought a snow cone for a dime. Wild Cherry.

The stereo blared so loud the speakers coughed ragged distortion.

—Iɟ ꞀЙ!—

Just surrender your shadow before you bleed in the sand . . . ǧive tħę dešȝrt it's dũe!

Ken hissed, head buzzing with hornets, their numbers swelling, stingers at work on the backside of his skull. The hive bloomed behind his forehead; a pain so God-awful he wondered if the bone had actually *moved*.

Fearing his eyes would pop like a champagne cork, he glanced at the speedometer before that could happen. Seventy-three. A few hundred feet ahead, Flat-Top, corkscrewing into the road, churning up asphalt debris. Steel and insulators dared him to trespass.

V̌HBtṼ!

The wall, *the wall*, photos glued to it with old, yellowed cellophane tape: A fun night as an underage bartender in Twin Falls, a couple of months before he'd finished trucker school. He'd met a couple of hard-drinking guys from the Crow Reservation in Montana—Ernie Sunbird and Dulro something-or-other—and after his shift they drained two bottles of Jim Beam. Everybody puked, but it was fun.

Mouth-fuck yourself with that gun. Blow your Mongrel face off . . .

Ken did as he was told. He grabbed his S&W and cocked the hammer, the Flat-Top tower so huge in his windshield now that it filled the world.

Still able to smell the gunpowder from firing the weapon hours ago, he dropped his jaw and crammed the muzzle inside his mouth. The cannon smashed past his upper teeth in a wild explosion of hurt. The taste was ugly with oil, the bright yet bitter tang of steel. The desert blurred past him.

Do it, faggot!

The wall faded. The bricks began to look like those glass blocks rich people used in their rich people's showers, see-through and vague, so you could see only distorted shapes on the other side. But these shapes were wrong; they didn't make sense. Too many limbs, too many heads, like something the world had rejected.

A few stained bricks remained in that matrix, and upon one was taped a Polaroid he'd actually taken himself. A guy at a diner had gotten up to use the restroom, and Ken snatched the camera from his table. He stole a photo of an exquisite nineteen-year-old Little Star as she leaned against the cash register counter, flawlessly beautiful, eyes the shape and color of almonds, hips like Mulholland Drive.

Now at nearly eighty miles an hour, Ken, with a face full of Smith and Wesson, leaned right and took the wheel with him. The truck veered, tires screeching. The entire cab burst into an awful tornado of sound as the left fenders and fuel tank scraped the tower. Sparks flew into the window and peppered his face. The leading edge of the trailer smashed into Flat-Top.

ɯƎ *ƧΛĬD ĐƠ ỈṬ!*

Little Star leaning against the counter as he lined up the shot. Hippie fringe dangling from her purse, the sleeves of her jacket. She flipped her waist-length hair the way Cher used to back on that old TV show, and Ken laughed right before he hit the button.

He removed the gun from his mouth.

After he stashed the photo in her purse and returned the camera to the table, she whispered to him, 'Have you ever made love in a hammock?'

Ken unloaded the cylinder through the windshield. The absolutely deafening blast from the .44 dwarfed the horror show of the demon Signal. The glass (both the opaque squares in his wall and the Peterbilt's windshield) now had four new holes, split into a network of spiderweb cracks.

The revolver empty, a deafened Ken laid it on the seat. Despite the agony, he grinned.

You still have plenty of Polaroids, find them.

The Signal renewed the incursion, scouring Ken for more buried hurt. His mind's eye ached with images from the long-buried decades: Six-years-old and wetting his pants, gripped by the terror of entering the cavernous school restroom by himself; his yippy little mutt Frito Bandito, who his father had made him abandon on Route 73—citing a lack of money to pay for dog food;

the icy way he refused to acknowledge Hilde Fredrick after losing his virginity to her.

The years rolled roughshod over the memory wall he'd constructed, overrode anything fond with something dreadful. Little Star looked up at him with her glazed eyes and priceless hair chopped to her jaw line, their bedroom stinking, strangers passed out in the living room, all their second-hand belongings sold off. She coughed up a dismissive laugh when asked if she'd fed Bibi. As she opened her near-toothless mouth to speak, the signal commandeered her, her eyes rolled white, and the voice of Those Others poured from her lips.

AƆ⊣ ᒣ'H3Ɛ

Now Bibi ɯon't take ʎour phone calls becλusƐ she kΠōψs you let me ÐĪĚ.

Naked, a croaking Little Star crumbled out of the bed, dragging with her wet sheets and crammed ashtrays. Everything fell on the floor in a snarl. Her torso looked like a skinned stepladder. Her pelvis was visible through her buttocks.

ʰCp~ 2Ũʮ⅃x !r!

BʮƮ youʼRƐ reåɖy ƬOʼ laY it on Ƭ̵He line fⱺr STRANGEᴕS?
Y̊ᵾ ÃßAйɗʽòИƐɖ MƐƐ

She crabbed across the carpet on elongated, knobbly limbs, over the cigarette burns and beer cans, to where Bibi lay screeching in a playpen held together with duct tape. Head down, palms flat, ass in the air, Little Star tapped a madman's rhythm with one scrawny foot. She turned her head farther than anatomy should allow. The kingsnake of her tongue licked the hollow between her shoulder blades.

Little Star glared at Ken with white, empty eyes. Shadowless eyes.

You dèsEr̆Ve to have youⱺ shadow sɯa⅃⅃oweɗ.

At the sight of her mother twisting in a way not possible, tongue flicking, eyes polished pearls, a terrified Bibi shoved her face into her little hands.

Half memory, half Signal perversion, Ken's horrendous vision of Little Star smiled like a girl on her birthday. *I'm thinking about selling her.*

On Route 60, Flat-Top plunged a second leg into the Peterbilt's path.

Ken swerved into the giant, which sent the truck's rear end into a fishy, feral sway. Flat-Top reared as it was struck, steel groaning but remained steady. The wires flexed and wobbled, taking the raging insulators along for the ride.

The impact had been off-angle, too oblique to cause the unbalancing Ken had hoped for. He'd driven big rigs for two decades—this particular Peterbilt since 1990—so it was all second nature; he straightened out the vehicle and shifted the engine into thirteenth gear, realizing the mission had changed. His contingency plan, known only to him, would have to be implemented.

The substation, monstrous in its predator stance, thorns of raging insulators blazing, spit plasma tendrils into the early morning haze. The baritone thrum of the Signal bored into the ground, tunneling beneath Route 60 and rippling the asphalt. The lane lines warped, then gave way as cracks opened in the road.

I fucking missed, I won't be able to trip the tower. I'm going in.

Ken, his focus dead-ahead on his new target, plunged the accelerator to the floor. The twin turbos breathed raw fury into the motor. *Force equals mass times acceleration*, he crazily remembered from high school, right before he blew the dust of the Rez from his heel and hit the road for life. Although Ken Lightfeather was no physicist, he knew there was no way the Peterbilt would be stopped without serious interference.

Mr. Los Angeles' Cadillac handled like a bad idea.

The moment Otis realized this, he was in the middle of a westbound U-turn and had the thought—*this is a bad idea, I may get us all killed.*

A tower blocked the road, a cat-head tethered to Flat-Top, the substation's guardian which had just attempted to remove Ken. Spray painted on a piece of sheet metal that had been secured to block the ladder rungs from adventure-seeking drunkards, someone had spray-painted *Big Joey Chugs Pole*.

Nikki saw that and said, "Keep an eye out for Big Joey, Otis."

The rear tires churned in the mire of the shoulder, spinning and sliding as Otis yanked the steering wheel. The Caddy's windshield displayed nothing but a blur of the landscape until their squirrely turn pointed them west. Fishtailing out of the shoulder, he barely scraped Big Joey—now in Red Zeppelin's rear-view and planted in front of the Kwik Gas.

Everyone screamed, including Otis, but he kept his hands glued to the wheel.

He dropped the gas pedal, and the V8 power plant gulped as much air as the four-barrel carb would allow. It coughed, wheezed, and then caught. A fart of exhaust blew out the back, the wheels gained traction, and the huge cruiser lurched forward.

Childs unlatched his belt, leaned out the window, and pointed his rifle downrange.

Nikki looked over her shoulder. In the distance, Ken's trailer scraped Flat-Top and emitted a fountain of sparks.

Big Joey dragged a second leg into the road, gouging divots into the tarmac. The giant pursued them with a fervor which far eclipsed that of the slow drones she and Childs had encountered last night. Still, Nikki never imagined these colossal brutes capable of such speed and wondered if proximity to the substation infused them with greater strength, or worse, a burgeoning intelligence. She didn't know, but anything was possible.

"Floor it!" Nikki yelled, not turning away from the rear window. "Fuck Big Joey, he chugs pole anyway!"

Caleb, belted in so tight he could not turn around, watched wide-eyed in Ken's severed mirror. Big Joey excavated asphalt like a plow as it pushed another leg onto Route 60. A flare caught his eye, and he whipped the mirror to his left, past Childs, to the receding sight of Otis' trailer—and the satellite dish.

"Deathbeam!"

Nikki had no time to react.

The Deathbeam burst from the dish in a sawtoothed bolt, brilliant purple against the pastel tangerine of dawn. It slammed into the road just behind the Cadillac, hot as a welder's torch. Pulverized asphalt exploded from the highway and fell onto Red Zeppelin's enormous trunk like black hail.

Nikki's eyes danced with blue dots as her remaining fillings buzzed with agony. Childs cried out as searing heat scorched his shirt brittle. Caleb let go of the mirror and slapped his hands to his eyes. Pale moaned like a man on his deathbed. Otis smelled the ozone of an approaching Florida storm.

The interior swarmed with electricity.

Every interior and dashboard light swelled with luminescence, then popped as they flamed out. Glass sprayed the cabin as several gauges gave up the ghost.

When Nikki looked back again, she was relieved to see the satellite dish a sagging ruin. A second blast of Deathbeam had been too much for the dish and its components to endure, and anything attached to its electrical systems went up in flames. However, smoke now poured out of the open door of Otis' trailer.

"Good!" Nikki screamed. "That's *twice* you missed, asshole!" She gave the melted dish twin, bouncing middle fingers—but Big Joey was still very much in the game. The tower now had three legs in the road.

Otis had seen the flash of the Deathbeam in the rearview as he straightened the wheel and showed little surprise when the chunks of Route 60 battered the trunk. He managed a quick glance to his right, the boy Caleb pulling his hands from his face, eyes like saucers. His father in the middle, the poor sap, just sat with hands against the dash—no seat belt, no bracing his body with his legs, no sense of urgency.

Despite the electric surge which had gutted the Caddy's instruments, the stereo (the lone modification Pale had installed) snapped alive, bringing with it the knife language blare of the Signal.

It resonated through the steering wheel, moving straight through Otis's hands, arms, shoulders, and finally, teeth. Whatever dash lights remained snuffed out in puffs of acrid smoke. The sun visor flapped, and the rearview mirror, where dawn and Big Joey should have been gloriously illuminated, showed only darkness.

$\hat{A}\underset{\smile}{T}\tilde{\omega}n$!$f-\phi^w_w k$

Pale uttered a deep, ugly groan.

As endless aeons of hate poured into the cabin, a dark shape caught Otis' eye.

He saw Ruthie running alongside the Cadillac, her solitary eye a jaundiced poached egg. Between the thumb and forefinger of one corpse hand she held her bridgework, in the other, Franklin's high school baseball portrait.

Ruthie's circus tent burial dress billowed. What was left of her hair flapped like tufts of weatherbeaten carpet. Shreds of her coffin lining clung to cracks in her mummified skin at the clavicle, elbow, and mandible. Even though her tongue had been dust for years, a bloated, leathery version of it still wagged as it had in the generator shed, bulbous and shiny like some deep-sea invertebrate. Otis could see the Y-trail of her autopsy scar peering out from the frilly lace top of her too-big collar.

I see him! Ruthie screeched.

G^d'Eŋ!d−R!

I see Franklin. He's alone and afraid. There's so much blood, there's so many roaring voices.

Ruthie's words bored into the caves of his sinus, wormed its way behind his eyes. How Otis wished he'd never talked Franklin out of a baseball career, how he'd never raised a grieving, guilty fist to his wife of thirty-two years.

No Heaven or Hell for us, Otis. Just this endless, frozen Elsewhere. I live in a rotten box. Franklin fits in a lunch bag.

Ruthie tapped the portrait with her witch finger. Despite the road chaos he could hear her nails, now at grave-length (hadn't he'd heard a long time ago that your nails continue to grow after you die?), tap the glass.

Watch the smoke, Otis. Watch the smoke billow.

He wished he'd told Ruthie more often how he'd always loved her. He longed for the evenings on Green Willow Creek and their secret twilight cove. He wished he could change it all, rewind and repent, instead of living a life of desert exile.

But the coffin was open, the dead were furious, and they would be heard. Otis was taught that only God forgives; all men can do is ask one another to let it slide.

The radio screamed at him.

ИФ(G И ᴢEꞮ!

ŞE̦Ë̦ȊNG is þě̦ḶꞮÈvï̦ꭑg.

Ruthie slammed Franklin's baseball portrait against the glass. He was an infant in the photo now, but six foot three, an immense baby. Franklin peered from underneath his ball cap, his baby-fat face, adorable when he was just that little butterball, now possessed a full complement of teeth, perhaps more. The Louisville Slugger, resting on his shoulder like Paul Bunyan's axe, was covered in thick mats of blood and hair. Franklin's uniform was on fire, but that didn't stop him from taking off his hat and bowing to his father. The Medusa's Snakepit crawled over his scalp, hissing and flicking serpent tongues. All around this colossal infant, the meat of his Marine battalion lay dead, torn to shreds and turned to stone.

Otis screamed and tried to pull his face away. A part of him, that part that was still sane and present in the real world where high-tension towers walked and his satellite dish was capable of a death ray, saw a *third* tower in the road now, dead ahead, due west, an immense, defiant goalie from a giant's hockey match, blocking the net and the open road.

It's The Great Step Downward, Otis. Ruthie's voice was filled with bone splinters. *It's where Tȟő∫Ɛ OʈнɛʄЯ₂ find terrible ways to screw the world, so tossing an old spade like you to the woodchipper is easy-peasy.*

Just drive into the tower and know.

Otis didn't think; he steered Red Zeppelin in a straight line. He imagined the road disappearing and the lush banks of Green Willow Creek streaking by. Because it was a cicada year, the sound was immense, and the clouds glowed purple as the sun went down for the count. Ruthie was cute and alluring in her little green dress and sandals and always packed a lovely picnic basket.

Grease everyone. БLȍȍÐ on the road, ŞǫùL₂ on the highway.

Ruthie smeared her dead face against the window, a proud mom mugging for a snapshot with her framed portrait of Franklin. Her greasy eye dilated into an empty black sea. Breath, impossible yet so, frosted the glass as dirt clods tumbled from her mouth.

FraЙklin knɵ₦s, Ruthie gurgled, tongue licking the filthy glass. Her voice was now putrid, Florida swamp mud—all gator blood and water moccasins, buzzing mosquitoes, and forgotten murders.

Otis gripped the wheel. His face leaked tears and snot. Cicadas, millions of them, called from the treetops, their shadows long and lying across the creek, ghosts of bridges no longer there.

Give the desert its due, she gurgled. *Ʈhen ⱪou'll kNO'w.*

Ņőńt ƑÄÌĻ ʊŞ!!

Just over one-hundred-fifty yards away, the Goalie loomed. If he floored it, Otis figured impact at seventy-five miles per hour, which might be enough to give the desert what it wanted, or more importantly, satisfy Ruthie, pay the debt, then settle in their spot on the creek.

FRANkĻIN,NĘƎDS YOU— Ꮞ E'S JÜ₂T A BAßУ ÂꟻtER AĻĹ!

Childs looked at Nikki, who was prepared to leap over the seat and snatch the wheel. He grabbed Otis' shoulders and put his mouth to the old man's ear. *"It's not real!"* Childs screamed. *"Turn away from the goddamned tow—"*

Caleb shouted, "Ken said to think of something better, to remember the good things!"

Upon touching Otis, Childs could see Ruthie now, not as Otis wished she was on Green Willow Creek, he had no access to that, but a dried husk in the filthy burial rag, humping it along Route 60 like a grunt in basic training. She was the cryptkeeper, a teenager's Halloween prank, *but here*, shouting nonsense through the window as the tower up ahead stood its ground. Childs experienced Otis' agony—melded with it—and next to Ruthie, lashed to her waist with medical tubing, stumbled his father. Harry Childs, wearing a stained and drooping hospital gown and still tethered to his ventilator, which he dragged like a reluctant dog, struggled to keep pace. The ventilator hose dangled from the corner of his mouth, tape flapping, the pipe of some pompous academic. His bread dough face seemed smeared over the topography of his skull, a sculptor's rough draft, and the man's ears, just as Dumbo-huge as his son's, caught the blood-hue of sunrise.

WdÑƐIy [d!!

It's all over when they open The Gate, Ruthie and Harry Childs said in unison. *The Infinite Mouth.*

It was then that Otis and Childs both realized that *Pale* matched those ghost voices word for word.

"It's all over when they open The Gate. The Infinite Mouth."

Red Zeppelin's cab hummed with voices from stars long burned out. All three spoke in unison:

It denies redemption, even if the soul is in the blood.

Jenks, Nikki thought. *The blood centrifuge, those goddamn monster flashes of light, the screams from the tent. Lasers. Light frequencies, one of the guys at the MIT lab thought non-visible light could transcend time . . . Another dimension—is that the Gate? The screaming . . . was something killed in there? For its blood? It* Denies Redemption.

Is that why the Signal harvests guilt?

"That's it!" Nikki said, as close to a forty-niner shouting *'Eureka!'* as possible. "It's sacrifice—*blood sacrifice*—it's ancient, it goes all the way back to Leviticus! Goddammit, Jenks laid it right in front of us!"

She grabbed Childs and screamed into his face, *"You see?"*

Otis licked his lips as Red Zeppelin's engine growled. The Goalie harbored zero intention of relinquishing its position. The cicadas bloomed with sound.

"Leviticus, Randy! *You of all people* have to understand that!"

For half a second, Childs' face was blank. Understanding opened his features like a puzzle box.

"For the life of the flesh is in the blood?" he said.

"Yes! Earlier, you had a piece of it! Those symbols on my monitor weren't *occult*—they're *goddamn Aramaic!*"

Caleb's head twisted from Childs to Nikki and back again. He'd gone to church, never really thought much of it, liked the stained-glass windows and sculpture but had zero biblical knowledge. His mother, though, she'd had quite the run-in with tarot cards, preferring to stay in her hocus-pocus bedroom, wreathed in smoke and dark influence.

Childs quoted, *"I have given it to you upon the altar to make an atonement for your souls: for it is the blood that maketh an atonement for the soul—"*

S⟨ʒ [?] Ξω)/ЖИ—!

Drill this batch of monkeys into that tower, Gas Money . . .

Ahead, Goalie blocked escape. Its colossal cage filled the windshield. In the rearview, Big Joey, the entirety of its mass on Route 60 and soon to be clear of the Kwik Gas. There was little doubt the intent was to box them in from the rear.

Behind the mini-mart, Otis' trailer burned, while the substation, perched on that mile-away hill to the east, heaved its bulk into a war stance as the speeding challenger, Ken in his canary yellow Peterbilt, approached.

Death promised bloody ugliness, delivered with the indifference only machine or demon could summon.

MÄЖЄ IT ALL EⱯ Ọ!

Nearly a mile to the east of Pale Brody's Cadillac, the Peterbilt's speedometer hovered at eighty, and at this speed, no matter what the driver's skill level, this monster rig would be impossible to control when things got dicey. Without his driver-side mirror, Ken could not tell whether the Caddy made it through the gauntlet, but he saw the unmistakable glare of the Deathbeam and knew with absolute certainty this ticket was a one-way fare.

Dead ahead lay the roaring nemesis. The rising sun caught the substation's enormous spires, bristling with glowing, humming insulators, and cast enormous forks of shadow over Route 60. Those giant bars of darkness began to descend, and for the moment, with the horizon spilling dawn-fire across the belly of the storm, the perverse beauty of the scene captured Ken's eye and obscured the underlying intent.

The spires were *in motion*, tilting vertical toward horizontal. They leveled off, slowed by wire tension, a battleship's cannons aimed at the Peterbilt.

Now Ken saw through the distraction of watercolor light and moving shadow and realized the substation's offensive posture—it was well aware of his presence and intent, and would not allow him to succeed.

"So it's like that," Ken said.

Ken saw the first projectile hurl toward the rig, partially obscured through the windshield's bullet crack network. It screamed as it corkscrewed in flight, emitting a wispy purple trail; a giant, lethal bottle rocket.

Ken realized the spire had jettisoned a piece of itself toward the big rig, and it screeched overhead in a blur, barely missing the top of the cab. The plasma trail's electromag discharge made his skin crawl as it passed. He could taste a coppery, positive charge in his blood, leaking from teeth loosened by the .44's barrel in his mouth.

The cab smelled of diesel exhaust, ozone, and nervous sweat. Ken held the wheel. His eyes, separated by twin lines of glorious warpaint, narrowed behind his aviators.

In rapid succession, the substation unleashed three additional ingots. Upon launch, a few wires snapped away to the ground, arcing plasma and setting fires. Smoke billowed.

The first impaled the Peterbilt's grille, the impact rocking the cab. Steam boiled out of the engine wound, followed by a cough of molten aluminum, which, when caught by the wind, slapped against the windshield like hot blood.

The second impact sheared off the right fender with a horrendous shriek, converting it to blazing slag as it spun away, headlights and all. The right wheels caught fire and puked black smoke. The cab listed. Ken tilted toward the passenger seat and bit his tongue.

The third and smallest of the super-heated pieces went straight through the windshield.

Glass exploded into the cab, skewering Ken with a thousand tiny needles. The pain was everywhere, hot, urgent, a blanket of needles. Bloody glass stuck out of his face at any imaginable angle. Even his lips had been slit and sliced.

Ken screamed.

His right eye took the worst of it. Punctured by the wreck of his aviator sunglasses, the eye went dark. He clawed off the ruined shades, hissing when his hand came away red. Ken Lightfeather looked like a bizarre man-cactus that had been shot in the face.

When he tried to speak, the shards lodged in his tongue banged against his teeth, opened the tender underside of his lips, and brought more scarlet. He screamed again instead, but it turned into a madman's cackle, an Apache battle cry. His beaded eagle shirt and black mane were slick with blood.

The passenger seat burned, flames wrapping around the empty 629. Plunged into the padding of the seat back, the projectile made contact with the seat's metal frame—and that's when the Signal really went to work.

A nude Little Star now straddled the snarled ingot, long scrawny legs wrapped around it, her back leaning against the dashboard. Smoke crawled over her emaciated frame. Shoulders wildly out of alignment, she tucked her head into the crook of her elbow, clavicle and ribs visible through that yellowed snail-like skin. An invasion of acne occupied her once flawless face.

Bibi's with your MOMMY, not her FATHER, you gutless bedwetter.

Ken stared horrified at the contortionist gnarl of her broken knees, the impossible right angle as her floundering foot pounded against the smoking upholstery.

The speedometer needle reached eighty-eight. Head tucked into her elbow, Little Star jabbed one hand out and seized Ken's chin. Her shoulder made a ghastly snapping noise as she squeezed his cheeks like a pomegranate. The pressure forced an ugly jet of fluid to puke from his slashed eye socket.

Ken gagged, inhaling fumes and blood. He chewed glass, spat slivers of tongue and gum tissue. Ken's remaining eye wept from the sight of his ruined lover and invasive, toxic smoke.

I'm a carcass, kept alive by a mad machine, Little Star cawed. Ken saw the constellation of needle marks all over her arms, the soft flesh at the base of her thumb, her inner thigh.

Ken snapped his head away to see the Peterbilt's hood smolder and peel, the leading edge of the damage aglow, exposing the mortally wounded engine compartment. Something in the huge turbodiesel broke with a sharp *Clang!* and spiraled away in a helix of purple fire. Dollops of searing plasma bored into the engine block.

Take that one eye of yours and look at me when I'm talking to you.

Fire and fury, love and loss, guilt and ghost ruled the world. Nearly laughing despite it all, Ken batted Little Star's twig of an arm away, reached up, and blared the air horn.

WHAAAUNNK!

Even though it hurt like the end of the world, he did his best to bellow, "Come get me, you—"

D!ʿH3Yf−₵₳𝒩

"—motherfuckers!"

Heavy bloodsmoke poured out of Ken's mouth in a grotesque, black soup. His broken eye slipped from the socket and began its slow ride south.

Little Star unfolded her arm and threw her head back, way back—*too far back*—then flicked her ungodly black tongue. Her neck bristled with tendons and pulsing blood vessels. So many missing teeth. Dragonfire smoke everywhere.

Ten years from now, Fatherless and hopeless in some shitty trailer like her mother, Bibi will die alone—because of you, because you're going to die ŚⱧ₳ĐØ𝓌ĹɆšŠ₷.

She will never know you, but we do. 𝒲Ɇ ₭𝒩ʿØ𝒲 ɎOǓ!!

Childs let go of Otis, fell back, and Nikki caught him.

The Signal's hallucinations were now infectious between individuals, just as its presence was capable of transference from VLA to the power grid. Childs clutched the rifle, and the tangibility of it helped him push the image of the corpse woman and his bleached, dying father away, but these images had been harvested by dark forces, and if there was ever a time he needed to lean on his faith, it was now.

Otis saw only the massive tower in the road, The Goalie guarding the end of the line. Whether he would face damnation as a suicidal murderer, sacrificing others in a head-on collision with the tower, or blissfully awaken on a blanket between two willow trees brimming with cicadas, he didn't know.

"I know Ruthie," Otis muttered. "*I'm sorry, honey.*"

"*That's* Jenks' whole goddamn trip," Nikki said, pointing to the back of Otis' head. She didn't care if anyone was listening. "If *sacrifice* doesn't say ritual, I don't know *what* does."

Caleb, strapped tight, leaning against the door, watched, in the enormous mirror Ken had given him, the Peterbilt's approach to the substation. He kept his eyes on the truck, bellowing black exhaust as it shot between Flat-Top's legs. The hilltop enemy, raging and alive in the fire red of sunrise, pitched its spires toward Ken.

Even after all he'd witnessed, Caleb was stunned. He'd seen towers pull themselves from the earth, pursue a truck, even seen the Deathbeam in action (twice now, actually), but something about the substation assuming an offensive posture gripped his spine. As crazy as the thought was to him, the electrical grid had been commandeered supernaturally and had every intention of killing them. It would be nothing short of a miracle if they made it off this road alive.

Caleb watched in bewilderment as one of the spires, emitting light and smoke—an arc-welder electrode on a massive scale—extended lengthwise. It stretched forward toward the Peterbilt until the steel *snapped*.

The severed piece rocketed toward Ken's big rig, trailing hot, purple plasma. It missed the top of the trailer by a few feet, twisting through the air until it slammed into the steel grid of Big Joey.

The projectile exploded into a chrysanthemum of plasma-fire. The point of impact boiled and hissed. Molten slag ran like dense, glowing blood over the damaged tower, then dropped into the road. It spread on Route 60, impossible electric lava, its leading edges bristling with tongues of flame, seeping into the cracks caused by the tunneling Signal.

Caleb dropped the mirror and twisted in his seat. Big Joey, compromised from the wound, stumbled. A foreleg stabbed outward as the tower leaned back toward the Kwik Gas. The tower's cross arms pitched to-and-fro, perhaps in some attempt to retain balance, Caleb didn't know. The taut wires pulled, and the insulators buzzed their insanity at total concert volume. With a section of its support struts gone, there was little doubt Big Joey could stay ambulatory, or at the very least balanced, for long.

Before Caleb could utter a warning, he realized that Red Zeppelin was doomed—the flailing leg was sure to impale the rear end as Big Joey regained balance and reversed direction.

"The Nightword cast them out," Pale said. His voice was many and one, a chorus of nightmares. His lips were thin, bloodless lines. Most of the Band-Aids Caleb had stuck to his face had come off. Completely removed from the urgency of their situation on the road, Pale's exposure in the Hertz had led him into a completely different aspect of Signal intrusion, the territory of hubris so common to spectre and charlatan, demon and killer.

"Your broken souls are eager to welcome Us as your Shadowless Masters. We are here. We are everywhere. We sleep beneath the great brooding mountains of the world."

Caleb's attention was split between the croaking serpent voice from his father and the spear of half-molten horror about to slam into the Cadillac.

He had no idea Otis was on a suicide run.

But Nikki did.

"Otis!" Nikki screamed as the windshield filled with Goalie blocking the road, and the rear window promised impalement from a maimed Big Joey. "Cut the whee—"

The entire world pivoted. The horizon dropped.

Through the rising windshield, they could see nothing but the monstrous hulk of the Goalie, its ultra-wide cross arms, and the twin spikes of its cat head crown. Lightning smashed the early morning sky, which was, now that Red Zeppelin was at a thirty-degree incline, dead-ahead.

Big Joey, gouged and bleeding slag, broke its fall with the rear end of the Cadillac, a mammoth penitent genuflecting in the middle of the road. The mighty car's nose sprang upward, an empty teeter-totter with a fat kid on one side. Its enormous trunk, which caved like tin foil, began to bubble and burn as the substation plasma dripped from the tower's cage and onto the sheet metal.

Big Joey slid forward, cross arms yanked backward by wire tension, pushing the upended car with it. Bumper scraping the road, sparks flying, the Cadillac gained perhaps another forty feet down Route 60 before the hobbled monster extracted itself.

Red Zeppelin came down hard on the front end.

Upon impact, the mangled tail-end launched into the air. The trunk lid snapped open, and out flew three mangled guitar cases and Brody family luggage, everything trailing smoke. The lanced fuel tank bled gasoline in a sparkling rooster tail. The rear license plate flapped like a shutter on a haunted house.

Two and a half tons of automobile tilted onto its nose. The chrome bumper collapsed right before the hood surrendered with a terrible groan and the headlights exploded.

Twisting, the car came down hard on the roof. The passenger door sprang open like a bear trap being reset, and every bit of glass fled the vehicle in a shimmering burst of diamonds. It upended again, not as mightily this time, but the heavy passenger door had been damaged in the fall, and one of its hinges failed.

Pale launched through the opening. Ahead of the Cadillac, he tumbled airborne, boneless, and limp.

Caleb screamed. The world tumbled, and adrenaline snatched his heart. In that inverted world was the ragged outline of his father as he impacted the road in terrible slow motion, just like all the horrific Evel Knievel footage he'd seen on TV.

Pale's arm slapped against his back as his shoulder failed. One of his legs faced the wrong way. He bounced, soft and rubbery, chest arced upward, limbs dangling, neck a sodden rope. When he came down, he came down for good.

The left side of Pale Brody's face slammed into the asphalt. The last thing to hit the deck was his muddy Nikes, each landing ten yards ahead of his body. His jeans were shredded.

The Goalie stood directly over Pale. It didn't move.

The inertia proved insufficient to flip the car again, and in another second, the Cadillac fell back onto its roof. The wrecked door hung from one hinge. Glass covered the road.

Caleb struggled against the restraint, but his own inverted weight and panic, kept him pinned.

His senses overloaded, and the world went white. His ears rang, his hair tingled. Every possible emotion swelled in him as his mind slammed back to that February morning when he found his mother in the fetal position on the bathroom floor. *What To Do?* on the mirror and tarot cards littering the rug. One lay propped against the edge of the bathroom scale: *The Tower.*

Things are really going to change, she did this because of me, Caleb thought as the sound of his father's footsteps thumped up the stairs. *Val!* Pale cried over and over. *Valerie, talk to me!*

When Caleb could see straight again, he saw Randy Childs was half on the dashboard, half on the headliner. The man was awake, if not dazed, fumbling for his rifle. Otis was likewise inverted, his face and hands oozing red. The flying glass had cut him badly, and spatters of his blood painted the leather interior, the stainless-steel trim.

Caleb then heard Nikki shouting from behind.

"Oh God, *oh God*," Nikki cried. She smelled fuel and blood. "Everyone out of the car. Get out now!"

Caleb felt hands on him, Nikki's arms wrapping around his waist. She pulled him up against the seat back as best she could then opened the buckle, and he dropped on top of Childs.

Nikki was the first out of the vehicle. She crawled from the wreck on her belly, Artie Jayne's tool bag still around her shoulder and the Beretta tight in her waistband.

Once on the road, but on all fours, she caught a glimpse of Ken's rig down the road, pumping black smoke and the front end smothered in flames. Ahead of the truck, the substation looked like a battleship with cannons aimed at them. Fire and black smoke gurgled from the snarl of grids, wires, and transformers as random cracks of plasma stabbed at the rumbling storm and its scowling, accusing eye.

She saw the mangled hulk of Big Joey, metal screeching, the insulators fritzing and sparking. Behind it, a pile of slag spread on the road, boiling the asphalt and widening the cracks.

The Kwik Gas looked like a war casualty, awning shredded, gas pumps on their sides. Otis' satellite dish was toast, and his trailer spewed fire. Their rickety plan had gone horribly wrong, they'd traveled a quarter mile at best, and now their shit was deeper than ever.

Nikki crabbed over to the passenger window and snatched Caleb by the arm. She tugged, and the boy breech birthed, ass first and screaming. A few scrapes and a little blood, which was to be expected, but Caleb's eyes broadcast nothing but horror and confusion.

The Tower. Caleb conjured the tarot card leaning against the bathroom scale. Cracked and toppling, fire belched from the windows, its apex scourged by lightning, cartoon stars in the sky. Above it lurked some terrible, open eye. And here, in New Mexico, a true giant reeled on Route 60, slagged and limping. Another buzzing monstrosity stood defiant over his broken father. Above them all, real and remembered, The Gate, the accursed eye of Dragonfire. His mother had seen it. Perhaps she didn't know at the time, but *she had seen it.*

Childs was not far behind. He tossed the M-16 out onto the

highway and twisted out of the car. He looked like hell—peppered in Otis' blood and his own various scrapes, shirt scorched black by the Deathbeam.

"My dad!" Caleb screamed. He struggled in Nikki's arms, but she held fast, her nails digging into the boy's skin *"My dad's on the road!"*

Below the Goalie lay a barefoot Pale Brody, hips twisted, one chicken wing of an arm folded behind his back. Everyone saw the growing halo of blood around his head. His eyes were open. His mouth moved like a fish gasping in an angler's bag

"I'm so sorry, kid," Nikki said. "But we need to be off the road." She pulled Caleb away from the wreck. "I know it sucks, but if we move your dad right now, it may do more harm than good."

Childs ran to the driver-side and yanked the door open. With the Caddy's frame bent, the door only made it halfway and stopped. He crammed himself in, freed Otis, and pulled the old man out. Otis screamed when Childs tugged on his dislocated arm, but he either took the pain or risked a crushing death in the vehicle.

The old man gasped—nothing but storm and swaying wires between the Goalie and Big Joey—his mouth filled with the taste of warm copper. He smelled fuel as it spread from the ruptured fuel tank.

"Goddamn, I almost killed all of us," Otis groaned. "She, Ruthie . . . the tower, the cicadas, the soul . . . "

" . . . is in the blood," Childs finished with him.

Otis' dangling arm howled. Blood leaked from his broken nose. He looked at Childs with eyes wide with terror and low with shame.

"All of us are injured, so on your feet, you tough bastard," Child's said.

Childs' back hurt like hell, but as he yanked Otis up by the armpits, internal seals broke within both men. Otis yelped and coughed out a glob of fleshy goo, and Childs likewise began to taste blood.

"We're not done yet," Childs said as he pulled the charging handle on the M-16 and flicked the safety off. "By God, we're not done on the road yet."

An unstable Big Joey, dripping molten slag and pivoting, stumbled back toward the Kwik Gas.

The Cadillac bled fuel.

WHAAAUNNK!

Ken's air horn trumpeted into the dawn, and soon all would be fire.

-15-
ENDGAME

WHY, VALERIE? *Why didn't you want him? He's beautiful; he's a gift from God. We knew if things took off for me it would be hard, I'd be away a lot of the time, but you'd have our baby boy. When my road time was done, I would show him the way. We'd raise a fine young man.*

Pale remembered Valerie, spent on the delivery table, her feet still in the stirrups. Sweat had turned her face into a landscape of transparent beads. The immediate detachment Pale sensed from her was like a steel rod in his heart, worming around for the soft bits.

Now Pale lay on Route 60, skeleton broken, skull fractured, his left eye half-drowned in a scarlet lake. He could see into the distance, where Ken's burning Peterbilt seemed to be on a torpedo's mission into the growling substation; he could see the immediate, where his beloved son had been rescued from his beloved Red Zeppelin, and the micro, where the furious storm and the sunrise reflected in the stain of his blood.

The sunrise in my blood. I could have used that as a lyric if I wasn't about to die.

I did this for you, Valerie said one night in a cloud of alcohol-infused candor. Later she proved it as her distance from their son became a fissure, then a canyon. *There's something in him, Pale. There's an emptiness that's not noticeable to the eye—and yet I see it. There's something wrong with him. I carried him. I felt it inside of me, I knew that he could think before he was born. I felt his fingers glide against the wall of my womb. I could tell, even then, that he was drawing terrible symbols inside me. The soul is in the blood, Pale, and he set to marking mine. Months before you changed his first diaper, I knew. And now here we are.*

Moving effortlessly in several directions, Pale's mind, liberated from linear time, recalled Caleb as a toddler, playing in the sand with the other kids. Before long, his little playmates burst into tears. Their mothers scooped them up and drilled Pale with their icy, maternal glares. Pale thought it was about him, the long-haired rock and roll guy, perceived as a lowlife trying to up his game in the nice suburban park with his dimwit kid.

But no, Pale thought at night when the house was quiet, save for the ticking of the antique grandfather clock Valerie Starr had inherited from her family in Montana. *The truth comes out at night when the dogs run with Satan in every alleyway. The kids were repulsed by my son. Their instinct was to pull away, and their mothers—always in tune—knew.*

You're blinded by him, Pale, Valerie said years later as she stuffed her Samsonite and emptied the nightstand drawer into a grocery bag—an avalanche of bracelets, ChapSticks, Bic lighters, and prescription bottles. She wrapped a rubber band around her tarot deck and threw that in last. The top card: The Tower, catastrophic change beneath a glaring eye. *Whether you choose to be so, or it's something Caleb is capable of imposing on you, I don't know. Neither would surprise me.*

Pale convinced himself her exit was hastened by that horrendous "I Wish You Missed Me" video and the utter shitstorm of failure that followed; the label dropping the band, tour plans scuttled, the Capitol Records life raft going up in smoke. He short-changed her as a woman who yearned only to be a ritzy rock wife, the glitz girl from the Rocky Mountains made good. Again, all about *him*, and zero insight that it was *Valerie* who suffered. Not as a victim of direct abuse but as someone who feared she may have brought something dreadful into the world.

Already petite, Valerie Elaine Starr-Brody had dropped twenty pounds since Caleb's birth, and by the time Caleb was seven, she'd had taken to wearing wigs after most of her hair had thinned to a wispy scarf the color of dry wheat. Over the years, one of her eyes changed from hazel to a murky, seasick green. Most suspected Valerie of being a cokehead (or worse), but it was not the case. Valerie wasn't negligent; she was spent.

Remember how the flowers died only outside his bedroom window but thrived everywhere else? Why are there always spiders in the corner of his bedroom? How many exterminators

have we called? How about the times he'd arranged the magnets
on the refrigerator? My God, Pale, what in hell was that symbol
supposed to represent?

*Never any real friends from school. Great grades, but almost
no social life. Even two of your bandmates kept their distance.
You think that girl Yolanda Rivas from the next block likes him?
Hell, she's scared shitless of him. Remember the drawings he'd
make every year on his birthday? Sure as shit looked like his
refrigerator doodlings to me. How can you blot that out?*

*I know—part of me inside just knows—those birthday
drawings are exactly what he etched into my body. He carved a
witchery into my womb before he saw the light of day. He meant
it as a message, he knew that I would figure it out. Pete, he may
not be evil—I truly don't believe he is—but he is in touch with
something else, something from* Elsewhere.

A week before the incident in the bathroom (*let's just be
honest, Mac Daddy, and call it a suicide attempt*), Valerie sat on
the bed in the guest room, ashtray bulging with Kools, her wig
perched on the corner of the mirror. The cards were laid out in a
broken grid. Death. Prince of Cups. Ten of Swords. The Fool. She
looked at her husband with eyes that no longer matched.

*I know how this sounds, but even though he's not violent, we
should have had him put away.*

Pale remembered a pint-sized Caleb on the rug with his
GoBots, fashioning a world for them out of Legos and sticks, an
elliptical tunnel that looked to have been built by tiny masons and
birds. Pale had been changing guitar strings, and Caleb popped up
like a jack in the box, snatched the discarded strings, and
implemented them into his construction. He used the strings to
suspend the tunnel beneath one of the barstool-style chairs so that
it hovered above his collection of GoBots. That apparatus would
have kept Pale's high school geometry teacher stammering for
days.

The scene shifted as memory often does, and now Valerie stood
at the top of the stairs. She had her bags ready, a garment bag over
her arm, and wore her rabbit fur vest, and her wig was slightly
askew.

*For God's sake, Pete, wake up and smell the Weirdberries. If
I stay near him, he'll suck the remaining life out of me. Look at
me, I'm a dead woman walking the longer I stay.*

Valerie's eyes wet with regret, she touched her husband's face. She cracked a weak, bitter smile, and Pale finally noticed that her gums had receded, and her teeth looked like tiny dominoes.

In the bathroom that morning, you should have let me go.

When had she bandaged her wrist?

I have to go. Pale, I love you, truly I do—but you are blind and therefore unaffected. If I stay, I wither and die. I have to go. Now.

Valerie dropped into her Honda and was on the 101 South before Pale knew what hit him. That had been in 1989. In 1993, as he lay dying from blunt force trauma and internal bleeding, all the pieces slid together as he watched the eye of the storm, suspended over the fire-spitting snarl of the substation.

The substation assumed a total war footing. Like the world's most dangerous shotgun, the spires unleashed a flurry of plasma-fire projectiles at Ken's big rig. They screamed forward, twisting in their trajectory, trails brilliant. In as little as ten seconds, the spires were smoldering nubs, the entirety of their mass hurled toward the threat.

The Peterbilt had been stabbed to death. The engine block was on its way to becoming slag; the cylinders melted, the cams seized. Ken dropped the clutch and set the transmission into neutral, then took his hands off the wheel.

"Lord, it is up to you!" Ken coughed through a mouthful of glass. His face was a ruined glove, the remnants of his right eye had finished its southern migration and lay cradled in the crook of his belt buckle. He gagged on smoke and choked on blood.

ЧX\ώC —БоК!

A fierce blast of Signal tunneled in search of the darkest defilement, Those Others ravenous to bend Ken's final thought to be one of tragedy. Instead, he recalled one surviving Polaroid, face-up in the rubble of his brick wall.

As the world rattled and the truck disintegrated into flame, Ken focused on that Polaroid, a beautiful slice of time, back when the future was only the ribbon of road leading away from the Rez, squalor an unseeable future. Before drugs. Before servitude. Before shame.

Gooey in love, he and Myra Redcloud drove all the way to Lake Powell with nothing but a full tank of gas and eighty dollars between them.

He'd been lean and shirtless, jester and charmer, confidant and lover. Myra was flawless, tall, and stunning, lips like fuchsia nectar, eager to laugh and see new things. They escaped the dreary, blazing Rez for a few days, told no one where they were headed, reveling in one another and the perfect September sky.

They drank ice-cold beer, skinny-dipped in blue water, and slept by the fire. Ken remembered how his heart swelled when they'd made love beneath the swirl of the Milky Way, and later, as they gazed into the cosmos, he pointed to the constellation Lyra, which sounded like Myra, and given her the nickname of

"Little Star!"

One last metal ingot from the substation—a small dab about the size of a baseball—impaled Ken Lightfeather below the sternum. A gout of scarlet fire poured from his mouth and nose. With his wife's name on his lips, he collapsed onto the wheel.

The Polaroid, featuring Ken and Myra knee-deep in Lake Powell, tilting beer cans to one another's lips like newlyweds, bubbled and warped as fire consumed it.

His boot hit the brake, his weight pulled the wheel to the left, and the Peterbilt, now driven by a dead man, twisted into a jackknife at ninety-five miles an hour.

Otis and Childs backed away from the upturned Cadillac. Otis' left arm hung like a piece of broken pipe. The impact with the steering wheel had crushed something in there, but his right arm was right as rain, and he used that hand to grab a handful of Childs' shoulder and use him as a crutch.

Big Joey lurched forward and slapped the inverted Cadillac out of the way. Red Zeppelin scraped and screeched across the width of Route 60, a glistening fan spraying from the gash in the fuel tank. It slid to the shoulder; nose crammed into the ditch. Belly up, ass in the air, trunk mangled and glass gone, Pale Brody's 1968 Fleetwood had been officially sent to the great salvage yard in the sky.

Above, the tower raged.

FՉ!Ƕ'ƀ —BұdΦΛ!

Doesn't matter what you tried to show me, Harry Childs said. *I know where I'm going.*

Childs looked around for his father, sure he would see the

Poppin' Fresh Dough version of his dad in a hospital johnny, staggering alongside the road, pushing his ventilator like a homeless person with a shopping cart.

You could have read from the slabs of The Ten Commandments, and I'd still tell you that you're delusional. Just like your clueless hippie sister.

But it was worse; Childs was back in his father's sickroom, hair buzzed tight, face gaunt from his sole combat tour, practicing his Deathside manner. He had his Bible open, a King James he'd bought at the PX before the return flight from Okinawa, and read aloud from Psalms.

Like sheep they are laid in the grave; death shall feed on them; and the upright shall have dominion over them in the morning; and their beauty shall consume in the grave from their dwelling. But God will redeem my soul from the power of the grave: for he shall receive me.

The only other sound in the room was the robot hiss of the ventilator.

Harry Childs' eyes were old lemons, his hair gray spiderwebs in the garden. Even though tubes blocked his windpipe, he spoke, and his voice was that of The Great Step Downward, the bloody place where machines did awful things because their creators had gone mad.

Randy now knew there was a very thin line between the words *suffer* and s*ulfur*.

Harry Childs rolled his head sideways. *That jungle scared the piss out of you, didn't it, boy?* he sneered. *The Awakener of Stars squirms out of the Gate to devour the Light of the World.*

With each syllable, his ventilator tube bounced. The IV bag looked to be filled with yellow bile and eyes—eyes of some creature Randy didn't want to know about, something that watched him from Elsewhere—floated inside. *It'll be a new Nightworld, Randall, then, like this bag of eyes, you'll see real war. You'll see men do far more than just die. That's what's coming through the Gate.*

Harry Childs coughed and the same yellow bile from his IV bag bubbled into the ventilator tube. His hand, spider-thin with nails that hadn't been trimmed in weeks, stabbed toward his son. The heart monitor screeched as his pulse skyrocketed. The eyes in the IV bag pressed themselves against the plastic and gawked at twenty-two-year-old Randall Childs.

You can't save everyone, Childs' adult voice said through his young man's mouth. *Maybe I should just let him go.*

You'll wish we'd changed places when The Shadowless Ones arrive, his father said through a gurgle of belly grease. It bubbled out of the ventilator tube like lava, stained his gown, and pooled on the sheets.

And I'm gleefully going to the Elsewhere. So shoot everyone on this fucking road and join me.

Otis, connected by touch, stood behind Randy Childs in that room at St. Augustine's, experiencing every ounce of the man's misery. *You can't save everyone,* he heard, immediately realizing the dying man's commitment to oblivion turned the sickroom into cursed ground, and that's when the hospital room went dark, the walls suddenly covered in yellowed satin, Ruthie's tattered coffin lining, embossed with pretty roses.

Pulled from the dissolving room, Childs was thrust back to Route 60, but now, between himself and the limping Big Joey, Ruthie Thompson's single graveyard eye. Wet and dilated, bloodshot and crazy, she met his gaze. Tufts of mangy hair braided into worms—*no, snakes,* Childs thought—uncoiling into Medusa's hissing crown. Her enormous burial dress billowed in the Devil Wind like a Bedouin's robe.

Otis whimpered behind him, *the thin howl of grief,* he knew, the old man's hand gripping his shoulder.

Ruthie launched her corpse hand past his cheek and throttled Otis.

To Otis, it was like a king crab had seized his windpipe. He gagged, coughing up a wad of bright, red lungmeat. His ears filled with the scream of a million cicadas.

Ruthie pulled Otis in for a strangler's goodnight kiss. The wind wrapped the shreds of her coffin lining around both men's shoulders. Her autopsy sutures strained and flexed. The leather sea cucumber of her tongue flopped in the pocket of her jaw, and though long dead, her breath whipped past Childs in a frigid, reeking gale.

You belong to me, and your friend here is going for the ride, Ruthie said, her voice like an insect, a cicada with its clicking wings and clacking tymbals. Otis feared she'd sprout antennae through those sparse tufts of hair, and red, bulbous compound eyes would fill the empty holes in her skull.

Take your foolish faith and shove it in your ass, Harry Childs croaked.

Childs recoiled as Ruthie's face uttered Harry Childs' faithlessness; their two nightmares intertwined.

The sickroom now existed in tandem with the road, transparent yet there all the same. The EKG whined in flatline, the flooded ventilator worked Harry's corpse chest like the bellows in a blacksmith's livery. Otis saw Ruthie in a stranger's deathbed, morbidly obese, bursting out of a far too small hospital gown. The wheezing machine pumped her chest like some witch blowing into a bag. This was a cubist's playground, a nonsensical criss-cross of realities and horrors, here on this endless highway of blurred lines and rampaging giants.

Ðλԓӡӱ *bc I[!]*

You're just like your mother—years before me and just as dead, Randall, God or no God. Just. As. Dead. [FRANKLIN IS HERE, AND WE'VE GOT PLANS FOR HIM. HE CRIES EXACTLY LIKE AN INFANT WHEN HE BURNS . . .] *It's frozen black where I'm going, where you're going, where this whole shitty world is going, endless Zero, the Great Step Downward . . .* [THEY WON'T ALLOW HIM AS MUCH AS A LOOK AT HIS MOTHER, THEY'RE WEARING MY BABY'S GUTS TO ADORN INVISIBLE BODIES] *. . . where we're all Shadowless. You won't need one after you're dead, so I'll have yours . . .* [I'LL HAVE YOUR SHADOW!]

Childs screamed as his mind finally refused the ugly offer to lie down and surrender. *Free will is a bitch. You're gone, Pop, and I couldn't stop you.*

"You may not want to exist, but *I* do!"

Childs pushed Otis back with his elbow, breaking the connection.

The M-16 tucked into the soft hollow of his right shoulder, Childs raised the iron sight to his eye.

Despite the Devil Wind or the insect whine of Ruthie, Otis heard the screech of tires. He followed the rifle's line of sight and beheld a fury of black cancer smoke and frenetic, throbbing flares of blazing light, turning the substation into a crazy portal in a science fiction movie. *And perhaps,* Otis thought, *that's just what that blasphemy on the hill, or that storm hole above it is after all.*

As it punched through that smoke cloud, tires screaming, molten slag trailing behind it like blood from an open wound, Ken's flaming Peterbilt launched into a terrible jackknife.

God bless that man, Otis thought. The sun flared as it cleared the eastern hill, casting huge shadows through the snarling substation and vortices stirred by Ken Lightfeather's final ride. *I'll miss you, old buddy.*

Former Staff Sergeant Randy Childs, United States Army, 1979 M.I.T. Ph.D. Graduate, and Chief Systems Developer at Boston's Medusa Engineering Corporation, opened fire. Full auto.

Survival consumed the substation; fury drove the storm.

Above the flaring tangle of the electrical apparatus, with its buzzing transformers and banging circuit breakers, the cyclonic eye rapidly condensed into an aperture a quarter its current size. The sudden shift in pressure drew the hot Devil Wind to the eye of the storm, sucking in smoke from the substation, airborne debris, and dirt.

For a brief moment, there was no sound; even the death throes of Ken's sacrificed big rig were silenced.

Ozone and the motionless gulf between heartbeats, the hush of the prairie as a tornado writhes in the distance.

A massive blast of thunder, a sonic fist, barreled from the eye of the storm. This massive compression wave generated an opaque ring, a smoking torus of storm vapor that dropped like an anvil. The torus smashed into the ground, expanding with the speed of a high explosive upon impact, and the entirety of the substation's steel frame swayed. Several junctions, where girders met right angles, raised like shoulders. Each point bent and leaned, their bases twisting into the ground for purchase, a colossal bat walking on its wings.

Laboring to steady itself, the substation *roared*.

DÚHHRUÜÙ!

The remnants of the battleship spires collapsed, plowing into the nest of electrical fires below. Smoke belched upward in small mushroom clouds.

The thunder-ring narrowly missed the corpse-driven Peterbilt, which slid into the chaos like an enormous boomerang.

The cab was all but consumed by fire, and now that the hood was gone entirely, the engine had liquefied, pouring from the bottom as boiling slag. The remaining tires, which were only on the trailer, smoked and screamed as it swung around and broadsided an array of transformers. The impact sent a second wave of tremors through the substation's spider legs, toppling insulators' crowns.

The jackknifed truck leaned into a sideways roll. The trailer separated from the cab like the stages of a moon rocket. The trailer reeled toward the core of the substation while the cab—and Ken—tumbled away in the worst NASCAR crash imaginable, trailing fire and black, noxious smoke.

The cab collided with the wall of circuit breakers and wiped them from their mooring. Blue flashes arced and spat into the early morning. Power lines snapped. Support beams caved in, and large steel sections began to creak and shriek. More fires started as the cab broke apart and spread its destruction as far as physics allowed.

The trailer bullied its way through the substation's network of support beams, severing nearly everything in its path. Insulators popped off and twirled away like glowing batons. The wires to which they were tethered fell to the ground and arced millions of amperes into the earth. A totem pole-like structure of transformers tipped and made contact with another, resulting in a succession of strained connections—which ran straight to the towers.

The sun spread golden fire against the belly of the storm.

Devil Wind roasted the condemned highway while the towers, even the hobbled Big Joey, stood still—insulators fully alight, fully aware.

The cyclone hissed—that puckered storm hole actually *hissed*—a mammoth inhalation, it seemed, before it released a second brutal thunder-ring and a rebuking bolt of lightning directly onto the rolling trailer.

Bullseye. It blew apart like balsa wood. The shockwave pushed the ailing substation backward, a portion of it losing its footing upon the hill. Naked wheels flew into the air like bizarre Frisbees. Still intact, one of the trailer's rear doors landed at the foot of Flat-Top.

Another series of electrical discharges tore the substation's insides to pieces. Flowers of blinding plasma spewed from the site. A Bellagio fountain of debris twisted and spun away. Endless shards of metal and burning ceramic rained onto Route 60.

Finally, the transmission lines connected to Flat-Top's insulators pulled taut, and the tower floundered. It backed toward the substation, almost comically, then the wires that tethered it to Big Joey, already compromised by the plasma wound, tightened. Big Joey was pulled backward toward the Kwik Gas, lumbering like some vaudeville act given the shepherd's hook.

In the distance, the line of northwest towers also looked to be in real trouble. Several staggered on the New Mexico plain, a chain gang caught in the middle of a rebellion.

Then, Deathbeam.

Half running, half limping, Nikki kept one arm around Caleb and one eye on the substation. The thunder-ring was a mighty sight—from the pinched iris of the cyclone's eye it dropped like concrete, heavy and flat. The bludgeoning tone of the thunder was more painful than gunfire, as the volume was like nothing she'd ever experienced, even at the storm's furious birth at the VLA. The vapor ring expanded so rapidly it blurred, driving a cloud of dust and loose road debris into their highway battlefield. *A sonic-kinetic weapon,* her mind babbled.

Caleb turned at the colossal sound, suffering a pang of guilt as his interest was piqued, and he tore his eyes away from his crumpled father in that awful red puddle. Part of him knew his father was beyond hope. Another aspect of him knew that tremendous forces he'd always wished to see were at work, and if he missed the spectacle, he'd regret it. The giant blast and the accompanying shockwave slammed into his gut.

The substation reeled. It writhed, buzzed, piercing the dawn with its cry of agony.

DÚHĦRUÙÙ!

Molten scraps flew out of the snarl. Blinding flashes of light arced like a sea of gigantic flashbulbs.

They watched Ken's rig slide sideways, the front end burning. When the trailer slammed into the structure and began to roll, Caleb finally knew that Ken the Road Warrior was beyond hope. The trailer performed a grotesque tumble and the cab twisted off into the opposite direction, spreading fire. It was magnificent to behold: the scale, the destruction, the bravery—

Caleb cried out when the storm blew the trailer to smithereens. Even though he knew Ken was already gone, that solidified it.

The impact of both thunder ring and lightning bolt stunned the bellowing substation. Wires separated, and the structure began to collapse. The substation struggled to back away in the direction it had come, a fighter retreating from a street brawl.

"It's happening," Caleb said. "It's beginning."

Machine gunfire broke out. Nikki saw Childs moving backward with Otis, firing short bursts at Big Joey, Slayer of Cadillacs. The monster took one more step, but Childs blew off two of its insulators, and the wires broke free, arcing Dragonfire purple and buzzing like mad. The weight shifted, and Big Joey came down on its mangled leg with a metallic thud. Steel bent as the tower leaned forward like a man waiting to be knighted.

"*Hah-hah!*" Childs cackled. He dropped the spent mag and jammed in a fresh one. Debris from the substation explosions began to fall all around them. Ahead, the giant. "That's what you get, Jenks, you rat-lucifer-fuck!"

"Mr. Los Angeles is hurt," Otis said to Childs, pointing at the broken hump of Pale Brody. The poor bastard was done for, but he could not be left to die on the highway.

"I'm sorry, but he's gone, old-timer," Childs said. "And so are we if we don't do something."

The Signal blew one last furious accusation.

Ɔquɥʔ[?] ʃ!

ƆɅⱢƩβ—

You're fucked anyway, Randy's father and Otis' Ruthie spat into his ear. He could smell the rancid bile in the ventilator tube, feel her ghost breath freeze the nape of his neck. *Come down here into the Undervoid where we belong.*

"Goddammit, *that is not so!*" Childs screamed. "*You're not taking me with you!*"

"Randy, stop firing!" Nikki yelled. "Deathbeam, *I know it!*"

Childs ignored Nikki and fired again. A few rounds pinged off the leaning tower's frame, but more found their target. Another wire separated, taking the insulator with it. The burning pendulum swung in a vast arc, narrowly missing the fuel bled from the lanced Cadillac.

"Ten points, fucko!" Childs bellowed. Just as he nestled in for his follow-up shot, another enormous swell of purple light bloomed from the raging substation.

Flat-Top stumbled. In turn, it pulled on the giant in front of Childs.

Big Joey's cross arms were yanked back toward Flat-Top. The hot edges of its plasma-fire wound still burned as it pulled the chewed leg up with an awful squeal. Now Big Joey stood on three legs, the wire tension perhaps the only thing keeping it vertical. The severed insulator scraped the road as Flat-Top pulled Big Joey closer to the Kwik Gas.

ĈΛ£Σβ –

You'll die on this road, Ruthie said to Otis. She had Harry Childs' tube in her mouth and her bridgework pinched between her fingers. The burnt-meat smoke from Franklin's fire boiled around her. *Never forget that I'm taking you with me, Otis.*

[WE'LL HAVE A SON AND NAME HIM FRANKLIN, SHE'D SAID AS SHE LAID OUT THE PICNIC BLANKET. THE CICADAS CALLED, THE WILLOWS DARKENED, AND THE SUN BID THEM GOODNIGHT.]

"I'm ready, Ruthie," Otis whispered, just as the Deathbeam burst from the substation.

Nikki shouted, *"Randy hit the deck!"*

The Deathbeam soared the half-mile down Route 60 in a furious purple ribbon, its core the burning white totality of the stars. Wailing and screeching, it rocketed about six feet from the surface of the road, shot between the legs of Flat-Top, and narrowly missed the precariously tilted and stumbling Big Joey, all the while illuminating Route 60 in a magnificent strobe effect.

Ruthie screamed.

ĈąĻĘβ *!!– !!*

Harry Childs sneered.

The Deathbeam incinerated Randy Childs and, a nanosecond later, Otis Thompson. Neither man felt any pain, but they sensed the locomotive of heat and the overpowering electric fist as their killer hurtled toward them at just under the speed of light. The two men vaporized.

The weapon immediately snuffed out.

Caleb could not believe his eyes when he saw half a pelvis fall into the road and teeter back and forth like pottery, tangled in the burning tatters of blue jeans. The immediate area smelled like burnt meat, hot asphalt, and ozone. One of Otis' smoking work boots tumbled toward the crumpled pile of Pale Brody.

Pale witnessed the execution of Otis and Childs with an eye half-submerged in blood. He saw it coming before anyone else, right after the storm killed Ken Lightfeather's rig. The Deathbeam was alive, it was part of whatever the hell had been unleashed in the desert, and when it moved, when it sought recompense, it was voiced in a piercing, banshee wail.

Although Childs and his machine gun had had some effect on the limping Big Joey, there was no way he would be allowed to succeed. The Deathbeam's word was final, and that's all there was to it.

Pale watched Childs' head separate from his body, then just cease to be. Otis actually spun for a half-second as he was not hit as squarely as Childs, but the power was unstoppable and merciless. He lifted out of his boots and turned to both smoke and mist in mid-air like a Macy's balloon suffering a dreadful malfunction.

One of the last things I'll witness is violent death. Caleb has seen things no kid should see. Dear God, please prove Valerie wrong, and tell me he'll be different now . . .

The Signal made its demand known, confident its search for a host may soon be at an end.

ĈΛLΣβ– ĈΛLΣβ

Nikki dropped to her belly when the Deathbeam spooled up, and she attempted to bring the kid down with her. He was a strong one, this Caleb, and she just wasn't able to make it happen.

The weapon was terrible. It turned the two men into bloody steam in less than a second. Brave Randy Childs, who just a little more than twelve hours ago spun his index finger like helicopter rotors, warming the team up for some Good Old-Fashioned Space Shit, vanished.

Childs and the nice man from the filling station were gone, and the kid's dad was busted up like a scarecrow. Nikki didn't know when she'd find the time to be traumatized, but one thing was certain: it was not now.

When you're free and clear in some hotel room with a bottle of booze and the curtains shut, then you can lose your mind. Keep your shit tight. You have to make it out alive. That kid needs you, and his dad is good as dead, so don't you join him, Barlowe.

Besides, you have to deal with that cunt Jenks.

But there was another drama in play on Route 60: Big Joey teetered on three legs. The cross arms, perhaps sixty feet in width, were pulled out of true, bending backward toward the Kwik Gas, the struggling Flat-Top, and the fury of the retreating substation. Big Joey fought to stay upright like an angry horse straining against the reins.

Another wire gave way and swept roadward, taking a pair of insulators with it. Still, when Nikki heard the ugly metallic scream, the lazy howl of the substation meeting its end, she gazed in awe as Dragonfire, which began at the VLA, sure as shit ended at the Kwik Gas.

She knew she should move, but the sight momentarily froze her in place. The entire substation, spurting plasma-fire and belching smoke, crawled in retreat.

Them or us, she thought. *This is it.*

A good portion of the beast tumbled down the backside of the rise Otis, Ken and Childs had watched it crest right before dawn. Enormous pieces of steel flailed like the arms of a drowning man as it vanished behind the hill, an acre of steel sliding out of view. Dust rose from behind the hill as breaking sections tumbled down, and to save itself, the substation flung one desperate length of steel forward and clawed at the rocks and brush. Its weight was massive, the inertia too lopsided; neither Earth nor Route 60 could sustain the bulk of the beast.

The substation's last hope to maintain balance, a pair of strained extensions of scaffolding and insulators dug deep into the spine of Route 60, gave way with a deep, metallic groan. Realization seemed to hit home, and again, the substation roared.

DÚHHRUÜÙ!

Ladies and gentlemen, boys and girls, children of all ages, once gravity got a hold of that mass and pulled it downhill, the tension was too much for the towers to bear. A moment later, the chain reaction began.

Ashes, ashes, we all fall down, Nikki thought.

Big Joey appeared startled. Its plasma-damaged cage jolted and buckled, and the cat head spires rotated as the giant sought the source of its predicament: the descent of Flat-Top.

Wires pulled tight as piano strings as the substation crumbled behind the hill, and when all of its lines—the sum of its tension to be measured in thousands of tons—suddenly released, Flat-Top, now halfway up the hill as the substation tugged it along, was cut off from everything that kept it alive.

Down went Flat-Top, the fainting heroine, stiff-legged and blind, with still a few of the white-hot insulators attached. The sound it made was a long deep moan of fatigue—*resignation*, Nikki thought—a massive gridwork of galvanized steel returning to its natural state. It fell sideways, crumbling at hard forty-five-degree angles. Now bent into a weird delta shape, it began to slide down the face of the hill, churning dust and debris into the Devil Wind dawn.

Before Nikki could secure Caleb and back away, the wires over Route 60 snapped free with an audible *fwack!*, and Big Joey, back where it started when they fishtailed onto the highway, crashed directly into Thompson's Kwik Gas, your last stop for fuel before Magdalena.

Big Joey fell dead, and the naked frame of the awning was its tomb.

There was absolutely no way the awning could tolerate the force of being T-boned by one hundred and ninety tons. They collapsed together in a tremendous orchestra of dumb steel and concrete. The corpse of the Hertz truck was fully engulfed by the calamity and, likewise, the mini-mart. The cross arms crushed the tiny store like a shoebox. Sparks, dirt, and debris (and who knew how many Slush Puppie cups) puked into the air.

A hot insulator broke free from the tangle of tower and awning and tumbled through the steel maze in a series of clanging impacts. It landed on a wide beam, tipped for a second, then slid off. It fell like a lawn dart, straight down, into one of the holes left behind by the severed gas pumps, banging the edges all the way down.

A roaring column of flame erupted from the exposed throat of the underground fuel tank. The sound was like a rocket engine, and even from the crash site of the late Red Zeppelin, Nikki and Caleb could feel the heat.

A minute earlier, the thunder-rings had fallen with mighty, cacophonous rage, but the Kwik Gas detonated with a burly, no-nonsense *Boom!* It was a battering ram of sound, almost a tangible thing, its presence similar to the destruction wave from the first dish destroyed at the VLA, which now to Nikki seemed like weeks ago.

Nikki grabbed Caleb, who finally crumbled like a bag of sticks. She cocooned herself around him as he rolled, wrapping one leg over the boy's body and pulling his torso to hers. She tucked his head down, then her own, and waited for the pain.

The blast sent pond ripples through the puddle of Pale Brody's blood. Merciless heat, today's last rider on Route 60, charged toward him. If God was kind enough to take him now, he would gladly accept, and if he saw *Those Others*, he'd either go insane in their Deathrealm or, more likely, spend eternity grappling with them.

The Tower, Caleb's card, he thought. *The Fool, mine.*

The wall of fire was an engine of death, rolling, *searing*, coughing black smoke. The marauder crawled over the highway, and he knew that when it reached him time would stop.

He managed to move only his eyes and saw Nikki shield Caleb. Her clothes were filthy, her smoldering hair a dirty old rug. She tightened her grip and held his son in a way Valerie never had.

This is what it's like to die in a nuclear war.

Oh Valerie, I wish you missed me.

An inferno, this strip of Route 60.

The remaining towers began to fall.

-16-
YOUNGBLOOD

NIKKI HEARD THE rhythm of tires on tarmac and felt the sun on her skin, but my God, did everything hurt. Eyes still closed, she winced, and every fold of her face screamed bloody murder. She raised her hands and pressed them against her neck. *Ow. That smarts.*

Her hands crawled north and touched . . . *gauze? Is that gauze? Is my head wrapped? What the—*

Her last minute of consciousness slammed back into her mind—The Deathbeam erasing Randy Childs and Otis the old-timer. The substation sliding off hill like a stoned crab. The immense tower groaning as it fell, clobbering the gas station like something out of a disaster movie. The pillar of fire, that massive tornado of heat—then tucking herself into a ball, wrapped around . . . *who?*

The kid! Where's the boy?

She recalled the second heat punch of the Cadillac's fuel tank going up, the *whoosh* as flaming parts spiraled by. She reached further back and relived the crash of the first gunship as they fled the VLA, the trail of flames, and the frightening hail of exploded ammunition. Further still, she saw Gary DeLeon with the bloody fire extinguisher over his head.

We should be dead. Am I dead? The kid's dad has to be toast.

"Whrr nn eeyy?"

"What's that?" said a male voice, from perhaps three feet away.

The sound of the tires was unmistakable now. Imperfections in the road. The feel of the Naugahyde seat and the belt that secured her in it.

I'm definitely in a car, but who's driving?

"Whurr an eye?"

"Where are you? You're in a Socorro County Sheriff's Department cruiser, ma'am. I'm Deputy Youngblood and you're on the way to a hospital. You have . . . injuries."

"Inurhee?"

"Yes, ma'am. I took the liberty of wrapping some of the burns. It would have been impossible to get EMTs out here, so I'm hightailing it. You're *so* lucky to be alive."

Nikki's mind condensed toward a single point of darkness. She thought about her cat, Greasy Bob, and that her neighbor Carol had agreed to take care of him for a few days, the sound of *It's Only Rock and Roll (But I Like It)* blasting from her oldest brother's new Marantz FM receiver, the boozy in-flight party on the Fun Jet, a dead language interwoven with the DragSat data, Artie Jayne's dangling severed lips, the vulture face of Armand Jenks . . .

Jenks. I know what you are—

She pressed her hand against the puncture wound in her neck, then sleep once again took Nicole Lynn Barlowe all the way down.

INTERVIEW VI

DEFENSE INTELLIGENCE AGENCY
CASE No. NB-18266-00
October 17, 1993 09:21 HRS
ATTACH TO PREVIOUS INTERVIEW

INVESTIGATORS AND SUBJECT UNCHANGED

CLASSIFIED.
PRESS BLACKOUT.

BEGIN TRANSCRIPTION

Oberon: Quite the yarn, Doctor Barlowe.

Castillo: No doubt. A tall tale, as we say out here.

Barlowe: You bet, Julie. You wanted it in gritty detail, so there it is. Not a bad recollection, I have to say. The more I chew it over in my mind, the clearer things become, and I think I'm pretty clear now.

Oberon: I'm thinking along the same lines as Detective Castillo.

Barlowe: Then I guess the night he had planned for you two at the Red Roof Inn is a go? I'll send a bottle of Cold Duck, keep it classy.

Oberon: Burn trauma, the disaster at the VLA, and the truck crash might have, well, you know, tossed a monkey wrench into your works.

Barlowe: Ah. I see. That's the easy way out classify me as a nutcase to begin the discrediting process. You may want to remember that *discredited does not mean disproved*. By the way, I'd sure like to check on my cat. Maybe talk to my folks, you know, normal shit.

Oberon: Calamity has a way of altering memories.

Barlowe: Memories have a way of sticking around, sister.

Oberon: *You* may have a way of sticking around this facility for a while. *Sister.*

Barlowe: Here we are. Finally, the nitty gritty titty committee is called to order. Let 'er rip. You've been waiting to drop an ultimatum for two days. But before you lay your offer on the table, let me ask you something. Why are you so quick to defend Medusa Engineering maybe not directly, but certainly you're casting shade on everything I've told you. The dishes are destroyed, the towers are down. The Kwik Gas is an ash pile, all those people are dead.

Oberon: The lawyers will be here at ten, and they're very interested in talking to you. It stands to reason that a company the size of Medusa Engineering, congruent with the broad scope of government contracts they possess, holds some sway in the way certain aspects of sensitive matters are handled. They can be very persuasive. Sometimes generous. *But never at a disadvantage.*

Castillo: Picking up what she's putting down, Doctor Wise Ass?

Barlowe: So they're going to stroll in here smelling like Wall Street. Sure to stink up the room with a cash payout. You're just here to broker the deal, then. I'm sure that always falls under the purview of the DIA, am I right?

Castillo: Maybe something like that, who knows? It's all confidential.

Barlowe: Good Cop: Money. Bad Cop: Destroyed Reputation. Or is it something else?

Oberon: It is in the interests of all involved that discretion and the avoidance of let's call it *inflammatory hyperbole* be employed to sew up any fissures concerning interpretations of the events of October 14, 1993.

Barlowe: Ah, a trip to Payday, New Mexico, wreathed in a very stringent set of conditions, then.

Oberon: That is usually how settlements work.

Barlowe: Don't think I've forgotten about the kid. I have *not* forgotten about Caleb. The boy is missing, and I am detained the only two who apparently were not affected by the Signal. Do you think I couldn't put that together?

Castillo: There's no missing boy, Doctor Barlowe. Best if you just forget all that. Maybe he's someone you knew as a child. Trauma and memories again, you know.

Oberon: The defense industry is a very large web. You have to look at it from the spider's point of view.

Barlowe: That's exactly what I saw, the spider's point of view. But I can tell you, it's a *helix, no*t a spider. And the helix intertwines, just like this sham interrogation and paper-thin attempt to gaslight me. Other than spitting out a few fillings, I was not affected by the Dragonfire influence. Why is that? Does that make me special?

Oberon: Sounds like *Weekly World News* and their Batboy stories. No one is signing off on that.

Barlowe: Yeah? What's *your* theory?

Oberon: A terrible malfunction of some kind if I were pressed to answer in layman's terms.

Barlowe: And the Signal? I can't fathom that being part of anything *but* occult influence. I saw the symbols Aramaic I now know on the monitors right before it all went bloody. A dead language transmitted by a CME. Technology may kill, but not like that.

Oberon: The homicide claim is yours alone.

Barlowe: That's because anyone to refute it is dead.

Castillo: No can do, Doctor Barlowe.

Barlowe: An electrical substation forty *miles* from where it should be, and you just blow right past that? If you're supposed to be an MK-Ultra mind specialist, you really do suck balls at it.

Oberon: We said nothing in the way of influencing your answers or made any attempt to sow internal doubt. Your story contains nothing but a lot of hearsay and would never hold up in court.

Barlowe: And why would I be in court? You have to accept, Julie, that your gig is up. You're not DIA.

Oberon: I'm just using court as an analogy to illustr

Barlowe: [INTERRUPTING] Alight, alright, everyone is in the club but me. Medusa Engineering is the *Medusa Cult*, and there's two sides: those who know, and those who just do the work. We're like little minions for you bloodsuckers, little Renfields all.

Oberon: Honestly, Doctor Barlowe . . .

Barlowe: Remember when we talked about compartmentalization, Castillo? *That's* what I didn't get until the black tent. But now, here in the dark, *now I see.*

Oberon: Cute.

Barlowe: Why the Sun? Is there a relationship between Black Magic and the *fucking STARS*? Why did it need *blood*? I'll tell you it's all sacrifice. Some real old school, no-kidding-around Old Testament fireworks. Armand Jenks brought something terrible into the world on purpose. *The Awakener of Stars.* Who says shit like that unless you're some occultist viper? There's something there in us, myself and the boy Caleb that Jenks wants, I'm sure of it. I was young and hopped up on nerd-cool, now I've pissed my life away working for Dr. Mengele. The Indian was right . . . The Old Conflict. The Oldest Conflict.

Oberon: [INTO COMMS DEVICE] Red Team, we've going to need evac and sedation. Kilo Delta Kilo, seven seven, Oberon, Julia. Terminate recording

BUZZER SOUNDS

Barlowe: It's all fun and games until someone opens the goddamn Gate, isn't it? The Medusa Cult can wear their little robes at night, give each other knowing nods in the hallway, engage in worldwide fuckery with access into every major artery that keeps the world alive.

DOORS OPEN.
CLATTER OF SEVERAL INDIVIDUALS ENTERING ROOM
INDISTINCT SHOUTING

Barlowe: You knew all about the black tent. Was the blood sacrifice the bait that brought that shitty entity, whatever it is maybe Jenks' Architect of Zero purple helix pal down from the CME? Did that laser light show somehow assist in that? Open a . . . a . . . . fissure? Easy to see why generator truck was there, it powered the fucking laser. I think when Jenks realized it had gotten away from him, he had to call in the airstrike.

Castillo: The trauma has you completely unreason

Barlowe: *Medusa Engineering is the Medusa Cult.* It's that simple. Where is Caleb? Where is that boy, is he bleeding on an altar somewhere for you monsters? Hooked up to a centrifuge?

Oberon: Hector, kill that recorder, please.

SEVERAL VOICES INDISTINGUISHABLE

SOUND OF SCUFFLE, GLASS BREAKING.

Barlowe: [VOICE ELEVATED] Makes you wonder just how far back they go. His father said it: *The Nightworld cast them out, through The Gate.* And Jenks is trying to open that Gate. I'll bet we only sampled a taste of what's to come . . . how bad things will get if it's allowed to continue. Just look, just look at me now . . .

Oberon: Hector, I said *shut that goddamned tape off!*

Barlowe: Those Others, The Shadowless Ones, whose eyes are they using to see into our wretchedness, whose teeth do they use to *gnaw* into The Great Elsewhere

RECORDING ENDS

-17-

THE GARDEN AND JENKS

THE WORLD SMELLED of fuel and ash. The sun was lava orange, the waning clouds red as blood. The destruction was total; the Kwik Gas all but removed from the map, three twisted towers in the road, the remains of the substation smoldering behind the hill. Smoke was caught by natural wind, and it moved east in black, reeking patches. Spot fires burned everywhere.

In the far away lay the unmistakable shapes of downed towers, the motionless giants resembling the aftermath of a bridge collapse or a roller coaster disaster. Transmission lines snaked toward the hill from which the substation had fallen, silent and stripped of power. A dead Flat-Top laid at the foot of the hill, smoldering.

Route 60 suffered massive damage. Molten slag took its toll where the substation made its last stand, and the site where Big Joey flipped the Cadillac was rife with gouges and a glowing plasma sinkhole. Shadows played over the war zone Route 60 had become; they crawled across the bent steel of downed towers, the twisted aluminum of the Kwik Gas, the smoking corpse of a 1968 Cadillac Fleetwood, and of course, Pale Brody.

A dazed and exhausted Caleb stood next to Nikki, who had taken the brunt of the fire's fury. The poor lady's face was terribly burned, her hair singed so severely in places it resembled steel wool. It appeared to Caleb as if her eyelids had been burned away, or at least so crippled by blisters it seemed she couldn't blink. Peeling skin covered her cheeks and forehead, and her lips were swollen, glistening inner tubes. She grabbed Caleb by the elbow. When she breathed, it sounded like sandpaper.

"We're alive," Nikki croaked, but it sounded like *Eer U-a-Yvv*. Her tongue was covered in ash, the inside of her mouth and throat likewise dusted. Even though it seemed they'd endured the inferno for several minutes, at this distance from the Kwik Gas, they'd only been exposed to its fading leading edge. It was actually no more than three seconds until the firestorm dissolved.

The immensity of the towers when standing was one thing, but to see them smashed on the ground was another entirely. They were staggeringly huge, just monstrous. The insulators that raged and threatened all night long were now a burnt corn cob about the size of a small sedan. How furious they had appeared last night, in the storm, through the slanted rain as they screamed purple and orange, buzzed their insect nonsense, and helped transmit the awful tones that drove men to homicide or worse. Now here they were, nothing more than discarded and charred composite material.

Caleb ached at the sight of his father.

Between the hulks of Big Joey and Goalie lay the bent body of Pale Brody. Caleb broke free from Nikki and ran to him. He stood there a moment with his hands out like he was trying to explain something to a toddler, then the lad's knees gave way, and down he went. He set his hand on his father's destroyed shoulder, then snatched it away.

Nikki thought for sure Pale was stone dead; there was no way to survive that blood loss and head trauma. When she saw Pale's jaw move and his eyes flutter open, she gasped.

"You made it," Pale whispered, his voice nearly gone. His eye, the one on the road, was filled with burnt blood. The stain surrounding his cracked skull was the size of a truck tire. His clothes were nearly ashes. "Playboy."

"Oh, Dad, please," Caleb said. "Please hold on, we'll get an ambulance here."

Caleb's face crinkled into a rubber glove. His cheeks and nose flushed with heat and pressure. Tears very soon. His mouth tasted of gasoline.

Pale managed an anemic chuckle. "No, son. No."

"I don't know what to say," Caleb sobbed. *"I don't know what to do."*

Now that Pale could truly *see*, he recognized so much of Valerie in their son, from her hazel eyes to the flare of his nostrils as his young beautiful face surrendered to grief.

"You said chain gang—all we needed to know." Pale's lips

pulled back from his teeth, the last smile of a dying man. "Stay with me. Watch the sun close The Gate."

I'll miss him so much, Pale thought. *I'll miss the man I'll never know.*

They stared east. The sun, huge and fully clear of the horizon, set the desert alight. Above, the mother cyclone rapidly condensed to a central point, where its war-eye spun over the moaning, arcing ruin of the substation. Though the sky tumor was still miles wide, it was now far less intimidating than it had been at first light. Soon it would be gone. Stubborn thunder prowled its surface, aware that time was short.

A weave of impossible light shot into the sky from behind the hill, a wispy helix of brilliant micro-stars screeching into the morning air. It rocketed upward into the rapidly shrinking eye of the storm.

The collision of the Dragonfire helix and cyclone brought a sound as if God had punched the world in the eye. The remnants of the storm burst with a searing, electric purple flare, then simply blew apart in all directions, leaving in its wake only the soft violet dawn.

Caleb remained on his knees, petting his father's head, tucking Pale's burned and filthy hair behind his ear, smoothing his cheek, and murmuring things only a father would understand.

If the soul is in the blood, Pale thought, *then mine is where it belongs, on the road.*

Pale stiffened. He coughed once, and a weak mist sprayed from his lips and landed on Route 60, where a battle had been fought against giants.

"Dad? Dad? *Oh, God . . . Dad!*"

Pale breathed the words, "I see a garden."

And he was gone.

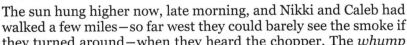

The sun hung higher now, late morning, and Nikki and Caleb had walked a few miles—so far west they could barely see the smoke if they turned around—when they heard the chopper. The *whump whump* of the rotor blades was a faint echo at first, but in the minute or two it took to bear down on them, Nikki already knew who it was.

The jet-black Bell 206 came in low, parallel to the highway, not far above a tower that lay with its legs straight out like a fainting goat. The nose dipped as it swung around, the rotors kicking up a wall of stinging dust. Nikki and Caleb had to lower their heads to shield their eyes, and the helicopter came out of its bold turn and landed in the middle of Route 60.

She stood beside Caleb, burned and filthy, face ruined, strung out from fatigue, and scoffed at the sight of the first person to exit the helicopter. He looked like he just walked out of an army recruitment ad: fit, V-shaped torso, buzz-cut, aviator shades. She would have been slightly amused by this if he hadn't been holding a bolt-action rifle.

Has to be that dipshit Randy mentioned, she thought.

He was followed by a man in a pristine white suit, impeccably tailored. Black hair slicked back. Slim face. That Basil Rathbone nose, those icy, pale blue eyes.

"Well, it's Darth Jenks," Nikki shouted so she could be heard as the chopper's engine wound down. Her throat was still a red, painful membrane. "You even had time to change outfits!" She was so exhausted she honestly didn't care what she said to him. "I hope you're thrilled with what you've done."

Armand Jenks stopped just beside Colonel Taymour. Nikki was right; this was the man Childs had told her he'd seen outside the tent, the military-looking gent with the heavy earmuffs, now secured to his belt by a D-ring.

"A long night," Jenks said. He didn't raise his voice, but there was no difficulty hearing him over the engines. "I ordered you and Childs to stay on station. You disobeyed me."

Nikki's hand went to the Beretta. Taymour had the rifle to his shoulder in under a second. He leaned in. He had Nikki dead to rights.

"Doctor Barlowe, do you want to join the dead in the desert?" Jenks said.

She took her hand off the pistol and splayed her fingers into a starfish. She looked at Jenks through a cloud of blisters.

"I gotta ask," Nikki said.

Armand Jenks stared at her, then shifted his eyes to Caleb.

"You *knew* the Signal would arrive, didn't you? But something needed blood, something had to be *sacrificed*; first in the tent, then us. The soul is in the blood—didn't think I'd put that little puzzle together, did you?"

"Is that your question, Doctor Barlowe? Or are you looking to impress someone with your ceaselessly running mouth?"

Nikki watched Jenks' breath fog in the desert sun. A thought jumped into her head and dropped anchor: *Time to put this demon down.* Jenks has to be greased for Randy, Artie Jayne, that poor kid Billy Urus, the crews aboard those gunships. Otis, Ken, everyone. Especially Caleb, who had just watched his father die.

And for the crime of witchery.

"Although your survival instinct is commendable, I owe you nothing by way of explanation," Jenks added. "But as I told Doctor Childs, there is an Architect, and his name is Zero. Whatever happens to you from this time forward is my decision alone. Doctor Barlowe, think about the type of future you would like that to be."

Taymour took a step forward, his breathing slow and steady.

"Don't you fucking *touch* this boy," Nikki snarled.

From now on, I will never hesitate, she'd told Ken. With her left hand, she moved Caleb behind her. With the other, she pulled the pistol.

"Lights out, Jenks."

Nikki squeezed the trigger.

Click.

"Goddammit!"

Click.

Surprised at her stupidity, she fumbled with the thumb safety. Hard to miss, but miss it she did.

Armand Jenks put his crustacean index finger to his lips.

"Shhh," he said. *"Sleep now."*

Colonel Taymour fired a tranquilizer dart into Nikki Barlowe's neck. Her eyes, though swollen nearly shut, snapped wide in disbelief. With a gun in one hand and the other on Caleb, there was no way to remove the dart without disarming herself or letting go of the boy.

The ketamine worked fast.

She stopped and stared at the pistol, then her fingers simply opened. Her vision turned to soup, and she dropped the Beretta.

Nikki staggered backward like a rodeo clown, arms flapping, then dropped unconscious onto Route 60.

Caleb, who was carrying Nikki's bag, dropped it and turned to flee. Before he could gain five yards, Taymour had him. Caleb fought at first—he thought Nikki was dead—but when he saw her breathing, he stopped struggling.

"Don't you hurt her anymore!"

The hand on his neck squeezed just enough to shut Caleb up; there just was no besting a powerhouse like Taymour. And the man with the timber wolf's eyes, the guy in the white suit who had his own helicopter, he was clearly not to be messed with.

Taymour pulled a radio from his belt. "Logistics, this is Colonel Taymour. I'll need an appropriately marked road evac vehicle on Route sixty, at mile marker . . . " He looked around. "Mile marker ninety-two. Copy?"

"Mile marker ninety-two, copy," came the squelchy reply.

Taymour picked up the bag and Nikki's gun. He searched her, found the two additional magazines, and headed back to stand near Jenks with his rifle slung and the bag hanging.

Jenks saw the caricature drawn on the bag by Artie Jayne, features exaggerated, wearing a sombrero and working on a huge stogie. He scoffed and adjusted his cuff links.

"What are you going to do with me, mister?" Caleb said.

Jenks eyed him. "You heard The Summoning?"

Caleb shook his head, then shrugged. "What do you mean?"

"The Control Voice. When it speaks to the powerless, it brings their weaknesses to the water's edge. Everyone that is, but people like you and me."

Caleb thought of his father on the telephone and the agony that had gripped him when the weird music spat from Otis' little radio; what he was like after the tower had its way with him inside the truck. The way Ken's hands went to his ears. Otis weeping.

"I can tell that you are . . . impervious to certain agonies," Jenks added.

"Am I in trouble?"

Jenks shook his head. His slender mouth nearly smiled.

"No trouble," he said. "Not even close. It is a Summoning, as I said. We are called, while others are consumed."

"That noise didn't do anything to me, if that's what you mean. Nikki too."

"Doctor Barlowe is unique in that way as well."

Caleb looked at Nikki, flat on her back and breathing deeply. "So why did you do that to Nikki? She's been nice to me."

"Doctor Barlowe is my *employee*, and I am sure you will agree I cannot allow anyone to point a firearm at her *superior*."

"She had a long night too."

"Nights run long in the desert." Jenks nodded toward the distant pile of steel and the smoldering wrecks beyond. "This entire place is a battlefield."

Caleb looked around. Steel and smoke, war and tragedy. *These are Old Forces, Caleb m'boy*, his father had said last night. *Old Commands.*

I guess I'm an orphan now, he thought. *Maybe when Nikki wakes up, we'll think of something because Mom will never take me.*

"My dad died in the car crash; it was awful. But I'm not blind, there was no way to live through that. I don't know. I should be dead, too. But I'm not. Last night he rescued Nikki and the Spacedoctor."

"Childs?" Jenks asked, interested only in that, completely blowing past the death of the boy's father. "Older gentleman? Where is he now?"

"Yeah, that was his name. I think the sounds got to him, as well as my dad. He had an army gun, M-16, I think. *Machine* gun. He shot at one of the towers, he almost killed it. The Deathbeam . . . well . . . made sure he *didn't.*"

"The Control Voice, yes. Interesting choice of words, young man. *Deathbeam.*"

"I figured it out, though. I figured out how to stop all of it. Just break the circuit. Maybe the plan didn't go just as we thought it would, but we still broke the circuit and ran the Signal to ground. You should have seen how brave they all were, mister. Nikki too."

Jenks looked back toward the chopper. He nodded to the pilot, and the idling engine began to wind up.

Jenks placed his palm on Caleb's forehead and closed his eyes. His lips parted slightly, and a cold sheet of air hissed between his teeth. Caleb saw an exhale of barely there, wispy white fog.

"You. The Gate," Jenks said, pulling his hand back. "How long have you known?"

Caleb shrugged. "I've always been able to see it," he said. He didn't know where that came from, but it seemed fitting.

Caleb had always known, but not entirely. It had danced on the periphery, like a word on the tip of his tongue. How could this scarecrow man in the white suit know? Didn't Dad mention it too, thunderstruck on Otis' sofa, after he'd stared bewildered into a bag of potato chips?

The Nightworld cast them out. Through The Gate.

"I even built something that looked like it one time."

"Then we should talk about your future," Jenks said. He moved his hands behind his back, shifting his posture to that of a soldier at ease. "Young man, have you ever thought about what it would be like to be King?"

Caleb stared at Jenks.

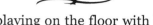

Caleb remembered playing on the floor with his GoBots, looking up at his father, who sat at the dining room table, restringing one of his guitars. The glare from the sun outside the window that day was as it was this morning in New Mexico, lava orange and deep blood red. It caught Pale's long hair and made it glow. Caleb thought he looked like one of the saints depicted in the stained-glass windows of Our Lady of Guadalupe church.

"We leave for the road on the seventeenth, Caleb. First show is on the twentieth. Every night I'll dedicate my solo to you, just to make sure the world knows I have the best son in the world."

"When will you be home?" Caleb said in his little voice. He was six then and had adjusted to his father being away for days, or even weeks, at a time than most kids his age. When asked at school: *What does your dad do?* Caleb always straightened his back and proudly replied, *Rock Star. How about yours?*

"Top of June. Then you and I are off to the Sequoias for a whole *four days*, Playboy."

"Mom isn't going?"

Pale shook his head. "She says she just wants you and me to go and have a good time. Boys' club, don'tcha know?"

"I want to see the giants. In the school library, I have three books about the Sequoias on hold. Lots of pictures."

Pale stopped and looked at his son. "And you *will* see giants, my man! Tell you what. Bring those books home tomorrow, and we'll look at them together—then you make a list of all the places you want to see while we're there. I'll make it happen."

"King's Canyon too?" Caleb's hazel eyes opened kind of wide, a little wet, and a lot of wonderful.

"King's Canyon, too."

Caleb nodded. He looked at his GoBots, arranged in intersecting V-Shapes. Next to them was a cyclopean piece of geometry he'd built from Legos and sticks he'd found in the yard, lashed together with rubber bands, dental floss, whatever he could get his hands on. He noticed the used guitar strings on the table and grabbed them.

Caleb busied himself beneath one of the barstools for a few minutes, fastening his creation to the legs, suspended like some sort of floating tunnel. He thought it looked pretty cool. One finishing touch remained: he used a yellow post-it note to mark this structure as *The Gate*.

"I read there's a cave," Caleb said, sticking his little face out from beneath the chair.

His father glanced at his custom creation. To Pale it looked like something from a sci-fi novel cover. John Berkey does Lovecraft, perhaps.

"We can go inside and see crystals and stuff."

Pale raised his eyebrows. "Sounds rad, Playboy."

"Maybe there's bats."

"Maybe worse!" Pale said as he made a monster face and growled.

Caleb laughed and raised one of his GoBots, the one that bristled with gun barrels. He made a squealing space-laser sound, and Pale dropped his head to the table with a hard thunk.

"Gotcha, monster—Deathbeam 2000!"

Airborne.

As they pulled up, Caleb's mind left the memory of his father feigning death by GoBot and focused on the police cruiser pulling up next to Nikki. The cop walked over to her with a black case in his hand. He knelt and began to wrap bandages around her face, which Caleb thought was pretty tricky in the presence of helicopter rotor turbulence. He reached again into the bag and jabbed a syringe into her arm.

The last thing Caleb saw before the Medusa Engineering chopper turned away was the policeman dragging Nikki into the backseat of the car. She was going to be in bad shape for a while, he knew. A burned face is about as horrible as it gets and ten times worse for a woman. He liked her, and she liked him—plus, Nikki also could not be swayed by the Signal, The Control Voice. He admired that about her and hoped to see Nikki Barlowe again.

One of these days, he told himself, *we'll need each other*.

Heading east, they flew over the site of Thompson's Kwik Gas. The gas station was a scorched ruin, the awning and fallen electrical tower intertwined like battling snakes. Otis' double-wide had burned to ashes. Red Zeppelin's charred metal corpse poked out of the ditch like something from a junkyard, near a huge wound the molten slag had burned into the road. And not far away, the Deathbeam had vaporized two men, just erased them from the world.

Ahead Caleb could see the death site of the substation. Most of it had melted, still smoking and glowing in the dark, nocturnal eye Dragonfire plasma had burrowed into the world. Pieces of it jutted from the ugliness like those people at Pompeii, caught by surprise when Vesuvius claimed them—and somewhere in that mess was Ken Lightfeather.

Downed wires ran from the hole toward the wrecked chain gangs, the wreckage stretching for miles. Most of the giants were down, lying on their sides and bent out of true. If he looked far enough in the distance, some towers still stood, wires down, stranded miles from home.

As they moved beyond the war scene, Caleb put his hands against the window and looked back. The patrol car that had picked up Nikki approached, careful to stay between two fallen giants and the black eels of grounded transmission lines. The officer got out, hauled something that looked like a heavy plastic sleeping bag from the trunk, and stepped toward the body of Pale Brody, the Mac Daddy.

I see a garden, he'd said.

2019

From Independent-News-Hound.com, August 4, 2019.

The January 2018 incursion of Medusa Engineering's D-Wave Quantum Computer core—by the White-Hat hacking collective known as Legion Th1rt33n—was made available on the Dark Web Onion Servers for approximately nine days. During that time, several of the documents went viral, appearing mostly on conspiracy boards, encrypted chat apps, alternative media news sites, and were discussed at length on several podcasts.

A focused attack on these Dark Web servers resulted in a literal, near-total *incineration* of the Dark Web. The attack was seen as purely retaliatory (speculation points to Medusa Engineering themselves) via an electronic signal that not only caused the interior components of the servers to burn—but in some cases, rumor had it—led the server administrators to commit suicide. By that time, of course, many of the documents had been backed up on such sites as *Cryptome, DarkWebEyeball, SilencerNet,* and *SubStack*, so putting the horse back in the barn, as they say, became impossible.

Whether these documents or the urban legends that surround them are genuine remains to be seen, but they have stirred enough internet controversy to be lumped into the same pool as *The Protocols of the Elders of Zion, A Closer Look at Crosius,* and *The Report from Iron Mountain*. Further revelations have drawn direct connections between Medusa Engineering and the CERN disaster of 2017, which will be explored in depth in my documentary film, *Medusa Engineering and The Shadowless Underground*.

Garrison Elliot Pomerantz

Editor-In-Chief
Independent News Hound

**MEDUSA ENGINEERING
PROJECT DRAGONFIRE VLA INCIDENT SUMMARY
EXECUTIVE EYES ONLY**

**MEDIA BLACKOUT
FILE PENDING FURTHER MODIFICATIONS**

Archive Catalog #DF: 45S 33K
Filed: November 6, 1993

From: Armand Jenks
Medusa Engineering Corporation
1017 Silver Star Road
Boston, Massachusetts 02163

To: ████████████████████████████████ ,

CC: Jacqueline Rawlings

The tragic events at the Very Large Array
in Socorro, New Mexico were undoubtedly a
setback of major significance for Project
Dragonfire. Not only did the team suffer a
mass casualty event, but external damage to
the VLA will also likely render it
inoperable for several years. NASA and DOD
liaisons will attend a debriefing at MEC
headquarters in February 1994. They have
already requested a complete breakdown of
events, as well as a turnover of pertinent
data leading to the malfunction.

It is my recommendation that we keep these
two agencies on a very narrow NTK basis and
compartmentalize as much as possible.
Knowledge of B-Team and their parallel
efforts during the Dragonfire episode are
to be considered extremely sensitive and
privileged information and *not* to be

disclosed under any circumstances.

I further call to have the large format data storage media sequestered but reported as destroyed. The DAT backup, recovered from Doctor Barlowe, should also fall under these restrictions.

DRAGSAT III construction is currently on schedule and should deliver on time. The software engineers and ancient artifact specialists, however, have been alerted that information harvested from the VLA data may impact software requirements. Therefore, the completion date for additional systems, at this time, remains flexible.

The damage to the New Mexico power grid apparatus is unfortunate, but our current Media insertions detailing an Iraqi retribution operation appear to be holding. Operation Desert Storm patriotism and fervor is still high, and that works in our favor.

The VLA damage is another matter entirely. Revealing it to be a software malfunction will make for a difficult sale, and unfortunately, the downing of the two Air Force gunships complicates the problem. I suggest another angle, and that is an embedded terror cell within the US Air Force colluded with the aforementioned Iraqis for simultaneous strikes. As the power grid operation commenced, the terrorist-acquired aircraft attacked the VLA to some success, but inept piloting compromised their effort. We have several people at Industrial Light and Magic who will assist in enforcing that narrative.

It is my deep regret that The Summoning revealed a greater danger than anticipated. It is clear now that The Architect of Zero is closer than previously speculated, perhaps now within the solar system. But allow this clarity: *The Gate can be opened,* and our recent recruit should be considered the silver lining in all of this, despite the trying days ahead for Public Relations in New York.

PRELIMINARY DAMAGE ASSESSMENT: 1.83 billion USD.

Medusa Engineering casualties: 9 confirmed dead, 4 presumed deceased, 3 severely traumatized/institutionalized at Kincaide Hills Psychiatric Recovery Center [a Medusa Engineering holding], Lansing, MI. One employee in permanent detention at V-Facility.

Current Status of VLA Dragonfire Team (as of 10/21/93)

- Chang, Jin (deceased)
- Childs, Randall R. (presumed deceased body never recovered)
- DeLeon Gerald P. (deceased)
- Fenga, Albert (deceased)
- Feingold, Ana N. (deceased)
- Greenwald, Victor (presumed deceased body never recovered)
- Hurosawa, Kenji (deceased)
- Ifrate, Kristin P. (presumed deceased body never recovered)
- Jackson, Mitchell (deceased)

- Jayne, Artemis D. (deceased)
- Kurtis, Johnathan Q.(deceased)
- Orlando, Antonio F. (presumed deceased body never recovered)
- Petersen, Rachel K. (institutionalized)
- Shipman, Serena H. (deceased)
- Urus, William A. (institutionalized)
- Voorhees, Sharon (institutionalized)
- Barlowe, Nicole L. (detained at V-Facility, Roanoke, VA.)

It is recommended that Doctor Barlowe remain at V-Facility until such time staff Medical and Psychological evaluators are confident her recovery is solidified, as the delusional narrative of her recollection must *always* be stressed. Her debriefing documents have already been inserted into the Defense Intelligence Agency archive and appropriately marked as such. Again, I strongly suggest she remain in Medusa Engineering custody.

I look forward to Management's response and suggestions.

Deos Sine Umbra,

Armand Jenks

THE END?

Not if you want to dive into more of Crystal Lake Publishing's Tales from the Darkest Depths!

Check out our amazing website and online store
or download our latest catalog here.
https://geni.us/CLPCatalog

We always have great new projects and content on the website to dive into, as well as a newsletter, behind the scenes options, social media platforms, our own dark fiction shared-world series and our very own webstore. Our webstore even has categories specifically for KU books, non-fiction, anthologies, and of course more novels and novellas.

AUTHOR'S NOTE

I can't thank you enough for taking hours out of your busy lives to read *Live Wire*. The story has a long history, starting with a ham-fisted draft in the mid-eighties, a complete reworking in the early nineties (the bones of which are buried in this version), then a full-on rebuild in 2020. Four drafts after *that*, here we are.

Was the action over the top? You bet. Was the tech/science a little screwy? Yep. But if I did my job correctly in this, my first published novel, you spent time with characters that felt plausible despite the insane situation and the exploitation of their inner torments. That's the juice.

I want to acknowledge the invaluable contribution of J. David Osborne, who executed a painstaking developmental edit of this novel. Without that level of input, I don't know how long this manuscript would have languished on my hard drive before I had the stones to send it out. He even squashed typos.

An enormous *Thank You* goes to Joe Mynhardt and his crew at Crystal Lake Publishing for getting behind this book and its unknown author. When I was young, a band I was in finally got noticed. Same thrill when *Live Wire* was accepted for publication. That *never* gets old.

In one way or another, my entire life has boiled down to this: Make Up Crazy Shit. I write because I love it. Know that we'll go on many adventures together; we'll burn things and blow stuff up; exorcise demons and torch witches; battle monsters and collapse glaciers; meet ghosts and the killers that protect them—and ultimately confront an ancient terror bound by even older rules.

So feel free to come back for more, as the Medusa Cult may have fallen short in 1993 . . . but they are one tenacious cadre of evil and are not easily discouraged.

See you soon . . .

ABOUT THE AUTHOR

Kyle Toucher (rhymes with *voucher*) was raised on a diet of Frankenstein and Godzilla, Black Sabbath and Black Flag, Lovecraft, Blatty, Barker and King. Through his twenties, he fronted the influential Nardcore crossover band Dr. Know, made records and hit the road. Later, he moved into the Visual Effects field, which led to eight Emmy nominations and two awards for *Firefly* and *Battlestar: Galactica*. Recent credits include *Top Gun: Maverick*, *The Orville*, and defense industry clients.

He lives with a lovely woman, five cats, two dogs, and several guitars in a secure, undisclosed location.

Crystal Lake Publishing has run several of his stories in their Patreon-only Shallow Waters series, most of which have ties to one another, and some to the novel you just read.

FLIGHT 2320: Wire-Witch
December 21st, 1984
Witchfyndre
Exile From Cicada Street
The Red-Eye to Salem
This is a Greedy, Jealous House
We Should Be On Our Way From Here
The Nightman's Last Shift
Note to Sanderson
FLIGHT 2320
Freezer Burn

Life Returns, a horror tale based on the popular Dr. Know song of the same name, can be downloaded in EPUB and PDF format here: https://getbook.at/LifeReturns.

www.kyletoucher.monster
twitter: @kyletoucher

Readers . . .

Thank you for reading *Live Wire*. We hope you enjoyed this novel

If you have a moment, please review *Live Wire* at the store where you bought it.

Help other readers by telling them why you enjoyed this book. No need to write an in-depth discussion. Even a single sentence will be greatly appreciated. Reviews go a long way to helping a book sell, and is great for an author's career. It'll also help us to continue publishing quality books. You can also share a photo of yourself holding this book with the hashtag #IGotMyCLPBook!

Thank you again for taking the time to journey with Crystal Lake Publishing.

Visit our Linktree page for a list of our social media platforms. https://linktr.ee/CrystalLakePublishing

Our Mission Statement:

Since its founding in August 2012, Crystal Lake Publishing has quickly become one of the world's leading publishers of Dark Fiction and Horror books in print, eBook, and audio formats.

While we strive to present only the highest quality fiction and entertainment, we also endeavour to support authors along their writing journey. We offer our time and experience in non-fiction projects, as well as author mentoring and services, at competitive prices.

With several Bram Stoker Award wins and many other wins and nominations (including the HWA's Specialty Press Award), Crystal Lake Publishing puts integrity, honor, and respect at the forefront of our publishing operations.

We strive for each book and outreach program we spearhead to not only entertain and touch or comment on issues that affect our readers, but also to strengthen and support the Dark Fiction field and its authors.

Not only do we find and publish authors we believe are destined for greatness, but we strive to work with men and woman who endeavour to be decent human beings who care more for others than themselves, while still being hard working, driven, and passionate artists and storytellers.

Crystal Lake Publishing is and will always be a beacon of what passion and dedication, combined with overwhelming teamwork and respect, can accomplish. We endeavour to know each and every one of our readers, while building personal relationships with our authors, reviewers, bloggers, podcasters, bookstores, and libraries.

We will be as trustworthy, forthright, and transparent as any business can be, while also keeping most of the headaches away from our authors, since it's our job to solve the problems so they can stay in a creative mind. Which of course also means paying our authors.

We do not just publish books, we present to you worlds within your world, doors within your mind, from talented authors who sacrifice so much for a moment of your time.

There are some amazing small presses out there, and through collaboration and open forums we will continue to support other presses in the goal of helping authors and showing the world what quality small presses are capable of accomplishing. No one wins when a small press goes down, so we will always be there to support hardworking, legitimate presses and their authors. We don't see Crystal Lake as the best press out there, but we will always strive to be the best, strive to be the most interactive and grateful, and even blessed press around. No matter what happens over time, we will also take our mission very seriously while appreciating where we are and enjoying the journey.

What do we offer our authors that they can't do for themselves through self-publishing?

We are big supporters of self-publishing (especially hybrid publishing), if done with care, patience, and planning. However, not every author has the time or inclination to do market research, advertise, and set up book launch strategies. Although a lot of authors are successful in doing it all, strong small presses will always be there for the authors who just want to do what they do best: write.

What we offer is experience, industry knowledge, contacts and trust built up over years. And due to our strong brand and trusting fanbase, every Crystal Lake Publishing book comes with weight of respect. In time our fans begin to trust our judgment and will try a new author purely based on our support of said author.

With each launch we strive to fine-tune our approach, learn from our mistakes, and increase our reach. We continue to assure our authors that we're here for them and that we'll carry the weight of the launch and dealing with third parties while they focus on their strengths—be it writing, interviews, blogs, signings, etc.

We also offer several mentoring packages to authors that include knowledge and skills they can use in both traditional and self-publishing endeavours.

We look forward to launching many new careers.

This is what we believe in. What we stand for. This will be our legacy.

Welcome to Crystal Lake Publishing— Tales from the Darkest Depths.

Printed in Great Britain
by Amazon

31143415R00150